THE SUNDAY WIFE

Also by Cassandra King

Making Waves
The Same Sweet Girls

Cassandra King

THE SUNDAY WIFE

HYPERION

New York

Mass Market ISBN: 0-7868-9070-3

Hyperion books are available for special promotions and
premiums. For details contact Michael Rentas, Manager,
Inventory and Premium Sales, Hyperion, 77 West 66th
Street, 11th floor, New York, New York 10023, or call
212-456-0133.

FIRST MASS MARKET EDITION

10 9 8 7 6 5 4 3 2 1

To my not-just-Sunday husband, Patrick,
who has given me faith, hope, love, and a room
with a view.
From your biggest fan.

Acknowledgments

In deepest love, I lift a glass to the perfect sons and families: Jim, Liz, Jason, Jake, Tyler, and Michael; the beautiful girls and families: Jessica and Elise; Melissa, Jay, and forthcoming baby; Megan, Terry, Molly, and new baby; with a prayer for Susannah's return; to my irrepressible Daddy; the precious sisters: Beckie, Reggie, and the boys: Nancy, Jim, and Will; to the terrific in-laws: Carol; Mike and Jean; Kathy, Bobby, and Willie; Jim, Janice, Rachel, and Michael; Tim and Terrye.

In humble gratitude, I lift a glass to the best agent anyone could ever have, Marly Rusoff; to my superb editor, Leslie Wells; and to my gifted publisher, Ellen Archer.

In joyous friendship, I lift a glass to Mary and Gregg; Melinda and Doug; Zoe and Alex; Suzanne and Peter; Annie and Heyward; Cynthia and Cliff; Jane and Stan; Terry and Tommie; Dottie and Peter; Flooz and Tom; Loretta and Bill, teacher extraordinaire; Joan and Norman, big boss man; Connie and Mika; Linda and Michael; Barbara and Tom; to Kerry; Tim Belk; Gene; Mrs. Randal; Bad Mary; Kazue; the original Jakey-poo; and the Same Sweet Girls, subject of the next book.

I went to the Garden of Love,
And saw what I never had seen:
A chapel was built in the midst,
Where I used to play on the green.

And the gates of this chapel were shut,
And 'Thou shalt not' writ over the door....
And priests in black gowns were
    walking their rounds,
And binding with briars my joys and desires.

WILLIAM BLAKE, from "The Garden of Love"

THE SUNDAY WIFE

Prologue

LEAVING MY LIFE BEHIND me, I follow the sun, blinking against its late-afternoon brightness, my swollen eyes burning. When I turn off Highway 98, the scenic route that spans the Florida Panhandle from Tallahassee to Mobile Bay, my memories close in. I long to turn off the air conditioner and roll the windows down and let the salt air blow back to Crystal Springs, where my memories belong. Stopping at the pedestrian walk in the Victorian village of Seaside, I watch sun-browned tourists cross from the Gulf, loaded down with wet towels, beach bags of sunscreen, bottled water. The driver behind me honks his horn, and, startled out of my daze, I turn into the parking area in front of Modaci's Market. Supplies, Celeste said—don't forget to stop at Modaci's for groceries and stuff, soap, toothpaste, toilet paper. Her place has been closed up, needs restocking. Celeste the fortune-teller, the outcast. The only one I could turn to when my life fell apart. She was the one who put the keys in my hand, who guided me to the car and said, *Go. Go to Grayton Beach. No one will look for you there.*

The road to Celeste's beach place is sugar-white sand, spinning the wheels of my car as I turn off the highway. Grayton Beach isn't like the other resort areas on the Emerald Coast—it's the real Florida, the locals say. Maddox told me that years ago, when leaving the Miracle Strip of Panama City, you could drive all the way to Grayton and see nothing but the thick scrub that covers north Florida like kudzu covers the rest of the South. Now there's one development after the other, clear to Mobile Bay. Grayton's little shops and cottages are tucked away in gnarled pines and stunted oaks, not one condominium blocking the view to the ocean. If the neighboring Seaside is a fairy-tale kingdom, then Grayton Beach is the enchanted forest, hiding the little people.

I drive for half a mile before coming to the trailer park, deep in a grove of pine flatwoods, overgrown with blackberry bushes and scrub. Although I can't see it, I feel it—the Gulf of Mexico, right behind the moss-hung oaks. I roll the window down, breathing the hot salt air. *Open the door of my trailer,* Celeste had said, *and the ocean is your backyard.*

At the end of the road is Celeste's trailer, hidden in low-hanging magnolia trees, the branches scraping the top of my car when I park. Sea oats wave in the sandy yard like welcoming banners as I make my way up the path overgrown with sticker-burrs. The tiny silver trailer is a doll's house with zodiac signs painted around the door frame, Aquarius pouring water from a pitcher, Pisces the fish, Scorpio a skeletal crab . . . emblems of her trade, Celeste's star signs. Climbing the concrete block steps, I fumble with the key, all of a sudden dead tired.

Everything is as Celeste described inside, the late afternoon sun flooding in as I pull the shades one by one. The front windows are dark, obscured by magnolia branches, but those across the back offer a breathtaking vista of white sand and beach foliage. I wish the sand dunes weren't so tall, weren't covered by tangles of sea-grape vines, blocking the view of the ocean, then scoff at my ingratitude. If Celeste hadn't offered me this place, I'd have nowhere to go, ocean view or not. Moving to the tiny kitchen area, I put away my meager groceries, fruit and bread and cheese. I'd never bought so few things; Ben, the classic meat-and-potatoes man, demanded big meals, a pantry stocked with junk food, groceries the biggest chunk of our budget. From a plastic bag I bring out two bottles of wine, a good bordeaux and a pinot grigio for variety. Augusta's legacy. In my upbringing, there was no such thing as wine with dinner—my people drank Jim Beam from a brown paper bag in the back of a pickup truck.

I'd bought a pound of fresh shrimp at Modaci's, gasping when the clerk rang it up. Ten ninety-five. Holding up the checkout line, I went to the back of the store and returned with fishing equipment and bait. Setting up poles and lines and pulling my supper from the sea was something I was born knowing how to do. A country girl can survive. Retrieving the equipment from the car, I walk to the beach. As I top the biggest dune, the emerald splendor is spread out before me, a banquet of blue sky and green sea on a white picnic table. Kicking off my flip-flops, I run to the water with the pole banging against my bare legs. The hot foamy waves cover my feet as I throw my head back to shout: "Yes!" My voice rises and joins the song of seagulls overhead: as far as the eye can see, only the wide expanse of sea and sky, and for a moment, I forget why I've run away. I don't know what I've done to deserve this hideaway, this healing elixir of sea and sun, but I thank God in a prayer snatched from my lips by the sea wind. I thank Him that we don't always get what we deserve. Sometimes, we get what we need.

Low and pink, the sun hovers over the horizon like an iridescent bubble suspended by a playful angel. I bait the hook of my fishing pole with a gray shrimp and cast the line way out into the waves. After anchoring the pole firmly in wet sand, I walk far enough to see the town of Grayton. Last time I walked those streets, peeping in the little shops and art galleries, Augusta and Gus waited for me in the outdoor café beneath banana trees. The town blurs as my eyes fill with tears, and, remembering, I turn my head away, toward the setting sun. How many sunsets will it take before I can think of them without crying? I guess that's what I've come to Grayton to find out.

One

I ENDED UP AT Grayton Beach because I came to Crystal Springs first. It was three years ago, the first Wednesday in June, that Ben and I moved to the town of Crystal Springs, across the state of Florida from the Jacksonville area where we'd lived for twenty years. With the moving van a few minutes behind us, we pulled our cars, me following Ben—a metaphor for our life together—into the driveway of our new house. We'd moved before, several times, but this was the most momentous one yet. Ben motioned for me to join him before we walked up the brick walkway to the house. A welcoming committee awaited us inside, and I was nervous. A few weeks before, Ben had met with them and won them over; now it was my turn.

"Dean, listen to me now," Ben said in a low voice, as we stood next to his blue Buick. "I was thinking on the ride over—a couple of things I forgot to tell you about these folks." Although I was skittish, worried about making a good impression, Ben was poised and confident. His brown eyes were alight, his dark hair in place. Almost fifty now, Ben looked better than the first day I saw him, standing in the back of the First Methodist Church of Amelia Island. As a young man, he'd been good-looking in a boyish, clean-cut way; as an older man, he was remarkably handsome. Trim and muscular, he always dressed well, impressive in dark suits, starched shirts, silk ties, and fine leather shoes. He was one of those men who became more distinguished with age, his silvered temples giving him an air of authority. A helpful trait in his profession.

I folded my arms and leaned against his car with a sigh. "I don't know how," I said, "since you've given me every detail of their lives. Bet I know more about them than they do." Looking around, I saw that the church, next door to the parsonage, was big, much bigger than I expected, with a towering white steeple and stained-glass windows gleaming in the sun like jewels. The saying went, the more stained glass, the higher up the ladder the preacher was. Ben was halfway to heaven here.

"Remember this, because it's *very* important," he said in a whisper, although there was no one around to hear him. "The Administrative Board chairperson is Bob Harris. Bob Harris, president of First Florida bank, a real big shot in town, so be especially nice to him."

"Bob Harris," I repeated dutifully, looking away from the church. I didn't know it would be so big. I longed for the safety of our little church in Lake City, wishing we'd never come here. Earlier on, I'd been as excited as Ben, thrilled with the move, his appointment to Crystal Springs. Now I was just apprehensive.

Ben bent his head close to mine and I smelled his spicy aftershave. "Got everyone's name right? Bob's wife's Collie, I think. Collie something-or-other."

"Collie dog?"

"Collie Ruth, I believe. No—wait, that's his sister-in-law. His wife's Lorraine. Or Loretta. Loretta Harris, that's it."

"Which one, Ben?"

"Lorraine, just like I said. You've got to pay attention, Dean, or you'll mess up. Now, remember who the president of the Pastor-Parish Relations Committee is?"

I shook my head and held up a hand, annoyed. "You're confusing me. Trust me, okay? I'll get their names right." Ben had trouble with names, not me. "I'm not the one who stood in the pulpit and introduced the guest soloist Peter Littlejohn as John Littlepeter," I reminded him.

"You'll never let me live that down, will you?" Cutting his eyes my way, Ben tried not to smile, to maintain his look of piety. It was a look he was good at.

"Never. Anytime you get too self-righteous I'll be here to remind you," I told him, smiling. We'd spent twenty years together with me being his foil; he was the esteemed man of God, me the thorn in his side. "I'll be fine, Ben, don't worry. I'll be on my best behavior."

"You'd better be. Let's go in, then." As Ben straightened himself up, I readied myself, too, smoothing down my long denim skirt, reaching under the waistband to tuck in my best white cotton blouse. Licking my fingertips, I smoothed back my hair, tugged on the ponytail at the nape of my neck, fidgeted with the wide barrette that held it in place. But when I retrieved a tube of lipstick from the small purse hanging over my shoulder, Ben took my arm and pulled me forward, his grip firm. "You don't have time to primp," he said in a low voice. "They're peeking out the windows at us! Let's go."

As we walked up to the house, I was taken aback by the difference in it and Ben's description. When he'd returned from meeting with the committee, I'd probed him to describe the town, the church, and the house in minute detail, but he'd been vague. He did okay with the church and town, but all he remembered about the house was that it was big, yellow brick, Colonial in style, and very formal. He'd not told me it was such a fine place, that the front lawn with its lush green grass was so neatly landscaped, abloom with white daisies and orange daylilies. He'd neglected to say that the wide grounds sloped toward the street to a sidewalk shaded with palm trees. Towns with sidewalks seemed more welcoming to me. The brick walkway leading to the front porch of the house was bordered in purple pansies, their sweet faces turned toward us in greeting.

Ben put his hand on my back, steering me forward, and I swallowed nervously as we climbed the brick steps, moving toward our new life, to meet the people who'd decide if we'd make it here or not. I glanced at Ben, praying he'd tell me it would be all right. He ignored me, eyes straight ahead, and I forced down the panic building somewhere deep within, causing my knees to go weak and my heart to thud. I can do this, I repeated to myself, I can do this for Ben.

I had no idea what I was getting myself into when I married Ben. Had I known, would I have done it? It's impossible to answer that now. All I know is, when I first laid eyes on the Reverend Ben Lynch, I knew he was the man I'd marry. I'd taken a job right out of college, as pianist of my foster parents' church on Amelia Island, when the Reverend Ben Lynch was appointed our pastor. It was his second, maybe third, church appointment since he'd gotten out of seminary. His first Sunday, he was standing in the back of the church, greeting the congregation, when I walked into the choir loft to prepare for the morning worship service. I stopped and stared at him. Although not much taller than me, he was well-built and broad-shouldered, with thick brown hair and shining dark eyes, good-looking as a movie star. I pulled the choir director aside and whispered, "Who is *that*?"

"Our new preacher," she replied, smiling slyly. "Good-looking, isn't he? We're lucky to get him. He's on his way up."

He was. Had he not made the career-fatal mistake of marrying me, Ben Lynch would've been where he wanted to go, top of the ladder of the United Methodist Church. Almost thirty years old then, the son of a prominent minister, he'd been on his way. To be a successful preacher, however, he needed a wife, and he needed one quick. He was too good-looking, too smooth and charming to stay single; younger women in his churches fell in love with him, and the older ones plotted to marry him off to their daughters. The bishop didn't like single ministers; there was too much potential for trouble. But Ben had been too preoccupied with getting his doctorate, preparing himself for a life of service in the church, to look for a wife.

Lucky me; I came along at just the right time. Because of my moony-eyed crush on him, the church ladies conspired to marry us off. With no idea that they'd set a trap for him, Ben took me on as a project, educating me in the ways of the church, molding me to be the perfect preacher's wife. Even though I'd not been raised in the Methodist church—had been a rebellious foster child and an object of charity—Ben was sure he could make me into a worthy mate. Some cynics say all preachers have God complexes, and Dr. Ben Lynch thought himself a miracle worker. Henry Higgins in a clerical collar, maybe. Since I'd not been schooled in the church, grown up with its traditions and modes of behavior, I lacked all the necessary graces to be the kind of preacher's wife the church expected. So this move was my chance to make a fresh start.

The welcoming committee surrounded Ben and me as soon as we opened the front door, and I was enveloped in hugs and kisses. A quick count told me there were two men and four women. A determined smile on my face, I eyed them warily, my defenses up. I knew from past experiences that this committee would be the one to tell everyone in town about the new preacher and his wife. Before the sun set today, Crystal Springs would know exactly how we dressed, how we acted toward each other, and the contents of every single box we brought in.

"So this lovely lady is your better half, Dr. Lynch," said the first man to greet us. He had to be Bob Harris, chairman of the Administrative Board, exactly as I pictured him—in his early sixties, with bright silver hair and a politician's smile and handshake. Standing next to him, his wife wasn't Lorraine or Loretta but Noreen, and I shot Ben an exasperated look when I called her both before getting it right. Chairwoman of the parsonage committee, Noreen was petite, with beige hair that wouldn't budge in a hurricane. "Why, Dean, you're so pretty. And so much *younger* than we expected," she said as she kissed my cheek and fluttered her eyelashes at Ben. Her breath smelled of cigarettes and her perfume, gardenias.

The next one to introduce herself was exactly as Ben had described her: Collie Ruth Walker, sister to Noreen and the president of the most powerful organization in the church, the United Methodist Women. Immediately I was drawn to Collie Ruth, a handsome woman in her sixties, tastefully dressed in a silk dress and pearl choker. According to Ben, she was active in community and civic affairs as well as in groups like the Historic Society. I figured she was a widow, wealthy, who lived in a big old house that'd been in the family for years, richly furnished with antiques. The sunlight through the windows of the entrance hall caught the sparkle of diamonds on her fingers.

"Everyone's been dying to meet you, Dean." Collie Ruth smiled, hugging me close. Her face was open and friendly, and her brown eyes twinkled youthfully. Somehow I knew she'd be an advocate, which wasn't always the case. The UMW president often expected a lot of the preacher's wife: She had to attend all meetings, serve on several committees, always be available to host teas and give programs. The parsonage living room stayed in a state of readiness for such occasions. "Meet Lorraine Bullock, our music director," Collie Ruth instructed, turning me to face the rest of the committee, "and her husband A.H., chair of the Pastor-Parish Relations Committee. With them's our talented organist, Sylvia Hinds."

I told Ben afterward that I smelled trouble with those three right away. Preachers' wives develop a sort of radar where church people are concerned. A.H. Bullock was easy; both Ben and I soon found out that he was a pompous ass, a troublemaker. His wife, Lorraine, however, was a bit more subtle. I guessed her to be about my age, mid-forties, and she smothered me in a hug, a saccharine-sweet smile on her face. A big-boned woman, slightly overweight, she'd tried to disguise her plump cheeks with blusher, applied to create the illusion of high cheekbones. "We've heard *all* about you, Dean," she said, eyeing me with mascara-laden, cunning eyes. Everything about her was overdone; she wore too much makeup, too much perfume, and was overdressed in a bright-red pantsuit with several gold necklaces and bracelets. Although I hated myself for smugly assessing new acquaintances, I surmised that Lorraine was an uneducated country girl trying to pass herself off as a member of the country-club set. Something about her didn't ring true, and I suspected the carefully hidden presence of the redneck South. I always recognized one of my own. As we moved through the house, she stayed close to me and patted my arm, as though to let me know she was on my side. I'd learned to be wary of the church ladies who pretended to be supportive while lying in wait for a crack in my armor. With me, it wasn't a long wait.

The organist, Sylvia Hinds, I disliked immediately, so much so that I felt guilty and went out of my way to be extra nice to her. Although young, probably in her thirties, she was as dour-faced as an old woman. Unlike Lorraine, Sylvia could have used a trip to the beauty parlor. Besides wearing old-timey black-rimmed glasses, she won the prize for the most unattractive hairdo ever—cut close to her ears, then flaring out like an upside-down mushroom. "I hope you like the house," she said to me, extending a cold, limp hand, "because we've worked ourselves to death getting it ready." Her high, nasal voice was another charming feature; eventually I'd nickname her Sylvia Whiney-Hiney. I figured that she was the church's martyr; the woman who had her finger in every pie, yet complained of all the work involved. The church was her only social life, the doors never opened without her—she let everyone know that and expected the same of others. Without a smidgen of joy in her faith, she looked down her thin nose at any activity not church-related. If a book or interesting article was mentioned, she'd let everyone know that *she* didn't have time to read. She was much too busy serving the Lord.

Ben and I were walked through the house ceremoniously. I tried not to cringe at the too-formal living room, done up in shades of gold and beige and decorated with velvet and brocade and heavy mahogany furniture. I shouldn't have been disappointed; parsonages were always stiffly formal, uncomfortable places. In the adjoining dining room, a chandelier was suspended like a crystal spiderweb over a long table so highly polished, it reflected like a mirror. I oohed and ahhed because I had to, even though the whole place had the feel of a funeral home. I expected a brass stand with a placard: *The Reverend and Mrs. Ben Lynch. Viewing hours 7–9.*

In the rest of the house, Collie Ruth showed me the practical things—the disposal, the linens, storage areas, light switches—while the others delivered a running commentary that provided some insight into the politics of the church. The dynamics of a church could make or break a preacher; he had to know where the power lay, who ran the church, and who only thought they did. "Use the best paste wax on this sideboard, Dean," Noreen Harris said when we entered the pine-paneled den next to the kitchen. "Bob's dear mother donated it to the parsonage, and it's a priceless family heirloom."

Priceless or not, it was apparent that Bob's dear mother had dumped it in the parsonage because it was so ugly, she wouldn't have it. Bob Harris got down on his hands and knees to show Ben how to work the wide brick fireplace. "Gotta be careful here, Preacher," he said to Ben. "Couple years ago Brother Penfield didn't open the damper and got a faceful of soot. I called the bishop and told him Crystal Springs wasn't ready for a black preacher." Laughing, he slapped Ben on the back, and Ben grabbed the mantel to steady himself, a weak smile on his face.

Since we didn't have furniture of our own, just personal belongings, the movers had quickly unloaded our boxes and made their departure while we were being shown through the house. A. H. Bullock summoned the church's maintenance workers, two Hispanic men, their sleeves rolled up and muscles bulging. When no one made a move to introduce them, I stuck out my hand and introduced Ben and myself. They smiled shyly and lowered their eyes, then got busy distributing the boxes. In the master bedroom, the older man put a box marked *Kitchen* on the floor and A.H. jumped him. "Hey, you, Pedro," he yelled. "Can't you read? No-hablo-the-English? Take that box to the kitchen, like it says."

Ducking his dark head, the man hurried out with the box, red-faced. A.H. looked at Ben and rolled his eyes. "For years we had the best janitor in town, an old colored fellow who worked till he dropped dead at age eighty. Nowadays, you can't get nobody but the migrants. Can't speak English, lazy, steal anything that's not nailed down." When Ben shook his head sympathetically, I glared at him, wishing I were standing close enough to poke him with my elbow. I glared at A. H. Bullock, too, but he didn't notice. His wife, Lorraine, did, though, and her eyes narrowed. At least she stopped patting my arm.

"Be careful cleaning this shower, Dean," Noreen said in one of the guest bedrooms. Her eyes moved over me meaningfully. "The stall's real little, and one of our preachers' wives was so—ah—large, she almost got stuck in it once."

"Poor old Mrs. Ledbetter," Lorraine said, shaking her head sadly. "Crazy as a bessie bug. By the time they left here, she'd lost her mind completely."

"Happens to a lot of preachers' wives," I said, giggling. Everyone looked at me in horror, and Ben threw me a warning glance, one dark eyebrow raised to his hairline. My face burning, I turned my attention to the guest room. What the good church folks didn't know was that after they left, I'd fix this room up as my own. Ben and I hadn't shared a bedroom for years. Except for occasional visits allowed me, he preferred to sleep alone, since he got up all through the night and worked on his sermons. Or worse, practiced them out loud. He insisted I keep my toiletries on the dresser in the master bedroom and a frilly robe hanging behind the door, to keep up appearances.

The church ladies were especially proud of an extra room in the back that they'd converted to a music room for me, furnishing it with a piano once they heard that I gave piano lessons. They watched for my reaction, and I was genuinely touched, in spite of my dismay at the decor. The piano was fine—a small black upright—but the rest of the room was appallingly tacky, overdone with pink lace curtains, an ornate desk, and tiny velvet chairs, surely too fragile for sitting on. I tried not to stare at the wallpaper, which had romanticized seventeenth-century figures dancing the minuet in dizzying circles around the room. My suspicions about Lorraine's background were confirmed when she leaned over and patted my arm again. "Sylvia and I were thrilled to find the precious border," she said proudly. "I've never seen anything quite like it."

The wallpaper border appeared to be musical notes on a scale, but on closer inspection, I saw that in each note was a fat cherub, pink mouth opened, singing angelically. "I've never seen anything like it, either," I said with a straight face.

"We hear you play the guitar as well as the piano," Collie Ruth said to me, her bright eyes curious. "Plan on giving guitar lessons, too?"

"Actually, I play the dulcimer," I told her.

"Dulcimer!" A.H. Bullock scratched his balding head and frowned. "What on earth's that?"

"Surely you know what a *dulcimer* is, A.H.," Sylvia Hinds hooted.

"One of those doohickeys that you play with hammers, honey," Lorraine told him.

A.H. gasped. "Hammers like I stock at the hardware store?"

"Actually, it's a mountain dulcimer," I said. "It's strummed instead."

"Mountain dulcimer, huh? Come from those big mountains y'all have over in east Florida, Preacher?" A.H. said, slapping Ben on the back and laughing heartily at his own humor.

"How . . . interesting," Sylvia said, her voice implying the opposite. "How long you been playing it, Dean?"

As he was apt to do, Ben answered for me. "Dean started her music career early. As a child she performed in her family's bluegrass group." Ben always worked that information into a conversation, thinking it provided me with just the right touch of respectability, explained my backwoods heritage. He knew the church would have heard I was orphaned at age twelve and taken in by a good old Methodist family as a foster child. As long as no one probed further, he could conveniently omit the true character of my foot-stomping, hard-drinking ancestry.

"How wonderful, Dean!" Collie Ruth smiled. "Anyone we would've heard of?"

I shook my head. "No, just a local thing. We called ourselves The Cypress Swamp Band and performed at barn dances, weddings, things like that. It was a long time ago." I wasn't about to describe the backwoods juke joints where we performed every Saturday night.

"And you played the dulcimer as a child?" she questioned, her interest making me like her even more.

"That's right. It was my grandmother's, and she taught me to play it at age six." I didn't tell her the story behind my learning to play, the significance it had in my life. Nor did I tell her that my dulcimer was safely locked away in the trunk of my car since I always moved it myself, not trusting Ben to touch it. In a rural church a few years after we married, I'd played it for a wedding and caused a mild uproar. The preacher's wife playing a guitar in the Lord's House—a guitar! Next thing you know, there would be drums and dancing in the aisles. Ben hadn't liked my dulcimer since, preferring that I stick with the piano. He avoided anything controversial, but it was unlikely to be a problem here. One good thing about larger churches was that they tended to be more liberal.

"Dean's going to be a good addition to our choir, Brother Ben," Lorraine Bullock said to Ben, as though I weren't present.

"Well, ah, Loretta," Ben said, "Dean was tickled to hear First Methodist had a full-time music director on staff, since she's been doing the music in my churches for years and is ready for a break. Right, honey?"

"As both pianist and organist," Sylvia protested, her voice rising, "*I'm* the one who needs a break."

"But—Dean can't do that!" Lorraine said, horrified. "Everybody in Crystal Springs has heard that our new preacher's wife has a degree in music. What will the Baptists say if she doesn't join our choir?"

Her husband chimed in, his voice indignant. "A musician like your wife not being in our choir? Ridiculous!" Like his wife, he addressed Ben, ignoring me.

I looked at Ben. He'd promised to help me get off the hook when we moved here. Although I loved music with my body and soul, I'd looked forward to sitting with the congregation, letting the paid staff do it. When Ben avoided my eyes, I knew he'd let me down, and I swallowed the anger that rose like heartburn. Suppressing anger had become an art form, something I'd perfected with a lifetime's practice.

"Ah, I-I'm sure Dean'll help out with the music once we get settled," he muttered. Looking around the room, he rubbed his hands together, smiling. "You ladies did a fine job with this room, Collie Sue. Now, why don't we go see how the unloading's coming?"

I didn't want them helping us unpack our boxes, handling my things, looking at the contents curiously. But they did, and there was nothing I could do, short of ordering them out of the house. Their house, not mine. I watched helplessly as they arranged my dishes in the cabinets, stood by as the boxes were emptied and my life put in order for me. Even the men helped out, Bob and A.H. putting books and whatnots on the shelves in the den as the women readied the kitchen. Bob joked and laughed amiably as he worked, but I caught A.H. eyeing me speculatively.

It was during this time that the Holderfield family was

first mentioned. We'd heard about them before we moved, of course; it was impossible to talk about Crystal Springs without mentioning its most well-known residents. It was the Holderfields who made it such a coveted appointment among Ben's colleagues. One of the most prominent families in northern Florida—in the history of the settlement of Florida, for that matter—the present Holderfield family, made up of Maddox, Augusta, and their young son, had attended Crystal Springs First Methodist until recently. Apparently, they'd drifted off and no one knew why, nor could anyone lure them back. So the bishop hatched a master plan to restore them to the fold. That Ben, of all the eager contenders, was the one chosen to bring the Holderfield family—and fortune—back to the Methodist church seems beyond coincidence to me now.

"Brother Ben?" Collie Ruth said as she wiped off my everyday china. "I ran into Maddox Holderfield at the country club and told him I'd be mad if he and Augusta don't come to your reception Sunday afternoon. I reminded him that his mama was one of my best friends, God rest her soul."

I looked up from the floor, where I sat unwrapping tea goblets. Ben stepped into the kitchen, eyebrows raised high. "Think they'll come?"

A.H. came in behind Ben, pulling out a handkerchief and mopping his sweaty brow. Although he appeared to be Ben's age, he had the flabby, overweight body of a much older man. "They haven't darkened the door of the church for years," he said.

"Have either of you seen Mimosa Grove?" Noreen Harris asked.

"No, but I'm dying to," I answered. The Holderfields' historic estate was one of the few left in the Panhandle, and I read that it'd been a working cotton plantation of thousands of acres earlier this century, though reduced now to a few hundred acres. Pictures of the house, which dated to the early 1800's, were in the Florida history books. It was called Mimosa Grove because of a unique avenue of giant mimosa trees, brought from Spain by an early settler. As a certified tree-hugger, I was as anxious to see the famed mimosas as the house.

"Don't know if you've heard this, Brother Ben," Bob Harris said, "but Maddox Holderfield saved this town. He's a fine boy." I knew from Ben's meetings with the bishop, the "boy" was in his late forties.

"I've heard all about that, Bob," Ben said, leaning on the door frame between the kitchen and den, watching everyone else work. Something he was good at, I'd noticed before.

Bob stuck his head in the kitchen and addressed his remarks to me. "When his daddy died, Miss Dean, Maddox reopened the tomato packing plant and put a lot of people to work. Hard to do with agribusiness taking over everything nowadays."

I nodded, not sure what response was expected of me. "As you might imagine, he's kind of a town hero," Bob continued, and I nodded more vigorously, smiling.

Lorraine Bullock blinked her eyes coyly. She was unpacking my dinnerware, arranging knives, forks, and spoons into a slotted holder in a drawer. "Folks in these parts think Maddox Holderfield hung the moon. And he's so *nice*, too. If you didn't know he was such a big shot, you'd think he was just a regular human being." I ducked my head to hide my smile. As opposed to *what*, I wanted to ask her.

Sylvia Whiney-Hiney put her two bits in from the kitchen table, where she unpacked place mats and napkins. "Unlike his wife. She's never had anything to do with any of us. Thinks she's too good, I guess."

"Now, Sylvia," Collie Ruth said quickly, "that's not

true. I've always adored Augusta, no matter what everybody says about her."

That was certainly intriguing. "Collie Ruth?" I said, glancing up from my seat on the floor, hoping I could prod her to say more. "The bishop told us that Augusta was raised in this church but Maddox wasn't?"

"That's right." She nodded. "First Methodist's only claim to Maddox is through Augusta."

Ben stood with his arms folded, listening avidly. He glanced my way in approval, knowing I was probing for information, something that might help him win the Holderfields back. "Although Augusta's family was one of the founders of our church, the Holderfields are Episcopalian," Collie Ruth explained. I knew that Augusta's family was as prominent as Maddox's, her father having been a well-known state senator for decades. "After Maddox and Augusta married about fifteen years ago, I think, they ended up here, in Augusta's home church, though Maddox has never joined," Collie Ruth continued. "Their only child, Gus, was christened here, but soon afterward they quit coming and none of our preachers have had any luck getting them back."

"There's no reason to hope they'll come to the reception Sunday," Sylvia said, sniffing. Evidently she was nearsighted; she peered through her glasses like Mr. Magoo, narrowing her eyes and squinting.

Collie Ruth smiled at Sylvia smugly. "Actually, Sylvia, I have a good reason to think they might. At the country club, Augusta was with Maddox, and she seemed very curious to hear about Dean."

"*Me?*" I said at the same time that both Ben and Sylvia said, "*Dean?*" Pleased at getting everyone's attention, Collie Ruth took center stage. The unpacking stopped and everyone watched her. Taking her time, she put away a couple of plates before turning back to her audience.

"Why, yes," she said. "Augusta asked me numerous questions about Dean, and seemed really interested in meeting her."

I caught my breath, excited. It wasn't often I'd upstaged Ben. Matter of fact, it had never happened. All eyes were on me, as though the onlookers—Ben included, I feared—were trying to figure out why Augusta Holderfield would be interested in someone like me. I wondered how they saw me—as the pious preacher's wife I was trying so hard to be, or as the unsuitable one they'd surely heard about? "What's Augusta like?" I asked, addressing Collie Ruth, although everyone else jumped in, each with a different response.

Sylvia twisted her lips like she'd just bitten into a sour persimmon. "I told you, she doesn't have anything to do with any of us. I guarantee she won't come." *Especially to meet you*, her look implied.

"Perfectly charming," Collie Ruth said quickly, glaring at Sylvia. "Very warm and fun-loving."

"She's a wild one," A.H. contributed. "Had quite a reputation as a teenager."

"I never figured out what Maddox saw in Augusta, myself," Lorraine said. "Have y'all ever seen anyone as mismatched?" I dared not look at Ben, figuring he'd answer that the same way as me: Every time I look in the mirror.

Bob Harris laughed and slapped Ben on the back again, and this time Ben had the door frame to grab hold of. "If they come to the reception, you'll know what he sees in her, Preacher," Bob said. "She's a looker. I mean, a real looker."

Noreen'd been quiet, watching us as she wiped off china cups with a dishcloth. "That's true, but . . . Augusta's one of those women too beautiful for her own good." Another intriguing statement, I thought, my interest piqued even more.

"To be honest, nice as he is, Maddox is . . . well, attractive but not especially good-looking," Sylvia added. "What you'd call ordinary-looking, I guess." Like a regular human being, I thought.

Noreen looked at Ben, her eyes thoughtful. "Oh, I wouldn't say that, not at all. Though not like Brother Ben here, Maddox is certainly appealing in his own way. Women all over the state were after him, y'all might remember. He surprised everyone by up and marrying Augusta Spencer. Then after a few years, it looked like she wasn't going to be able to give him children. I feel sorry for any woman who can't have children."

To give her credit, she realized what she'd said as soon as it came out of her mouth, and her face flamed red. There was an awkward silence as everyone looked my way, and I lowered my head to the box I was unpacking. Collie Ruth came to my rescue, which she was to do many times during the duration of my time in Crystal Springs. She glared at her red-faced sister, then turned and shook her dishcloth at the men standing in the doorway. "Tell you what," she said. "Why don't you men go over to the church now and help Brother Ben unpack his office things? We'll have this whole house in order by supper time."

And they did. Boxes were unpacked and hauled away, pictures hung, clothes folded in drawers. The women gossiped constantly as they worked, filling me in on the rest of the congregation. I only half-listened, my mind going back again and again to the intriguing idea of Augusta Holderfield being curious about me. My fascination with the Holderfields started that afternoon amidst the boxes and Bubble Wrap of my new house, although I had no way of knowing then how my fate would become so intertwined with theirs. Everything I believed about destiny was about to change.

Standing in the receiving line in the church's Fellowship Hall the following Sunday, I wondered with every hand I shook if the Holderfields would be next. Bob Harris, silver hair smooth and shining, was first in line with Noreen next to him, dressed in a beige silk suit the same shade as her artfully colored hair. Noreen had surprised me by bringing me one of her cast-off suits to wear, saying it was much too big for her but would look nice on me, a double-edged statement if I've ever heard one. A minister's family is often the object of a certain kind of benign charity, as I discovered in mine and Ben's first church, where I almost ruined his career. The board chairman's wife brought me a sack of cast-off clothes and I froze instead of thanking her as I flashed back to my humiliation as a foster child and object of charity. Since that incident, I learned to take their hand-me-downs more graciously, even developing an appreciation for expensive castoffs, which I couldn't have afforded otherwise. Ben approved since it left more money in our budget for his costly wardrobe. When I'd appeared in Noreen's double-breasted white suit, he'd been pleased until I leaned over to buckle the straps of my heels. "Good heavens, Dean," he'd gasped, "that jacket's cut too low. Go back and pin it. You can use that cameo my mother gave you." I tried to tell him I wasn't planning on bending over, and I didn't want to wear his mother's heavy, old-fashioned cameo, but he refused to walk to the church with me until I did as he commanded.

Ben stood next to the Harrises, turning with each well-wisher to introduce me. Collie Ruth, in charge of the refreshments, hovered at our elbows. I was grateful every time she whispered a name to me when I faltered. I was nervous and distracted, worried about not making a good impression. In my paranoia, I imagined raised eyebrows and sideways glances from the church members, sure word had gotten around that I was an imposter, not to the manor born. *You've heard about the wife, haven't you?* they'd whisper. *She's held back Brother Ben, that rising star of the clergy, for all these years. Several years younger than him, yet didn't even give him children! And look how she's dressed, poor thing, in that old suit of Noreen Harris's, pinned halfway to her neck.* I couldn't win. If I dolled myself up, somehow slipped past Ben's disapproving eye, the congregation thought I was a floozy. If I didn't, letting my long straight hair hang loose and not putting on makeup, they whispered that I looked like a country bumpkin, right off the turnip truck.

Ben and I dutifully played our parts for more than an hour, shaking hands and smiling and making small talk. We carried on over babies and toddlers and grandchildren; we tried to show the teenagers how cool we were, and listened patiently as our older members told about the church in the good old days, when dear Brother So-and-so was there. There was a big turnout since the other churches came in full support: the Baptists, Presbyterians, Episcopalians, and Catholics, their elderly white-collared priest in tow. I gave up on the Holderfields coming and took a punch cup from Collie Ruth, my mouth dry from smiling so much. "What a crowd," Ben said, grinning as he drank his punch. Unlike me, he was good at these occasions. The men respected and liked him; the women in his churches fell in love with him. I should know; I'd been one of them.

Ben was raising his punch cup to his mouth when Collie Ruth gasped and took it right out of his hand. "Lord have mercy, Brother Ben, give me that cup. Here come the Holderfields!" There was a rustle of excitement in the crowded room, and everyone turned toward the main door. A man and woman and young boy were coming through the double doors, nodding and speaking to those standing nearby. The crowd parted as though Moses were coming through the Red Sea, and Ben straightened his tie and smoothed down his dark hair.

Intrigued, I focused on Maddox Holderfield first.

Watching him move toward us, I saw that Noreen's description of him was much more accurate than Sylvia's and Lorraine's. Far from ordinary, there was a kind of casual elegance about him that I found much more attractive than mere looks. In this crowd of people in their Sunday best, he was cool and aristocratic, casually dressed in a white shirt, khakis, and loafers. Tanned, with crisp, gray-streaked hair, Maddox Holderfield moved through the crowd like a crown prince, and I watched in admiration.

As soon as I saw Augusta Holderfield, draped in a pale blue dress that clung to her willowy frame, I realized that describing her as a "real looker" was an understatement. She was quite simply the most beautiful woman I'd ever seen. Her blond hair was spectacular, falling to her shoulders in tendrils like a painting of a Renaissance angel; her cheekbones were sculptured, her dark-fringed eyes bright blue. She was as stylish and elegant as a fashion model, and I suddenly felt plain, gawky, foolishly dressed in a too-big suit and clodhopper shoes. As she walked languidly toward us, every single person in the room turned to look at her. I glanced over at Ben to make sure his mouth wasn't hanging open.

The boy with the Holderfields was their nine-year-old son, Gus. Although cute, with hair like sand-colored silk and round little glasses, Gus was without his father's poise or his mother's spectacular looks. The church ladies had told me that Gus was a sweet, diffident child but painfully shy and quiet, very sheltered by his parents. When he caught my eye, he blushed and lowered his eyes.

Augusta was detained by an elderly lady who hugged and kissed a red-faced Gus, so Maddox left them and held out a large tanned hand to Ben. "Dr. Lynch, welcome to Crystal Springs. I'm Maddox Holderfield," he said. Ben fell all over himself, about to shake his hand off. At Ben's introduction, Maddox turned clear gray eyes on me, and I gulped.

Had I not been so nervous, his open, beguiling gaze would've put me at ease. Like Gus, he wore round wire-rimmed glasses, which gave him a gentle, scholarly look. "A pleasure, Mrs. Lynch," he said, shaking my hand.

"Please call me Dean." Under his scrutiny, I felt like a bug impaled on a collection board, especially since Ben's eyes were on me, too, along with those of the congregation and half the town. With the highly tuned radar of the long married, I knew Ben was nervous for me. It was imperative that I make a good impression on the Holderfields if Ben had any hope of bringing them back to the church.

"Only if you call me Maddox, Dean," he replied smoothly.

Augusta managed to free herself from the elderly lady, and she spoke to Bob, Noreen, and Ben briefly before reaching me and taking both my hands in hers. "Dean? I'm Augusta Holderfield."

Like an idiot, the only thing I could think to say was "I know," and everyone laughed. Augusta laughed, too, tossing her marvelous blond hair. Up close, she was so utterly beautiful that I stared at her like a fool. "Dean's a great name," Augusta said, studying me. "I don't think I've ever heard it before. I mean, not for a woman."

"It's short for Willodean. My grandmother's name," I told her, wincing.

"Could be worse—I'm named after my father," she said, then tilted her head. "I came this afternoon just to meet you, Dean. I hear you and I have a lot in common."

Although I'd thought the same thing—both of us were married to highly revered older men, others didn't approve of us, we were gossiped about—I didn't know how to respond. I was sure the crowd hanging on our every word couldn't imagine what on earth she was referring to. No two women could've come from more different backgrounds.

"Here's something you have in common with both Augusta and me, Dean, from what I hear," Maddox Holderfield said. The room became still, all eyes on us. "Like the two of us, you're that rarest of all birds—a native Floridian."

"Oh, no, not me," I blurted out, not understanding him. "I was born and raised in Florida."

Out of the corner of my eye I saw Ben shuffle his feet and Collie Ruth turn her head in surprise. A loud guffaw in the background came from A. H. Bullock. "I meant . . ." I said, my face burning. "That's right! I was. Am, I mean. A native. Ben was raised in Georgia," I added lamely.

"I know that you and Augusta love music," Collie Ruth said to Maddox, in a too-obvious attempt to divert attention from my gaffe, "so you'll be interested to know that Dean is a musician." In her eagerness to be helpful, she moved in on us, stepping on my foot in the process. "Dean has a degree in music education and plays both the piano and the guitar!"

"No kidding?" Augusta said, tossing her head again, a habit of hers, I was to find. Every time she did it, her hair brushed her white shoulders and Ben's eyes widened appreciatively. "I don't know many women who play the guitar," she added, still looking at me curiously.

"You a folksinger, Dean?" Maddox asked, and the church members standing around us laughed in surprise. No doubt I fit their image of a leftover from the sixties with my long straight hair pulled severely back in a ponytail at the nape of my neck, no jewelry except for the cameo, and very little makeup.

"D-dulcimer," I said, rubbing my palms on the side of my skirt. My hands were wet and clammy. This meeting wasn't going as I'd hoped. Cutting my eyes his way, I saw that Ben was not only shuffling his feet but also tugging on his tie, even though he wore a big smile plastered on his face.

"Pardon me?" Maddox said.

"I play the dulcimer, not the guitar," I told him, glancing around at our audience. I felt like I'd announced that I played voodoo drums for satanic rituals.

Augusta Holderfield let out a whoop, and her husband groaned. "You've got to be kidding," she said, her eyes shining. "How fabulous."

Maddox rolled his eyes at the crowd of onlookers, then turned back to me. "I'm afraid you're in for it now, Dean," he chuckled, shaking his head. "My wife has a thing for dulcimer music."

Murmurs rippled through the crowd. Among those closest to us was our oldest church member, Mr. Clyde Morris, here from the nursing home in a wheelchair. We'd met him and his nurse shortly before the appearance of the Holderfields. In his nineties and deaf as a post, he cupped a hand around his ear and said in a voice heard throughout the Fellowship Hall, "Huh? What kind of thing does she have?"

Augusta hooted again, putting her hand over her mouth as her dancing eyes met mine. Mortified, I managed a weak smile before lowering my head. I heard Maddox's polite cough, as though to hide a snicker, before he came to my rescue. "Augusta's always dragging me to concerts, especially if anyone's playing a dulcimer. We just got back from Nashville, where we heard some great bluegrass."

"Bluegrass?" Collie Ruth said, her face lighting up. "Then you'll be tickled to hear that Dean played in her family's bluegrass band. Our preacher's wife is a real-life, performing musician."

"Oh, no, not at all," I protested with a gasp, knowing the next question from the Holderfields. Sure enough, Augusta grabbed my arm.

"You actually played in a bluegrass band?" she asked. "How wonderful! Are they still performing?"

Ben wouldn't let the spotlight stay on me for too long,

and sure enough, he quickly stepped in, much to my relief. "Dean's family is . . . ah . . . no longer with us, Augusta," he said. "She was orphaned at a young age and taken in by the Richardson family on Amelia Island." He turned to Maddox. "Maybe you've heard of them, Maddox. He's got a big tomato farm, too."

Maddox looked from me to Ben. "I don't think so, Ben. I'm afraid I don't get to that part of the state much."

Augusta, as tall as Ben, blocked him from my view when she leaned toward me. "So, you're a performing musician, Dean? I can't tell you how that fascinates me. Hope I'll be able to hear you play soon."

"Then y'all have to come to our fellowship supper this Wednesday night," Ben said, stepping forward, his voice booming. His pulpit voice, I called it. "Lorraine asked Dean just this morning if she'd play a special for us." His eyes caught Gus's, who'd successfully hidden behind Augusta until now. "And we have lots of games and things for this young fellow here."

"You've been awfully quiet, Gus," Collie Ruth said. "Can't you come out from behind your mama and talk to us, let the Lynches see what a fine little boy you are?"

Gus blushed, but didn't move from behind Augusta. Instead, he looked up at Collie Ruth and asked, "C-could I have some refreshments first, Miss Collie Ruth?"

"Gus!" Augusta laughed indulgently, but Collie Ruth moved quickly and grabbed a tray from the lace-covered table next to us, after pushing past the wheelchair of a still-bewildered Clyde Morris.

"Sure you can, honey," Collie Ruth said to Gus. "I'll fix you right up. How about some of these?"

Gus nodded eagerly, and Collie Ruth brought a tray of punch cups and cookies forward, passing them out to each of us like party favors. My hands shook as I took a cup, but I was grateful to have something—anything—to hold on to.

Just as I raised the cup to my parched lips, Ben made his move. Beating Collie Ruth to the honor, he took a cup and a handful of cookies from the tray and knelt down in front of Gus. Even though Ben had not wanted children of his own, he prided himself on being good with the kids of his congregation. "Here you go, young man," he said to Gus. "Where we come from, we call these cookies 'sand tarts,' and they're my favorite. My wife makes them for me all the time."

Gus turned his face up to me, and the chattering crowd quieted. "You mean that lady there is your *wife*?" he gasped, his eyes wide behind his glasses. The crowd burst into laughter.

"Gus Holderfield!" Augusta exclaimed. At that very moment, I lost my grip on the sticky punch cup and it slipped from my hand, splashing frozen strawberries on my white suit, hitting the front of my jacket like a sash. The silver cup hit the tiled floor with a clatter loud enough to wake the dead in the cemetery behind the church.

"Oh, *Jesus Christ*," I cried out, horrified. Realizing what I'd said, I looked up, my hand going instinctively to cover my mouth. Collie Ruth and the rest of the church members gasped; Ben's eyes widened in shock, and Maddox Holderfield smiled his ironic smile. Everyone's eyes were on me, the splash of red strawberries on my white suit as bright as a scarlet letter.

I think I'd be standing there today, frozen in mortification, if Augusta hadn't come to my rescue. "Come on, Dean," she said briskly. "Let's go wash that stuff off your pretty white suit before it stains. Will y'all excuse us?"

In my low, clunky heels I stumbled after her as she led me out of the main room of the Fellowship Hall toward the kitchen. The crowd parted to let us through, murmuring. I turned my head to look back and saw Collie Ruth, Noreen, and Lorraine Bullock all heading toward us. Augusta held up her hand to stop them. "I'll take care of this, ladies," she said. "Y'all stay here and talk to Maddox till we get back. Get Gus some more of those sand tarts, okay?"

I assumed we'd go to the kitchen and wash up, but Augusta pushed open the swinging doors to the hallway. I wasn't sure where she was taking me until we stopped before the ladies' room. "Here we go," Augusta said, pushing me inside. "Glad I remembered where this thing was."

The pink wallpapered ladies' room smelled like rotten peaches, and I headed straight for the sink to turn on the water faucet. With one hand I grabbed a paper towel from a basket while splashing cold water on the front of my suit with the other. Flustered, I knocked over the basket, scattering the towels like rose petals all over the floor. When the basket fell and bounced on the tiles, I heard a noise from Augusta. Raising my head, I saw her reflection in the mirror over the sink. She was hunched over, leaning against the door frame.

"Augusta! Are you all right?" I cried out, wondering what else could go wrong, if she was having some sort of seizure or something. Through the tears of humiliation that stung my eyes, I saw that she was laughing.

"What's so funny?" I demanded. The frozen glob of strawberries stuck to the front of my suit came unglued and fell at my feet, causing me to jump back, startled, and Augusta laughed even louder.

"Oh my God in heaven," she tittered. "To think what I'd've missed if I hadn't come today. When Clyde Morris said what he did, I managed to keep a straight face, but then Gus! That broke me up. Who'd he think you were—the Virgin Mary?"

I stared at her, my eyes wide, my mouth open. Then I couldn't stop myself. It started with a giggle and I, too, laughed, leaning weakly against the sink.

When our hilarity was spent, Augusta wiped her eyes and smiled at me. "Bet you feel a lot better now. The tension in that room was so thick, you could cut it with a knife. Has it been like that all afternoon?"

I nodded, leaning toward the mirror as I wiped my eyes, too. "Oh, yeah. Everybody's always real uptight on occasions like this."

"Good Lord," she said, clucking sympathetically. "How do you stand it?"

I shook my head. "It can be pretty trying," I admitted. "I get so nervous. That's why I always do something to mess up, I guess." I shrugged, trying for nonchalance, not wanting her to know how mortified I'd been. "Gives them something to talk about."

"You sure gave them something to talk about today," Augusta giggled. "If you could've seen Ass Hole Bullock's face when you said 'Jesus Christ' after dropping that cup of punch! He looked like he was going to have a coronary."

"*Who?*" I asked.

"You know—A. H. Bullock."

That was all it took to get me started again, and Augusta laughed, too, throwing her head back. Both of us jumped when the door rattled and shook. "Augusta?" It was Collie Ruth, standing in the hallway trying to open the door. "The door's not locked, is it?"

Like me, Augusta tried to pull herself together. "Collie Ruth? I locked it till we could get Dean all cleaned up. We'll be out in a second, okay?"

There was a pause, then Collie Ruth's voice again, muffled by the door between us. "But . . . is everything all right, honey? I thought I heard somebody crying."

"Oh, no, ma'am," Augusta said. "We're fine. Just getting cleaned up, is all."

The door rattled again. "Let me in and I'll help y'all. People are wondering what's going on."

Augusta pulled on the door a couple of times, then turned to me and winked. "Goodness, it seems to be stuck. But I'll get it open, don't you worry. Go back and tell everybody that Dean and I'll be out in just a minute, okay?"

"Well, okay," Collie Ruth replied, her voice uncertain. "I'll come back with a screwdriver if y'all aren't out in a few minutes, you hear?" We stood still, holding our breath, until we heard her heels clicking down the hallway as she returned to the reception.

"Guess we'd better go," I said to Augusta. "If she comes back and tries to pry us out with a screwdriver, I'll crack up." Our eyes met as we hooted again, covering our mouths to mute the sound.

Her arm draped over my shoulder, Augusta pulled me to her, hugging me close. "My God, Dean Lynch, this is too much! I was dying to meet you after hearing all the talk going around town, and I sure got my money's worth."

"The church ladies told me about you," I said, "so I was dying to meet you, too."

"Oh, shoot, I know what they say about me," she said, rolling her eyes. "Tell you what, let's me and you get together next week and compare notes. Now that we've met, I can tell—you and I would make a great team."

Two

BEN WAS HIGH AS a Georgia pine the night we went to Mimosa Grove for the first time, thrilled that he'd already scored with Maddox Holderfield and we'd only been in town for two weeks. The church folks told him that although Reverend Penfield, his predecessor, paid official visits to Mimosa Grove, he'd never been invited socially. The very next day after the reception, Augusta had called, asking us to dinner. Because of all the church meetings and civic clubs, it was a few days before we could make it. By then I'd worked myself into a frenzy of dread, resigned to committing another faux pas. I'd been out of the backwoods for twenty years, had a college education, and had lived in several different places, but I still carried childhood fears of social disgrace.

Ben let out a whistle when we turned off the main highway and drove through the iron gates that led to Mimosa Grove. "Would you look at that?" He'd changed twice, first dressing in a suit and tie, then deciding a short-sleeved shirt and khakis were more appropriate. He'd been annoyed that I hadn't asked Augusta if it was a formal dinner. "Always ask,

Dean," he'd said, scowling as he combed his dark hair. "Simple enough, isn't it? Then we won't have to wonder if we're underdressed." I'd looked down at my sandals and denim sundress, a thrift-store special, and sighed.

It was early evening, just past sunset, as we turned onto the winding driveway leading to the big old plantation house. I bent down to look out the window, gaping like a country bumpkin. "The house is something," I said to Ben, "but what I like are the trees."

"Because you're a hopeless tree-hugger," he said, and I glanced over at him, surprised.

"There was a time when you couldn't even say that, much less joke about it," I said, and he rolled his eyes.

"Good Lord, who can blame me? The bishop still mentions it, every time I see him."

"I was a hero to some people," I said in a small voice, and Ben hooted.

"Bunch of fanatics is all; old hippies, environmentalists, nobody in our church. But at least you didn't chain yourself to the tree or get arrested with them. It could've been worse."

"Only because I was too big a coward," I muttered, not loud enough for Ben to hear. No point in rehashing that incident, especially since it'd brought us to the brink of divorce.

"Well, nobody's going to bulldoze these trees, that's for sure," he said, slowing down.

The giant mimosas leading up to the house had been planted from seedlings brought over from Spain by the first Mrs. Holderfield, rumored to have been a Spanish contessa. Unlike the local trees, they were tall with thick trunks and placed close enough together to form a green-and-pink tunnel over us. It was like swimming underneath flowers. At the end of the avenue we circled a lily pond in front, and Ben stopped the Buick in the graveled parking area. Craning my neck, I stumbled getting out of the car, staring upward at the white stucco mansion with its columned portico and iron-laced balconies. It was more impressive up close than from a distance, though time had left its mark, leaving the grand old house as elegantly shabby as an aging Southern belle. Ben chuckled as we climbed the steps. "Close your mouth, Dean. You're gonna catch a fly."

Maddox opened the front door with such a gracious smile that I relaxed. As far as I could tell, he was every bit as nice as everybody said. In his own domain, he looked exactly as he had the first time I saw him, relaxed, charming, and oh-so-aristocratic. Ben greeted his host a bit too heartily, shaking Maddox's hand as though he were the pope. I halfway expected to see him fall prostrate and kiss his ring.

In the entrance hall, my eyes widened looking at the mahogany staircase with its wrought-iron balustrade, big enough to drive a car up. "Augusta'll be right down," Maddox said. "She's getting Gus tucked in for the night." Embarrassed, I knew we'd been too punctual; Ben's insistence on being a few minutes early wasn't the norm in the Holderfields' world.

"It's all so beautiful," I blurted out as we went into the living room. "What's this unusual wood?" Pine paneling was a familiar sight, narrow and blondish with knotholes, but this wood was as dark and rich as chocolate fudge.

"Native cypress," Maddox said as his fingers traced the dark etchings of the pattern. "It wasn't considered a show wood when the house was built. Cypress was plentiful, was all. We removed seven layers of paint to uncover it."

"Who would paint over something this gorgeous?" I said, then blushed. Foot-in-mouth disease again. Of course it had been some of his ancestors.

Although Ben glared at me, Maddox gave no sign that he'd heard me. "Would you like a tour?" he asked instead.

"Oh, yes," I said. "Did you know, when I was in fourth

grade, Mimosa Grove was in our Florida history books? I've always wanted to see it."

"Bet you have to do tours and things like that, living in a historical monument," Ben said, and Maddox nodded.

"Yeah, and it's a pain in the ass, too. Oops, pardon me, Reverend," he said, grinning.

"Don't worry," Ben said. "I live with Dean, so I've heard worse." My face flamed, but Maddox winked at me behind Ben's back.

As we started out of the living room, Maddox paused by a silver serving tray on an old sideboard and lifted up a crystal decanter of white wine. "Chardonnay?" he asked.

Trying to appear casual, I took a glass, as though having a drink with our church members was no big deal. Ben piously refused, having Perrier instead, and I ignored the look he gave me when Maddox turned his back to twist open the green bottle of mineral water. The wine was brisk as a cold splash of rose water, the crystal glass delicate as a dragonfly's wings.

We sipped our drinks companionably as Maddox walked us through the house. It was hard to imagine anyone living in a place grand as a museum, with fragile-looking Oriental rugs tossed everywhere on the wide-planked pine floors. I assumed it was Augusta's touches that made it feel like a home, such as an oversized vase with a surprising arrangement of sunflowers, their heads the size of pumpkins. Along with gold-framed paintings of Holderfield ancestors, informal family snapshots were in groupings all over: Maddox and Augusta on their wedding day; Maddox in surgical greens holding a newborn Gus; Augusta holding out her arms to her toddling son. Augusta looked much different in her twenties, young and innocent instead of sophisticated as she was now.

It was obvious that Maddox loved the house in spite of the pitfalls of living in a historic monument. "Yeah, it's a great place, but an awful drain," he responded to Ben's enthusiastic questions. "The upkeep's unbelievable. I've often thought we'll have to donate it to the historical society or else go bankrupt keeping it up. It's absurd to maintain it for the three of us, but I'm determined to keep it in the family so we can pass it down to Gus." He opened the door to the family room. "The original structure was built in 1848, a few years after Florida became a state. Very few white people settled here, you know. Why would they try to survive in this hellhole of a swampland when the rest of the South was so fertile? Florida was full of snakes and gators and mosquitoes and Seminoles, all of them deadly on any given day."

"So the house is antebellum?" Ben asked. "Parts of it remind me of New Orleans. French influence, I'll bet."

"You're observant," Maddox said, and Ben beamed. "It's written up as antebellum, but it's really a hodgepodge, like our Florida heritage. My ancestors were English intermarried with French and Spaniards, thus the balconies and porticoes and iron lace. Mix that with antebellum neoclassicism and you get Mimosa Grove." We peered into the black-and-white tiled kitchen, where a heavenly aroma floated from a copper pot on a restaurant-size stove. "Augusta's gumbo," Maddox told us. "She's a great cook. Gardener, too. Grows her own herbs and vegetables."

"So Augusta doesn't have household help?" I asked, cutting my eyes to Ben. When we were driving out, he'd bet me we'd be served dinner by a uniformed maid.

"Oh, yeah, we have help. This place is way too big for the two of us to manage. There's my foreman, Carl Hernandez, and his wife, Theresa, who helps us out with Gus and around the house. Their son's getting a degree in horticulture, so he does the grounds."

Ben beamed. "They're members of our church," he announced, as though Maddox wouldn't know that. He was proud of the social activism of the Methodist church, proud we had both Hispanic and African-American members. He couldn't take credit for the Hernandezes, but he'd recently landed the new doctor in town, a black man.

"I'm lucky to have Carl, I tell you, Ben," Maddox said. "They're Cuban exiles, and he has a master's degree in agriculture. I couldn't run the farm without him."

In the dining room, Maddox pointed out that the cypress paneling had been painted white by his mother, so he'd not removed it. "She couldn't take the darkness of the wood, so she added Georgian windows to let more light in. But here, in the library," he said, continuing our tour, "the cypress was left natural, dark and gloomy as hell. Looks like something out of Edgar Allan Poe, doesn't it?"

It did, but I fell in love with the library and pulled out one of my favorites, *Cross Creek*. Sure enough, Marjorie Kinnan Rawlings had personalized it to Maddox's parents. "Oh, my God," I said, my fingers tracing her scrawled signature.

Maddox said to me, "I'll bet you're interested in Florida history."

"Very much so. But Ben's not, since he hails from Georgia, the *real* South."

Maddox chuckled. "To a lot of folks, Florida history is an oxymoron, but I find it both unique and fascinating. Look at this." He pointed me toward a glass-fronted bookcase. "I have a small collection of rare books you might be interested in." He handed me a fragile brown book, and I gasped when I saw the title: *Travels* by William Bartram.

"I've read it a dozen times!" I told him. "His descriptions of the early days of Florida are unbelievable." Losing interest, Ben wandered over to a globe on a tall stand, twirling it impatiently.

"This one actually belongs to my sister," Maddox said, turning the yellowed pages.

I looked up at him, curious. "So you have brothers and sisters?"

He shook his head, replacing the book on the shelf. "Just my younger sister, Kathryn. Since she lives in North Carolina, we don't get to see much of her. She went to college in Chapel Hill and married a local boy. Got a houseful of kids, so Gus has cousins to play with when we get together."

"Ah—you have a wonderful collection of children's books for them," I said, pulling out a tattered copy of *Raggedy Ann and Andy*.

"Borrow whatever you'd like, or you're welcome to take some to the window seat over there," Maddox said. Turning, I looked at the cushioned seat nestled in an alcove. Books had been the great escape of my childhood, and I'd read every single one in the school library. To be snug on a window seat at Mimosa Grove with a lapful of books would be about as good as it gets.

Augusta swept into the room, Gus trailing behind her, just as Maddox ushered us onto the sunporch, a glassed-in room of rattan and potted palms and orchids in hanging baskets. Slow-turning fans overhead stirred the night air, and candles flickered on a wicker table set for four.

"Dean!" Augusta smiled, giving me a tea-rose scented hug. "It's great you're finally here." She greeted Ben, shaking his hand formally and calling him Dr. Lynch, even though he asked her to call him Ben. I flinched looking at her, for she was dressed in jade-green silk pants and top, elegant as a well-cut jewel. Now that she'd made her appearance, I felt like a middle-aged matron in my denim and sensible sandals, a brown wren next to a peacock.

"I promised Gus he could come say good night, then it's straight to bed for his royal hiney," Augusta said, tossing her glorious hair.

Gus peeked from behind his mother, ready for bedtime

in Batman pj's, his silky hair wet and plastered to his head. He lowered his eyes when he greeted us, his eyelashes long and dark. I longed to take him in my arms, but contented myself with patting him on the head. He squinted at me without his glasses, and smiled.

"I have to say, Maddox," Ben said after Gus had gone and we'd seated ourselves around the wicker table, "that I don't envy you at your age raising a young child. Makes me tired to think about it. Don't think I'd have married Dean if she'd had her heart set on having kids."

In the awkward silence, I lowered my eyes to my plate. For someone so well-known for his people skills, Ben could be incredibly tactless. Everyone in town talked about the early years of their marriage when it looked like the Holderfields wouldn't be able to have children. Surely Ben knew people didn't like to talk about those things, knowing how I avoided discussions of our childlessness. It always surprised me when church members asked us whose idea it was that we didn't have children, mine or Ben's. By my silence, I gave the impression that it was mine, another mark against me. Oh, well. I raised my wineglass defiantly. Might as well be hung for a goat as a sheep.

"Thanks for reminding me of my advancing age, Brother Ben," Maddox said lightly, but there was an edge to his voice. Ben had the grace to look uncomfortable, and Augusta winked at me as she ladled the gumbo from a silver tureen into our bowls.

"Mimosa Grove is fabulous, Augusta," I said to her, desperate to change the subject.

The candlelight caught the sparkle of tiny diamonds in her earlobes. "Yeah, but it's an unbelievable pain. I'd love to have a house at Key West, but every penny we have goes into keeping this old place afloat. Not a day goes by that something isn't leaking, peeling, cracking, stopping up, or falling down."

I couldn't respond because I'd never had a house of my own, and never would. After parsonage life ended, the Methodist church furnished smart little duplexes for the retirement years, rented out at a nominal cost until their inhabitants ended up in the nursing homes also provided and run by the church. The thought depressed me so much, I couldn't think about it, especially since Ben found it an ideal solution.

"Dean doesn't agree with me," Ben said, "but I *love* having a house furnished by the church. The stuff you complain about, Augusta, we don't have to think about."

"I'd much prefer to think about it," I snapped, then blushed to feel Augusta's eyes on me.

"Jesus, I don't blame you," she said, her voice soft. "Don't they come in and inspect it, peek under the bed to make sure you didn't miss any dust motes?"

Ben picked up his water glass and smiled. "A common misconception. The parsonage committee inspects, but only to see if we need anything. Isn't that right, Dean?"

I wanted to kick him under the table, for he knew I wouldn't argue in front of Augusta and Maddox. "They're good about asking if we need anything," I muttered instead.

We fell silent eating the gumbo, dark brown and thick with oysters and crabmeat and big fat shrimp. Augusta turned to me, her eyes bright. "Dean, I've waited long enough to hear about your dulcimer."

"Oh, Dean was the music director and organist at our church on Amelia Island," Ben answered for me, spooning gumbo into his mouth with gusto. "She plays all sorts of instruments. Y'all should come to our fellowship suppers, since she plays the piano for group singing afterward."

"Dean?" Augusta kept her gaze on me as she passed a napkin-covered basket of fragrant bread.

"Actually," I told her, "I grew up playing the dulcimer. The one I have is handmade, and was my grandmother's. She taught me to play it." I took an herb-studded roll and inhaled the fragrance of rosemary. "It's a mountain dulcimer. Fits right in my lap." My baby, I wanted to add, but didn't.

Augusta said, "What kind of wood is it? And does it have hearts and thingamajigs carved on it?"

I smiled at her. "Solid walnut, top and sides. And the sound holes are carved with bluebirds and leaves instead of hearts."

"Do you know anything about its history?"

I shook my head, touching my mouth with my napkin. "I wish. My grandparents moved to Florida from the mountains of Kentucky, bringing it with them, is all I know."

"A true heirloom, whatever its history," Augusta said.

"The only heirloom Dean can claim," Ben said, chuckling.

"So your grandmother was a musician, then? She was part of your family's bluegrass group?" Augusta asked. "I'm still dying to hear about it."

I smiled. "Not much to tell. We performed for local weddings, dances, even funerals. But I wouldn't call my grandmother a musician. She was more like a—ah—she did odd jobs, nothing special. She died when I was twelve."

"We've heard that you have no relatives left," Maddox said gently. "That must be really tough."

I shrugged and looked down at my plate. "You get used to it." I didn't want questions about my background tonight. Augusta began removing the soup bowls, putting a hand on my shoulder when I tried to get up and help her.

"More wine, anyone?" Maddox held the carafe poised over my glass, but I caught Ben's look out of the corner of my eye and shook my head.

Augusta brought in plates of stuffed sea bass, the aroma like the ocean heavy with rain. When I complimented her, Maddox put a hand on his wife's arm. "Augusta's a great cook, great mother, and great wife."

Augusta shot him a look of disgust. "Oh, please."

"I don't mean to embarrass you in front of these nice people, but it's true." His warm gray eyes were so full of his love for her that I ducked my head, reaching for my water glass. Again, Augusta scoffed at her husband's praise.

"Goddammit, Maddox," she said. "I mean it."

Unabashed, he looked over at Ben, grinning. "Shame on you, talking like that in front of the preacher."

Augusta shrugged. "You know I don't sugarcoat things for anybody," she said. Like Maddox, I looked at Ben, who was staring at her, astonished. He was used to being treated much more reverently.

"It's not like you to be rude to guests, Augusta," Maddox said.

After a pause, she relented. "I apologize, then. I certainly don't intend to be rude, Dr. Lynch. I say what I mean, and if anyone doesn't like it, well . . . I'm sorry. I am who I am."

"Fair enough," Ben said. He seemed unaffected, but his disenchantment with Augusta had begun.

We finished our meal in silence, somewhat uncomfortably. I wasn't sure what Augusta's comments meant, but I wondered for the first time about her and Maddox and their seemingly perfect existence. We were eating dessert, mango sorbet on a rum-soaked sponge cake, when a cry pierced the stillness of the summer night. Ben and I froze, spoons poised over our plates. For one crazy moment I thought of Jane Eyre and the wife in the attic. Augusta stood up, then hurried from the room, her white napkin falling to the stone floor like a rose petal.

"It's okay," Maddox said, getting to his feet to pour us coffee from a silver pot. "Just Gus having one of his bad dreams. Augusta'll get him back to sleep."

"Poor baby," I murmured, relieved. I remembered only too clearly the terror of childhood nightmares.

"Monsters under the bed." Maddox smiled at me, his round glasses catching the yellow glow of the candles. "Cream and sugar?"

"Should I go up and see if I can help out?" I asked him after the second cup of coffee. An awkward silence hung over us like the moon as time stretched on and Augusta still hadn't returned.

"Dean," Ben said, putting his hand on my arm, "I'm sure Augusta can handle her child without your help."

"Oh!" I looked at Maddox, my face burning. "I—I didn't mean to imply—"

"No, no, don't be silly. Why don't you go up and peek in on them? Second room to your right, top of the stairs." Maddox rose to his feet. "Ben, come with me and I'll show you some pictures of Crystal Springs in the old days, when your church was first built." He held the door open that led from the sunporch to the library as I hurried out, finding my way through the maze of gloomy rooms. I went upstairs cautiously, not sure if I should or not. The second door to the right was closed, so I stood in the hallway uncertain, feeling like an idiot.

A door opened at the other end of the hall and Augusta came out. If she was surprised to see me lurking in the hallway, she didn't let on, just came to me and smiled wearily.

"Gus get off to sleep okay?" I asked in a whisper.

"He's just high-strung like his mama," she replied. Outside Gus's door, she turned the handle and indicated for me to look inside. "But he sure looks like an angel asleep."

He did; one arm flung over his head and the other clutching a teddy bear close. I turned to smile at her but her expression stopped me dead. "Augusta?" I said. "Is something wrong?"

"Nothing," she said, shaking her head. "It's nothing."

"Is Gus—he's not sick or something, is he?" Surely if he had a fatal illness, we would've heard by now.

She shook her head again and pushed her hair back with both hands. "No, no, he's fine. He's great. It's not that." She managed a weak smile. "I didn't think I'd ever have kids, Dean, and sometimes . . . it's like, I don't deserve him. He's so dear to me, so very special."

"Of course he is," I replied, not knowing what else to say.

"I can't believe . . ." I wasn't sure what she was going to say because she stopped herself and looked away. "Oh, never mind," she sighed. "Don't pay any attention to me, okay?" She pulled Gus's door to and motioned for me to follow her down the hall.

Back downstairs, Augusta tossed her head, and in doing so, seemed to toss off that strange moment. There was no trace of it when we joined our husbands, waiting for us at the foot of the stairwell. We were saying our good-byes by the front door when I made my faux pas. Ben told me later that he was surprised I'd made it that far without making a fool of myself.

As Maddox opened the heavy front door, I spotted an unusual hanging in the hallway. A piece of tapestry, long and narrow with a silk tassel on the end, seemed to descend from the molding of the ceiling. "Is it just decorative, or what?" I asked him.

"Originally it was connected to the kitchen," Maddox explained, shrugging. "Used to call the servants forth, I guess."

"Which explains why you didn't know what it was, Dean," Ben said with a grin. "Servants don't come with the parsonage. Don't guess either one of you can relate to that, can you?"

"That's not true, Dr. Lynch," Augusta said, and her voice was cool. "We don't have live-in servants. I wouldn't even if we could." Although Augusta's family was well-to-do, her politician father had been notorious for his liberal views, so she'd been raised quite differently than the Holderfields, the church ladies told me.

"Unlike Dean," Ben teased, patting my shoulder. "She'd have a maid to fan her and feed her grapes."

"Come on," Augusta said. "Would you, Dean?"

"Hardly," I said, my voice sharper than I intended. "I'd have trouble with that kind of exploitation since my own grandmother cleaned rich people's houses when she wasn't picking cotton in their fields."

Ben grabbed my arm and pulled me toward the open door, a grin plastered on his face. "My sermon's not going to be worth doodly-squat if I don't get home and work on it, folks," he said heartily. "Thanks for inviting us. Don't know when we've had a better dinner!"

Outside in the car, Ben put his head on the steering wheel. "God in heaven, Dean, I can't believe you made that crack about rich folks," he sighed.

I swallowed and shook my head. "Me neither. I feel terrible—"

"You should," he said, backing the car out. "It was embarrassing. You don't have to rub people's noses in your white-trash background. I've told you, generally people are sympathetic and understanding, if you'd stop being so defensive."

"I know, I know . . ." I moaned.

"You need to reread the chapter in my book about Jesus and the Samaritan woman. The Samaritans were the lower class of Jesus' day, looked down on by everyone. Seeing how Jesus accepted her ought to make you feel better about yourself."

"*Love yourself as Jesus loves you*," I muttered. The title of Ben's devotional book, published last year.

"Exactly. That's my girl!"

Although we talked on the phone every day after our dinner at Mimosa Grove, almost a week went by before I saw Augusta again. After my turning down her lunch invitations each day, she grew exasperated with my schedule, her persistence making me suspect she was as lonely as me. "Tell the old biddies of First Methodist to kiss your behind, you're not going to another one of their boring meetings," she said.

"Oh, Augusta, I *can't*."

"Why not? Surely you don't go to everything at the church, do you?"

"I ought to. You know, for Ben, since we're trying to make a good impression."

"Oh, bull," Augusta snorted. "Ben doesn't need your help to make it. I hear the talk going around. Last night we had drinks at the country club with that incredible bore Bob Harris and his dingbat wife, Noreen. They raved endlessly about Ben."

"Bet they didn't rave about me," I sighed.

"Not true. Bob told Maddox you had a good-looking ass."

"He did *not*," I squealed.

"Naw, I made that up. How long do you think it's been since him and Noreen have done it? She might mess her hair up."

I laughed, and Augusta persisted. "Come on, Dean, skip the ladies' luncheon and come to Pensacola with me. I could tell you some stories about my life that'd make everybody else's look tame."

"How can I resist?" I said. "Okay, you win. I'll make up something so I can sneak away for lunch."

It was the beginning of my rebellion, my eventual estrangement from the church people. After the first time, it became easier; every now and then, I went to a meeting, sat near the back, and slipped out quietly once it got under way. Like a school kid skipping classes, I delighted in my truancy even while consumed by guilt. My prayer life flourished, for the

more I sneaked away with Augusta, the more time I spent on
my knees, begging God's forgiveness.

For the duration of our friendship in the months that followed, Augusta showed as much curiosity about my life as I
did about hers. She never understood how I could live the way
I did, the itinerant life of a preacher's wife. After we spent
more time together and got to know each other better, Augusta confessed that it was more than that—she just couldn't
imagine me and Ben together. "Jesus Christ," she said to me,
"you with a *preacher*, Dean! It makes no sense to me. I just
don't get it."

I knew that Augusta could never truly understand my
background, see how it made me what I was, or how Ben had
seemed to be my salvation, my way out. It was impossible for
someone like her, raised in wealth and privilege, to comprehend the degradation and humiliation of my childhood, the
way it shaped me into the person I was when she met up with
me so many years later. Not that she didn't try. "You mean
you were real poor?" she'd asked me, wide-eyed.

"After my parents died and I was put in foster care, I
was a ward of the state," I replied. "I had nothing, Augusta.
Nothing. The people of my church sent me to college."

"So you were an orphan?" she persisted.

"Little Orphan redneck Annie," I answered.

"And your parents were alcoholics?"

"No," I told her, sighing, shaking my head. "They were
drunks. Both of them, sorry people. Sorry as gully dirt. They
drank all day and played their music in juke joints all night
and died the way they lived, drunk. The two of them, shit-
faced drunk."

Augusta understood enough to see that I had to get out
of the backwaters of north Florida, away from my pathetic,

white-trash upbringing. But she didn't quite see how Ben figured into it. According to her, I was smart and pretty and talented, so I could've gotten myself out without anyone's help. It wasn't as though I was desperate, she said. Why would I marry Ben, so different from me and a holy man to boot? It intrigued her, and it would be a long time, toward the end of our friendship, before I understood her fascination with my choice of a husband. "A man of the cloth," she'd tease me. "What's it like to be married to a man of God?"

What was it like to be married to a minister, a proclaimer of the Word, a man ordained by God to perform the holy sacraments, to baptize, marry, and bury? When I told Augusta that I hadn't realized what I was getting into, that I'd considered myself so lucky to marry Ben that I wouldn't have cared what his profession was, she'd scoffed. "Gimme a break. He's the one who was lucky to get you."

"Not so. I still don't know what Ben saw in me; why he married me when he had so many others to choose from," I confessed.

"I can't believe you're so naive," she'd said. "Either that, or Ben's brainwashed you. Dean, don't you have any idea how beautiful you are? One look at you, and the good reverend was a goner. He committed the deadly sin of lust in his heart, so he had to seek penitence. Wasn't it Saint Paul who said it's better to marry than to burn?"

Even though Augusta was curious about me, it took a while before I found out much about her. From the beginning, things didn't quite add up. Something about the relationship between her and Maddox struck me as off balance, but I couldn't put my finger on it. Unlike Ben and myself, the two of them should've been perfectly matched; both were from privileged backgrounds and shared histories. I'd even secretly wondered if Maddox, the town hero, was a drunk or wife-beater or something, but Augusta'd admitted that he was as goody-goody as his reputation. "Oh, Maddox," she'd said dismissively. "He's so polite, so controlled, so damn *nice* that I could scream." If that were the case, then the problem must be with Augusta, though that didn't make sense, either. In spite of her scoffing, she seemed to adore her husband, and he obviously worshiped her. Augusta was too flamboyant not to have gossip associated with her, however, and I heard plenty from the church ladies, once our friendship became known around Crystal Springs. They loved telling me about her wild ways, saying her poor widowed daddy sent her off to boarding school as a teenager because he couldn't control her; that she slipped out at night and went God knows where with God knows who. Word of her beauty was so widespread that boys—and men—from everywhere flocked to the Spencer house day and night, causing one scandal after the other. I hated gossip, having been the object of it myself, but I'd not been able to resist the stories. Everything about Augusta intrigued and fascinated me.

Ben was required by the bishop to attend seminars for professional development, and he usually insisted on dragging me along. A few weeks after our dinner at Mimosa Grove, he went to a workshop on pastoral counseling in Tallahassee with some of the local ministers. Although he offered to forgo their company if I wanted to come, I assured him I'd make the sacrifice. When I told Augusta that Ben would be out of town for two days, she changed her plans to go to FSU with Maddox and Gus. Maddox was taking Gus to a big alumni event to meet the college baseball team, and Augusta begged out by convincing Maddox that it'd be an opportunity for him and Gus to do some male bonding. As soon as the car was out of the driveway, she was on the phone. "Get a bag packed and your behiney out here, baby girl," she said breathlessly. "We're having a spend-the-night party! I'll tell you all about what a bore Maddox is if you'll let me in on the secret life of the not-so-Reverend Lynch."

"You mean we're going to spend our precious hours of freedom talking about *men*?" I said.

"What else is there to talk about? Bring your makeup, because I'm going to change your image as the pious preacher's wife. When the reverend returns, his eyes'll pop out. You'll be transformed into a bigger floozy than Vanna Faye Bell."

I giggled. Vanna Faye Bell, the main soloist in our choir, was a local icon, a former Miss Florida who wore enough makeup to keep Revlon in business for a year. She traveled the state giving her testimony and singing her heart out at church events. Ben thought she hung the moon, especially when she welcomed him on his first Sunday by singing "You Light Up My Life," and dedicating it to him. I'd not dared make fun of her since she was so highly revered in the church, but of course that wouldn't stop Augusta. Our mutual irreverence was part of our attraction for each other; Augusta said the things I thought but had learned over the years to suppress.

On the third floor of Mimosa Grove, away from the master suite, study, and Gus's bedroom and playroom on the second floor, was a guest room with windows that looked out over the lily pond and wide grounds and hardwood forest surrounding the plantation. "This is fabulous," I said as Augusta hung the slacks and blouse I'd brought for our excursion into Pensacola. Plans included a facial, pedicure, and massage. I looked around, enchanted. It was like a room in a museum, with a wide-planked wooden floor and antique wallpaper, cream-colored with sprigs of rosebuds.

She made a face. "Too old-fashioned for me. Come sit on the dresser stool."

I sat down in front of the dresser, facing my reflection in

an old oval mirror as Augusta, chewing her lip, studied me. "What?" I asked.

"Umm. What can be done for this little church mouse when we go for our makeovers tomorrow?" She walked first to one side of the dresser then the other. "Have you ever thought about wearing makeup?"

"Oh, thanks a lot," I snorted. "I *am* wearing makeup!"

"Oh. What about fixing your hair, then?"

"I call this fixed. Let me up. I'm not going to sit here and be insulted by someone who looks like you!"

"You hide your light under a bushel, baby girl. You have a drop-dead body, but hide it under hand-me-downs buttoned to your neck." She took my ponytail in her hand as though weighing it, and nodded thoughtfully. "Hmmm. Your hair's looking good now that the sun's highlighted it. Get a few more highlights tomorrow, which will be a good contrast to your dark complexion. This severe style suits you, pulled straight back. I was going to persuade you to cut it, but I've changed my mind. Anything else would take away from your almond-shaped eyes; they're your best feature. You need shadow to bring out that unusual green color, though," she added.

"No way," I said. "I'm hopeless with stuff like that. When I put on eye makeup I look like Tammy Faye Bakker, or whatever her name is now."

Augusta sighed, throwing her hands up. "When Ben runs off with Vanna Faye Bell, don't come crying to me."

I laughed at her reflection. "Ben's not running off with anybody. He might lust after her, but he'd never do anything to cause a scandal."

"He conveniently forgets the part about committing adultery in his heart, huh? Typical preacher. Has Ben ever fooled around?"

"*Ben?*"

"I withdraw the question." She went to the door, laughing. "Okay, I'll leave you alone for now. Get yourself settled in, then come downstairs and let's swim before supper."

When Augusta left, I lay down on the bed, my head cushioned in mounds of pillows, feeling like the Little Match Girl gone to heaven. I couldn't believe I was here, in Mimosa Grove, a house I'd seen in a history book and fantasized over as a lonely child. Once Augusta left, quiet and serenity settled in heavy as fog. If I lived in a house like this, I'd disappear on the third floor and play my dulcimer without anyone to hear me, interrupt me, or intrude on that moment when my soul merged with my music. No Ben coming in to ask if I minded fixing him a sandwich or listening to a run-through of his sermon. Privacy was a commodity more precious than gold. I'd not had it in the tiny house of my childhood nor with my foster parents, in a room I shared with two other girls.

After a swim and a supper of shrimp salad, Augusta and I settled into the cushioned furniture by the pool with a pitcher of margaritas and my dulcimer. When the blood red sun slipped into the dark woods, we raised our glasses in a salute.

"You're worse than Maddox about mooning over sunsets," Augusta said, reaching for the frosted pitcher. I sat on a lounge chair next to her, cross-legged.

"So he's a sun worshiper, too," I smiled, closing my eyes and feeling the warmth on my face. I was also feeling a nice buzz from the margaritas.

Augusta laughed. "Oh, goody—we're getting to the part where we talk about the men. Yeah, Maddox puts up a good front, acting all macho, but he's a poet at heart. That's how he courted me, sending me romantic poetry."

"You're kidding," I sighed. "Better shut up or I'll be falling in love with your husband."

"No big deal. I'm used to it—women always been after him like flies on a cowpatty."

"That doesn't bother you?" I glanced over at her curiously. The reddish-gold light of the sunset gilded her face and hair, giving her an unearthly beauty. As though she'd have to worry about her husband looking at another woman!

"Naw." She grinned wickedly. "Nobody woman enough to take my man."

I laughed and turned my face back to the sun. "The first time the church ladies talked about you and Maddox? They said you'd known each other all your lives. That must be kind of strange, marrying a man you've grown up with."

Augusta's voice floated over to me on the soft, sweet air. "Not really. He's several years older, so when I was a little girl of ten, snaggletoothed with pigtails, Maddox was in high school. Our parents were friends, so I spent a lot of time at Mimosa Grove. But Maddox was a distant figure to me, like an older cousin or something."

"When did things change?"

I thought for a minute she wasn't going to answer, then she was somewhat hesitant. "Oh, I came back from college one weekend and my parents dragged me to a social function out here. Or rather, my daddy did—my mother had died years before. Anyway, Maddox was home from graduate school, and we sort of discovered each other."

"Your eyes met across a crowded room, huh?"

Augusta snorted. "Not hardly. I was bored and he was someone to talk to. Plus, he was engaged then; had been for years."

"No kidding?"

"Yeah, so I didn't really think of him as an unattached male."

"Guess not, with a fiancée in the picture. Who was she, anyone from around here?"

"You'll run into her eventually. Libby Legere. They're Episcopalians, richer than God. A lot richer than the Holderfields. As you might imagine, not one of my favorite people, and the feeling is mutual."

I had to prod her to finish the story. "Well? Don't leave me hanging. You're home from college and your daddy drags you to Mimosa Grove. What happened then?"

She sighed. "Maddox was just an old family friend, Dean. Of course, I was aware of the way other women threw themselves at him, the eligible Holderfield heir, even if he was taken by Libby. I teased him about it, the women fawning over him. He claims he fell in love with me that very night."

I'll just bet he did. "He knew you weren't like the rest, don't you think? You didn't care about his name or money, like those other women," I said. It was a romantic story.

"Probably. But you know how that is, Dean, all the women in town carrying on about the good-looking new preacher. Let's hear about your courtship now. Instead of poetry, he read you the Bible, I'll bet. Some of it's pretty good stuff, like the Song of Solomon: *A bundle of myrrh is my well-beloved unto me; he shall lie all night betwixt my breasts.*"

I giggled and raised myself on my elbows. Augusta grinned. "Another margarita, preacher's wife? Not used to after-dinner drinks, are you? Describe the unbearable horror of being a preacher's wife now, baby girl. Details. I want details."

I shook my head. "No way. You've heard all about me, but I don't know much about you. I want to hear about Maddox sending you poetry. Is that how your courtship began?"

"Sort of. Actually, he sent me flowers the next day. White roses, my favorite." We could see her prized white rose beds from the pool. "I called to thank him for the roses, and he asked for my address at school."

"Where'd you go?"

"Little place in Palm Beach, all-girls' school. I go back to college, and he starts writing me, sending me poetry. Nothing romantic then. It didn't get romantic until I came home for the summer. He broke his engagement, we started seeing each other and . . . that's it."

I was quiet for a while, thinking, then asked, "Is he the only man you've ever loved?"

To my surprise, Augusta looked uneasy and busied herself poking the straw into her frothy green drink. "Yep. I'd dated lots of guys, but once I fell for Maddox, that was it."

"You're lying," I cried, surprising myself with my boldness. Maybe I should rely on margaritas more often to loosen me up. "I can tell you're lying! Who was it—a high school boy?"

She shook her head, not looking at me. "No. It was high school, but no boy. A married man."

"No kidding," I whispered drunkenly. "One of your teachers?"

"Not exactly. But you're close. Someone like that." She shrugged before continuing. "I haven't had quite enough booze to tell you about that one yet. Plus, I'm *not* telling you anything else until you fess up about the reverend. What'd he do—slip his hand up your dress while you played his organ?"

"Augusta!" I screeched. "Ben's too goody-goody for stuff like that."

She looked at me curiously. "No kidding? I mean, he looks uptight as all get-out, but you can't always go by that. He didn't make a pass at you?"

"Of course not. Can you see Ben doing that?"

"It blows my mind picturing him doing *anything*. Does he close his eyes and pray while y'all are doing it?"

"You have a truly evil mind," I said.

"It's hard for me to imagine you married to such a tight-ass, tell you the truth. I'm not insulting you, am I?"

"Oh, no. God forbid that you say anything outrageous and insult anyone."

She laughed. "So, why'd you marry Ben?"

"Why do you think?"

"Beats me."

"Augusta! You're awful, and I'm not telling you anything else."

"You're right," she agreed, "we're both too wasted for true confessions now. Before you get any drunker, why don't you play some music? I don't even know if you're any good."

"On the piano and organ, I'm passable," I told her, putting my drink down and getting my dulcimer out, placing it on my lap. "But I can play the *hell* out of this baby here."

Again Augusta threw back her head and laughed. "José Cuervo—you are a friend of mine! A little tequila sure loosens you up, preacher's wife."

She laughed even more when I began plunking out the tune "José Cuervo." Jumping to her feet, she grabbed a candle from the table, holding it like a microphone. "You know what I've always wanted to be?" she confided. "A country singer. I got the stuff to do it, too."

"*José Cuervo*," she began singing, in a surprisingly good voice, and I plucked away on the dulcimer, though I'd never played such a song before. The two of us sang together, laughing.

Augusta pranced across the stone patio around the pool, tossing her hair back and forth as she sang in the fading red light of the sunset, and my laughter encouraged her wild performance. When darkness fell, fireflies came out and applauded our songs with their tiny sparks of light, twinkling in the dark like an unseen audience. When Augusta sat back down on the lounge beside me, we moved on to more familiar tunes, "Amazing Grace," "Just as I Am," and "Will the Circle Be Unbroken?"

When our laughter died down and our voices were hoarse from singing, Augusta turned to me. "Bet you don't know my favorite gospel song," she said, her voice soft in the black night. " 'Drifting Too Far from the Shore.' It's real old."

"I can't believe you know that one!" I cried. "I haven't played it since I was a kid. We always closed with it in my family's band." Frowning, I began to pick out the tune. "Hope I haven't forgotten the words."

"I know them," Augusta said. "Listen." She closed her eyes and started singing, her voice floating over the dark grounds like smoke. "*Drifting too far, you're drifting too far from the shore,*" she sang. I don't know why, but all the craziness of the evening left me and I felt sad and lonely, as sad and lonely as the sound of Augusta's voice floating in the sweet night air. Tears stung my eyes, and although I strummed chords, I didn't join her in singing.

The sadness that swept over me was a temporal thing, brought on as much by the tequila as the words of the song. Fireflies glowed; cicadas sang their sweet mourning song in the flowerless azalea bushes around the pool, and tears eased down my face for no reason. Overcome with half-drunken melancholy, I wiped my eyes and looked at Augusta. She had become the playmate I'd never had in my lonely childhood, the longed-for best friend of my miserable adolescence, and the woman friend denied me by Ben's itinerant profession.

Three

OUR FIRST SUMMER TOGETHER, Augusta introduced me to Celeste. On one of those days when I'd sneaked away from a church meeting, Augusta and I were lounging around the pool as Gus splashed in the shallow end, squealing, "Mama! Beanie! Watch me swim." Although Gus and I had become buddies, he couldn't get my name straight, exasperating Augusta and amusing Maddox by calling me Miss Della or Deb. "Gus," Augusta had said, "listen to Mama. It's *Dean*. Rhymes with *bean*. You can remember that, for Christ's sake—you'll be in the fourth grade." So the next time I came over, Gus squealed, "Look, it's Miss Bean!" This was shortened to Beanie, and Beanie I remained.

Augusta passed me a margarita, and I raised up from my patio chair to drink it as I watched Gus swim. He wasn't as fair as Augusta; the sun had turned his skin brown and highlighted his sandy-colored hair. "Gus is getting a good tan," I observed.

"The Spanish contessa's genes," Augusta said. "Maddox's so proud of his royal-ass blood, but I tell him it's really Gypsy blood."

"I've read that 'Gypsy' in some Eastern European countries is the equivalent of the 'n' word here."

"They've suffered a lot of prejudice. But I've always had a thing for Gypsies. Have you ever met a real one?" Augusta asked.

"Can't say I have. They're not real abundant in the north Florida swamps."

She jumped up, almost turning over the chair in her excitement. "Then you and I have got to go to Madame Celeste. She's a real, honest-to-God Gypsy woman. A fortune-teller! She just moved into town and opened up a store on West Bay Street. Tomorrow I'll get Theresa to baby-sit Gus, and we'll go. You're not going to believe the stuff she's got in that store."

"Have you been there?" I pushed my sunglasses on top of my head, intrigued. Augusta was constantly surprising me.

"The old biddies at the country club were gossiping about her the other day, so on the way home, Maddox stopped and I peeked into her store window. He was so embarrassed, he ducked down in the seat. We've gotta have our fortunes told, Miss Bean."

I frowned, shading my face with my hand. "I don't know. Ben has some old-fashioned ideas. Me seeing a fortune-teller might strike him as weird."

"Oh, bull. He may be a tight-ass, but he's a cool, with-it kind of preacher, isn't he?"

"He's not a Holy Roller, if that's what you mean. He's more conservative than he likes to admit, but you have to act like a forward-thinking preacher to make it in the Methodist church nowadays, and whatever else he may be, Ben's ambitious."

"Maybe you can convince him he should have his fortune told, too. He might find material for a new book: *Let Jesus Be Your Fortune-Teller*."

"Shame on you, girl," I said, "making fun of Ben's pride and joy." She'd shocked me by buying one of Ben's devotional books, then taking it home and reading passages out loud to me and Maddox, laughing at them shamelessly. Some of it was indeed pious and corny, but out of loyalty to Ben, I'd been determined not to laugh. Naturally, Augusta had read the part on the joys of a Christian marriage, her favorite. "Oh, my God, you two—listen to this," she'd cried. "*Wives, you will do well to remember that your beloved husband is nothing but a little boy at heart, no matter how strong and masculine he might be.*"

"It's the truth," Maddox'd said. "Old Brother Ben knows of what he speaketh."

"Listen, listen," she'd continued, in spite of my trying to grab the book from her. "*He longs for your praise and admiration more than anything. Brag on his accomplishments, tell him how much you admire him, and watch how he responds. Give him your complete devotion and I can promise you, you will have a happy home.*" Making gagging noises, she'd made a big show of throwing the book into the trash can, where she said it belonged.

Augusta and I stood outside the door of Madame Celeste's store the next day, as excited as schoolgirls. As Augusta tried the doorknob, I looked around. I'd feel like a fool if the church ladies saw me here. The palm trees in the grassy median of Main Street swayed in the warm summer breeze, cars went back and forth, and folks bustled along the sidewalks. We'd gotten here too early; the store didn't appear to be open. Augusta had heard that Madame Celeste had moved into an apartment over the store, so I stepped back and looked up at the two dusty windows of the second floor.

Above the scarlet door a new sign swung in the breeze: *Celestial Things by Madame Celeste*, it read in bold black letters. *Spiritual Healer and Guide. Crystals, the stars, the tarot, palm readings, healing herbs.* No wonder Maddox had hidden in the car.

Augusta pushed the door open and a brass bell jingled. The shop was smaller than it looked from outside, with scarlet-red walls and a black ceiling dotted with glow-in-the-dark stars. The crude wooden floor was scattered with rag rugs that looked hand-loomed, the air thick with the sweet smell of incense. On a glass counter across the back was an old-fashioned adding machine and cash register. We peered inside the case of jewelry: black-and-white yin-yang necklaces, Celtic crosses, zodiac signs, sun and moon earrings. Behind the counter, an area was curtained off with a red-patterned curtain. When the curtain rustled, I whirled around, and Madame Celeste herself stepped out.

Central casting couldn't have done a better job. Augusta and I stared, thrilled. Exotic as her name, Madame Celeste was tall and voluptuous, with frizzy jet-black hair halfway down her back. She was dressed in black with a fringed shawl draped over one shoulder, brass earrings dangling from her ears. Although I guessed her to be middle-aged, her dark face was smooth and ageless, with prominent cheekbones and a pouty-lipped, sensuous mouth. She raised a large hand, rings on every finger, and beckoned to Augusta. Her fingernails were so long, they curved toward her palm.

Augusta held out her hand as though to introduce herself, but before she could open her mouth, the fortune-teller took Augusta's hand in both of hers and shook her head to silence her. Her black eyes, rimmed in kohl, were painted like Cleopatra's, heavy brows arching over them. She was beautiful in a strange kind of way, like a vampire in an old black-and-white movie.

"Your aura is very disturbing," she said to Augusta, and her voice was marvelous, throaty and heavily accented. "Dark, very dark. And red, a sign of danger."

Augusta gasped. "Real danger? Like *danger* danger?"

Her earrings swinging, Madame Celeste pointed a red-tipped finger. "Once you heard voices of the universe, but you have wandered from the path, have you not? You must allow me to help you find the way back. Before it is too late," she added ominously.

When I saw Augusta's eyes widen, I was afraid she was crazy enough to believe that mess, so I stepped forward. "Madame Celeste, I'm Dean Lynch, and this is Augusta Holderfield. We stopped by to say welcome to Crystal Springs." She squeezed my hand, looking me over from head to toe.

"Please call me Celeste," she said. "Your aura disturbs me as well, Dean Lynch."

The last thing I wanted to hear about was my aura, so I turned back to her store. "What an interesting place you have here, Celeste. You make a lot of this stuff yourself, right?"

Her black eyes were bright with pride as she said, "With my herbs I not only scent the candles and potpourri but also make many old remedies." But I hadn't succeeded in distracting her, for she turned back to Augusta. "You came for a reading?" She obviously found her a whole lot more interesting than me, probably because Augusta was staring at her like she'd just had a religious vision.

Augusta nodded. "Could we do it right now?"

"The present moment is the only one we have, is it not?" Celeste said. Her voice sounded too much like the Wizard of Oz for me, and I stifled a giggle. "I was making morning tea when the universe led you two here. You will join me?"

"Oh, no, we couldn't possibly—" I began, but Augusta told Celeste that we'd be delighted. Celeste led us behind the counter and through the red curtain, up a steep and narrow stairway of weathered wood.

The apartment was just one room, like the store downstairs, with Gypsy-looking shawls over the windows and black-shaded lamps burning. As a teapot whistled on a white-enameled stove, Celeste pointed us toward a wooden table surrounded by an odd assortment of kitchen chairs. "Please sit. I hope you like the tea I grow myself."

Augusta and I seated ourselves at the table, and Celeste handed us brown mugs of a greenish, strong-scented peppermint tea, as delicious as it smelled. Celeste looked like a Gypsy queen, wild and alien, drinking from a golden goblet instead of a cheap mug from Wal-Mart. She raised her dark head and looked at us, first me, then Augusta. "You have lived in Crystal Springs all your lives?" she asked us.

"Not yet," I said, but was the only one to laugh at my humor. "Augusta has, but I just moved here. How about yourself—where are you from?"

She shrugged. "Ah, mostly in Florida, the last few years. My native land is Romania. The time came to settle down, and I love the Florida sun. In my search for the perfect town, I found Crystal Springs. More tea?" She'd said all she was going to about herself.

Both of us held out our cups. "Are you really going to tell my fortune?" Augusta blurted out.

"Your sign—Pisces?" Celeste said, and I marveled at how close she was.

"Aquarius," Augusta said.

Celeste nodded. "Ah, the water-bearer. Your feelings flow too easily with water as your medium. But you must take care. There's much heartbreak ahead, I fear."

After such an encouraging start, I hoped Augusta would not want to hear any more. But no such luck. At Celeste's motion, she opened her palm. Celeste's face was impassive as she turned Augusta's hand this way and that, but for some crazy reason, I felt uneasy, like she'd seen something scary in the lines and creases. I realized I had no idea who Augusta was, even though we'd been together so much lately, grown so close in such a short time. In the dim lamplight, her perfectly molded face was as impenetrable and mysterious as a shroud. I studied her, the pale blond hair hanging loose to her shoulders, a tendril falling across one eye. Feeling my gaze, she winked at me and pushed her hair off her face when Celeste let go of her hand.

"Let's try the cards instead," Celeste said. She got up and turned to a red lacquered cabinet behind her, taking out a deck of cards folded in a black silk cloth. As she shuffled them, her eyes stayed on Augusta. When she handed Augusta the deck to cut, I pulled my chair closer. The cards were twice the size of regular playing cards, solid black on one side. Celeste spread them on the black silk cloth and I watched, intrigued by their strange-looking symbols and characters, suns and moons and knights and ladies and dragons and castles. Beautiful, but somehow creepy-looking.

"The cards come up with a separation . . . a loved one, a heartbreak." Celeste's voice was low and mysterious. Augusta leaned over the cards, her eyes wide. Separation! I thought of a bit of gossip I'd recently heard from the church ladies, that Maddox and Augusta had separated once several years ago; something Augusta hadn't yet told me about. Oh, Lord—what if it were true; what if Celeste really could see into people's lives?

Celeste dealt out another row of cards, her movements quick as a magician's. The center card had zodiac signs around it and a knight in the middle, holding a sword high over his head. "Much conflict is coming into your life. A man is central to the conflict."

"A man's always central when there's conflict," I said lightly.

"And a woman? A woman has entered your life, bringing the conflict out. The dark woman."

"She's here," I whispered to Augusta. "Her name's Miss Bean." Augusta tore her eyes from Celeste long enough to shoot me an exasperated look.

I leaned closer, disappointed. Celeste hadn't said anything that couldn't be applied to anyone, much like the horoscopes in the paper. I perked up, however, when she turned over a facedown card. The ancient symbol of death, a black-hooded skeleton holding a scythe. "Well, that one's pretty obvious," Augusta said dryly.

But Celeste wagged her finger. "In the position of the Crossing, the card of death represents the bridge over which all must go." She swooped the cards up, reshuffled them, then arranged them facedown on the cloth, this time in the shape of a cross. I could imagine what Ben would say about that one!

"You must be very cautious as events unfold in the future," Celeste told Augusta as she turned over a card depicting a tower crumbling into a stormy sea. "The old order of your life falls apart, you see?"

When Augusta showed no reaction, Celeste shook her head and the earrings swayed. "Skepticism is very harmful, my friend. You must open yourself to the truth." Augusta's reading was pretty gloomy until Celeste turned over another card and smiled. "Ah! The King of Cups, a good sign."

"The King of Cups?" Augusta repeated.

"It's like this. The signs correspond to the four basic elements of the universe: fire, water, air, and earth. The Cups hold the element of water, of life, and flow of the emotions, including love."

"Oh goody—a love interest," I whispered. "The tall, dark stranger. Tom Cruise will come through town, see you, and fall madly in love."

Augusta shook her head. "Won't work. Tom Cruise is short."

Celeste looked at us sternly. I put on my best poker face and Augusta laughed. Celeste continued, speaking like a biblical prophet. "Indeed, the King might indicate a new love." Although I'd never heard anyone begin a sentence with "indeed," I managed to keep a straight face. "But what it means in the Overhanging Position? Unclear at this point."

"Wonder if it's like the missionary position." I giggled, nudging Augusta with my elbow.

"So this King is a real person, then? A man?" Augusta said, ignoring me.

Celeste's expression was dark. "Know this, Augusta. The cards are only a guide. They do not reveal the answers but uncover the keys so *you* find answers."

"But I don't want keys. I want the answers," Augusta replied saucily.

"Of course. As eternal as mankind." Celeste's black eyes twinkled. "Or should I say womankind, if you think back to our mother Eve. Right?"

She turned over the rest of the cards, and again I felt uneasy, for her face was dark and troubled. "Ah . . . more time is needed, I see. You must come back, Augusta. Open your soul to the universe. Then come back to me, yes?" She swooped up the cards and restacked them, wrapping the black cloth around them.

Augusta chewed her full lower lip. "Umm. That's all you're going to tell me today, even with stuff like a skeleton in my cards?"

"You are not ready, Augusta. The universe will lead you back," Celeste said. She surprised me by standing up, ready for us to go. "This is how I know. The High Priestess was in your spread. You shall have Madame Celeste as a guide! You will not wander down the wrong path."

Neither Augusta nor I spoke as she backed her car out of the parking place. George Strait sang about exes and Texas on the CD player, and Augusta leaned forward to turn the volume up. Because she had sunglasses on and her face was composed, I couldn't tell what she was thinking. Finally, I could stand it no longer. "Well?"

"Well what?"

"Augusta! You have a hissy fit to go to that fortune-teller, who tells you your aura looks like Armageddon, a skeleton and a crumbling tower's in your cards, and that's all you can say?"

"She must've seen something really bad, don't you think?"

"No, I do not. You're far too intelligent to be scared by that crap."

"I appear intelligent to you? Goes to show how deceiving looks are."

"What'd you think, really?" I persisted.

"I thought she was wonderful. I loved the way she looked, and her place upstairs. I can't wait to go back." She pulled the car into the driveway of the parsonage and turned off the ignition. Next door at the church, the Migrant Day Care Program was in full swing, and we watched the children running and laughing on the playground. The program was Augusta's pet project, and lately she'd gotten me involved, too. She had persuaded local churches to rent out their facilities to house the day care facilities for the hundreds of migrant workers who came to our area every spring and summer. Ben cleverly offered our day care center, thinking Augusta would return to church in exchange. It had partially worked; Tuesdays and Thursdays were the days Augusta and I volunteered.

"Come inside and I'll fix you a tomato sandwich," I said, opening the car door. "The reverend asked me if I'd bring you by his office when we got back. He wants to talk to you about the day care."

"Oh, crap. After such an intriguing morning, I'm in no mood to talk business," she groaned.

"Listen, I thought Madame Celeste was a hoot, too," I admitted. "It was fun. Just don't make the mistake of taking her seriously. The whole thing was a ploy to get you to come back. I'll bet she does that to everybody."

"Does what?"

"You know. Tells you some stuff on purpose that'll intrigue you, kind of scare you, then says it's not clear, that you have to come back, let her be your spiritual guide."

"It's not true she does it to everybody, Miss Smarty-Britches. She didn't say it to you."

"For obvious reasons. She's been in the business long enough to know I'm a skeptic, not a sucker like you."

"O ye of little faith," Augusta said. She was halfway out the car door when she slid back under the wheel. "Oh, I just remembered—I can't do lunch. Theresa can't stay with Gus this afternoon."

"What about the meeting with Ben?"

"Tell His Holiness I'll give him a call this afternoon. And quit frowning, Dean; I'm not worried about what Madame Celeste said."

I stared at her as I got out of the car. "You're lying! You're going back to her, aren't you?"

She avoided my eyes as she restarted the car. "Why would I do that? She told me the time wasn't right yet."

"Because I was right—she scared you good. Augusta, surely you don't believe that bull?"

"O ye of little faith," she repeated, laughing at me. Then without another word, she was gone. I stood watching her car back out of the driveway, saw the casual wave of her hand, her diamond wedding band flashing like a star in the bright sun. Again, that weird little feeling of uneasiness came over me. Something about the whole encounter with Celeste didn't feel right.

I tried to talk to Ben about it over dinner that night. As chaplain of almost every organization in town, Ben had meetings practically every night, most of them starting with a free meal. In honor of our having dinner together I fixed his favorite foods, country-fried steak in gravy, mashed potatoes, butter beans, and homemade rolls. I sliced tomatoes from Collie Ruth's garden and chopped sweet Georgia peaches and whipped real cream to top the pound cake for dessert. I'd given up trying to get Ben to eat healthy. All this cholesterol would surely kill him, but he'd die with a smile on his face.

I let Ben tell me about his week first, what was going on with the congregation. It was no surprise to hear that he was feeling pressure to get Maddox and Augusta back. Folks figured he'd had the whole summer, socialized with the Holderfields, his wife had gotten buddy-buddy with Augusta, so why weren't they coming to church?

"I can't understand it, myself," he said, sopping up thick brown gravy with a roll. "Not that I'm worried about Maddox's soul, because I'm sure he's a Christian. The other morning? I went out to the plant and talked with him for over an hour."

"What did he say?" I asked, refilling his iced-tea glass.

"Meat's tough," Ben said, taking another piece from the platter, scooping extra gravy on it.

"What an odd response. Has nothing to do with why he doesn't come to church, though."

Ben raised his head and looked up at me, chewing, his dark eyes blank. "Huh?" He shook his head and rolled his eyes. "Oh—I get it. Very funny. Ha ha. Oh, the usual malarkey—he doesn't need to come to church to worship God, God is in nature, blah blah blah. Plus, everybody in the church is a hypocrite. You know."

"No hypocrites at First Methodist, that's for sure. Ready for dessert? Collie Ruth brought us a pound cake and I got you some Georgia peaches."

"Give me an extra helping of that whipped cream. Obviously something happened with Maddox and the church, but nobody'll tell me what."

"Oh, come on, Ben. As much as church folks love to gossip, they'd be falling all over themselves to tell you if anything specific had happened. When I've asked Augusta about coming back, she just shrugs it off."

Ben wiped whipped cream from his mouth before reaching for another piece of cake. "I'm thinking about talking to Dr. Vickery about it, next time I see him."

"Dr. Vickery who used to be the preacher here?" I asked, surprised. "Why him?"

The most famous preacher in Florida, John Marcus Vickery was Ben's idol. Several years ago he'd been the minister here at First Methodist, in the same pulpit Ben now occupied. He was now in the bishop's cabinet and was rumored to be our next bishop. Ben practically genuflected every time Dr. Vickery's name was mentioned.

"Hasn't Augusta ever said anything to you about him?"

"Dr. Vickery?" I repeated stupidly, and Ben rolled his eyes in exasperation.

"Good heavens, Dean. Don't you ever listen to the talk going around town?"

"Not if I can help it."

"Well, you should. You learn things that way. When she

was a teenager and the Spencers lived on the other side of the church, Augusta was the Vickerys' baby-sitter."

I was somewhat surprised that Augusta had not mentioned that to me, insignificant though it was. The house Augusta was raised in—the one her family occupied when they were not in Tallahassee—was actually behind the church on the next block, a rambling Victorian that was now a bed-and-breakfast. She'd pointed it out to me, saying we had something else in common, that we'd both lived next to the church. That's all I remembered of our conversation. "No kidding?" I said to Ben. "Didn't the Vickerys have a houseful of kids?"

Ben shrugged. "Just two, I think. Heard the whole family was crazy about Augusta. Ask her about them sometime."

"I will," I said, nodding. "But just because Augusta baby-sat for them years ago doesn't mean Dr. Vickery knows anything about her and Maddox not coming to church, does it? Here's what I think it was: They had a baby and their routine changed. Got out of the habit of going to church when Gus came along, is all."

"Well, whatever happened, I'm not going to give up on Maddox," Ben continued. "And I want you to use your influence with Augusta. I thought she was going to be here for lunch today."

"She had to get back home."

"What's wrong with you?" he asked, frowning when he saw that I was eating only peaches. "Collie Ruth's cake's the best in the church. When's Augusta coming back so we can talk?"

"You'll have to ask her fortune-teller," I told him, shrugging.

"What?" He held his cup up for me to pour him some decaf. "Oh, good heavens—don't tell me that Augusta, of all people, has gotten hooked up with that woman who's opened up that new store downtown!"

"Yep. We went there this morning."

To my surprise, Ben put his cup down and stared at me, narrowing his eyes. "You're kidding. Tell me you're kidding."

"I kid you not. Augusta had her fortune told."

"I hope to goodness that you didn't. How much did it cost? Surely you're not wasting our hard-earned money on that nonsense."

"She didn't charge Augusta anything," I protested. "And I liked the woman—her name's Celeste and she's a real Gypsy—but I didn't like her scaring Augusta, saying her future was uncertain and stuff like that."

Ben pushed his chair back. "A.H. and some of the others are not real happy that the city council let her open up that shop. They don't care for the kind of stuff she peddles in there."

"Last I heard, Florida was still part of the United States of America. You know, free enterprise and all that. Maybe somebody needs to tell Ass Hole Bullock that."

Ben lowered his cup and looked at me. "*Who?*"

"A.H."

He rolled his eyes and, though he tried not to, smiled. "God in heaven, Dean. Ass Hole Bullock! You're going to get me kicked out of the Methodist church yet."

"Ben, you know as well as I do that A.H. Bullock is one of the biggest troublemakers in the church."

"I know, I know. But, it's not just him saying it; it's some others, too. And they've got a point about that fortune-telling place. All they're saying is the kind of stuff in her store attracts a certain kind of clientele. Sends the wrong message to our high school kids, with all those earrings and tattoos and dope-taking things."

"I was in her shop just this morning, Ben. Sure, it's a bunch of hooey, but there was *no* drug paraphernalia in there." Annoyed, I flung the dishwasher open and began scraping our dishes. Ben took his coffee cup and leaned on the counter, watching me.

"I'd as soon you stay away from there, tell you the truth. Controversy's brewing."

"I had no intention of going back, but now I can't wait."

"Come on, Dean. Don't be ridiculous."

"No, I mean it. I'm going to get my lower lip, nostril, and belly button pierced, a marijuana plant tattooed on my ankle, and a rebel flag on my behiney."

"Now, why do you do that? Why do you do that every single time?"

"Do what?"

"Get on your high horse. Get that chip on your shoulder, that kiss-my-fanny, fighting redneck attitude. It'll keep you down all your life," he retorted.

"Oh, well, excuse me! Let's bring up my poor old white-trash background again. Can't let a single day go by, can we?"

"All I'm saying is, you can rise above it if you'll stop from reverting to old ways every time you lose your temper."

"I'll tell you what, Ben. If being in the same class as A. H. Bullock and the rest of the hypocrites like him means I look down my nose at everybody not like me, then you can forget it."

Ben's jaw tightened and his eyes turned cold. Before he could think up a good retort, the phone rang shrilly and interrupted what was surely working up to a good fight on the special occasion of his rare dinner home.

Four

A THURSDAY IN LATE summer, Augusta and I were doing our volunteer work in the kindergarten class, one of the rooms First Methodist provided for the Migrant Day Care Program, when she approached me with her latest scheme.

"The last day of August, the day care's having a going-away party for the kids before their families move on," she said as she glued cotton balls onto paper sheep. I nodded, my attention diverted by the animal shapes I was cutting out of construction paper. Around a small table, the children colored furiously, their little faces lost in concentration. I paused to marvel at their beauty, their heads bent together, hair like sheets of black silk, except for the towheaded Gus.

"Listen—I've got a plan," Augusta continued, whispering. "Remember when we did the beach unit and Julio had never seen the ocean? Well, he's not leaving here without going to the beach."

I looked at eight-year-old Julio Domingo, his thin shoulders hunched over the table as he colored pages of animals. With his mop of black hair, sad dark eyes, and ill-fitting clothes, Julio looked like an extra in a Latino version of *Oliver!* During the course of the summer, he and Gus had become buddies.

"A day at the beach? Good idea—" But Augusta shook her head before I finished.

"Not a day at the beach, Miss Bean—a weekend. Labor Day weekend, to be exact. I've already talked to Maddox, and he approves. We have a standard rental at Seaside every Labor Day weekend, so we're doing it—we're taking not only you and Ben, we're taking Julio, too."

I laughed, and the children looked up to see what was so funny. Señorita Bean—my nickname among the kids, thanks to Gus—is crazy, so please ignore her, Augusta told them in Spanish. The kids nodded solemnly and went back to their coloring.

"Oh, that should be no big deal whatsoever," I said in a low voice. "Especially since it's such a breeze arranging for Julio to come play with Gus." Although Gus and Julio were friends, his parents refused to let Julio come to the big house. The class structure of their native country wouldn't allow them to cross over the invisible borders that separated migrants from employers.

"I'm going to the migrant camp to talk to Julio's mother this afternoon," Augusta told me. "It was Maddox's idea."

I raised my eyebrows. "No kidding?"

"Sure was. So, as soon as we get the details ironed out, I'll go out to the migrant camp and sell Julio's mama on this trip. I promise you, it will work out."

It was not until we were unpacking our bags at the Seaside beach house that Augusta admitted how she got Julio to come with us. I stood suspended over my suitcase, swimsuit in hand.

"Say that again?" I said.

Augusta flung a closet door open and without asking, hung my sundress and beach robe in it. "I told Julio's folks that Mr. Holderfield insisted Julio come and keep Gus company, and that if they want to work for us next summer, they'd better do it," she said breezily, her back to me.

I sat down beside my suitcase on the single bed I'd claimed. "*Augusta*—I can't believe you did that."

"It was the only thing I could think of," she admitted. "And I was determined to give Julio and Gus a fun weekend together."

"Does Maddox know?"

Augusta shrugged, her back still to me. "Ah . . . not exactly."

We finished my bed and started in on Ben's, who'd said he might join us Sunday. Otherwise, he wasn't coming until Labor Day, claiming that, unlike everyone else, he was much too busy to take off. We'd had an argument about it, me begging him to call off church like everyone else; him mad at me for leaving. I'd never missed church for something as frivolous as a vacation, but this time, I defied Ben to come to Seaside. I asked Augusta, "Aren't you afraid Maddox'll be mad when he finds out?"

"*If* he finds out," she said.

"Okay, *if* he finds out. Even though he worships the ground you walk on, surely Mr. Perfect gets mad with you at times."

"Oh, yeah, plenty of times," she admitted. "Like most easygoing people, Maddox doesn't blow his cool often, but when he does, it's scary. You don't want to be around him then."

"Thanks for the warning," I said. "If he finds out what you did to lure Julio, all you'll see of me is heels and elbows."

"Maddox is already pissed with me about Libby and Simms, as you observed on the drive down this morning,"

Augusta said. The beds done, she opened up the French doors to the balcony outside.

I laughed. "Y'all kept me entertained, that's for sure." We'd driven down in Augusta's Volvo station wagon, she and Maddox up front, me in the back with the two little boys. We'd only gotten a few miles outside of Crystal Springs when Maddox casually mentioned to Augusta that he'd invited their old friends Simms and Libby Legere to join them for the Labor Day cookout, since the Legeres would be in Seaside for the weekend, too. Augusta was furious, yelling at Maddox in front of the wide-eyed Gus and Julio. It took me a minute, then I recalled that Maddox had been engaged to Libby Legere when Augusta came on the scene. Augusta'd sworn to me that it wasn't jealousy that caused her dislike of Libby; it was Libby herself. Augusta couldn't stand her. When I'd asked why, she'd said to wait until I met her, the snobbish, blue-blooded bitch.

Augusta stepped out on the balcony and the strong salt wind lifted her hair around her head like a halo. The sun was blinding off the waters of the Gulf, and she shaded her eyes with her hands. "Celeste warned me there'd be conflict on this trip, big time."

"Better take care, then," I snorted. "Throw salt over your shoulder, roll your britches legs up, and spit cross-eyed through your fingers." Augusta had been seeing Celeste regularly since our first visit, but I hadn't gone back. I stood by Augusta on the balcony, straining to hear with the strong wind snatching her voice away.

"You make fun of her, but I'm intrigued," Augusta said seriously. "Don't you believe there are things out there—unseen forces—that determine our fate?"

"No, I do not. Things happen like accidents and cancer and stuff like that, but mainly, we determine our fate by the decisions we make."

Augusta looked at me, the blue of her eyes the same as the sky overhead. "You're such a pragmatist, aren't you? Funny, you and Maddox cut from the same cloth. Did you know that?"

I shook my head. "I don't know him that well. And quit changing the subject. What did the lovely Celeste have to say about this weekend?"

Augusta turned back to face the sea. "Plenty. She has a premonition that our holiday will cause big problems between me and Maddox. Even suggested I call the whole thing off."

"Your aura still acting up?"

"Among other things. I don't like tempting fate, but—here we are." Augusta frowned, shading the sun from her eyes with her hands, then shrugged. "Well, come on, Miss Bean. Let's round up everybody and head for the beach."

Augusta stayed with the boys on the seashore since they wanted to build sand castles while Maddox and I swam together in the ocean.

"Undertow's rough," Maddox said when he surfaced beside me in the clear green water. "Good thing we didn't bring the boys out."

I nodded in agreement, then plunged back beneath the foaming water. I was still shy around Maddox. I'd had little experience with men like him, sophisticated and charming in his flippant, offhand way. I always stammered and blushed like an idiot in his presence.

Even though I swam as far as I could from him, Maddox followed and surfaced beside me again. "God, you swim like a sea creature, Dean," he said. "How about holding still long enough for me to ask you something?"

"Oh—sure! Okay," I said, spitting salt water out like a porpoise.

"Tell me this—what do you think of Augusta's going to that silly-ass fortune-teller?"

"Oh, she'll get tired of it, I imagine."

"Did she tell you that bull about the fortune-teller—what's her name, Madame Celestial?—telling her that no good would come of this trip? I caught her meditating and praying to the goddess, burning serenity candles all over the place."

I laughed. On the shore, Gus and Julio trotted back and forth to the water's edge, filling their buckets and running to the sand castle. "A white chickadee with a little brown duckling," I said.

"The only dark duckling on this beach, that's for sure," Maddox replied.

"Reckon we've disturbed the order of things here?"

Maddox chuckled. "Sure as hell hope so. These yuppies need something to talk about besides the stock market and their BMWs. But, Dean, don't change the subject. If Augusta goes off the deep end with this fortune-teller, I'm holding you personally responsible."

"*Me?*"

"Yep. I worry about Augusta because she can be kind of . . . unstable at times. So I'm counting on you to be a good influence."

"You've got to be kidding," I said, squinting at him. "Talk about the blind leading the blind. . . ."

"Not so. You're good for Augusta. She doesn't have any other friends, you realize that? The only person in Crystal Springs she's close to, besides you, is Rich Kingsley, and he's as wild and crazy as she is."

"Rich Kingsley?"

"You'll meet him soon—he's been in Maine for the summer. Anyway, I'm delighted she has a woman friend like you. You're as steady as she is reckless."

"Solid and steady, huh? You make me sound like a . . . a turtle or something."

Maddox laughed. His eyes were the same color as the ocean at twilight, I thought. "A mermaid'd be more appropriate. Bet you can outswim me. You be the turtle and I'll be the hare and let's race to the shore."

Instead of answering, I dove beside him and surfaced several feet ahead. Throwing him a challenging look over my shoulder, I began long strokes toward the shore. I was halfway there when he swam past me, his strongly muscled arms pulling him easily through the water, like a hot knife through butter. He gave me a victory sign as I swam toward the shore like a plodding, solid tortoise, and Maddox won the race easily.

That afternoon Maddox loaded all of us into the station wagon and announced that he was taking us someplace wild but fun. "Julio and Gus, you're in for an adventure," he said from his perch in the driver's seat. The yellow, blue, and pink tin-roofed houses of Seaside were as colorful in the bright sunlight as balloons at a child's birthday party. "You children are going to see some young asses," he said in Spanish.

Julio and Gus screamed with laughter and Augusta punched Maddox on the shoulder, hard. "What?" he yelped, pulling out onto the crowded highway.

"Maddox, don't say things like that—kids repeat everything," she said.

Maddox adjusted the visor to the glare of the afternoon sun. "I said I was taking them to see some baby donkeys, is all," he protested. "They have goats there, too, but I didn't know how to say it."

"For someone with supposedly Spanish blood, your Spanish is pitiful," Augusta taunted. "Besides, you need to speak English to Julio since he's learning this summer. You're taking us to Grayton Beach, aren't you?"

It was my turn to lean forward. "Grayton Beach? I've always wanted to go there."

"You would," Augusta said dryly, then settled back with a sigh. "If I'd known that's where we were going, I'd have stayed on the beach."

"Where's your sense of adventure?" Maddox asked her. "We're going on a safari."

"Safari, my as—foot. All they have at that place are a few scraggly chickens and some stinky goats."

I'd longed to see Grayton Beach, a little fishing village west of Seaside, because I'd heard how unspoiled it was, unchanged by tourism. When we arrived and Maddox pulled the car under a spreading magnolia tree, I fell in love with it, and saw why he'd brought the kids. A fenced-off petting zoo was spread haphazardly among moss-draped oaks, next to an area with shops unlike any I'd seen before, primitive wooden structures with packed-dirt floors. One was an art gallery, with paintings of local scenes; the others held T-shirts and hats and beach towels, and there was a small outdoor café shaded by banana trees. Gus and Julio squealed as they clambered out of the station wagon. Augusta was right; there were mostly goats and chickens and ducks, with a few ponies and potbellied pigs. Julio jumped up and down in delight, throwing his head back to laugh at a fat little pig rutting in a mud puddle, and Gus climbed the fence to pet the goats.

Later, I walked around with Maddox while the boys sat at the outdoor café eating ice cream and Augusta treated herself to a frozen daiquiri. She taunted me for taking Maddox up on his invitation to explore Grayton. "Go ahead," she said, rolling her eyes. "But don't say I didn't warn you. There's nothing to Grayton Beach compared to Seaside."

Maddox took my arm, pulling me away. "Ignore she who has no appreciation for the unspoiled beauty of nature, Miss Bean," he said, "and come with me for a look back in time."

It was two or three blocks to the beach from the outdoor café, and Maddox and I strolled along licking melting ice-cream cones. "Grayton has a feel of Key West, in some ways," he told me.

"Some of the houses look really old," I observed, noting the wooden structures with wraparound porches and old shutters. Most of them were small and modest, a contrast to the opulence of Seaside. "Turn of the century?"

"Early nineteen hundreds, I think, one of the oldest villages in this area." Maddox nodded, biting the top off his swirled cone. "What flavor did you get?"

"Banana and macadamia nut. But yours looks better. Peach?"

He nodded again and took another big bite. "It was a hard decision," he said. "Take another bite of yours and we'll swap. Then I want to show you something in town."

"There's an actual town?"

"Sort of. A few little shops, and the Corner Café's a famous place to eat, written up in a lot of mags. Here, take my cone. I can't bear for you to miss out on the fresh peach."

He was right, it was better than the banana. I finished it off and licked my fingers. When the road ended, we turned left to the Corner Café, and Maddox pointed to a sign on the door. "Here it is." The sign listed the days and times they were open for lunch and dinner, then read: *Hours vary depending on the tide.*

I laughed. "Joke, right?"

"Nope. That's the kind of laid-back place Grayton is." He turned from the café and pointed across the street. "Look.

The beach is right there, but the sand dunes and wild-grape vines are so tall, you can't see it."

"I love it here! If I ever run away, this is where I'll come," I told him, shading my eyes with my hands.

"You'll never run away," he said. "You're the tortoise, remember?"

Laughing, we strolled back companionably, and I realized that something had changed between Augusta's husband and myself. Since our swim this morning, I'd lost my uneasiness around him. When we reached the café, Augusta leaned over the rail of the porch and waved.

"Quit gawking, Dean, this ain't the Riviera," she said, loud enough that the other people in the café turned their heads and smiled.

Ben surprised us by appearing late that Sunday night, driving down after church. The boys had gone to bed, stuffed with shrimp and worn out from a day on the beach, and Augusta, Maddox, and I were sitting in rockers on the back porch overlooking the ocean, our feet propped on the railing, sipping wine and looking out over the dark moonlit water. My dulcimer, which Augusta'd insisted I bring along, was in the case, propped against the rail. We'd had a sing-along after dinner, when Augusta taught Julio to sing the FSU fight song and "Dixie" in his broken English. Maddox'd rolled his eyes and put his hands over his ears, causing Julio to giggle hysterically.

Maddox rose lazily from his rocking chair. "Anybody want a piece of key lime pie?" Ignoring Augusta's oinking noises, I nodded. "Sure. I'll take one," I said.

When Maddox returned with the pie, Augusta sighed. "I give up. After you drop dead of a heart attack, Maddox, I hope my next husband will be more careful about what he eats."

"After you dry up and blow away from not eating enough, I hope my second wife will be a big fat mama who cooks fried chicken and gravy, turnip greens with hunks of fatback, and key lime pies for dessert, every single day," he said, balancing the dessert plate on his lap as he sat back down.

"Not a very flattering portrait of Dean," Augusta said, and I raised my head from my plate, the taste of key limes sour on my tongue. I licked meringue from my lips and frowned at her, wondering what she was up to now. "You and her'd be perfect for each other," she added.

"Dean wouldn't have me," Maddox told her, stuffing another piece of pie in his mouth. "She has a thing for holy men, and I'm too much of a hedonistic, unrepentant, and hopeless sinner. When poor old Ben croaks, her next husband will be a cross between Saint Francis of Assisi and Jerry Falwell."

Above our laughter and the pounding of the surf, we heard a car drive up in front of the house, the crunch of tires on the oyster-shell-paved driveway, and we looked at each other, puzzled. When a door slammed, Maddox got to his feet. "Who could that be, this late?" He left his chair to walk around the porch to the front of the house.

When the wind carried the sound of voices to us, Augusta leaned forward in her rocking chair until she could see around the side of the house, then she quickly moved back, giggling. "Speak of the devil. Better hide your wineglass."

Ben turned the corner, Maddox right behind him, his hand on Ben's shoulder, and I jumped to my feet. "Look who the wind blew in," Maddox said, just as I said, "Ben—I thought it'd gotten so late that you wouldn't come till tomorrow!"

"Guess I should've called," Ben said, looking sheepish. "Sit back down, Dean. I didn't mean to interrupt y'all."

"Don't be silly, Ben," Maddox said, pulling another

rocker forward. "Take a load off—how about a glass of wine or a beer?"

"Beer sounds good," Ben said, sinking into the rocker, and Augusta and I exchanged surprised glances. I'd admitted to her that Ben and I had argued about my missing church.

"This trip to the seashore inspired me, Maddox," Ben said when Maddox handed him a beer. "I used the sea as the theme of both my sermons today. This morning it was about Jesus calming the seas, and tonight, Him walking on water."

Augusta hooted. "Well, that's a new one, Maddox—you doing something that inspires a sermon." She poured herself another glass of wine and raised it high, winking at me.

Maddox turned his attention to Ben, saying politely, "I hear from everyone in town what a good preacher you are."

I held my breath, hoping Ben wouldn't demonstrate. Instead, he put his beer down and leaned toward Maddox. I hoped even more he didn't choose this occasion to try and get them back in the church. "Calming the seas and walking on the waters both in one day was a big challenge," he said instead. "Preaching about the miracles of the Bible can be like walking a tightwire."

"How so?" Maddox asked.

Ben shrugged. "You know. Some folks are strict literalists when it comes to the Word of God. Others—like you two, I'm sure"—he nodded toward Augusta and Maddox—"are uncomfortable with the idea of miracles."

"Wait a minute, Dr. Lynch," Augusta said. "You're making an assumption, aren't you? I believe in the Virgin Birth. I believe Jesus turned water to wine, and have no doubt that He walked on water and calmed the seas. And I certainly believe He arose from the dead."

The only light was from the flickering candles, which cast shadows on Ben's face. I saw him narrow his eyes as he tried to determine if Augusta was serious or not. "Oh," he said lamely, then chuckled. "Nowadays, it's unusual for people to think that way. In this modern age . . ." He shrugged, letting the idea drop, and looked to Maddox for help.

Maddox leaned back in the rocker. "Miracles in our modern age. Fascinating subject, isn't it? What do you think, Ben?"

"Me? Well . . ." He rubbed his hands together and frowned, as though deep in thought. "Tell you the truth, Maddox, I have no problem with whatever theory my parishioners embrace. I can relate to both the literalists and the skeptics."

Augusta gave a whistle. "If you ever give up preaching, you could go into politics."

I turned to Maddox, curious. "Maddox? Which are you?"

His eyes met mine in the darkness. "I'm a skeptical literalist. Or maybe a literal skeptic."

"In other words, you don't know," I said. "Are you agnostic?"

To my surprise, he shook his head. "Not at all. The agnostic's cowardly. Either be an atheist or a believer. You can't have it both ways. Think about it—there's no maybe. It's either true, or it ain't."

"Then you're a believer," I said.

He raised his glass to me with a shrug. "I am. What about you, Miss Bean?"

I shook my head. "I don't know. I mean, I believe in God because of the order of nature, so I guess I believe in miracles. How can you look at a seashell or a spiderweb and not believe?"

"Ah! A pragmatist who's also a romantic," he smiled.

"How can anyone be a realist and not want to commit suicide?" Augusta said. "One good look at all the shit in the world today ought to be enough to turn anyone into a romantic."

"I'm more of a romantic than anything else," I agreed.

"Like me, Miss Bean, you're pantheistic," Maddox said.

"Well, sure, if that means everything's a miracle. What Jesus did, any of us could've done," I said.

"Whoa," Maddox laughed, startled. "Hold it a minute. Do you believe that, Ben?"

Ben frowned. "Ah—not exactly. I certainly wouldn't put it that way."

"Come on, Preacher," Augusta said. "Everybody looks to you for spiritual guidance. Tell us what *you* think."

Ben regarded her steadily. "I'm not here to tell you what I think, Augusta. I'm here to interpret the Word of God."

They stared at each other and I realized with a shock that Ben didn't much like Augusta. I wasn't sure why, unless it had to do with my relationship with her. He was beginning to resent the time I spent with her, as well as my being under her influence instead of his. Sometimes it made me feel like a rag doll, pulled between the two of them.

As though he, too, sensed their animosity, Maddox quickly intervened. "I'm interested in hearing more about Dean's theory on the miracles of Jesus. What He did, any of us could do?" His eyes glinted in amusement. "That's a pretty radical idea, Miss Bean. Are you saying that you could walk on water?"

"If I were as in tune with God as He was, of course I could."

"Ah. I see what you're getting at." He turned back to look over the ocean, quiet and thoughtful.

Ben's eyes fell on my dulcimer propped against the railing. "I didn't know you brought your dulcimer, Dean. Did y'all have a hootenanny?"

"Sure did, Preacher," Augusta said. Her voice was back to normal, light and mocking, the tension of the moment passed. "Dean played while I taught the children some nice Sunday school songs."

Maddox rose and leaned over the railing, looking up at the dark sky. "Uh-oh," he said. "We'll be in trouble if a storm blows up. At least one person on this porch is in danger of being struck by lightning."

Labor Day, I came back to the house after a swim in the ocean to find Simms and Libby Legere on the back porch with Maddox. I'd left Ben jogging, and Augusta under an umbrella on the beach, watching the little boys play in the surf. As I walked up the long wooden walkway to the house, I had a chance to observe the Legeres before they saw me. Next to the Holderfields, the Legeres were the most talked-about family in Crystal Springs. They were high-church Episcopalians, descendants of the town's founders, and lived in an old estate on the river that'd been in the Legere family for generations. Although the Legeres came from families as blue-blooded as the Holderfields, they were not as highly revered. Simms made big money as a land developer. Blood money, according to both old Floridians and the local conservationist groups.

Maddox was handing what appeared to be a Bloody Mary to Libby Legere, who reached out to take it with a slender tanned hand. Although not beautiful like Augusta, even from a distance she was stunning, one of those women whose beauty was in her bone structure, the way she held herself. Her bearing said that she was totally confident of her place in life. I doubted she'd ever had an unkind thought about herself. I was glad Augusta wasn't with me, for when Libby took the glass from Maddox's hand, her fingers touched his and she smiled up at him provocatively, tilting her head.

When Maddox handed a glass to Simms Legere, standing next to his wife, I blinked in surprise. I'd pictured him looking like Maddox, attractive and poised, but Simms Legere was a good inch or two shorter than his wife, and quite overweight, his face ruddy in the bright light of the sun. Like Maddox, he wore round wire-rimmed glasses. His reddish hair was sparse and fine, a few strands combed over in a futile attempt to cover the baldness on top. Dressed in a white knit shirt and khaki shorts, he looked like a little Humpty-Dumpty standing next to the tall, broad-shouldered Maddox. It was easy to understand why the church ladies insisted that Libby had married Simms on the rebound.

I'd have loved to slow down my approach, watching them, but Maddox spotted me and waved. "Dean! Come meet Simms and Libby." Pulling my towel tightly around my shoulders, I hurried up the walkway so they wouldn't realize I'd been spying on them.

Simms Legere stepped forward and took my hand in greeting, smiling with such genuine friendliness that I immediately felt guilty for my assessment of him. "So this is the lovely Miss Bean! What a pleasure to finally meet you," he said, his dark eyes shining. His plump hand in mine was firm yet gentle, his smile playful. "I'm Simms Legere, and this is my better half, Libby."

"I've been so anxious to meet you, Dean," Libby said, stepping forward and squeezing my hand, using my name as easily as if we'd known each other all our lives. Wealthy, well-bred women all seemed to have similar features—the combination of good genes and a pampered lifestyle—and up close, Libby was no exception. Her hair was a sun-streaked dark blond, thick as molasses, the kind that made me aware of mine scraggling down my back, dripping wet. She had skin given to many women of her class: flawless, golden-hued, and luminous, like I imagined their lives to be. Neither fat nor thin, big- nor flat-chested, muscular nor flabby, she was a perfect size, tall and slender, elegantly dressed in white linen shorts and shirt, expensive leather sandals on her well-shaped feet.

"I'll call Augusta in from the beach, get some steaks on the grill," Maddox said. "Gotta celebrate this day like red-blooded, flag-waving Americans."

Libby threw back her head and laughed at him, her lux-uriant hair swinging. "You're confusing it with July Fourth, Maddox, dear. Today's a redneck holiday."

"Ben'll stay for lunch, won't he?" Maddox asked me, raising his eyebrows. Ben had told us at breakfast that he'd probably return home after his morning run, since he had so much to do. Augusta had snickered and my face had burned, befuddled and helpless at their building animosity toward each other.

"Oh, he'll stay for lunch," I assured Maddox. I then turned to Simms and Libby. "If you'll excuse me, I'll go up-stairs and get ready." As I went into the house, I looked back over my shoulder to find both Simms and Libby regarding me intently. Simms's dark, myopic eyes rested on my bare legs appreciatively, traveling up to where I clutched the towel around my shoulders. Libby's look was more speculative. Her light brown eyes met mine curiously over her drink, unwa-vering as I smiled at her, then turned away quickly, running up the stairs to my room.

I soon had good reason to question my skepticism of Ce-leste on that unforgettable Labor Day. As we grilled steaks, skewers of fresh shrimp, and husk-wrapped corn on the cob, Augusta and Libby began sparring like two old enemies fac-ing each other in the wild, fangs bared and claws sharpened. It started with Julio's appearance. Augusta had allowed Gus and Julio to stay at the beach and build sand castles, telling them we'd watch them from the back porch while we cooked. I tossed a large salad on the round porch table, throwing in fresh vegetables from Augusta's garden. Augusta and Maddox were at the grill, Maddox frowning in concentration through the smoke from his steaks, and Augusta basting the shrimp kabobs with an herb-studded marinade. Ben and Simms sat side by side on two deck chairs, talking FSU football. Libby lounged on the porch rail, draped over it languidly as she watched the activity on the beach, shading her eyes with one hand, the other holding a drink.

"Who's Gus's friend, Maddox?" she questioned. I'd noticed that she avoided addressing Augusta as much as possible. "Not the little Adams boy, is it?"

Maddox shook his head. "Nope. It's Julio Domingo."

Libby peered at the distant figures of Gus and Julio, their small shapes bent over a rising sand castle. "Oh! That child is Hispanic, isn't he?"

Augusta didn't look up from the grill as she muttered, "Took you a while, Libby, but you figured it out."

"Come look at this one," Maddox said to Simms, holding up a steak, "and see if it's rare enough for you. Rest of them are about ready, too. Shrimp done, Augusta?"

She nodded, using long tongs to place them on a brightly painted platter. "All ready. I'll get Gus and Julio, and we'll eat."

Libby hugged Gus and shook hands with Julio when Augusta introduced him, keeping her hands on the boy's thin shoulders protectively. When the boys went inside to clean up for lunch, Libby thawed momentarily and smiled at Augusta. "That child's beautiful, Augusta! And his English is excellent, too."

"All he said to you was 'good morning,'" Augusta muttered. In cutoff jeans and a halter top, she glowed with a kind of erotic energy.

"Does little Julio live in Crystal Springs?" Libby asked.

Maddox raised an eyebrow and winked at Augusta, who was regarding Libby coolly. "No, they're just visiting," he said.

"Oh? Are his parents with that group of visiting South American professors at the junior college?" she asked.

"No, Libby," Augusta said. "Julio's folks are with a group of South Americans visiting in the tomato fields. They're migrant workers."

Libby's eyes widened. "Migrants?" she said, forcing a smile. "You mean, Mexicans?"

"Honduran," Augusta said. "Dean, why don't you put the salad over here?" She motioned to a wooden table next to the grill. "And go ahead and add the dressing, if you want."

Libby came to stand beside the grill, hands on hips, her big dark sunglasses pushed up on her head. "But—I don't understand! Surely you don't allow Gus to play with those children, do you?"

"Gus and Julio've become big buddies over the summer," Maddox said absently as he distributed the steaks to the waiting plates. "Y'all come get them while they're hot."

"But . . . you don't let Gus go out to the *migrant* camp—" Libby began, stopping at the appearance of Gus and Julio.

"Oh, goody—Daddy's steaks!" Gus cried, running and grabbing Maddox around the waist. No matter that Gus was long and lanky, Maddox picked his son up and held him. "Daddy's a better cooker than Mama," Gus announced to us when Maddox put him down.

"Like his daddy, Gus is a philistine," Augusta snorted. "He prefers steaks, hot dogs, and hamburgers to my gourmet cooking. Y'all fix your plates and sit wherever, okay?"

Simms Legere laughed, his face even ruddier now that he'd had a few drinks. "Our kids always loved the junk food I make, too." Piling his plate high, he turned to Ben, who stood next to him filling his plate. "How 'bout you, Preacher? You cook much?"

Ben turned to look at me, grinning. "Uh-oh, Brother

Simms, you're going to get me in trouble with the little lady. Right, Dean?"

I took my plate to the table and pulled out a chair, ignoring him. Simms looked from me to Ben and grinned, saying, "As an old married man, I can tell I hit a sore spot. Come on, Dean—tell us the story."

I shook my head. "It's nothing. Silly, actually . . ."

Ben brought his plate and sat down next to me. "Silly's right. Dean got mad at me because at our last church, the men's group did a cookbook and asked me for my favorite recipe. Like Maddox, only thing I ever cook is grilled stuff, so I gave them my recipe for steak." He stuffed a big piece in his mouth, chewing with relish. "Mmmm—steak's perfect, Maddox."

Libby put down her plate, nothing on it but one kabob and a tiny bit of salad. "I don't get it. Why would Dean get mad at that?" She smiled up at Ben.

"Tell her the recipe," I said.

Ben laughed heartily. "It went like this: 'Have wife prepare grill, salt and pepper and marinade steaks. When charcoal's just right, put steaks on till wife says they're done, then remove to platter wife stands holding.' For some reason, that irritated Dean, and I've never heard the end of it."

Libby and Simms laughed with Ben, but Augusta and I exchanged glances as she put her plate down next to mine. "Gus, why don't you and Julio sit at that little table over there?" she said when they brought their plates over.

Libby turned her head and watched them, her hair swinging on her creamy shoulders, then turned back to Maddox. "Shouldn't you cut their steak for them?"

"Naw, they're eight, nine years old," Maddox told her, sitting down heavily across from her. "God, I'm starving."

"But . . . little Julio might not know—ah—how to," she said.

Augusta's head jerked up. "This might surprise you, Libby, but I'm pretty sure they have steaks in Honduras."

Libby met her eyes coolly. "*Some* Hondurans have steaks, I'm sure. But you don't know about little Julio's family—"

"Oh? And what do you know about them, Libby?"

"Let it drop, Augusta," Maddox said, an edge to his voice. "This food looks good, if I do say so myself."

We ate in silence for a minute, then Libby pointed to Maddox's plate. "Normally I don't eat red meat, but your steak looks so good. Could I have a little bite?"

He obliged, and Libby closed her eyes as she chewed, sighing, "That's fabulous."

"Fire's still hot. Be glad to cook you one," Maddox said.

"No, no," Libby smiled. "Just let me have another piece of yours."

"Won't take but a minute to cook you one."

"Oh, it won't be the same as sharing yours, Maddox, darling," Augusta said, and Ben stared at her, wide-eyed. I looked down at my plate quickly before I laughed out loud.

Maddox shot Augusta a warning look as he cut his steak, putting a large portion on Libby's plate. "There you go, Libby. A little-bitty bite for you."

As though to break the tension, Simms said hastily, "Ah—how'd the crop go this year, Maddox? Pretty good harvest?"

Maddox nodded. "Great year. I plan to give out some nice bonuses this Christmas."

"You're lucky. Don't have the problems with your workers that a lot of folks do," Simms said.

"Luck has nothing to do with it," Augusta said shortly. "Maddox is good to his workers, pays them well, provides nice housing."

"Too good, you ask me," Libby said, cutting the steak she'd gotten from Maddox into delicate strips.

"No one did," Augusta said pointedly, then glanced over at Julio. "However, I don't think our subject's appropriate, if you get my dig."

Simms's face turned even redder. "Oh! I apologize, Augusta—I wasn't thinking—"

"No problem," Augusta said breezily. She was more tolerant toward Simms than his wife, I'd noticed. To my surprise, Libby turned to me.

"Dean, I've heard all about Brother Ben from the townspeople, but I know very little about you," she cooed, laying a hand on my arm. "I hear that you're a musician."

I nodded, reaching for the iced-tea pitcher to refill my glass. I doubted that Libby had heard very little about me; if so, she was probably the only one in town. Her next question confirmed my suspicions. "You were raised on Amelia Island, weren't you?"

Again I nodded, concentrating on my plate and hoping she'd leave me alone. No such luck. "Such a lovely resort area," Libby continued. "Guess you lived on the Atlantic?"

I shook my head. "The swamps, actually. It wasn't a resort island when I was growing up there."

Libby raised perfectly shaped eyebrows. "The *swamps*? Really? How . . . fascinating. What did your daddy do?"

I was used to Ben answering for me but not Augusta, so I looked at her in surprise when she said, loudly, "Dean's family were musicians, Libby. Had a successful bluegrass band, right, Dean?"

I knew what she was trying to do, but it would only work if not pursued too closely. Libby gasped, her hand to her throat. "No kidding? I'm certainly impressed. Simms has quite a collection of bluegrass music, don't you, darling?"

Simms nodded eagerly. "Sure do. Who were your folks, Dean?"

"Ah . . . we called ourselves The Cypress Swamp Band."

Simms scratched his balding head, then carefully patted the strands of hair back in place. "Hmm . . . don't believe I know that group. Y'all cut a lot of records?"

"Not really," I hedged. I rose quickly, hitting my knee on the table. "Anybody but me want another corn on the cob?" I called out from the grill.

"We do, Beanie!" Julio and Gus both raised their hands eagerly, and I took them each one, hoping the subject would be changed by the time I returned to the table.

"Did your family's band travel a lot, Dean?" Libby asked me as soon as I sat down.

I smothered a smile, picturing my daddy's rattly old pickup going back and forth to the juke joints in town, where he and my mama sang and played every night. "You could say that, I guess," I said solemnly.

"I'll get on the Internet, see if I can find some of your records," Simms said. Good luck with that, I thought, but smiled at him over my corn on the cob. It was impossible not to like Simms's open, engaging friendliness.

Gus and Julio came to the table, holding their plates out to us. "Look, Mama!" Gus cried. "We ate everything on our plates. Can we have our cookies now?"

"I promised you could, didn't I?" Augusta said as she wiped off her hands with her napkin, then pulled Julio to her, kissing his cheek. He blushed and hung his head with a shy smile. I was glad Augusta didn't see Libby's expression. She eyed Julio as though he were lice-infested, now that his true identity had been revealed.

"Can we take the cookies to the beach?" Gus pleaded.

"Sit under my umbrella, don't get in the water, and don't feed the seagulls," Augusta instructed him.

After the boys had gone to the beach, Augusta brought out a raspberry cheesecake she'd made for the adults, lavishly pouring framboise over each slice. She'd been instructing me on the proper consumption of liqueurs and wines, and the framboise was part of my education. "Don't get drunk on the dessert, Preacher," she said to Ben, then rolled her eyes as he pushed the liqueur-soaked raspberries off his slice. "This is why I made cookies for the boys," she explained, puddling Simms's slice with the luscious-smelling framboise as he watched eagerly. She shaded her eyes with her hands and looked out to the beach until she spotted the boys safely under the umbrella, waving at us as they stuffed themselves with cookies.

"I'm really surprised little Julio's parents let him come with you," Libby said, turning up her elegant nose at the cheesecake as she selected a few raspberries instead. "They're usually pretty good about staying in their place. That Mexican family who did my yard work, remember, Maddox? I couldn't even get them to come in the house to pick up their paycheck."

"I was surprised, too," Maddox admitted, biting into his cheesecake, "since we've had the same problem getting Julio over to play with Gus. How'd you pull it off, Augusta?"

If Augusta'd not been so intent on licking the framboise off her fingers, she might've hedged the question, but she shrugged nonchalantly. "I was so determined for Julio to have a weekend at the beach that I told his parents they'd lose their jobs if they didn't let him come."

Libby gasped, Simms choked on a big bite of cheesecake, and Ben's head shot up from his plate. I swallowed nervously when I saw the fire flash in Maddox's gray eyes.

"You told them *what*?"

Augusta blinked, and stared at her husband, as though just realizing what she'd said. I figured she'd try to brazen her way out of it now that she was caught, which is exactly what she did. "The ends justified the means," she said breezily. "They wouldn't have let Julio come otherwise."

Maddox slammed his hand down on the table and everyone jumped. "Goddammit, Augusta, how could you do such a thing? Don't you know what that does to my relationship with them?" He glanced over at Ben, who was watching wide-eyed. "Excuse my French, Preacher."

Augusta threw her napkin down and glared at Maddox. "Nothing will come of it, Maddox—don't get your panties in a wad."

He ran his fingers through his hair and moaned. "God-almighty damn! You had no business doing that, Augusta. I try so hard to have a good relationship with my workers."

Libby leaned toward him and placed a long slender hand on his arm. "Maybe you could go to them, Maddox, explain—"

Augusta jumped to her feet. "Maybe *you* could mind your own business, Libby."

"Hey!" Maddox snapped. "That's enough, Augusta. You've been rude to our guests all morning, and I'm fed up with it. You owe Libby an apology."

Augusta turned on him, her eyes flashing. "Why don't you apologize to her for me, Maddox? You'll find her right under you, lips puckered, as usual."

"Wait just a minute—" Simms gasped, at the same time Libby tossed her head and said, "No apology necessary, Maddox. I knew when you invited us that Augusta'd be pissed off and make you pay for it."

"Oh, poor baby Maddox," Augusta said. "But he always has you on his side, Libby, doesn't he? Quite literally, too."

Maddox got to his feet, so furious, his face was as red as Simms's. "Stop it, Augusta!"

Libby rose, too, unruffled as she faced Augusta across the table. "Maybe he needs someone on his side, Augusta. Some of the things you've done . . ." She let her voice trail off meaningfully while Simms got up unsteadily, knocking against the table and sloshing the glasses of tea.

"Guess it'd be better if we go home now," he muttered, shaking his head sadly. "Ready, Libby?"

Maddox held his hand up. "Wait a minute, Simms. Nobody's going anywhere until Augusta apologizes. I won't have my guests treated this way."

I expected her to turn on Maddox for that, but instead Augusta took a deep breath, faced Libby and Simms, and said, "I apologize to the two of you. It was extremely rude of me."

His relief obvious, Simms mopped his brow with his handkerchief and grinned at Augusta with a nod. "No problem, no problem. Everything's fine, then!"

Libby inclined her head. "I accept your apology, Augusta. But I think Simms is right; we should be going now." She walked over to Maddox, and, cool as ice, kissed his cheek. "Thank you for inviting us." Turning to me, she laid her hand on my shoulder briefly. "Lovely to meet you, Dean. I'm sure we'll be seeing you around town."

Ben jumped to his feet, knocking his chair over. "Let's hit the road, then!" he said. Earlier, Ben, Maddox, and Simms had worked it out that Ben would ride back with the Legeres and leave his car for me and Augusta to drive back. The boys had brought so much down, and bought so much more at the souvenir shops, that Maddox didn't think the station wagon would hold it all.

After Ben and the Legeres left, Augusta turned her full fury on Maddox, with me as an uncomfortable witness as the three of us cleaned off the table. "Maddox, you son of a bitch," she screamed, "how dare you humiliate me like that in front of the high and mighty Libby Legere?"

"Me?" he yelled back. "You were worse than usual with

Libby. And what you did to bring Julio—that pisses me off to no end!"

They continued their fighting as we loaded the dishwasher and cleaned up the kitchen, carrying it to a new level as we moved back to the porch to watch the boys playing in the sand. Later, I wasn't exactly sure what it was that pushed Augusta over the edge, but before I knew what was happening, she got right in Maddox's face and shook her finger at him. "I hate your self-righteous, goody-two-shoes guts, Maddox Holderfield. I knew I should never have married you, and I never, ever want to see you again!"

To my utter astonishment, she flounced inside the house and came back on the porch with her suitcase in hand, her purse over her shoulder. "You've got Dean to help you, so the two of you can get everything packed up, take care of the boys. I'm leaving here."

His face flushing, Maddox stared at her. "Oh, no, you're not. You're not going home and leaving me and Dean to—"

"You're right," Augusta yelled. "I'm *not* going home. I'm going somewhere as far away from you as I can!" And with that, she left, slamming the door. I ran to the front door, my mouth hanging open, just in time to see the station wagon pulling out of the driveway. Horrified, I rushed back on the porch to find Maddox opening a beer nonchalantly.

"Don't worry, Miss Bean, she'll be back," he sighed heavily, drinking his beer and shrugging his shoulders. "It's not the first time she's left me."

Five

A WEEK AFTER THAT wild Labor Day, Maddox called me from Highlands, North Carolina. He'd found Augusta, and he and Gus had gone to bring her home.

"Is she okay?" I asked. Maddox's voice on the other end sounded harried, exhausted.

"She's fine, Miss Bean. Just overwrought. Gus, too."

"Do you think—I mean, could I speak to her?" I asked him.

Maddox was gone for a while, then returned to the phone to say Augusta didn't feel like talking. In a low voice, he said for me not to worry, that she'd call me back when she was feeling better, but she never did.

Since the afternoon that Augusta had driven away from the Seaside house, tires squealing, I'd heard nothing from her. I worried, concerned about her state of mind, disturbed by the signs of instability she'd shown on Labor Day. The week rolled by, and I waited to hear from Augusta, wondering where she could be and if she were all right. Maddox seemed exasperated but nonchalant about it, telling me when I'd called to find out if he'd heard from her that everything was fine, that she was just cooling her heels, and she'd be back. I'd paced the floor, jumped every time the phone rang, sure she'd disappeared or been in an accident or something. By the time he called me from Highlands, I was convinced Augusta had gone for good.

The Wednesday after Labor Day, I entered the kitchen to find Ben at the table with his coffee cup, hunched over reading the devotional. He and I had been at odds since we'd returned from Seaside. Although not as fiercely and passionately as Maddox and Augusta, we'd argued every moment we'd been alone. It wasn't just that he'd been offended at Augusta's behavior and my defense of her; I expected that. I was furious at him for telling the church ladies what happened, even if unintentionally. Labor Day, I'd gotten home late since I had to take Maddox and the boys home in my car, loaded down with beach stuff. We'd hardly been able to get anything in my small Toyota, so Maddox was to send Joe, the Hernandezes' son who worked at Mimosa Grove, after everything else. Because his mother wasn't there, Gus had cried while Julio looked on wide-eyed. Maddox had been irritable, telling Gus to quit crying, that his mother would be back. Slipping into my room at midnight, I'd inadvertently awakened Ben, who demanded to know why I was so late. I'd reluctantly told him about Augusta's leaving. To my horror, the next day he told Bob Harris—in confidence, he swore—but evidently Bob told Noreen, for the story was making the rounds all over town.

"Tonight's the fellowship supper, and—" he began, but I interrupted him.

"I'm not going," I said. "I don't feel like talking about what happened. The phone's been ringing off the hook, all the gossips trying to get the scoop. I'm sick of it."

Ben glared at me. "Things will be a lot worse if you don't go tonight. People will say you're hiding something."

I closed my eyes and heard Ben push his chair back, get to his feet, open the back door. "It won't look good if you don't go to the supper tonight," he repeated.

Opening my eyes, I looked at him. I rarely defied him, but suddenly I knew I was going to. "Tell everyone I have a headache," I said faintly. "I mean it, I'm not going." Ben was so surprised that he stared at me, speechless, then left in a huff.

When Collie Ruth stopped by to check on me that night, she said everyone was talking about Augusta at the supper. "You know how people are," she'd said, her voice tight. "Folks are saying they don't know what's worse—Augusta's leaving Maddox, or her taking that poor little migrant boy to the beach with y'all. Can you believe it? Augusta's liberal ways don't set well with some folks. Just like her daddy, they say, and he was unpopular with a lot of the community. I tell you, Dean, there's more prejudice around here against migrants and foreigners than there ever was toward blacks!"

I was to remember those words later, but at the time I just shook my head, depressed by thinking of the prejudice some people carried with them like heavy backpacks. I could tell Collie Ruth a thing or two about the prejudices against poor whites as well.

Another week passed before I returned to the normal activities of the church. The Holderfield migrant camp was empty now, all its occupants returned to faraway lands. It would stay empty until next spring's tomato crop. Thankfully, the talk began to die down about Augusta's leaving Maddox. Bigger and better stories came along. A hurricane brewing ninety miles off the coast of the Dominican Republic, posing a threat to the Florida mainland, was the news the following week.

The United Methodist Women held their monthly meetings in the room of the Fellowship Hall that they'd claimed as their own, and I took my seat reluctantly. My mind wandered during the proceedings, the endless reports from missions and socials and the altar guild, all presided over by Collie Ruth Walker. I perked up once, hiding a smile, when a heated discussion erupted as to whether an arrangement of flowers or a card should be sent to members who'd had a death in the family. It amused me that the most insignificant things caused the most passionate discussions—something Jesus called swatting at gnats and swallowing camels.

I always hated the last item of business: the report from the parsonage committee. I kept my eyes averted until it was over, squirming as the committee reported on the condition of "my" home. Noreen Harris leaned forward and peered over gold-rimmed half glasses.

"After the meeting tonight," she announced, "I've arranged for two of the young men from the youth group to come to the parsonage, remove the oak sideboard from the dining room, and return it to the Lord's Handmaidens."

Whispers ran around the room like an electric current. Collie Ruth raised herself full height at the podium and glared at Noreen. "First time I've heard about this," she said frostily. "Don't you like that sideboard, Dean?"

All eyes turned my way and my face flamed. "I-it's not a matter of *me* not liking it," I stammered.

"But you use it, don't you?" Collie Ruth persisted. "Even though there's a big sideboard in the dining room, you use the little oak one to store linens in, right?"

"Yes, ma'am," I said, my voice trembling. "Actually— this is the first I've heard of it being moved, too."

"*What?*" Collie Ruth glared at Noreen. "You're going to move something from the parsonage and haven't told Dean?"

Sylvia Hinds raised her hand. "Madame President, if I

can have the floor I can clear this up." I resisted the urge to roll my eyes at old Whiney-Hiney.

Collie Ruth stepped aside as Sylvia prissed up to the front of the room. Last Sunday, I'd discovered that her children were as charming as she was. Sylvia let the youngest one, Dixie Lee, sit beside her at the organ because the child, though eight years old, had flung a fit and refused to sit with her daddy. Then she'd petulantly kicked the foot pedals all during the service. Whenever Ben came to a critical point in his sermon, the attention of the congregation would be diverted by a loud *whamp!* from the organ. From the choir, I could see the tips of Ben's ears turning red and knew he was furious. Sylvia'd better watch out; Ben would get even. Soon he'd be preaching on kids who were overindulged and how rotten they turned out.

Sylvia adjusted her horn-rimmed glasses and cleared her throat. "Now, ladies," she began, "y'all know that Miss Lilly Henson donated that sideboard to my circle, the Lord's Handmaidens, before she went into the nursing home. Our former preacher's wife had it moved to the parsonage, but we're fixing up our room and have decided we want it back. I called Noreen, and everything's arranged." She looked at Collie Ruth and shrugged. "And that's all there are to it."

The room burst into startled laughter, and Sylvia's face turned bright red. Her voice rose an octave higher as she corrected herself. "That's all there *is* to it." She made her way back to her seat, her nose held high.

Collie Ruth turned to look at me, while the other women averted their eyes. "Dean?" she said. "This all right with you?"

Sylvia glared at Collie Ruth before sitting down. "This has nothing to do with her."

"Dean's using that sideboard, Sylvia," Collie Ruth responded.

"There's a perfectly good sideboard, a beautiful antique given by Noreen's mother-in-law, in the dining room. Why does she need two?"

"I have two in my dining room," Collie Ruth said.

"So do I," the vice president, Janice Johnson, said, leaning forward. "And besides, why does your circle need it, Sylvia? Y'all don't use it." Janice was the kind of woman I'd always both feared and envied: pretty and self-possessed, from one of the town's oldest families. Leading members of the country club set, the Johnsons lived in a classic house in the best neighborhood and had exemplary golden-haired children. With her blond hair in a perfectly angled cut, Janice looked like a sorority girl grown up. I always felt like the Little Match Girl in her presence.

"That's not the point," Sylvia whined. "Tradition's very important to us."

The others in the Lord's Handmaidens joined in a chorus of protest. I raised my hand to get Collie Ruth's attention. My voice trembling in humiliation, I said, "Please, let the Lord's Handmaidens take it. But could the boys possibly wait to pick it up? I'd like to get my stuff out." I had an overwhelming urge to tell Sylvia where she could put the damn sideboard.

"No problem, Dean," Noreen put in generously, her voice full of conciliation. "The boys'll help you move your things out." She looked up to Collie Ruth and smiled. "Now, then. All taken care of. That concludes our report."

Collie Ruth was skeptical, looking toward me for a sign. I gave her a weak smile, too proud to let anyone know how humiliating the whole thing was. She would have gone to bat for me, but I couldn't endure the squabbling that would follow.

It was during the social hour when I heard Augusta was back at Mimosa Grove. Lorraine Bullock, still a contender for my least-favorite church member, though outclassed by Sylvia Whiney-Hiney tonight, was doing refreshments. She and her committee began handing out plates and coffee cups as soon as the benediction was said. I looked down at my silver-edged china plate in dismay: two halves of a pimento-cheese sandwich, one on wheat and one white, salted peanuts, a piece of frozen Jell-O salad, and a huge chunk of chocolate cake, piled high with whipped cream and topped with a cherry. I'd insult them if I didn't eat it, so I nibbled on the pink Jell-O salad, which tasted like Pepto-Bismol.

It was Lorraine who started it. Settling her wide rear end on a peach-colored sofa, she looked around the room until her eyes fell on me. She was a woman as unattractive as her personality, with big hair, a big butt, and an even bigger mouth.

"Tell us, Dean, since you and Augusta have gotten so chummy, when did Augusta get back to Mimosa Grove?" she asked, stuffing half a sandwich into her mouth.

"I'm not sure," I murmured. Augusta was back and hadn't called me! I put my fork down and picked up my coffee cup, trying for nonchalance. The coffee was lukewarm and weak as dishwater. Raising my eyes, I looked at Lorraine. She'd devoured the sandwich and moved on to the cake, and I had the unkind thought that without her makeup and big hair, she'd look like a bulldog. Winston Churchill in drag, Augusta once called her.

"My daughter-in-law Grace Anne teaches fourth grade, as y'all know," Lorraine said, looking around the room, "and she's appalled that Gus missed school when him and his daddy went to look for Augusta. Poor little thing, Grace Anne told me that Gus didn't understand why his mama wasn't there, was scared to death she'd never come back. Grace Anne says Gus is in Becky Schuler's room this year, and he's about to drive poor Becky crazy. Got all sorts of problems, that one does."

A murmur went around the room like bees buzzing a hive. I looked up sharply, but Janice Johnson beat me to a retort. "That's ridiculous," Janice snorted. She and Lorraine were notorious for their clashes, since the snooty Janice didn't take well to social climbers like the Bullocks. "Gus is as well-behaved as any child I've ever known. Certainly better than Grace Anne's kids."

Lorraine bristled and I swallowed a smile, chalking one up for Janice. Augusta would be laughing out loud if she were here. I couldn't tell her about it, though, without revealing Lorraine's snide remark about Gus. I had to call her, find out when they had gotten back, and why she hadn't gotten in touch with me. I covered my untouched food with my napkin and rose quickly, before anyone could see what lay beneath. Muttering that I'd go to the parsonage and get the sideboard emptied out, I put my plate down and beat a hasty retreat.

I was surprised when Maddox opened the door the next morning at Mimosa Grove. In spite of slipping away from the UMW early last night, it was too late to call by the time I got through with the sideboard. The boys from the youth group were obviously uncomfortable at finding me on my hands and knees, pulling my linens out of the lower drawers. In spite of Noreen's offer, neither one helped, standing by and shuffling their feet as I lugged out the assortment of tablecloths and napkins the church provided for every occasion. I'd called Augusta several times in the morning, but the line had been busy. Finally I drove out to Mimosa Grove, puzzled.

"Maddox!" I said, looking down at my watch. Ten-thirty. He couldn't be home for lunch yet. He wasn't dressed for work, but was in rumpled jeans and a gray T-shirt.

Smiling at my confusion, he took my arm, pulling me into the entrance hall and closing the door behind us. "Am I glad to see you, Miss Bean. Come in."

"I—I didn't mean to show up like this," I stammered, "but I've been trying to call—"

"My fault," he said briskly. "I've been on the phone, working out of the house this morning." He kept his grip on my arm, steering me toward the sunporch. "Let's talk a minute before you go up and see Augusta, okay?"

Maddox stopped by the kitchen and flung open the swinging door. I was surprised to see Theresa Hernandez at the stove, since she was never there this time of the morning. "Theresa, how about bringing us some coffee?" he said, then headed me to the sunporch. We sat facing each other on brightly covered wicker chairs, but didn't talk until Theresa, quiet and efficient, her demeanor solemn, brought the coffee in china mugs on a rattan tray. Theresa was almost sixty years old but was as trim and agile as a girl, and didn't have a single wrinkle on her placid face.

"Theresa working for y'all in the mornings now?" I asked Maddox, sipping my coffee. It was rich and aromatic, scented with cinnamon and pale with cream. Cuban coffee.

"She'll be coming in more often now," he said, not offering further explanation, though we'd had numerous discussions about how Augusta balked at having her help full time.

We were silent as we drank our coffee, and I wondered why he'd asked me out here if not to talk about the Labor Day weekend. When he still didn't say anything, I cleared my throat and poured myself another cup. "Maddox? I haven't seen you since—ah—Labor Day. You okay?"

He sighed and looked out the windows. Bright and sunny today, it was still hot, though mid-September. "I was thinking how beautiful today is, how I wish we could avoid talking about—all that. Somehow the word got around about Augusta leaving, and the gossips have been having a field day."

I hoped and prayed he never found out that it was Ben who unintentionally started the talk. "It's been awful," I said. "People love talking about you and Augusta, don't they?"

Maddox smiled weakly. "That's for sure."

"Did Gus handle everything okay?"

He removed his glasses and rubbed his eyes. "He's such a great kid. He asked all the right questions, why grown-ups fight, why his mother doesn't like Miss Libby, stuff like that. Of course, I haven't been able to quite explain why Augusta left." He lowered his head and rubbed the back of his neck. His eyes, usually clear as crystals, darkened. "Augusta's been on Zantac ever since she got home. Been on Jack Daniel's myself."

"I've been really worried about Augusta...." I said hesitantly.

"Listen, about her not calling you, Dean ... Everything was so crazy—"

I raised my hand in protest. "It's okay. I understand, really."

He leaned toward me, elbows on his knees. "Bullshit. I bet you don't."

Under his direct gaze, I shook my head. "I—I guess not. When I heard y'all were back and Augusta hadn't called me ... I didn't know what to think." I lowered my eyes, embarrassed. Augusta didn't owe me anything. Maybe I'd misunderstood our friendship.

"Augusta hasn't wanted to talk to anybody," Maddox said softly.

"Even me?" I couldn't help it, I was hurt. As close as we'd gotten, and in a time of need, she shut me out.

"Especially you."

I blinked, stunned. Evidently my distress showed on my face, for Maddox placed a hand on my arm. "Don't take that the wrong way, Dean. As I told you at the beach, you and

Rich are the only friends Augusta has, and I appreciate your friendship. She needs you right now."

"Then—why has she shut me out?"

He shrugged. "My guess is, so you'll see only what she wants you to see of her life, the way she wishes things were. She's much more vulnerable than she lets on."

I smiled a shaky smile. "Augusta vulnerable? Like the proverbial steel magnolia, maybe."

"It's a mask, Dean. Trust me."

But I didn't, not then. Instead I thought that I understood Augusta, whom I'd known only three months, better than her husband of almost two decades. When I stuck my head in her bedroom, she jumped out of bed and ran to me on bare feet, grabbing me in her arms. "Oh, Beanie, Beanie," she sighed. "I knew you'd come see about me eventually."

"How come you didn't call me?" I asked. Augusta shrugged, and I could see her shoulder blades through the thin material of her white cotton gown. There were dark smudges under her eyes, and her hair was a mess.

"I haven't wanted to talk to anyone." She turned her head, and even in her disheveled state I marveled at the classic beauty of her profile. "Come on, let's sit over here in the sun," she said, motioning me toward the sitting area, under tall windows draped in lace curtains.

"I was worried sick about you, Augusta," I said, sitting in a rocker across from her. "If you'd called me, I'd have been out here in a heartbeat."

"Celeste brought me some things. Herbal tea, serenity candles, stuff like that."

It hurt that she'd called on Celeste, but not me. "Do you think we could talk?"

Augusta shook her head in protest, closing her eyes. "I'm not ready yet. You understand that, don't you, Dean?"

"Well, sort of. But . . ." I searched for the right words that wouldn't offend her. "Have you thought about talking to a counselor?" I blurted out. So much for the tactful approach.

The look she gave me was disdainful, her blue eyes blazing. "Counselors are so full of shit, thinking they know everything, have all the answers."

"That's not true. Certainly there're some bad ones, but not all of them. Ben's a trained counselor, you know."

"I rest my case."

I wasn't about to run with that one, so I tried another tactic. "I hate to see you so unhappy," I began. "Maybe . . . you and Maddox could see somebody together?"

Her anger dissipated and she studied me. "Oh, Dean, it's not that. My marriage is fine, and Maddox and I are doing great now, I swear. It's just me. I'm always flying off the handle, saying things I regret later. I got so pissed off with Libby, then with Maddox, and the whole thing got out of control. Everything's okay now. Mainly I'm feeling ashamed for carrying on in front of Gus and Julio. I wish we'd never gone to Seaside! Celeste warned me—"

"Bull. Celeste didn't know what was going to happen any more than we did."

Augusta shook her head. "One of these days, Dean, you'll see things differently."

"Maybe. Or maybe not." I shrugged.

"I shouldn't have said what I did to Julio's parents, Dean. That was wrong."

"True. But your intentions were good. You did it to give that little fellow a day at the beach that he'd never forget."

"Well, he sure as hell got that, didn't he?" she said, sighing.

"We all did, didn't we?" I rubbed my eyes, trying to figure out how to express my concern for her, when I heard a strange sound—a giggle.

"Especially Maddox," she said, putting her hand over her mouth.

I stared at her, astonished. "Surely you don't think this is *funny*?"

"I can't help it. I get tickled every time I think of the way Miss Priss-ass Libby looked when I told her to mind her own business."

"Augusta, listen to me . . ." I began, startled at the change in her, the swing from despair to hilarity. But she ignored my plea as her giggles turned into laughter. The old Augusta was on her way back.

When I left Mimosa Grove, I stopped to pick up dry cleaning. I was lugging the plastic-draped clothing back to my car when my eyes fell on the store across the street, with its sign hanging overhead: *Celestial Things*. Celeste's unsettling prediction about the Labor Day trip caused me to shiver, even in the warmth of the early afternoon sun overhead. Sheer coincidence, surely. Hanging the clothes, I had to crawl in the back; my hair caught on one of the hangers, and I scowled climbing into the driver's seat. Had it not been for the delay, however, I wouldn't have seen the entourage across the street.

While I wrestled with the hangers, a big white Cadillac had parked in front of Madame Celeste's store. Car doors slammed and I watched as three people—one of them my husband, Ben!—got out of the Cadillac and entered Celestial Things. I couldn't have been more astonished if I'd seen Ben going into an X-rated movie theater. Dumbly, I watched them through the rearview mirror. The reflection of the bright sun on the store windows made it difficult to see clearly, but I could tell Celeste was inside, behind the counter. With Ben was a man and a woman. Who were they, and what could they be doing? Like a bad scene from an old spy movie, I slunk down and watched them talking and gesturing, shadowy figures in a sunlit room. The man was A. H. Bullock, his balding head and fleshy jowls easy to distinguish as he walked around the store, picking up objects, running his mouth. The well-dressed woman was middle-aged and attractive, with beauty-salon hair, blond and perfect, like an Eva Gabor wig.

Another car pulled up, an old Volkswagen Beetle, painted purple and graffitied with bumper stickers and peace signs. The driver got out and I watched her drop a cigarette, then grind it into the pavement with her heel. She was young, perhaps a student at the nearby community college, wearing platform shoes and a skimpy top with a miniskirt, tattoos spotting her arms and long, slender legs like bruises. Her hair was spiky and dyed black, her lipstick just as dark, making her look like a vampire. She went into the shop and apparently bought something, for Celeste went to the cash register. Ben and his companions came out and got into the Cadillac. A. H. Bullock was driving, but I still couldn't think who the woman was, though I was sure I knew her. She got in the back and Ben sat in the passenger seat. I slunk down further as they drove off. Looking back to the store, I saw the vampiress backing her car out. When she left, I crossed the street. Ben and A. H. Bullock in Celeste's store! One thing for sure, they weren't there to have their fortunes told.

The cloying smell of incense hung in the air like evening fog when the bells on the red door announced my entrance. Celeste had her back to me, behind the counter, and she didn't move. She was dressed as colorfully as when I saw her last, with a bright shawl draped over one of her erect shoulders. Her black hair was loose and wild. "Celeste?" I said finally, and she turned, brass earrings clanking.

Her face was completely expressionless as she looked at

me. If she recognized me from the visit with Augusta, she didn't let on. "Ah—how are you doing?" I asked, made uneasy by her rigid demeanor.

Her eyes, lined with dark kohl, regarded me warily. Her answer was a curt nod of the head. "I am well. Thank you."

I felt foolish, standing there with nothing to say, no reason for being in her shop. My eyes fell on a circular display of greeting cards, and I whirled it, pretending to look for a card. No way could I send one to our church members—they were too far out, the messages too New Age. "Ask the universe to heal you"; "Pray to the goddess"; "Nurture yourself." Then I spotted one that said, "The Christian Right is neither."

"I'll get this one for Augusta." I smiled as Celeste rang it up. When she handed me change, I tried again. "I guess you don't remember me, Celeste, but I was here a few weeks ago with my friend Augusta Holderfield."

Celeste inclined her head. "I remember. Augusta Holderfield is a good customer, and you're Dean Lynch."

I smiled, pleased she remembered my name, until she continued. "You are the wife of the priest," she said.

"Ah, not exactly," I said. "He's not called a priest in our denomination. Priests are usually not married—that is, some aren't. The Protestant ones . . ." But I stopped myself, waiting for her to tell me that my husband had been here, to explain the purpose of his visit. Instead, she met my gaze as silent as wood. But definitely unfriendly. Not like she'd been with Augusta and me, the morning we had tea together.

"Celeste, I saw my husband leaving here," I admitted. "That's why I came." When her expression didn't change, her heavily fringed eyes studying me, I continued. "Just a minute ago, before that girl came in. He was with a couple of other folks. One of them is a businessman in town, but I don't know the woman . . ." I faltered, hoping she would help me out, tell me if they were here to invite her to church, or what.

"You sent your husband here?" Celeste said, her tone sharp. I looked at her startled, then laughed.

"Me send Ben here? Hardly." Then, realizing how that must sound, I amended it. "I mean, he's not into New Age stuff." The understatement of the year. "I was shocked to see him here, actually. And A. H. Bullock." It hit me then. Ben was chaplain of the Chamber of Commerce, A.H. one of its members; the woman must be another member. "Of course!" I smiled, relieved. "They were here on Chamber of Commerce business, weren't they?" I felt foolish pumping her to find out their business. She could tell me it was none of mine.

Celeste tossed her head. "They came from their chamber meeting, but not on official business, no! They came about . . . the other." In the sunlight coming through the windows, faint frown lines around her eyes were more noticeable, making her look older, tired.

I laid my hands down on the counter, leaning toward her. "What other? Celeste, what is going on?"

"Do you not know, Dean Lynch? You are not a part of it?" Her tone was still guarded, suspicious. Of me, I realized.

"I have absolutely no idea what you're talking about," I said.

She hesitated, then said, "The incident at the high school."

"Crystal Springs High?"

She raised her chin, spots of color on her cheekbones. "I'm full of regret and sorrow, but I cannot be responsible."

It dawned on me what she was referring to. This past Sunday, at church, the talk between services. I'd been so preoccupied that I'd not paid much attention. There was always idle chatter about people and events in the community. "I heard some talk—something about some kids in our church . . ." I began, but couldn't quite recall what. I shook my head and shrugged.

Celeste and I stared at each other as she took my measure. She must have suffered over the years, I realized, a woman who by her vocation and ethnicity was an object of derision and ridicule. As we stood facing each other, I sensed a change, a letting down of her guard. Her eyes filled with tears, which she wiped away with the edge of her shawl.

"Come on, Celeste. Tell me what happened and what it has to do with you."

She told me the story. "The—the young kids, fourteen years old, maybe, came in my store, had money and bought things, asking me questions. I told them many stories, legends. . . . They were interested, and I liked telling them about the old country. But, after the ball game Friday night, they go to the river, have a party with some sort of rituals. I think, drink a lot of liquor and smoke pot. Things happened." She shrugged elaborately. "A—young girl was hurt. Maybe, she was raped."

"Oh, my God," I gasped. "I hadn't heard that." Surely Ben would've said something to me—had I been that wrapped up in worrying about Augusta?

Celeste's eyes were troubled. "I think—the story, it just came out. The girl was afraid to tell, maybe? I hear children of prominent families are involved."

"Oh, Lord," I breathed, shaking my head. Then I looked up at her sharply. "Wait—what did you say, Celeste? About a ritual?"

"I know only what I hear," she said defensively. "I do not know what ritual, what they did." She shrugged. "Things teenagers do when they drink too much. Get high on drugs."

I blinked at her, frowning. Something wasn't adding up. "But—what does it have to do with you, Celeste? What'd they buy from you?"

She drew herself up, closing me out again. "I cannot

keep up with everything I sell. Business is good, with the students of the college back in town."

"But, surely you remember something—"

Again she shrugged, and her narrowed eyes glinted with a black light. "Incense, books, jewelry, candles . . . the usual. Nothing of harm here, even if people say so. My herbs are for healing, not for evil!"

I took a deep breath and looked around me. Black candles flickered, reflecting off purple quartz deep as the bowels of caves, while sinister-looking gargoyles grinned at me, incense smoke drifting from gaping mouths. Brass wind chimes clanged, although no air stirred. Who knew how impressionable young kids would see such things? "I'm still confused. Why was my husband here?"

"Ha! The good Christians of a town, they always want me on the outskirts, in a trailer with a sign out front. They bother with me only if I move in their midst. Now they regret giving me a license to operate my store and lease the building. They plan to revocal it."

"Revoke it, you mean? Your license? They can't do that, Celeste. You have as much right to your business license as the Dollar Store, Hallmark, anyone else."

"For years I saved to have my own store," she said bitterly. "Maybe it does not seem like much to others, but me—I moved around all my life. I want to settle in a nice town and run my little shop. That's all I ask of Crystal Springs. Is it too much?"

I laid my hand on her arm. In spite of her rigid posture, the defiant gleam in her eyes, she was trembling. "Celeste, listen. I'll find out from Ben what's going on. From what you've told me, you don't have anything to worry about. Probably some parents are upset by what their teenagers did to that girl, and they're looking for someone to blame. I'll see what I can find out and get back to you, okay?"

Again I could feel her taking my measure, reluctant and

mistrustful. Finally, she nodded her head. When I left and turned my car around, I saw her standing as I'd left her, her shoulders slumped and her head hung down. Her defiant posture had melted like a candle left burning too long.

I didn't see Ben, who was speaking at a church in Pensacola, signing his books afterward. He'd been excited telling me about it, I recalled guiltily. He'd wanted me to go with him, but I couldn't since I had to practice for a musical special this Sunday. I'd already gone to bed when I heard him come in, late, and walk past my bedroom. After a while I went down the dark hallway and opened his door. Ben looked up from his perch in bed, books spread out around him. His reading glasses had slipped down on his nose and his face registered surprise at my entrance.

"Dean! Thought you were asleep," he said, putting his book down and taking off his glasses. Even though he moved his feet, making room for me, he wasn't particularly overjoyed at the interruption. His face was tight, his eyes wary. He didn't like being disturbed when working on a sermon.

"How'd it go?" I asked, sitting on the foot of the bed and folding my legs under me. Frowning, Ben replaced a book I'd knocked off a stack.

"Oh, fine," he answered. "Sold a dozen or so books. Got your music all ready?"

"Yeah, it's an easy song to pick up." He nodded, but his eyes were distant. It was too late for small talk. "Ben, I need to ask you something."

Again, he frowned, which irritated me. "Listen," I said sharply, "I hate to bother you, but you're never home so we can talk."

"Oh, for heaven's sake, don't be so touchy. What is it?"

"I saw you this afternoon, going into Madame Celeste's store," I blurted out.

For a minute Ben looked blank, then he rolled his eyes. "Oh. Yeah, that's a big mess. All I need now."

"What? What's a big mess?"

"You know. All that stuff about those teenagers this weekend. Then that—young girl . . ." I was surprised when Ben avoided my eyes, picking up a pen and putting the top back on it. It'd already leaked ink on the navy-and-white striped top sheet.

"What girl? What happened? And what does it have to do with Celeste?"

"I don't know why you're asking me, Dean. You know good and well what's going on."

"I swear I don't. Tell me."

His lips tightened. "The parents are trying their best to keep things quiet."

"What things? I swear—if you don't tell me I'm going to scream!" Exasperated with his evasiveness, I hit the bed with my palm, and the ballpoint pen rolled to the floor. Ben put it on his nightstand before turning back to face me.

He sighed mightily. "For God's sake, calm down. Here's all I know—a group of kids got in some trouble this past weekend, couple of them in our church. A young girl was . . . er . . . hurt. She's not in our church but one of the boys involved is."

"What kind of trouble?"

Again Ben sighed as though I were asking him to climb Mt. Everest, right now, in his pj's. "That's all I can say."

"I've already heard some stuff," I admitted. "About drugs. And rape. . . ."

Ben threw his hands up dramatically. "See? That's how things get around! No one has said the word 'rape' yet. No one knows if it happened or not."

"What does it have to do with Madame Celeste?" I asked him, scooting closer. Instinctively, Ben drew away. I was surprised to see his eyes narrow and his face darken at the mention of Celeste's name.

"That woman is bad news, Dean. The kids bought a bunch of crap—excuse my French, but that's all it is—from her, then she told them stories having to do with rituals and stuff. Of course, being young and impressionable, they have to try it out. That's so irresponsible that I feel she should be held accountable."

I frowned, chewing on my lip. "Is that why you and Ass Hole Bullock and whoever that woman was went to see her today? Because you thought Celeste was responsible?"

Try as he might, Ben couldn't keep a smile from tugging at his lips. "If you don't stop calling A.H. that, I'm going to slip up and say it myself one day." He rearranged his face back into his best pious expression. "After the chamber luncheon today, some of us decided to go to Madame Celeste's place and take a look around."

"Who was that woman with you?"

"You know her. Annie Laurie Glascock. Goes to First Baptist—"

"Oh, my God, Ben! I can't believe it. Annie Laurie Glascock, whose husband is the state representative from this district?"

Ben drew back in surprise at my outburst. "Yeah, that's the one," he said, as though there'd be more.

"Buddy Glascock's a dimwit Republican right-winger—though I guess that's redundant—and Annie Laurie's president of the Eagle Forum," I yelled. "The Eagle Forum, Ben!"

"Didn't they do a program at the church right after we came?"

"That's how I know her," I said. "And don't pretend you don't know who they are, because we've had them in all our churches. Bunch of dingbat antifeminists who've done more to hold women back than any organization I know of."

"You can hardly call Annie Laurie a dingbat," Ben snorted. "She has a law degree and serves on the city council. She's a sharp woman, whether or not you like her politics."

"Oh, yeah, real sharp, isn't she? I don't know why she has a law degree, because she's never worked a day in her life, since she and her organization believe that a woman's place is in the home. A real sharp woman, Ben."

"I don't see anything wrong with that myself," he said. "Back in my mother's day, homemaking was a noble profession. Women are made to feel ashamed to be homemakers nowadays."

"Oh, bull. It's about choices, don't you see? What infuriates me about the Eagle Forum—among other things—is how they put a guilt trip on women who don't have a choice about certain things in their lives."

Ben's look was cold. "You know who you sound just like? Just exactly like? Augusta Holderfield."

"So? I'd rather sound like Augusta Holderfield than that idiot Annie Laurie Glascock, any day. The Eagle Forum—Jesus!"

"My point is, you're becoming a clone of Augusta. Much as you've been under her influence lately, I can't help but worry."

"I refuse to let you do this. You're not going to change the subject when I want to know why those right-wingers are harassing Celeste, and why you're going along with them."

Ben closed his eyes. "I can't take this tonight. I want you to go back to your room and leave me alone."

I stood up and stared down at him. My face burned, and a hot flush of anger moved from the tips of my toes all the way to the top of my head. "Oh, you do, do you? Well, let me tell you, Ben Lynch—it'll be a pleasure," I said. "You're *always* too busy to listen to me. I have to listen to all your sermons as well as every detail of every boring meeting you attend, but if I want to talk, then you don't have time. You're a hypocrite, flaunting your feel-good book about loving marriages when you won't take time to listen to your own wife!" When I flounced out of the room and slammed the door, I had the satisfaction of seeing Ben jerk his head back in astonishment, so hard that his glasses fell to the floor.

Six

A FEW DAYS LATER, I went to check on Celeste and was surprised to find Augusta there. Busy with church work, I hadn't talked to her for several days. And now there was the tension between me and Ben. Since the night I accosted him in his room, he'd been cool with me, even though I'd apologized.

"You can't imagine the pressure on me here," he'd snapped, his voice strained. "I need you to help me out, be the best preacher's wife they've ever seen, but what do you do instead? Run all over the place, neglecting me and your church work; you only have two piano students—I don't know what's happened to you!" I didn't argue because he was right. He was used to having me as his number one help-mate; his biggest cheerleader.

Celestial Things was empty except for the sweet-smelling smoke of incense. I was coughing and wiping my watery eyes when the curtain parted and Celeste appeared. Behind her was Augusta.

"Augusta!" I cried between coughs. "I didn't know you were here." I didn't park in front of Celestial Things, didn't see her car, because I didn't want my car seen. As my daddy used to say, no point in pissing on a skunk.

Dressed up in a beige linen suit with bone-colored heels and a pearl choker around her neck, Augusta sure looked better than when I saw her last. When I whistled at her smart-looking suit, she twirled. "Didn't recognize me, did you?" she said. "Maddox is flying me to Atlanta later on. He's going to a meeting, but I'm gonna shop till I drop. We'll eat at Abruzzi's, then see a play. I came by to check with Celeste, make sure it was a good day to fly."

I looked at Celeste. "Is it?"

Celeste shrugged, her dark eyes wary. "Augusta gives me too much power," she said, gesturing theatrically, her armful of silver bracelets clanking. "I say, Augusta, listen to the voices of the cosmos! I am merely the guide."

"Celeste has helped me more than any doctor I've ever been to," Augusta said, her blue eyes warm.

"So, are things better now?" I asked Celeste.

Augusta looked from me to Celeste. "What're you talking about?" she asked me.

"Celeste obviously hasn't told you about her visit from the chamber."

"Gas chamber? Chamber of Horrors?"

"You're close," I said, explaining the scene with Ben, A. H. Bullock, and Annie Laurie Glascock.

Augusta scowled. "The gruesome threesome came to get their fortunes told?"

"They'd just come from a Chamber of Commerce meeting," I explained, watching Celeste. "Seems some of the town's folks aren't happy that Celeste invaded their midst. So they looked around to see if she really sells devil-worshiping and dope-smoking stuff."

Augusta rolled her eyes to the ceiling. "Nothing to worry about, surely?"

I sighed, unable to reassure her. "Some kids who bought stuff here got in trouble last weekend. Turns out the whole thing was mostly rumors. Word got around that a girl had been raped, but yesterday we heard it wasn't true. Has it hurt your business?" I asked Celeste.

"What business?" she said, her voice bitter. "I've had very few sales since the trouble. Even students of the college . . ." She shrugged, flinging her ringed hands high.

Augusta frowned. "Sounds like we have a little problem here after all, Miss Bean. Who'd you say was with Ben and A.H.?"

"Annie Laurie Glascock. Know her?"

She made a face. "Do I! She and her husband are members of the dreaded Christian Coalition. Maddox has had more than one run-in with Buddy Glascock, who's such an asshole he makes A.H. seem like Mr. Rogers. Annie Laurie's forever stirring up trouble, her and her Eagle Forum. What'd she do here, Celeste?"

"Asked me questions. What things are for, you know?" She picked up an incense holder, a squatty gargoyle with a grotesque grin and pointed ears. "Like this—she says this is for smoking dope? Do you grow marijuana in your pots? I tell her no, I cook in my pots."

Augusta hooted, but her blue eyes clouded. "If Annie Laurie gets her group of witch-hunters after you, Celeste, your business will suffer. They'll use this incident to scare people, convince them you're corrupting the morals of the youth, one of their favorite buzzwords. With all the crap going on with kids nowadays, Celeste, you'd be the perfect scapegoat. Next thing you know, the Christian Coalition will hold a prayer vigil in front of your store."

Celeste nodded grimly. "So she tells me. They'll block the door to Celestial Things."

"Blocking the door to celestial things is their speciality." Augusta smiled wryly, and I groaned.

"In spite of your double entendres, if they're talking prayer vigils, we've got to do something," I said. "The Eagle Forum scares me. First week we were here, they approached me. I said I didn't join civic groups, but I was terrified they'd put me on their blacklist. A group of fanatics like them, united for the sole purpose of making my life miserable, does not appeal to me. When they left, I locked the doors and barred the windows."

"You should've held up a cross and spit over your shoulder." Augusta grimaced. "You don't have to worry about being blacklisted, however; they're too dim-witted to take a hint. Even though my daddy was the most insufferable white liberal in the state of Florida, and I proudly carry on his tradition, they still—to this very day—ask me to join them. But I'm not chicken-shit like you, Dean. I tell them to take their brooms and stick 'em where the sun don't shine."

"Do you really?" I asked in admiration.

"Naw, I'm lying," she admitted. "Even I have sense enough not to get them riled up. But this is different. Now they're after Celeste, and we've gotta stop them."

"That should be a piece of cake," I sighed. "Unless, next time they ask, me and you actually *join* the Eagle Forum. We infiltrate their ranks and work from the inside, like the FBI and CIA do."

Augusta's face was serious. "Hmm . . . not a bad idea."

"You crazy fool, I'm teasing."

"Yeah, but you might be on to something. Let me think a minute." She looked out the window, her blue eyes thoughtful, then she whirled around. "You know what—we might can fix their wagon after all. Celeste, close the store. We're going on a little trip."

"I cannot close in the middle of day!" Celeste protested.

"Oh? Gonna disappoint the hordes lined up outside? Put up a sign, Out to Lunch, Back in an Hour." Augusta started out the door, then stopped. "Oops, almost forgot what I came after." She grabbed a bottle of herbal massage oil and dropped it into her pocket, telling Celeste to put it on her tab.

I had no idea what she was up to, but Celeste locked up and we crawled into Augusta's car. Augusta stuck a CD in the player as she backed the station wagon out. "Augusta?" I asked, fastening my seat belt. "Do you mind telling me what's going on?" She hit Play and Willie and Waylon filled the silence, singing, "Mamas, don't let your babies grow up to be cowboys."

"You'll see," was all she'd say, humming along with the music.

"Why are my hands shaking and my heart beating fast?" I moaned. "Why I am scared you'll get me into big-time trouble?"

"You're just hungry, is all. Low blood sugar. Y'all haven't had lunch, have you?" She turned nonchalantly off Main Street into a residential area.

"You're just taking us to lunch?" I said, relieved. "I was scared we were blowing up Jerry Falwell's headquarters or something."

"As though I'd do anything like that, Miss Bean." She smiled smugly. "Goodness, no. We'll have us a nice little lunch, is all. Ah! Here we are."

I watched in surprise as Augusta pulled in front of a restaurant named Past Times, a place she'd sworn she hated. An old Victorian house, Past Times was only open for lunch and catered to the ladies: birthday parties, bridal showers, secretaries taking one another out. Augusta made fun of it, called it Panty Hose Times. She admitted that the food, though faux-Southern, wasn't so bad; it was the ambiance—

the kind of place you couldn't get into without panty hose on. The clientele was snooty and prissy; the Victorian decor made her want to puke, and it had, she said, pink silk flowers in swags over the doors, lace covers on the toilet seats, and ceramic cherubs for light fixtures.

"What are we doing here?" I asked. The patrons in the car next to us got out and smoothed their skirts down. There were four of them, pretty young businesswomen in stylish suits and heels, clutching their purses as they made their way up the purple pansy–lined walkway.

Ignoring my question, Augusta got out of the car. "Well, don't just sit there, *ladies*," she mocked. "Let's get something to eat."

"Wait a minute—I'm not dressed," I protested. The contrast to the three of us was almost comical. Although late September, it was still hot, so I'd dressed comfortably in shorts and a white cotton shirt, tied at the waist. As usual, I'd pulled my hair back in a careless ponytail, and slid my feet into red plastic flip-flops. Although Augusta was dressed up, Celeste looked like she was costumed for a part in the *Addams Family*. Her flowered skirt was long enough so you couldn't tell if she wore panty hose, but the peasant blouse hung low to reveal a startling amount of cleavage. As usual, a patterned shawl was thrown theatrically over her shoulder. To top it off, her hair was wilder than ever today, flying about her head like a black cloud. She would definitely stand out in this crowd.

Yet both she and Augusta strode bold as you please up the walkway of the restaurant and into the darkened entrance. An elegant young woman sat at an antique desk scribbling with a plumed pen. "Reservations only, ladies," she said without looking up. "Name, please?" Smartly dressed in a black linen sheath, she had sleek short hair and a bored voice.

"Mrs. Maddox Holderfield." I'd never heard Augusta identify herself that way but understood when the young woman looked up.

"Oh—oh, yes! Mrs. Holderfield—I'm sure we can find a table for *you*." She glanced over Augusta's shoulder to where Celeste and I lurked in the darkness of the entrance. "How many in your party?"

"Three. And put us in the Magnolia Room, please."

"I'm so sorry, Mrs. Holderfield, a ladies' group eats there every Thursday, but I can put you and your friends elsewhere. The Camilla Room has plenty of empty tables."

Augusta shook her head haughtily. "Surely you can find places in the Magnolia Room for three more," she said, unruffled.

"Oh, there's plenty of room," the young woman replied, "but—as I told you, Mrs. Holderfield—a group meets there. You'd be happier elsewhere, believe me."

I tugged on Augusta's arm and whispered, "Let's eat in the Camilla Room or go somewhere else."

Ignoring me, she confronted the hostess. "If you'll ask your manager, it can be arranged, surely."

The young woman forced a smile, her defeat obvious. "Let's not bother her, Mrs. Holderfield. Come with me, and I'll show you to your table. In the Magnolia Room."

I dared not look left or right as I followed behind Augusta with Celeste at my heels. Heads turned our way, and a rustle of whispers followed us as we traipsed through the main dining room to a back room with a swag of silk magnolias hanging on the door, held up by two ceramic cherubs. The hostess reached to open the door. "Follow me, please."

But Augusta took the menus and opened the door herself. "We prefer to find our own table," she said. The poor hostess stood openmouthed as Augusta stuck her head in the door, peering around. A chorus of women's voices poured from the room as Celeste and I crouched behind Augusta, unseen.

"The waitress inside will take your orders, then," the young hostess told us, then shrugged and walked off. Augusta motioned for us to follow as, menus in hand, she led us into the Magnolia Room.

There was a stunned silence as Celeste and I walked in behind Augusta, regal and confident, chin high. I felt my face burning, horrified to be here in shorts and flip-flops. As ridiculous as I looked, I was upstaged by Celeste, who flung her shawl about theatrically. The chatter of the well-dressed matrons stilled, their faces as astonished as if the three of us had walked in butt-naked. As we made our way to an empty table, I saw there were about forty or fifty women present, looking as if they'd just stepped out of a beauty salon, their hair Clairoled beige-blond or russet-red or silver-white. I spotted two or three ladies from our church, and quickly averted my eyes.

After nodding a greeting to the room at large like the Queen of England, Augusta motioned for us to sit at a table in the middle of the room. Unlike me, Celeste took her time, pulling out her chair slowly, adjusting her long skirt just so. I grabbed a menu and buried my face in it. Peeking around it, I saw several tables like ours clustered around the main table, with groups of four or five women at each one, staring at us. Gold-rimmed china plates awaited them, holding salads.

Seated behind the podium at the head table was none other than Annie Laurie Glascock, her eyebrows raised like question marks. On either side of her, two women bent toward each other, whispering furiously. One of them I knew—Vanna Faye Bell, the head soloist of our church choir. "Augusta, what have you gotten us into?" I whispered. As soon as I asked, I saw it. On the podium in front of Annie

Laurie Glascock, a brass plaque. Engraved on it was an eagle perched on an American flag, wings full spread. I kicked Augusta under the table, hard. "Oh, no. Not the Eagle Forum," I hissed, hidden by the menu I held in front of me. "Please God, tell me I am *not* at a meeting of the Eagle Forum!"

"They meet every Thursday for lunch," Augusta whispered back, a smile on her face as she surveyed the room. "Lot of work involved, safeguarding the morals of our country. Takes a lot of chicken salad."

Annie Laurie Glascock rose to her full height, stood behind the podium, and clicked on the microphone, which issued a shrill shriek. "Goodness, ladies, look who's joined us—it's Augusta Holderfield," Annie Laurie announced. "What a pleasant surprise." Although she sounded friendly, there was an edge to her voice like sharp ice.

"Thank you," Augusta said, then motioned to the waitress with an imperial wave. "Bring three more salad plates over here, please."

"You and your friends are welcome to join us," Annie Laurie continued, bending toward the microphone with a smile that would frighten Count Dracula, "but we're in the middle of a meeting. We welcome visitors who share our ideals, but we don't encourage others to visit."

Unperturbed, Augusta said, "You welcome visitors? Well, good. We're visiting."

"Let's get out of here," I said behind my menu.

Augusta shook her head. "Oh, no, Miss Bean, Miss Double-O Seven. This was your idea, and you're not leaving. I got us in here, and we've got to see it through."

Evidently Annie Laurie Glascock decided the only thing to do was to ignore the intrusion and proceed with business, for she turned and whispered something to the women on either side of her before returning to the podium. "Ladies, as usual I'll ask you to eat your salads as we proceed," she said, picking up the glasses hanging on a chain around her neck and perching them on her nose. Probably in her fifties, she was an attractive woman, big-boned and blond, expensively dressed in a white knit suit with gold buttons. The thick gold chain around her neck probably cost more than I made from my piano students all year. From it hung a jeweled gold cross the size of a hammer. One thing about the Christian Right, they didn't bother themselves with Jesus' teachings about poverty and humility. "Vanna Faye Bell has our devotional," Annie Laurie announced. "And has consented to sing."

Augusta winked at me as Vanna Faye Bell, the pride of Crystal Springs, came forward. She was beautiful, with lustrous golden-brown hair and a white-toothed smile. I'd never seen her without the smile, actually. In choir every Sunday, she maintained it throughout the sermon. She never took her eyes off Ben, her crush on him obvious. Vanna Faye placed a small tape recorder on the podium.

"Y'all forgive me for bringing taped music," she said in a low, breathy voice. "I just spotted my dear preacher's wife, and if I'd known she'd be here, she could've played for me."

Several heads turned my way, and I picked up my fork nonchalantly, hoping Vanna Faye'd get on with her song and leave me alone. "Any of y'all who haven't been to First Methodist since Brother Lynch came," she continued breathlessly, "should pay us a visit. Every single Sunday, Brother Ben inspires me."

"Ooh, I'll bet he does," Augusta murmured, and Celeste snickered.

"Let me put in a plug for his book of devotionals, *Love Yourself Like Jesus Loves You*." Vanna Faye nodded toward a woman in the audience. "Y'all still have plenty of copies, Maylene?"

I recognized the woman, Maylene Herring, who ran Words of Life, the Christian bookstore downtown. She was always calling Ben, asking him to come sign copies for her customers. I cringed hearing her sugary-sweet voice, because she made no effort to hide her dislike of me, stemming from the time she ordered me to go find Ben at the church. I was teaching a piano lesson and had no intention of doing any such thing. One of these days I'd tell her what happened during Ben's first book signing: Maylene's husband, a leading citizen and deacon at First Baptist, caught me in the hallway and tried to feel me up.

Vanna Faye continued. "Before I sing for y'all, I want to share with y'all what's on my heart."

"That sums up why Yankees hate the word *y'all*," Augusta whispered to Celeste.

"I find great comfort in reading my Bible," Vanna Faye began, "but, ladies, we deal with issues in our modern age that weren't around in biblical times, things like television and video games and the Internet. I like Brother Ben's book because he deals with the real issues of today. Like, a chapter on the joys of a Christian home. And, you ladies will appreciate this—a special section on keeping the romance in your marriage!" To my horror, she wagged a finger in my direction. "Maybe I should bring the expert up to tell us about that chapter." There were polite chuckles, while Augusta bruised my leg kicking me.

"Yes, I read Brother Ben's book every night," Vanna Faye told her audience. "I keep it right beside my bed."

"Bet she wishes it were Ben instead," Augusta snorted, and Celeste laughed out loud. I plunged my fork in the mound of chicken salad, red-faced.

Vanna Faye turned on the tape recorder then looked upward, as though God were in the heavens above her, holding up a placard with the lyrics written on it. A dreamy look came over her face as she closed her eyes and swayed to the music, then started singing "Wind Beneath My Wings." With the final words, she leaned back, held her hand high, and shook it as though flinging fairy dust on her audience.

I thought Augusta was going to choke, trying to keep from laughing out loud, so I didn't dare look up until applause broke out and Vanna Faye returned to her seat, bowing and blowing kisses.

Annie Laurie regained the microphone, applauding as she looked toward Vanna Faye, who sat smiling idiotically at her grateful audience. I figured she'd sit through the whole meeting like that.

"Such a blessing to have Vanna Faye one of us," Annie Laurie declared. "And now, our agenda for today." She put her glasses on and resumed a down-to-business demeanor, opening up her speech with a long tirade against things that she said threatened America today—feminism, gays and lesbians, mixed marriages, and single-parent households. Augusta choked on her tea when Annie Laurie launched into a diatribe against having road signs in both Spanish and English. She begged her audience to keep the English language pure, and to fight the taking over of our beloved country by alien forces: immigrants. "Go to any motel or Seven-Eleven in Florida," she said, "and you'll find it run by foreigners—heathens!—*Indians* in turbans and *Orientals* from God knows where. It's gotten so you have to take a translator with you to put gas in your car." Her audience laughed appreciatively at her little touch of humor.

"Today I'll address a grave danger in our public schools; the main focus of our efforts this week." At this, Annie Laurie paused dramatically, taking a sip of water. The women in the room watched in rapt attention, their eyes shining. "You all know that Buddy and I are firm believers in public education, and that Buddy serves on the education appropriation committee of the legislation," she told them. "Our two precious children, Buddy Jr. and Laurie Anne, are in public schools because I'm determined to fight from within the system to make America better. Last week, my precious little Laurie Anne, a tenth grader, brought me the reading list for her Advanced English class." Augusta groaned, but I kept my eyes straight ahead.

Annie Laurie held up a piece of paper and waved it. "I have it right here in black and white! Any of you all know Mr. Jake Belk, that new English teacher at the high school?" Several of the women nodded their heads. "My friends, Mr. Belk has assigned books so filthy that I will not allow Laurie Anne to return to his class! Every day I've been to the school confronting the principal, who says his hands are tied. And, listen to this, ladies—Mr. Jake Belk is actually threatening me! He claims he'll have the First Amendment folks down here to fight me. Well, so be it. I said to Mr. Belk, I've fought them before and I'll fight them again!"

Applause broke out, and Annie Laurie beamed. "We must fight the pornography that's being passed off as literature today. I checked out these books from the library. In the very first one, I counted eight *shit*s, eleven *son-of-a-bitch*es, fifteen *goddamn*s, and twenty—*twenty*!—'*f-u-c-k*s,' right there in black and white. Another book had ten references to the penis and eight to the vagina. One described self-abuse in such disgusting detail that you could tell the author was a practicer. And this one." She held up a book I was not familiar with. "Mr. Belk actually laughed at me—*laughed* at me, ladies—when I said there were sexual acts in this book that my innocent children and their classmates have never heard of. Well, we'll see who has the last laugh, won't we?"

While waiting for the applause to die down, Annie Laurie stood with her chin raised high, with the look of a martyr about to be sacrificed to heathens. She held the piece of paper at arm's length. "Let me share some of the books on this list so you can see if your children have this so-called literature—

I call it trash—among their possessions. If so, you must take action to keep your children from reading them. Confiscate any book on this list immediately!"

She adjusted her glasses and began reading: "*Of Mice and Men. The Catcher in the Rye. The Color Purple. I Know Why the Caged Bird Sings. Beloved. The Prince of Tides. Are You There God? It's Me, Margaret. The Pigman.*" Annie Laurie stopped abruptly, frowning and putting her hand over her eyes, as though too pained to go on. She took a sip of water, regained her composure, and continued.

"Across the country, groups like ours have had these removed from schools and libraries before. Now the fight has come to Crystal Springs, and we won't let this pornography remain in easy access of our children! I have drawn up a petition that we will take to the school board meeting where we will ask the board to ban these books from the school library. Your support is essential, ladies. Don't let me down."

The applause was thunderous enough to drown out Augusta's groans. Glancing at my watch, I was relieved to see that the hour was almost up. In spite of my embarrassment, I was glad Augusta had brought us here, walking right in with Celeste, big as you please. It was an incredibly gutsy thing to do, and I was proud to be her friend. She'd accomplished her purpose, which was to let Annie Laurie Glascock know that Celeste had influential advocates, and she'd better not sic her group on her. I leaned over to pick up my purse, anxious to leave, when a stout woman two tables over stood up.

"Annie Laurie," the woman said, "I just wanted to let you know how much I enjoyed visiting today." At that moment my heart sank because I knew what would happen next. Sure enough, Augusta stood up.

"Me, too, and thank you ladies for letting my friends and me sit in," Augusta began, her voice as smooth as silk, and the ladies around us beamed. "I had *no* idea so many enlightened women were in Crystal Springs." I dared look around me, and saw that she had the complete attention of everyone in the room. Annie Laurie gripped the podium with both hands, glaring at Augusta, but she wasn't about to tell the wife of Maddox Holderfield to sit down and shut up.

"It wasn't an accident that we came here today," Augusta continued. "I've been asked to join your organization often, so I remembered that you meet here every Thursday."

Annie Laurie leaned toward the microphone. "Excuse me, Augusta; even though you've turned us down in the past, that invitation still stands. You'd be welcome to join the Eagle Forum."

The room burst into applause and Augusta bowed to them, like an actress accepting an Oscar. "Why, thank you," she said, and if I didn't know better, I'd swear she was genuinely pleased. "It was that very spirit of *sisterhood* that brought me here. I couldn't imagine that a group of women— *sisters*—wouldn't applaud the struggles of one of their own." She paused, and I groaned inwardly, knowing how the word *sisterhood* would go over with this bunch, a group who actively fought the ERA several years ago. What was Augusta up to?

"I brought two visitors with me," she continued. "Since most of you seem to know Dean Lynch, wife of the new Methodist minister, I won't introduce her. But I'd like for my friend Celeste Cozma to stand."

When Celeste stood, there were audible gasps as it dawned on the women who she was. Though they'd heard of her, I doubted any of them except Annie Laurie had seen her. Not a single woman applauded in welcome. Celeste sat back down to silence as heavy as the tension in the air, now that her identity had been revealed.

"I'm sure you'll all want to welcome Celeste to our community," Augusta continued, unperturbed. "She's a single woman, trying to make it on her own—as I know some of you are—who has started her own business, a nice little gift store on West Bay Street. We women have to stick together if we're going to survive."

When a wave of whispers broke the silence of the room, Annie Laurie tapped on the microphone to get the attention back to her. "Thank you, Augusta," she said icily. "However, since our organization deals with the *important* issues of today, we don't have the time nor inclination to endorse new businesses. Even worthy ones," she added pointedly. She raised her chin and looked around the room. "Time is up, ladies. That concludes our program, and thank you all for coming."

I thought that Annie Laurie had won that round, that she'd succeeded in effectively shutting Augusta up. Just as the audience brought their hands up to applaud the end of their meeting, Augusta stopped them. A few of them were getting to their feet, but sat back down when Augusta held out her hand like a cop stopping traffic.

"Just one more thing, Annie Laurie. You say you don't endorse businesses, even worthy ones," Augusta said, her voice loud. Too loud. "You don't realize how *worthy* Celeste's business is. Celestial Things is more than a simple gift store, for Madame Celeste offers a service to our community that you ladies must hear about. In her devotional, Vanna Faye talked about the Christian home and marriage. You won't need a book on your bedside table to read about a loving marriage, ladies! All you need to do is discover the amazing secrets of Madame Celeste's herbs."

To my utter astonishment, Augusta reached deep in the pocket of her beige suit jacket and pulled out the vial of massage oil she'd bought earlier, holding it high. With that movement, she effectively stole the show from Annie Laurie Glascock.

"I won't tell you more," she said with a mysterious smile, "except to urge you to try Madame Celeste's potions. Your marriage will be the beneficiary. Believe me, ladies, you will use this oil in ways you've never dreamed of." And with that, she sat down. Annie Laurie tapped angrily on the microphone but couldn't quiet the excitement that swept over the room. I dared look over at Celeste, who was smiling and bowing her head as though she'd just been awarded the Nobel prize.

In a panic, I grabbed Augusta's arm. "Let's get out of here," I hissed. Slowly and deliberately, Augusta retrieved her purse and stood up, nodding her head in a farewell gesture to the astonished crowd. Beside her, Celeste stood up and bowed to the audience. If I didn't get her out of here, she'd be throwing them kisses. I somehow got between the two of them, half pushing and half pulling them to the door, tripping over my flip-flops in the process. The voices of the roomful of women swelled around us, almost loud enough to drown out Annie Laurie's *Tap! Tap! Tap!* on the microphone. I felt like barring the door when I pushed Celeste and Augusta out the other side of it, slamming it with a noise that caused the diners in the other part of the restaurant to raise their heads in surprise, forks in hand.

Once we crawled into the car and locked the doors, I closed my eyes and let out a long breath. Augusta and Celeste were laughing so hard that Celeste put her head down between her knees. Augusta banged on the steering wheel with glee. "Oh, my God," she shrieked. "Did you see the expressions on their faces? They didn't know whether to shit or sing 'Dixie.'"

"Crank the car!" I yelled, beyond caring if anyone heard me.

"The lady who came in my store," Celeste wheezed,

"her eyes popped out of her head when Augusta said that about my herbs."

I grabbed Augusta's arm and shook her hard, like a naughty child, which only set her off again. "This is not funny. You hear me—not funny," I said.

"Aw, bullshit," she laughed. "It's the most hilarious thing I've ever seen!" And at that, Celeste fell over again, clapping her hands, gasping for breath.

"Oh, no," Celeste cried out, "I will pee in my panties."

"Don't you dare, Celeste," I said, searching for the car keys in Augusta's ivory-and-gold purse. "And, I swear to God, Augusta Holderfield, I'm going to kill you dead as soon as we get out of here." Seeing that she was laughing too hard to drive, I slammed out of the passenger's seat, ran around the car, and pushed her over.

"Move out of the way," I commanded. "I'm getting us out of here before those rabid women come flying after us on their broomsticks." I squealed the tires in my haste to pull out of the parking lot, which of course caused Augusta and Celeste to whoop even louder.

Augusta's outrageous performance at the meeting of the Crystal Springs Chapter of the Eagle Forum backfired and ended up causing Celeste more problems, not to mention further widening the gap between Ben and me. Maddox told Augusta that it was a foolish thing to do and she should have better sense. Since she returned after the Labor Day disappearance, they'd been getting along, but this incident threatened to blow everything apart.

"Jesus Christ, Augusta," Maddox groaned when I was at Mimosa Grove a few days later. "Best thing would've been to let the whole thing die down, but you've stirred up a hornet's nest."

Augusta glared at him. We were by their pool one last time before it was closed for the winter. I was sitting on the side, dangling my feet and watching Gus, who swam out of earshot in the shallow end. Augusta sat under an umbrella, drinking piña coladas. She finished off her drink and picked up the long-stemmed cherry bobbling in the white froth.

"How do you know, Mr. Know-It-All?" she said, biting into the red cherry with her perfect white teeth. "I won't stand by and see a friend of mine mistreated."

Dressed in a gray business suit, Maddox stood next to Augusta's chair with his hands on his hips. He'd just gotten home from the packing plant and was tired and irritable, his face red and sweaty. "You do enough stupid things to keep my blood pressure sky-high," he snapped. Then to my surprise, he turned on me. "Goddammit, Dean, I count on you to keep Augusta out of trouble, not lead her in."

"Me!" I screeched at the same time Augusta laughed.

"It was Dean's fault," she said, her eyes sparkling. "She was the one to suggest we infiltrate the Eagle Forum."

"Aw, crap, Dean," he growled. "I thought you of all people had better sense."

Before I could defend myself, Augusta continued. "Actually, Dean should've been a secret agent. Here was her plan: Once we were accepted in the group, we plant bombs in their chicken salad, which wouldn't kill them, it'd just take every hairdresser in Florida to get their hairdos in place again."

"Very funny," Maddox said. "What do you have to say for yourself, Dean?"

I shrugged wearily. "Honest to God, we were just trying to keep that bunch of crazed fanatics away from Celeste."

He went to the table where Augusta's glass pitcher of piña coladas stood tall, milk-white, and frothy. "Yeah, it really worked, didn't it?" he snorted. "That half-page ad they took out in Sunday's paper shows how effective you were. Not to mention the little prayer vigil they held. They're trying to get that woman's business license revoked, you know that?" He made a face after drinking from a glass of piña colada. "This stuff tastes like shit."

"Jesus, Maddox," Augusta said. "Lighten up."

"You drive me crazy, the way you're always charging at windmills. Now that you have Sancho at your side, you're downright dangerous." He scowled at me, and I kicked listlessly in the cool water of the pool.

"You don't fool me," Augusta teased him, throwing her head back and closing her eyes. "You adore me, no matter what I do."

"Here's what I don't understand—why the fuck have you taken on that ridiculous fortune-teller?" he continued. "Frankly, I hope the Holy Rollers run her all the way back to Miami, or wherever she comes from."

"She's from Romania," Augusta said, but Maddox hooted.

"Romania my ass. Maybe Arab, Alabama. Or Rome, Georgia. That woman's a phony if I ever saw one."

He'd gone too far. Augusta's playful mood vanished and she rose up in the lounge chair. "You don't know what you're talking about, you pious know-it-all."

"This is not about me, Augusta, it's about you and your foolhardiness. You need to—" Maddox began, but we were spared his tirade by Gus.

"Look, Daddy," Gus squealed as he ran to us, oblivious to the tension of the grown-ups. "Beanie taught me how to do a cannonball!" And with that, he jumped into the pool, pulling his little legs close and landing with a splash that sent water splattering over Maddox.

"Go change, then come back for a swim, Maddox," Augusta laughed. "Or just jump in like that. You're wet enough."

"Wish to hell I could," he said, removing his glasses and wiping them with a towel dropped nearby. "But health inspectors are coming tomorrow and I've got to go back and help Carl finish the reports."

"Why you're so irritable." Augusta smiled. "It's not about me, after all."

"It's always about you, sweetheart." He snapped the towel at her legs and she grabbed for it angrily.

"That hurts," she yelled, taking the towel away and glaring at him. "So, are you telling me you won't be home for supper, Maddox? I've been marinating a beautiful red snapper all day."

"Can't help it. You and Gus eat it."

"Yuck!" Gus grimaced. "Not that fish Mama's fixing— he has his eyeballs in."

"You are not my child, Gus," Augusta told him. "No child of mine could be such a philistine."

"Takes after his old man," Maddox laughed. "Dean, why don't you stay and eat my portion of the snapper? Pay your penance for leading my wife astray."

"I'd love it," I said, easing into the pool. October had come and the water was cool. "But I'll have to see if Ben has a meeting or not."

"Bull," Augusta said. "You tell me constantly that he's never home for supper. Stay, and we'll eat out here."

"Yeah!" Gus cheered. "Beanie's gonna eat fish eyeballs with us." And he did another cannonball, further dousing his ill-tempered father. I dived underwater and stayed there until Maddox was gone.

As soon as I got home and turned on the overhead light in the kitchen, I saw that I'd messed up. There was an unfamiliar sight: a stack of dirty dishes piled in the sink. Ben had fixed his own supper. The kitchen was a disaster, grease splattered on the stove and vent overhead. The lingering smell told me he'd fried a steak in the iron skillet on top of the other dishes in the sink. I'd just squirted Ivory liquid over everything when Ben walked in. He was ready for bed, in plaid pj's buttoned to the neck.

"Thought I heard you," he said, opening the freezer door. "Where've you been?"

"Mimosa Grove, eating supper."

"Really? I tried calling out there and didn't get an answer. I was getting worried."

"We were at the pool and couldn't hear the phone. I had no idea you'd be home."

"You could've called and I'd have told you."

"I just figured you'd have a meeting . . ." I let my voice trail off as I scraped at his plate with my fingernail. He'd fried eggs with the steak. "Next time, could you run some water over the dishes? Keeps the food from sticking so bad."

"Hope there won't be a next time—you know I like my supper on the table when I get home," he said.

"I'm sorry . . . I don't always know when you'll be here."

"You fuss all the time about that, so I made a special effort to be home tonight. No telling when I'll be here again."

"Saturday night," I told him, wringing out the dishrag. "I've already planned it—I'm fixing grilled shrimp. You know, with garlic and butter? And, I've put on reserve at the video store that new Hallmark movie you want to see."

Ben shook his head. "Can't do it. I told the Isabel Gissendanner Circle we'd come to their social."

I grimaced. "Oh, Ben, there's no reason for us to go! It's not my circle, and if we go to theirs, we'll have to go to everybody's."

Ben nodded, cocking his head to the side. "Yeah, you're right. Okay."

I almost dropped the dishrag. I was getting myself braced for another big row tonight. "Okay? You mean it?"

To my surprise, Ben turned me around, took me in his arms, and kissed me. It was brief, not much more than a brushing of mouths, but a kiss, nonetheless. "Good heavens," I breathed afterward, looking up at him. "What brought that on?"

"You're right and I'm wrong," he said. "We haven't spent any time together lately, why we've been so at odds. So, I'm circling Saturday night on my calendar. We have a date. And after the movie, I want you to come to bed with me."

"We never do it on Saturday night," I reminded him, then put my head on his chest and rubbed his back. He felt so secure, so familiar. How could I have envied what Maddox and Augusta had when this was so much more comfortable? "Ben? There's nothing in the rule book that says we have to wait till Saturday night." He laughed and shook his head. Even as I said it, I knew he wouldn't listen. Our lovemaking was always written on his calendar. Penciled in, in case anything came up at the church.

"Only a couple more nights," he said.

"Come on, Ben," I tried again. "Don't you think we should be more spontaneous?"

"Nothing wrong with spontaneity. I talk about it in the marriage chapter in my book," he said, pulling away from me. "But I've got a Pastor-Parish Relations meeting early in the morning, so I'm gonna go to bed now." He paused. "By the way, you could have left a message on the machine."

For a moment I couldn't think what he meant. "I know. I wasn't thinking."

"When you're with Augusta, you forget everything else. Including me." He sighed, rubbing the back of his neck. "Or maybe I should say especially me."

"Oh, Ben, I'm so sorry—I had no idea you felt that

way." I took a step toward him, but he turned away. "You're rubbing your neck. Need your back rubbed or something?"

"Nope. I'm heading to bed. And you'd better, too. Don't you have a homecoming committee meeting first thing in the morning?"

I groaned, but before I could answer him, he was gone down the dark hall, closing the door to his room emphatically. I sighed and finished the dishes. After turning off the lights, I stood for a moment in the darkness, looking out the kitchen window to the sidewalk, lit with the muted yellow glow of the streetlights. I stepped closer to the window when I saw the startling sight of a full white moon moving high in the darkness, suddenly revealed as the wind blew a heavy cloud away. Augusta and I had not seen the moon tonight when we ate our supper on the patio. It had been hidden, as though a black velvet curtain had been pulled in the heavens. I wanted to run down the dark hall and wake Ben. I wanted to pull up his window shades and say, "Look! A full moon is out, and we almost missed it, Ben. We almost missed it."

But I stood where I was, watching until another cloud came and blocked out the moon's pure white light. I turned then and walked back to my room. Although I paused for a moment by Ben's door, I didn't go in. I'd wait until Saturday night.

Seven

DESPITE THE ENCOUNTER WITH the Christian Coalition and the on-again, off-again tension between Ben and me, things were going pretty well, and I was settling into our new life. Before we'd moved to Crystal Springs, the busy work of serving God had made Him seem as remote and inaccessible as a faraway star. Without time for introspection, my devotion withered on the vine, dried up by the endless details of meetings and committees. It wasn't quite so bad at Crystal Springs. A good thing about our being at a larger church was that it was easier to be anonymous in a congregation of six hundred. Though I still had a myriad of duties as the minister's wife, I didn't feel so overwhelmed. My sheer love of music was restored to me; my music once again a sacrament, a way of worship instead of a dreary duty.

Maybe because it was so unique, my dulcimer became very much in demand. That fall, I was asked to play for several gatherings in and around Crystal Springs, outside the confines of the church. For some of these, big weddings and birthday parties, I was paid quite well. Surprisingly, I was making more from my dulcimer than teaching my piano students, which had kept me in spending money in the past. I began creating my own musical style. I reached back into my childhood and the guitar-picking, harmonica-wailing music of my family's bluegrass group. I played and sang folksy classics for my performances, and the audience loved them: songs like "Whispering Pines," "Red River Valley," and "You Are My Sunshine." On some of the songs, I sang a capella. I had found both my style and my repertoire.

My next performance came as a result of Augusta's plan to give Celeste more exposure in Crystal Springs. Things had cooled down considerably, both with the weather and the mood of the town; otherwise, I'd not have listened to her. In spite of occasional bursts of rebellion, my basic nature was neither daring nor adventurous. The Christian Right had done their dirty work on Celestial Things. With a clever smear campaign, the Eagle Forum had spread the notion that Celeste was into strange rituals and satanic ceremonies. So Celestial Things was seen by most as a weird rather than a unique little gift shop. Augusta was determined to rectify the damage, this time in a more carefully thought-out way.

To my way of thinking, Augusta's business alone should've been enough to keep Celeste in high cotton. Augusta filled her home with tranquility candles and sweet-smelling potpourri, her language with terms like "listen to the universe," "tune in to the cosmos," and "celebrate the goddess within." She changed her image and began wearing organic cotton clothes in exotic shades as well as saris and silky shawls, with sandals on her feet and numerous silver bracelets on her arm. She let her hair go loose, and looked more stunning than ever.

"I've got the most fabulous idea," Augusta said one bright morning in late October. We were in her kitchen, making apple butter. She and Maddox and Gus had just gotten back from the mountains of north Alabama, bringing two bushels of small tart apples.

"I don't want to hear it," I said, cutting an apple peel in a long strip. "After our little visit to Past Times, I never want to hear another of your ideas."

"You know your problem, Dean?"

"I have a sinking feeling you're about to tell me."

"Other than your being the biggest chicken-shit ever?" she said. She stirred a pot of bubbling apples, deep brown and filling the air with the scent of cinnamon.

"You knew that about me from the beginning, Augusta. You've had to drag me kicking and screaming to everything since we've been friends."

"Whimpering and crying's more like it. It takes guts to kick and scream. No, here's what it is, O Gutless One. You don't know who you are."

I laughed. "Thank you, Dr. Freud. That's an original."

"You're not the woman you appear to be," she said, her blue eyes thoughtful. "She's a creation, actually. You've created her. And I'll bet you're terrified someone will find you out."

Her words hit so close to the truth that I became defensive. "I've never heard such a silly idea. Actually, I'm completely uncomplicated. What you see is what you get."

"Nothing could be further from the truth. You've put yourself into a role, the good little Sunday wife. You play the part—actually, you play it quite well—though your heart's not in it. But if you stopped, you might have to figure out who you really are."

I turned my back to her, running water over the apples in the sink. I didn't want her to see my face flushing. "Okay, I take it back. I do want to listen to your latest idea. Please, please tell me."

Augusta chuckled. "Don't wanna hear the truth, do you? Celeste and I figured it out."

"You've run out of things to talk to Celeste about, so y'all have started in on me?" My voice was sharp. "Are you ready for these apples?"

"Dump 'em in. I'd give anything if you'd go to Celeste, have a reading. You'd be amazed how it'd help you," she said, licking the apple-coated wooden spoon in her hand. The heat from the bubbling apple butter turned her hair into a mass of ringlets around her damp face.

"You can forget it. I don't want to explore the goddess within me. I don't need a guide to my inner child. And I sure don't want to feel the healing powers of the cosmos. You'll have to find a loonier friend than me to keep Celeste in business."

"Exactly my plan. I'm throwing a party, a big one. And you're going to be the entertainment. All Maddox and I hear lately is how you've become the Emmylou Harris of Crystal Springs. So, I want to hear you perform."

"No point in throwing a party. Couple of margaritas and I'll sing for you, as you know."

"Won't do. I want to see you in context, surrounded by an adoring audience. So, I'm giving a costume party here at Mimosa Grove, on Halloween night. You'll entertain us, but Celeste will be the main attraction. She'll give everyone a reading! Once people get a taste of her wares—so to speak—they'll come back for more."

"I don't know, Augusta . . ."

"Godalmighty, how did I ever get to be friends with such a tight-ass?" she sighed, shaking her head sadly. "My best boyfriend thinks it's a brilliant idea, even if my best girlfriend doesn't."

"I can't imagine Maddox going along with another of your crazy ideas."

Augusta hooted. "Not Maddox. Rich. Rich Kingsley. He and Godwin will be back in Crystal Springs by then, and they think it's a great idea." Rich Kingsley and his friend

Godwin St. Clair had been in Maine ever since we'd moved here. Augusta had told me that they were longtime companions, obviously gay, but everyone in Crystal Springs pretended not to know, since the St. Clair family was such an old and revered one.

"I'm glad they'll be back then, because I can't wait to meet the only other friends you've made after living here a lifetime," I teased her.

She laughed, tossing her head back. "They're dying to meet you, too. But tell me the truth, baby girl. What do you think of my party, really?"

My laugh floated over the kitchen like the scent of apples and cinnamon. "As much as I hate to admit it, it sounds like you've come up with a brilliant idea, for a change."

The Halloween party at Mimosa Grove was in full swing when Ben and I arrived. I parked beside him and slung the strap of my dulcimer case over my shoulder as I looked up at the big house, all lit up. I'd sneaked away from my church meetings last week, and Augusta, Gus, Theresa Hernandez, and I had spent every day getting it ready for tonight, polishing and shining and scrubbing. Then the fun part, scouring the countryside for decorations. From Augusta's garden we brought in armfuls of orange chrysanthemums and yellow daisies, along with harvest vegetables: yellow squash and purple eggplant and dried brown okra. We hauled in branches of oak leaves, turning gold and red, as well as bales of hay and stalks of sugarcane from the fields. Then we'd taken Carl's pickup to the farmer's market in Defuniak and returned with our treasure: twenty-five pumpkins. We spent a whole day carving them as Gus placed them, lit with candles, everywhere: lining the portico in front, the big windows, the curved staircase. Their crazy faces grinned lopsidedly, and their golden glow made me feel happier than I had in a long time. I was nervous about performing for such a large crowd—the whole front yard was full of cars—but I was also exhilarated. In some ways I was more anxious about performing with Ben in the audience. He'd hurt my feelings terribly when I'd first told him I'd be singing tonight.

"But . . ." he had said, looking confused, "you can't sing."

"Thanks for saying that, Ben," I'd replied. "Helps my confidence a whole lot."

"No point in getting huffy," he'd sighed, exasperated. "Me and you have different tastes, is all. I don't care for bluegrass, country, folk, stuff like that. No reason to take it personally."

"You like the kind of music Vanna Faye sings better," I'd said.

"Which doesn't make me the Lone Ranger—so does everyone else in town. It's called 'popular' music for a reason. Did I tell you she's doing a special on Sunday?" he'd said, unaware that I turned my head from him so he couldn't see my face.

"I can't wait."

Oblivious to my jitters, Ben took my arm and led me up the wide brick steps of Mimosa Grove. "Come on, cowgirl," he said.

Augusta had insisted on dressing me in a cowgirl costume. I'd planned to wear a witch cape and pointed hat, but she wouldn't hear of it. "Would Emmylou be caught dead singing for the elite of the Panhandle looking like a witch? Puh-leeze! You've got to work on your image," she declared as she pulled out a sequined, fringed cowgirl outfit from the attic, something she'd worn years ago in a rodeo parade. "There'll be folks here who can make your career."

"My career?" I'd screeched as she squeezed me into her clothes, two sizes too small. "I don't want another career. I have a career."

"Oh, bullshit. Being Ben Lynch's adoring wife doesn't count. The chairman of FSU's music department's gonna be there, and so's the entertainment director of Seaside."

"Oh, God, why'd you tell me? I'm not going to sing, then. And, I'm not going to wear this—it makes my rear end look like I've spent one too many days in the saddle."

She'd ignored my protests, as she always did, and I gave in to her, as I always did. I arrived melted and poured into her white satin cowgirl suit with its long fringe flapping in the cool breeze. I thought Ben'd have a fit but for once, he barely noticed. Although I'd told him everyone else would be in costume, he wore a dark suit instead, saying he wasn't staying long, the reason we both drove our cars. Halloween fell on a Saturday night, and he was anxious to get home and put the finishing touches on his sermon. I couldn't help but wonder if the party-goers would be secretly relieved, our church members tanking up on the free-flowing booze once their preacher left.

Gus opened the door for us, dressed as Quasimodo, complete with a humped back stuffed with pillows. "You look great, Gus," I told him.

"So do you, Miss Bean," Maddox said, suddenly materializing. "All of my heroes have been cowgirls." Ben and I both laughed when we saw him, dressed in black with a satin cape and white vampire fangs. Augusta had slicked his hair back with gel and smeared greenish-white makeup on his face. "Can I take your coat?" he asked Ben, but Gus pushed in between them.

"No, Daddy—that's my job! You're supposed to ask people if they want a drink," he whined. "Can I take your coat, Reverend Lynch?"

Ben shook his head, "No, thank you, son. I'm just going to stay long enough to hear my wife sing, then I gotta leave."

I made my way through the crowded drawing room,

holding my dulcimer close as I smiled and nodded to folks I recognized. People were in all sorts of costumes, skeletons and witches and devils, holding their drinks and plates of goodies. Augusta had set me up on the stair landing, decorated with hay bales, candlelit pumpkins, a cane-bottomed stool, and a microphone borrowed from the radio station. I wondered if Celeste was already in her fortune-telling den, the downstairs guest room, the furniture pushed to one side. We'd put a cloth-draped table in the middle with a candelabra on it, lit with black candles, and taped a sign on the door: *Tarot Reading by Madame Celeste of Celestial Things, 107 West Bay Street, Crystal Springs. Walk-ins Welcome.*

I didn't recognize Augusta when I saw her, coming toward me with a tray in hand. Like Maddox, she was draped from head to toe in black satin with a cape billowing behind her, her hair plastered down and a widow's peak painted on. She had to remove the vampire fangs to talk.

"It's about time you got here," she cried, catching up with me through the shoulder-to-shoulder crowd, the cape flaring out behind her. "Let's get you situated. Celeste is a hit—already told a dozen fortunes. Let's get you singing and plucking and folks'll be dying to sign you up for their next party."

"Why'd I let you talk me into this?" I moaned, stumbling after her.

In spite of my fussing and carrying on, the hall was dark enough that I could forget my nervousness. Augusta had told me to play three or four songs, break for about half an hour, then play again. She took the microphone to announce that I'd be entertaining on and off throughout the evening, then there'd be dancing in the library.

I'd been learning new songs for the occasion: "Wayfaring Stranger," "Queen of the Silver Dollar," "House of the Rising Sun." Before I knew it, I'd finished and was bowing to the applause. When I started down the stairs, my cheeks burned, but I felt lighthearted. A number of people stopped me as I made my way through the crowds to the dining room, where cold punch was waiting for my parched throat. Flushed with success and excitement, I'd finished my second cup when Augusta came into the room, blowing me congratulatory kisses. Celeste was with her, wearing a getup Augusta had ordered her from a speciality shop in Miami. Clusters of party-goers whispered together, cutting their eyes at Celeste, who sailed through them like a ship in full regalia. When she reached my side, I held her at arm's length and looked her over from head to toe. "My God," I gasped, "look at you!"

Celeste's long, heavy dress was spangled and exotic, colorful as a peacock's plumage. Anyone else would have looked ridiculous in it, but Celeste was fabulous. Under the tasseled headpiece, a braid was wrapped like a wreath around her head; without the black hair falling in her face, you could see the beauty of her high cheekbones and slanted eyes, and the men in the room stared.

There was a movement in the crowd near the door, and I turned my head to see the vampire Maddox leading Libby and Simms Legere our way. Though not in costume, both were dressed in black and held Mardi Gras–style masks. I'd not seen them since the Labor Day weekend.

"Dean," Maddox said when he reached us, "Libby and Simms wanted to tell you how much they liked your singing."

"Just marvelous, Dean," Libby said, touching my hand. Her demeanor was perfectly controlled, as though the embarrassing scene last time we were together had never happened.

"Libby, Simms . . . glad you could make it." Augusta's voice was cool until she took Celeste's elbow, pulling her into the circle. "Meet my friend and spiritual advisor, Madame Celeste."

Libby's golden eyes widened in surprise as she bowed her head. "So nice to meet you, Miss . . . ah . . . *Madame Celestial.*"

Libby's husband had a different reaction. Looking up at Celeste—she was several inches taller—Simms Legere's eyes lit up. "Madame Celeste," he said, bowing over her hand as though she were the queen of England, "I've been anxious to meet you." Celeste smiled at him sideways, inclining her head. Maddox caught my eye and winked, but I looked away, afraid I'd laugh out loud. Simms was practically drooling.

"What an interesting costume, Madame Celeste," Libby said, her eyes traveling over Celeste with a slight raising of her eyebrows.

"It's not a costume," Augusta said. "Celeste is in her native dress." I hoped I was the only one to hear the snort Maddox disguised as a cough.

"Oh, really? It's—Russian?" Libby said.

"Romanian," Celeste told her, her head held high, her chin tilted. Her accent was heavier tonight; evidently the dress inspired her.

"Romanian," Libby echoed. "What part are you from?"

Celeste gazed at Libby haughtily, her eyes guarded. "From everywhere, and nowhere. My people have no place."

Again I heard Maddox's disguised guffaw, his hand covering his mouth. When Augusta glared at him, he raised the wineglass to her, eyes twinkling. "Celeste is Roma," she said to Libby curtly. "What we call Gypsy. Her people are itinerant. What's happened to them historically is as shameful as what we Floridians have done to the Seminoles."

Libby laughed lightly. "Speak for yourself. I refuse to be burdened with that age-old guilt." She turned, her hair swirling about her shoulders. "Tell me, Madame Celeste, can I have a reading next?"

At first I thought Celeste wasn't going to answer her.

Unblinking, she stared at Libby until I looked away uncomfortably. Anyone else would have, but to her credit, Libby stared right back. Celeste finally nodded in agreement. "You may, since I see that you are not—how do you say?—the skeptical."

This time Maddox hooted aloud, not bothering to disguise his derision. "If you mean skeptic, Celeste, then you're describing Libby to a tee."

Libby turned to take a glass of wine from Theresa Hernandez, who circulated among the guests with a tray. Libby said to Maddox, "Remember confirmation class?"

"Oh, my God," Maddox laughed. "Dean, you'll get a kick out of this. At age twelve, Libby asked our poor old priest, Father Shaw, if Adam and Eve had belly buttons. Father Shaw almost swallowed his false teeth."

Libby kept a hand on Maddox's arm as she laughed, leaning close to him. I expected Augusta to disapprove of such intimacy, but instead she turned to Libby enthusiastically. "I'm glad you're more open-minded than Maddox, Libby, and will have your cards read," she said, ignoring Maddox's groan. Throwing me a look, she winked, and I knew what she was thinking: Her plan was at work. Celeste could make a good living off Libby Legere and her rich friends.

When Celeste motioned for Libby to follow, Simms stepped in front of her. "My wife can go with you now," he said to Celeste, his hand on her arm, "as long as you promise that I'll be next." Augusta beamed, giving me a thumbs-up sign behind his back.

Before my next performance, I saw Ben opening the front door and hurried to stop him. "Ben," I said, taking his arm, "wait! I'm about to sing again."

"I've heard all the country music I can stomach tonight,"

he said, brushing my arm off and going out the door without a backward glance. Stung, my face burning, I turned from him and stumbled up the stairs, taking my place at the microphone. After I'd finished, I made my way to the library, where all the furniture had been pushed aside and the rug rolled up for dancing. The room glowed with yellow candlelight, and the dancers moved dreamily to Ray Charles on the stereo, singing "Georgia on My Mind." As I stood inside the doorway watching, someone came up behind me, touched my elbow, and a voice I didn't know said, "May I have this dance?"

I turned and looked into the face of one of the most gorgeous men I'd ever seen. Tall and slender, he was fine-boned and delicate, with pale silky hair pulled back in a ponytail. Wearing boots with jeans and a black turtleneck, he had on a heavy black cape that swirled when he moved. The entertainment director at Seaside, I thought, or that actor from Pensacola who Augusta had hoped would show up. Startled, I stuck my hand out and he led me to the dance floor. Had I not been so stunned by his sheer beauty, I'd have refused. I'd danced very little in the last twenty years.

"I loved your music," he said as I moved into his arms. He smiled down at me with one of the most devastating smiles I'd seen off a movie screen. "I've always adored the dulcimer."

"Th-thank you," I stammered, stumbling over his feet. "Sorry, I'm a lousy dancer."

His eyes were blue-green, like the ocean on a good day when the tide's low. "Just follow my lead," he said. "How'd you get interested in the dulcimer? Not a mountain girl, are you?"

I shook my head. "No, but my grandmother was. I know little about her, except that the dulcimer was handed down to her on her wedding day, and she taught me how to play it when I was big enough to hold it. Only thing of value that anyone in my family ever taught me."

He looked down at me and raised an eyebrow. "I'd be willing to bet that's not the case."

I nodded, relaxing. "You're right. She also showed me how I didn't want to live my life."

"Ah! Which lesson is the most valuable?" His smile revealed a slight gap between his front teeth that added to his boyish looks.

"It's hard to say," I replied, "because my music has been my salvation. That sounds melodramatic and ridiculous, I know, but it's the truth. My music has saved me."

"It doesn't sound ridiculous, Dean Lynch. My art has done the same for me."

"I knew you were an artist!" I said, pulling back and looking up at him. "You obviously know me, but I'm sure we haven't met."

He tossed his head to get the fine blond hair out of his eyes. "Everyone here knows you because you're the Methodist minister's wife."

"Augusta calls me the Sunday wife," I smiled.

"I'm a member of your church," he said. "I confess, I haven't been to church since you've been here."

"Since you know me, it's only fair that you tell me who you are." It came out sounding coy, and I normally didn't flirt with the men in our church.

"I prefer to remain mysterious. After all, it's a costume ball, right?"

"But that's not fair," I protested, batting my eyelashes.

"I not only know you, Dean, but since you're *my* preacher's wife, you'd better behave. Don't drink too much or laugh too loud. Or God forbid, flirt with me too much. Because if you do, someone'll tell the church ladies, and your name will be mud."

"My name's mud anyway."

He whirled me around, laughing. "You're a beautiful and passionate woman, though you work hard at hiding it."

This time I was so startled that I stopped dancing and stared at him. "I don't think anyone's ever called me beautiful before. And certainly not passionate."

"Then it's about time." He laughed, loud, at the expression on my face, and people glanced our way curiously.

"What did you say?"

"Think I'm hitting on you, don't you?" he said, a twinkle in his eye. "Actually, I'm with someone who's dying to meet you. Come on, and we'll both hit on you." He took my hand and guided me, stunned, from the dance floor.

The cape twirling behind him, my mysterious dance partner led me through the swaying couples to the dimly lit hallway outside the library. The hall was large enough to hold the overflow from the library, and several people stood around chatting and laughing. My hand still in his, my partner took me to a secluded alcove in the hallway. I was surprised to see Augusta there, but even more so to see her talking to a man I'd not seen yet, a man in a wheelchair with a blanket over his lap. Augusta was leaning over him, her hand on his shoulder, whispering in his ear, and the man was laughing.

"Oh, there you are, Dean," Augusta said, straightening up at our approach. Unlike Maddox, she was still in full makeup and costume, though her fangs had disappeared. "I sent Rich looking for you an hour ago. Godwin and I'd about decided you two had fallen in love and eloped."

"Dean and I got acquainted on the dance floor," my partner said. With a gasp, I turned on him.

"You're Rich Kingsley!" I cried. Laughing, he held out his arms and I went into them, shaking my head as he kissed my cheek.

"Rich, you devil—don't tell me you didn't introduce yourself to Dean," Augusta laughed. "Shame on you! What'd you think, Dean, that Prince Charming had arrived?"

"You should've told me that your friend Rich was the most beautiful man alive," I said, still in his arms. "I was so dazzled, I kept stepping on his feet."

"Rating a dance with Rich will make you the envy of every woman here," Augusta said. "But now I want you to meet my dear friend Godwin St. Clair. If Rich is the most beautiful man alive, then Godwin's the most elegant. Godwin, I present Dean Lynch, your preacher's wife and my best friend."

I turned my attention to Godwin St. Clair, who was watching us and laughing. I felt like a fool now, remembering that Augusta had told me that her friend Rich was gay, and that his companion Godwin, much older, had had a stroke and was confined to a wheelchair. "Godwin St. Clair," I said, offering my hand. "I've been waiting for *months* to meet you and Rich."

"As I've longed to meet you, Dean," he said, eyes shining. "Augusta's told us all about you." When he took my outstretched hand and kissed it, I giggled like a schoolgirl.

"I've always wanted someone to do that," I said. His long hand was as lovely and fine as antique paper. In spite of his illness, he was a handsome man, with long white hair and a debonair goatee. Like Rich, he was in a black turtleneck, and the throw over his legs was black velvet. His eyes were dark and warm, taking in everything with an intense interest, and I immediately liked him.

"I thoroughly enjoyed your music," he said. "I've heard about your performances, and have so looked forward to hearing one."

"Dean was so nervous that she drove me crazy," Augusta said.

"Don't feel bad, Dean," Rich said, resting his arm around my shoulders lightly. "Every time I have a showing, I drink too much and show up shit-faced. Right, Godwin?"

Godwin chuckled and nodded. Augusta pointed to the painting over his head with her black-tipped fingernails. "Remember, Dean? You raved over this painting when you first came to the house, and I told you a friend of mine gave it to me and Maddox for Christmas?"

"Of course I remember. Don't tell me you did that painting, Rich."

"Yep," Augusta answered for him. "He should be world-famous, but instead he has a modest little studio right here in Crystal Springs."

"My God, Rich," I gasped. "It's wonderful!"

Rich ducked his head modestly, but I could tell he was pleased. Godwin held out his hand to me and I took it, moving closer. "We had the pleasure of meeting Dr. Lynch before he left to work on his sermon," he said. "We're so looking forward to hearing it tomorrow."

"I can't tell you how thrilled I am that you and Rich are members at First Methodist," I said, squeezing his hand.

Augusta laughed. "Let me translate that. Poor Dean's already had a clash with the more, ah, conservative element of our church, so she needs all the allies she can get."

"Rich and I heard about your escapades with the Eagle Forum," Godwin said sympathetically.

"We've had the pleasure of meeting that fortune-teller you were championing, Augusta," Rich said. "What fun!"

"Did you have your fortunes told?" I asked, looking from him to his companion. Godwin answered me first.

"Wouldn't have missed it," he told me. "She's quite good. Told me to watch out for fair-haired young artists, though." His dark eyes twinkled as he smiled up at Rich.

"You'd better listen to her," Rich teased, then turned to

us. "Godwin's fortune was better than mine. My cards were full of dragons and demons and crumbling castles. Scared the pure hell out of me. Is she really Romanian?"

"Of course," Augusta said. "She's the real thing, I promise you."

"Not according to Maddox," Godwin said, winking at me.

"Oh, crap, Godwin," Augusta sighed, "you know not to pay attention to Maddox. He has no imagination."

"No reason for you to leave him stranded on Labor Day," Rich said, then laughed when Augusta hit his arm.

"Don't you dare tease me about that, Rich Kingsley," she cried. "I'm very sensitive about that incident."

"Not as sensitive as Maddox, I'll bet," he retorted.

"Rich and I can't wait to hear all about your wild escapades, Augusta," Godwin said. "We're dying for a visit from you, the sooner the better."

She pouted. "I'll come see you, Godwin. And Ollie, of course, but I'm never speaking to Rich again."

Rich grabbed her and kissed her cheek. "Like hell. You know you find me irresistible, Augusta my darling. You can't stay away from me."

Pushing him away, Augusta turned back to Godwin. "How is Ollie, my favorite member of the family?"

"Ollie's great," Godwin answered. "Survived the plane ride back from Maine quite well, though he cried at first, quite loudly."

"Soon as you're up to it, give me a call and I'll bring Gus over to play with him," she said.

I tried to keep my face expressionless but couldn't believe Augusta'd failed to mention they had a child. I wondered if he was Godwin's or Rich's, and what the story was.

"When Gus greeted us tonight," Rich told her, "he

asked why we didn't bring Ollie. Said Ollie could've borrowed his Batman costume."

Godwin leaned forward and put his hand on Augusta's arm, chuckling. "I told him that unfortunately, Ollie's ears would hang out of the Batman hood."

Rich caught my puzzled look. "Look at the expression on Dean's face!" he exclaimed.

"We're being thoughtless and rude," Godwin said in dismay. "Ollie's our dog," he explained, and I laughed. "Do you like dogs, Dean?"

"I do," I told him, "especially since I've never had a pet. What kind is he?"

"A basset hound," he said, the corners of his mouth turning up impishly. He turned to Augusta and said, "Bring Dean over to the house later on next week to meet Ollie and to catch us up on what we've missed this summer. Y'all come for lunch."

"We'll do it," she said, then she suddenly whirled and took Rich's hand. "Patsy Cline's 'Sweet Dreams,' one of my favorite songs. Rich, you owe me a dance, and Dean and Godwin can spend some time together, the good little preacher's wife ministering to her parishioner."

After they danced off, hand in hand, I pushed Godwin's wheelchair nearer to the door. "Here," I told him. "You should be able to see them now."

But he shook his head and motioned toward a small antique chair in the hallway. "I'd much rather talk to you, my dear. Why don't you pull up that chair and tell me how you learned to play the dulcimer?"

When Augusta and Rich reappeared, flushed and laughing after their dance, they found Godwin and me with our heads bent together like old friends. I leaned over the wheelchair and kissed his cheek when Rich announced they had to go, that it was way past Godwin's bedtime. "I'm looking forward to our lunch next week," I told him. Augusta was right about one thing: I'd found allies in Rich and Godwin.

Augusta left me alone, seeing Rich and Godwin out and checking on the refreshments. I had no business staying since tomorrow was Sunday, such a busy day, but I went to so few parties outside the confines of the church—parties with dancing and champagne—I couldn't make myself go home, to my solitary room. I wanted to bask in the afterglow of my performance a little longer. Maddox had brought me plenty of contacts, and I'd had dozens of invitations to play.

As though my thoughts conjured him up, Maddox appeared by my side out of the candlelit darkness. "Could I get you a glass of champagne?" he asked, touching my arm.

"Sure." I shrugged. Might as well. The thought of facing another Sunday full of church work suddenly settled over me like a damp, heavy blanket, and I felt tired.

"Want to dance first?"

I shook my head. Maddox disappeared, then came back with two glasses. We stood sipping companionably, watching the dancers whirl past us.

"It's the Baptists who don't dance, not you broad-minded Methodists," he said.

I smiled. "It's not that. I have two left feet."

"That I can sympathize with."

Someone came up on the other side of Maddox and dragged him away. Soft slow music floated over the room, sad old songs: "Crying Time Again," "Unchained Melody," Willie Nelson singing "Blue Eyes Crying in the Rain," the dancers swaying in the semidarkness. The champagne was beginning to make me dreamy, wistful. Maddox had made it to the dance floor after I turned him down, Libby Legere moving sensuously in his arms. Then Augusta swirled by, her vampire cape flaring, dancing with Crystal Springs's portly mayor. Someone touched my arm and I jumped, startled.

"May I have the honor?" Simms Legere asked. "Saw you dancing with that artist fellow, so you can't refuse me."

"Both of us danced on his feet," I said, but Simms pulled me to join the swaying couples anyway.

"I've never danced with a preacher's wife before," he said in my ear, his voice slurred, and I realized he'd had a few too many. "Hope you don't mind me saying this, Dean, but I like you."

"I—like you, too, Simms," I said, feeling foolish.

"Like the way you look, too. Built like a woman. Don't know why Libby and Augusta wanna be so skinny. Men might like to look at fashion models, but it's women like you we want on a cold night."

"Wow, thanks," I said, laughing in spite of myself, trying to keep in step with him.

"I meant it as a compliment. You're one hell of a good-looking woman. And you play a mean banjo."

"It's a dulcimer, Simms."

"A what?"

"Never mind."

"Dean?" he breathed down my neck. "Can I talk to you?"

"Okay, but let's go out in the hall. Maybe you should sit down."

"You think I'm drunk?" he chuckled, swaying. Behind the thick glasses, his eyes were red and bleary. "Naw, I'm fine. I want you to tell me about Celeste."

"Celeste? What do you want to know about her?"

"Everything. She told my fortune six times."

"I didn't know it worked that way. Was it different each time?"

"Celeste listened to me, Dean, really listened. I told her

that I'm the unhappiest son of a bitch in the world." His breath was strong with bourbon, but his grip was so tight, I couldn't pull away.

"Let me guess—your wife doesn't understand you, right?" I said dryly.

"My life is meaningless, but since you're a preacher's wife, you have no idea what I'm talking about."

"You're not going to get any sympathy from me, if that's what you mean."

Simms sighed. "Celeste actually listened to me; only woman who's ever done that. Goddamn, she's gorgeous, too, don't you think? C'mon, Dean, let's go find her." To my surprise, he stopped dancing and began pulling me through the room. As we went out the door of the library, I caught Maddox's eye and mouthed "Help!"

His hand tight on my wrist, Simms pulled me to the guest bedroom where Celeste was. I tried to free my hand, but casually, not wanting to cause a scene. Several people spoke to us as we passed, but no one realized I was being dragged along. When we reached the end of the hall, the door to the guest bedroom was closed. With his free hand, Simms rattled the doorknob. When there was no response, he stared at the sign on the door, his face drooping as if he were about to cry.

"Come on, Simms," I said gently. "Celeste's busy. Let's go find your wife and see if she's ready to go home."

"I'm not going home with her," he muttered. "How'd you like to go home with her? Long as she can be near Maddox, she'll stay here." He raised his head and moaned when he saw someone approaching. "Son of a bitch! Speak of the devil."

Maddox was there, his hand on Simms's shoulder, and I let my breath out, relieved. "Simms?" Maddox said, his voice low. "What are you doing, man?"

"Waiting to see Celeste," Simms replied. "Me and her like each other. I like Dean, too, but she's a preacher's wife. I've never seen a sexy preacher's wife before. Makes me want to commit all seven of the deadly sins."

"Looks like you're well on your way. Let Dean go, Simms."

"I need her to come with me to see Celeste," Simms said, but when he tried to pull me with him, he lost his footing and fell against the guest room door with a bang. Reaching out to cushion his fall, he let go of my hand. I sighed in relief, rubbing my wrist. Maddox took a step to help Simms stand upright at the same time the door to the guest room opened. Celeste peeked out, looking at the three of us quizzically.

"Celeste!" Simms cried out. A drunken smile lit his face and his dark eyes glowed like those of a cat given a bowl of milk. "Tell my fortune again, okay?"

"Come with me, Simms," Maddox tried again. "Celeste can't see you now."

But Celeste shook her head and reached past Maddox, taking Simms by the arm. "It's fine, Maddox. I will see him."

"He's drunk as a skunk," Maddox snapped, exasperated. "Let me get Libby and we'll get him home."

Celeste shook her head sharply, taking Simms by the shoulders as she led him into the darkened room. "Simms and I, we understand each other. Go. Maddox, you and Dean go back to the dancing." And, pulling Simms into the room, she closed the door in Maddox's face.

For a moment Maddox stood stunned, then he turned to me. "Well, I'll be goddamned," he said.

I couldn't decide whether to laugh or cry. "I'm about partied out," I said instead, rubbing my eyes. "I'm going home."

"Oh, no, you're not, Miss Bean. The last dance is coming up and we're going to dance, by God. I'm a hell of a lot better dancer than that drunk fool Simms."

And he was. Unlike Simms, he held me at a respectable distance, and we danced comfortably together. Augusta smiled at me over her partner's shoulder as her husband whirled me past.

"You should be dancing this one with Augusta," I said to him.

"I would have, but I wanted to tell you something. Simms is really a good guy, Dean. We go back a long way. Don't judge him by his behavior tonight."

I shrugged. "I was raised in the backwoods, Maddox. I've seen plenty of drunks, so I'm not judging anybody."

"Simms has more money than God, but he's an unhappy man."

"So he told me."

"You don't sound convinced."

"Not true." I looked up at him. "In my stupid impoverished life, here's something I've observed. It's such a cliche, but money's just money. It buys a lot of nice things, and having it's a lot better than not having it, but I've yet to see it buy contentment."

"Well said. Guess that's what Simms has found out. So . . . he drinks too much. Way too much, and too often, and—"

Before he could continue, Libby Legere stopped us and took Maddox by the arm, her coat and purse in hand. "Dean, please forgive me for this," she said, "but, Maddox, have you seen Simms? Someone just told me that he, ah"—she glanced at me—"is feeling a little sick. I need to take him home."

"Sick? He's shit-faced drunk," Maddox said sharply, "and Dean knows all about it. Come on, we'll find him for you." He took her by one arm and me by the other, and led us out of the library. The crowd had thinned out now, as it was after midnight. From the stereo, Garth Brooks singing "The Dance" floated in the air like the dying smoke from the candles.

Maddox escorted us to the foot of the stairs, where most of the partygoers were gathered, saying their good-byes. "Simms was here a few minutes ago," he lied to Libby. The closed door of the guest bedroom, where Simms was still with Celeste, was down the dark hall. "Stay here with Dean, and I'll go find him."

If Augusta hadn't walked up at that moment, no doubt Maddox could have slipped Simms out of Celeste's room unnoticed. Unaware of what was happening, she came up just in time to hear Maddox. "Simms? I'll get him," Augusta said. "He's back here with Celeste."

Quick on his feet, Maddox hurried to his wife and took her arm. "No, no, sweetheart—go see about your other guests! I'll take care of this."

Uncomprehending, Augusta brushed his arm off. "No problem, Maddox." Although he tried to stop her, Augusta walked down the hall, excusing herself as she made her way through the last of the partygoers standing around the guest room door. Maddox hurried behind Augusta, still reaching for her arm, and Libby followed. Shrugging, I went with her.

Augusta flung open the door to the guest bedroom, which was dark and appeared empty, and Maddox sighed with relief. "Guess I was wrong," Augusta told us over her shoulder. "No one's in here."

She reached over and turned on the lamp on the bedside table, and there were gasps all around us. Libby pushed past me roughly, heading into the room now illuminated by a circle of yellow light. "Libby, wait!" Maddox said, grabbing her as she passed him, but she threw his hands off.

Celeste and Simms were on the bed, wrapped in each other's arms. Celeste's hair was down, spread out on the white pillow like a black cloud. Her blouse was undone, revealing her breasts. When she raised up on her elbow, she gasped and pulled her blouse up. Simms let out a cry when he saw Libby, then stumbled out of bed without his glasses on, his shirt unbuttoned and his pants down. With a loud whoop, Augusta threw up her arms and laughed like a lunatic.

Unlike Augusta, Libby was not amused. She charged into the room and grabbed Simms by what little hair he had left, her composure gone, her face red and distorted. "You son of a bitch!" she shrieked. "You no-good whoring *son of a bitch*!" When Maddox reached her, she was flailing her arms wildly. While Augusta rocked with laughter, the crowd of guests around me stood in stunned silence, mouths agape. On Halloween night, they looked like they'd just seen a ghost.

Maddox grabbed Libby, encircling her with both arms while he motioned toward the door with his head. "Simms, you fool," he cried, "get your ass out of here, man. Quick!" Simms stumbled to the floor in a heap as he plunged toward the door, trying to pull his pants up. He began to cry drunkenly, which caused another scream of laughter from Augusta.

"Augusta, shut up and go get Carl to drive Simms home," Maddox hissed over his shoulder, holding Libby as she struggled, trying to reach her husband, her arms going like windmills. She was out of control, red-faced and yelling, no longer the elegant woman of a few minutes ago.

"Simms, you whore-hopping son of a bitch—I'll kill you, do you hear me? How dare you humiliate me like this!" Libby screamed.

"I'm here, Maddox—I'll get Simms," someone said from the crowd, and I saw it was Carl Hernandez, hurrying into the room to get Simms to his feet. Hopping like a rabbit trying to pull up his trousers, Simms managed to hold on to them long enough to leave, Carl dragging him along. Celeste covered herself from the crowd gaping at her.

"Dean, get Celeste out of here," Maddox snarled, but

Augusta, sobered up, stepped in as she wiped her eyes and the smirk off her face.

"Celeste should stay here tonight," she said. "Why don't you take Libby home?" Before Maddox could move to do so, though, Libby pulled away from him and lunged across the bed at Celeste.

"You Gypsy slut!" she yelled. "How much did he pay you, you whore?"

"Men married to women like you," Celeste shot back, tossing her wild black hair, "they always come to me." Her face was burning with color and she looked glorious, untamed as a hurricane.

"Libby, Libby, come on," Maddox said, looking exhausted and bleary-eyed, not at all amused. "I'll drive you home."

The crowd had begun to fall away, quiet and subdued. When Augusta turned out the lamp and Maddox led Libby from the room, sobbing, the shocked whispers ceased, and everyone began to say their hasty good-byes. Augusta slammed the door to the guest bedroom so hard that the sign she'd taped up there—*Tarot Reading by Madame Celeste*—fluttered to the floor.

Eight

I HAD NO WAY of knowing the bright November day I had lunch with Godwin St. Clair and Rich Kingsley that they'd come to play such an important role in all of our lives. In spite of all that followed, I wouldn't do anything differently. I learned a lot from Rich and Godwin. I learned that none of us can love without commitment; that friendship, like love, requires its own kind of covenant. The components of loving are like the ecology of sea and sand and seagull, each a part of the other, dependent on the fragile bonds holding them together.

But that glorious November day, I wasn't thinking any of that. So eager was I to escape the confinement of the parsonage and the demands of the church that I practically ran the four blocks to the St. Clair house, a route I was to follow often in the months to come. Though still bright and yellow, warm on the top of my head, the sun had that watered-down look that we get in the few cool months Florida has. Pleasant and refreshing, the breeze was as bracing as a splash of salt

water. I wore a light sweater with my jeans, and had exchanged my flip-flops for clogs.

I stopped on the flagstone walkway to look at the big old
Victorian house after letting myself in the wrought-iron gate.
The church ladies had provided me the story of the St. Clairs,
one of the oldest and most beloved families in town. Godwin's father had run a prosperous antiques store and his
mother had been a gracious lady, active in our church. Godwin, also an antiques dealer, had lived in the family home all
his life, staying on to take care of his elderly parents until
their deaths. His mother had died several years ago, Godwin
and Rich taking care of her after she became bedridden. The
church ladies called Godwin an old maid, and told me that
he'd befriended a young artist whom he met on an antique-
dealing trip to Sarasota. Godwin brought Rich Kingsley
home with him and set him up in an art studio on the
grounds of the St. Clair house. Even though Rich and Godwin had been together for so many years, no one in the town
said the word "gay," at least not aloud.

Rich and Godwin greeted me as though we were already
close friends when I joined them on the sunporch in back of
the house. Even though Rich was even more artsy-looking today in a sweater with jeans and boots, Godwin was frailer in
the daylight, his skin pale and his white hair slightly damp,
even though his eyes sparkled and his spirits were high.

"Ollie, come out and meet our new friend Dean," Rich
said, leaning over a round table in the corner and snapping
his fingers. "He barks like a pit bull, then hides under the
table when you appear." The tablecloth rustled and a
mournful-eyed Ollie appeared, hanging his head and thumping his tail on the wooden floor. I knelt down and petted him
as he looked up with deep brown eyes, his long ears drag-

ging. He was a beauty, a dark reddish color spotted with white.

Godwin pointed to a chintz-cushioned rocker. "Sit down, my dear. You must be exhausted."

"Dean's assistant pastor of First Methodist," Augusta snorted. "Unpaid and unappreciated." She was perched on a wicker sofa, nibbling cheese and crackers. She looked wonderful in a long gauzy skirt and white peasant blouse, a quartz on a black cord around her neck.

Rich mixed a Bloody Mary and handed it to me, then picked up a brass tray of drinks on the low table in front of Augusta. "Okay, folks," he said over his shoulder as he headed to the kitchen, "now that Dean's here, I'll bring our lunch out. But no one can say a word about our biggest scandal in years while I'm in the kitchen, you hear?"

Augusta laughed but I put my hand on my forehead, groaning. "Do we have to talk about it?" I said. "I've heard nothing else since Sunday morning."

Godwin shook a long thin finger at me playfully. "Now, Dean, you can't deprive Crystal Springs of the most tantalizing gossip of the decade. Poor old Simms Legere caught in bed with a Gypsy woman!"

"Oh, that wasn't the best part, Godwin," Augusta said, her eyes bright as the sky. "The high and mighty Libby Legere screaming like trailer trash was the highlight for me."

"Not as good as Augusta cackling like a hyena," I told Godwin, who chuckled appreciatively. "Everyone else was shocked speechless, except Maddox, who stepped in to save the day."

"Shame on you, Augusta," Godwin said. "Poor Libby. And of course Maddox would save the day—it's what he does best."

"He's such a damn Eagle Scout," Augusta said, wrinkling her nose.

"No fair," Rich cried from the kitchen. "Y'all cannot talk trash till I get there." He opened the door and backed out carrying a large rattan tray, and Augusta pushed Godwin's wheelchair to the table. We sat down and shook fine linen napkins out, soft as cotton bolls. I averted my eyes when Rich tied Godwin's napkin around his neck. Behind his white head, the sun poured through the louvered windows of the porch, and Augusta raised her glass of white wine.

"To beloved old friends," she said.

"And new ones," Rich added, lifting his glass toward me.

Lunch was as much a feast for the eyes as the palate. The crab salad was laid out on green and red lettuce, the molded butter surrounded by lavender blossoms. Rich had cooked a huge loaf of dark bread and etched a pattern in the dough before baking it. Our plates and serving bowls were antique china, the center arrangement of day lilies in an exquisite piece of porcelain. Both Augusta and I pretended not to notice the difficulty Godwin was having feeding himself, but caught the moment when Rich reached over and tenderly wiped Godwin's mouth for him. Augusta's eyes met mine, and she launched into a play-by-play description of everything that happened at her Halloween party after they left. Soon they were laughing, the awkward moment passed.

Over a cup of café latte, Godwin turned to me with a twinkle in his dark eyes. "By the way, Dean, Dr. Lynch is paying us a pastoral visit later today."

Augusta pushed back in her chair. "What time's he coming?"

Godwin held up his cup for Rich to refill. "About five," he replied. "Why?"

"Just want to make sure I'm gone by then," she said.

Rich looked startled, then glanced at me. "Oh! Well . . . ah . . ." he stammered, his face red.

"Oh, my God, Augusta," Godwin laughed, "you're the

most irrepressible woman I've ever known. But tell me—if you can without embarrassing Dean—what do you have against Dr. Lynch?"

"He's a pious, self-righteous tight-ass," she said.

Godwin's eyes widened, and Rich moaned, "Don't sugar-coat it for us. Poor Dean."

"Poor Dean's right," Augusta said.

"But I don't understand you, Augusta," Godwin said, leaning forward. "Rich and I are delighted that First Methodist has such a distinguished minister, one who's so in-volved in the community."

"He's involved in the community, all right," she muttered.

Godwin furrowed his brow. "But, Augusta," he said, "your . . . ah . . . dislike of Dr. Lynch? That's not why you and Maddox don't come to church anymore, surely."

Augusta twirled a piece of her hair on the end of her fin-ger. "Maybe I just don't like preachers."

"But, that's not true, is it?" Godwin questioned her, still frowning. "As I recall, you were quite fond of John Marcus Vickery."

I glanced her way as Rich and I gathered up the dishes. "You've never told me that, Augusta," I said. "I've heard it before, but not from you."

"Dr. Vickery!" Rich said. "He was here when I first moved in, remember, Godwin? He's the most intriguing man I've ever known, minister or not."

"Don't worry about Godwin's feelings," Augusta teased.

"'Except for Godwin' goes without saying," Rich added. "Do you know Dr. Vickery, Dean?"

I shook my head. "Never met him, but of course I've heard all about him. He's my husband's idol."

"I hear he'll be our next bishop, and no wonder," God-win said. "He's unusually gifted."

Rich paused with an armful of dirty dishes. "You know,

I can confess this now, Godwin. I had the most awful crush on Dr. Vickery. He's unbelievably good-looking."

"So I've heard," I told him. "But I can't picture a sexy bishop. They're usually old as God."

"Actually, Augusta, you were close to the Vickery family, weren't you?" Godwin said, turning in his chair to face Augusta, who'd risen and was heading to the wicker sofa.

She shrugged, her back to us. "Not really."

Godwin tilted his head to the side. "But—you baby-sat for them when you were young, right? And didn't they take you with them on vacation a number of times?"

I didn't hear the rest of their conversation because I carried a stack of dishes to the kitchen, then helped Rich load the dishwasher. Rich nodded his head toward the porch and lowered his voice. "Augusta's getting her purse to go. Godwin must've hit a sore spot. That she's never told you about her relationship with the Vickerys is weird. You think it has something to do with them not coming to First Methodist?"

I rinsed a plate and handed it to him. "I avoid the subject with her." I wiped my hands on a towel and looked around. The kitchen looked like a spread in *House Beautiful*, with Mexican tiles and colorful woven rugs tossed with seeming carelessness onto the shiny floor. "I adore the kitchen, Rich. It's just the way I'd do one, if I ever had the chance."

"If I were you, Dean, I'd just come out and ask Augusta to tell you what's going on. Let me explain why." To my surprise, Rich put both hands on my shoulders and turned me to face him. Up close, I noticed what I'd not seen earlier, the pain in his eyes. Life had not been easy for Rich. His boyish face looked much older at close range. His fine blond hair was threaded with gray, and there was a weariness about his mouth.

"Out on the porch, I noticed your discomfort with the teasing about Godwin and me being gay," he said. When I opened my mouth to protest, he put a finger on my lips to stop me. "Your face is turning red."

I put my hands to my cheeks, which were hot to my touch. "I—I'm just not used to talking about it . . ."

"Of course you're not. Most of us aren't, especially here in the South. Let me tell you something, Dean, which will help you, I think. I don't know anything about your background except what I've heard around town."

"It's all true," I said. "I had a horrible childhood."

He smiled. "Then we have something in common. Although I came from a comfortable middle-class background, I was raised in a small, close-knit town, much smaller than Crystal Springs. My dad was a coach, my mother a teacher. I was different, Dean. I mean, really different—artistic, effeminate, and fragile. Imagine the torment I lived through, in a small-town environment, a coach's son. I can't tell you how many times I was beaten up by the town bullies. Battle scars." He pointed to a scar by his eyebrow. "By the time I turned eighteen and left for good, I'd tried to kill myself three times."

"Oh, God, Rich. You've really suffered, haven't you?"

He shrugged. "We all suffer in our own ways, don't we? That's not why I'm telling you this. It was only when I dealt with my true nature, the source of my difference, that I found any peace. So, I made a vow twenty years ago, when I was twenty-six years old and met Godwin, that I'd never deny myself again. And that I'd never be in any relationship— friendship, love affair, family, whatever—without honesty. It's been really difficult, Dean, and it's cost me a lot—my dad and my grandparents don't speak to me, I've lost a lot of people along the way—but I have to do it. I have no choice."

I nodded and smiled. "I think I know why you're telling me this."

"Hey!" Augusta called from the porch. "What are you

two doing in there? Rich, you'd better not be putting the make on Dean when I've been trying to change your mind about women for twenty years. Come on, Dean, I've gotta go now."

Rich winked at me. "Talk to Augusta, Dean. You're the closest friend she's ever had. There's something hidden in her, something that needs to come out."

"I will, Rich," I said. "I promise."

But of course I didn't. Not then, not until much later, when it was too late. My conversation with Rich in the kitchen on that sunny November morning would come back to haunt me many times in the months to come.

Augusta underestimated her old rival Libby Legere by thinking Libby would forgive Celeste for her public humiliation on Halloween night, insisting nothing would come of the escapade between Celeste and Simms Legere. "Simms is scared shitless of Libby, Dean," she'd told me scornfully. "Can you blame him? He's had his little flings, but nothing serious. Libby likes his money too much to boot him out for good. If either one of them had any sort of self-awareness, they'd realize they were miserable and their lives were empty, but that ain't going to happen."

After we left Rich and Godwin's, Augusta and I stopped by Celestial Things to check on Celeste. We found the door locked and Celeste's scrawled handwriting in big black letters on a taped-up piece of white poster board: "Closed until after Thanksgiving. Reopening December 1st."

"Oh, Jesus," Augusta muttered, "I told her not to do that." She pressed her face to the glass pane in the door and banged with the palm of her hand.

"Not to do what?" I said. "Why are you banging on the door when it's locked and Celeste is obviously not here? And why is she closed for Thanksgiving this early?"

Ignoring me, Augusta rattled the door handle until I

grabbed her arm. "Celeste has obviously skipped the country," I said. "Maybe she's taken the priceless heirloom dress that she wore to your party and gone back to Romania."

"Very funny," Augusta said. "Get your butt over to the window and look for her."

Like a nitwit, I stepped over to the front window and climbed up on the cement planters underneath, which wasn't easy since Celeste had planted shrubbery in them. I straddled a holly bush and pressed my nose to the glass. At first I saw nothing except the store, lights out and deserted, but then there was a movement behind the counter. "It's Celeste!" I told Augusta. "Looks like she's hiding from us."

"Bang on the window," Augusta ordered, and I banged away. Sure enough, Celeste peeped out from behind the counter like a scared rabbit. I motioned to her, and she crept across the store and unlocked the door. I jumped down from the holly bush without being scarred for life and sneaked in behind Augusta when Celeste cracked the door. As soon as we were inside, she slammed the door behind us and turned the key.

"Celeste, what the hell is going on?" Augusta said. Celeste put a finger to her lips, then motioned for us to follow her. Upstairs, Celeste turned on a lamp beside the sofa and indicated for us to sit down.

"What's happened?" I asked her, plopping down. "You on the Ten Most Wanted List or something?"

Augusta perched on the arm of a stuffed chair next to the sofa. Celeste stood and looked at us, her arms folded over her chest. She was dressed in tight black jeans and high-heeled boots up to her knees. With them she wore a hot-pink oversized sweater, spangled with silver, and her jet-black hair tied back with a colorful scarf. More normally dressed than in her fortune-telling attire, she still managed to look exotic. Probably because of the Cleopatra eye makeup, and the earrings hanging from her ears made of peacock feathers. "Simms's wife has someone following me," Celeste explained, "so I've been hiding from them."

"Is Simms here?" Augusta whispered, and I jumped to my feet.

"Simms? Oh, hell," I groaned. "If he is, let me out. I don't want anything to do with this."

Augusta rolled her eyes to the ceiling. "Oh, come on, preacher's wife. Don't be so pious."

"You know I'm not pious," I protested. "But you saw what happened when Libby caught Simms with Celeste. Ben's furious at me for the part I played in it. I mean it, I'm not having anything to do with this. Simms Legere is a married man, and from what I've heard, has every intention of staying that way."

To my surprise, Celeste came over and sat by me on the sofa. "Please, Augusta," she said, her voice low. "I will talk to Dean about this, no?"

I swallowed, glancing from her to Augusta. "Don't tell me that Simms is unhappily married, that his wife doesn't understand him, Celeste. If you want to have an affair with him, fine. That's your business. But I don't want to know about it. I don't want to hear about it, and I will not let Augusta drag me into it."

"Ah! Your aura disturbs me, Dean, for is very angry, with many dark colors. Tell me what I can say to make you feel better," Celeste said.

"For starters, why do you have a sign on the door saying you've gone away? And why did you hide when we banged on the door?"

She shrugged, turning her pink-painted mouth down at the corners. "But I am going away, Dean. I must. Too much

disturbance is in my energy field of late. It has become necessary for me to—how do you say?—reconnect with the
sources of power."

"Will you go to your place at Grayton Beach?" Augusta
asked.

"Grayton Beach?" I echoed. "I didn't know you had a
place there, Celeste."

Celeste nodded serenely. "Ah! But very small. Only for
one, yes? The trailer, it was my home for the many years
when I was with the carnival. Now that I have Celestial
Things, the trailer is parked in Grayton."

"So you have a getaway," I said.

Again, she nodded, her kohl-lined eyes slanted like a
cat's. "Where I go for the renew all."

"Renewal," Augusta corrected, smiling at me.

I threw my hands up. "Okay, okay. I overreacted.
Sounds like a great idea, Celeste. Go away to Grayton Beach
and commune with the universe, or whatever it is you do. Let
the talk about the Halloween party die down. Believe me,
Crystal Springs will have something else to talk about by
Thanksgiving."

I was right about that prediction, but wrong to trust Celeste and Augusta. The weekend after Thanksgiving, Augusta
and I found ourselves in the midst of another of our misad-
ventures. Augusta and Maddox had always taken Gus to the
biggest football rivalry in the state, the Florida-FSU game.
Kathryn, Maddox's sister from North Carolina, her husband,
Bill, and their two young children went with them, making it
a big family outing. This year, Augusta had another plan.
Thanksgiving Day, I was dressing to go to the church for a
turkey-and-dressing dinner for the less fortunate when Augusta called me, breathless with excitement.

"Oh, baby girl," she cried, "the most wonderful news!
Remember meeting Steve Sanders at the Halloween party?"

"Doesn't ring a bell," I replied, distracted. "Listen, could I call you back? I'm running late."

"Don't you dare run off until you hear this," she said. I groaned, feeling about as enthusiastic today as the Thanksgiving turkey. "Steve Sanders, the entertainment director at Seaside—he said he'd left a message for you," she continued breathlessly.

"Oh. Yeah, I remember now," I said, propping the phone on my shoulder and pulling my hose on. "I haven't had time to call him back, getting ready for this dinner at the church."

"Yeah, yeah, Mother Teresa. Listen: He wants you—you!—to play at this thingamajig they have every year at Seaside on the Saturday after Thanksgiving, an arts and crafts festival or something, filling in for someone who got the flu."

"Augusta, I can't possibly do it—that's the day after tomorrow."

"So? You've already told me that you and Ben didn't have anything planned."

"Well? That plan hasn't changed. We both need some time off, believe me."

"You need to play at Seaside much more. Besides, I've already told Steve you'd do it."

"Augusta! Call him back and tell him I can't, then."

"But you've got to, Dean—you simply have to."

"No, I don't. Ben would have a hissy-fit, me running off and leaving him now."

"Betcha Ben won't turn down a chance to go to the football game with Maddox and the brood of relatives. Didn't you tell me he'd give his eyeteeth to go, but couldn't get a ticket?"

"Yeah, but—"

"But nothing. I've already talked Maddox and everyone else into it. Maddox is giving Ben my ticket and taking him to the game. I'm going with you to Seaside."

"*What?*"

"Got to. I told Steve I was your manager. Don't worry, O blessed Saint Dean, we'll leave early enough to get you back for church Sunday morning."

"*Augusta,*" I screeched, hopping around with one shoe on and one off, "listen to me. This is another of your last-minute, wild-ass schemes, and I'm not doing it."

"I gotta go now. My Thanksgiving guests are arriving. Maddox'll call Ben later this afternoon to arrange everything. Oh—I got you a great dress to wear from that place in Miami, you know, where I got Celeste's Halloween outfit?"

"I wouldn't be caught dead in whatever you got from there. Send it back."

"It's an artsy-looking crushed velvet, perfect for Seaside. Kind of a smoky goldish-green color, same as your eyes. And I've gotten Rich and Godwin to come to the festival, too. Think how much good it'll do Godwin to have an outing."

"Augusta, you low-down, blackmailing—"

"I'm hanging up now, baby girl. See you Saturday."

It was impossible to stay irritated with Augusta once we got to Seaside and checked into our room. She'd pulled this whole thing off without a hitch and was full of herself, sassier than ever. I loved being with her, walking into the front lobby of the Seahorse Bed-and-Breakfast, having heads turn our way. Even though I was the one carrying a dulcimer in a case slung over my shoulder, the young woman at the front desk gushed over Augusta, thinking she was the performer, until Augusta corrected her. It was easy to understand the mistake. A head taller than me in her high-heeled boots, Augusta was wearing a fringed suede jacket with her jeans and big dark sunglasses. I slunk behind her, unnoticed.

The musical entertainment was part of an arts and crafts festival set up on the grassy-green amphitheater of Seaside, an early introduction to the holiday season, with artisans making decorations using the elements of the seashore. A perfect day for an outdoor event, it was cool and slightly breezy, with the late November sun high and bright. The sky was completely cloudless, so blue it hurt your eyes. A platform with microphones was set up for the musicians to perform as tourists sauntered through the displays; when Augusta and I arrived, a bluegrass trio was singing "Cotton-Eyed Joe," and the lively tune floated over the crowd like the sweet aroma of the funnel cakes sizzling in hot oil at one of the food booths. My performance was scheduled for two o'clock, allowing Augusta and me time to stuff ourselves with fried oyster sandwiches as we chatted with the other musicians. A couple of them had a small TV set up in the back of their pickup truck to catch the Florida-FSU game, and Augusta and I peered over their shoulders, searching the tiny screen for a glimpse of Maddox, Gus, or Ben in the crowd of faces painted like Gators or Seminoles.

The camaraderie with the other musicians was exactly what I needed to relax for my performance. Just before Steve Sanders introduced me, Augusta pointed to the audience. "Look, Dean, your cheering section, all the way from Crystal Springs, just like I promised." Sure enough, there was Godwin St. Clair in his wheelchair, a plaid blanket over his lap, with Rich Kingsley beside him, waving to me. Rich blew me a kiss and Godwin held up two fingers in a victory sign.

I did my usual repertoire, playing and singing "Wayfaring Stranger," and "Red River Valley," then the music only of the old tunes, "Shady Grove" and "Red Wing." I was unprepared when the continuing applause resulted in Steve asking me to do an encore, and I knew then that Augusta had been right about this trip and I'd been wrong, completely wrong.

I was even more convinced later when we went for an early supper on the outdoor deck of Bud & Alley's with Steve

Sanders, some of the musicians, and Rich and Godwin, watching the sun set over the Gulf while we ate. As I raised a glass of wine to the others, it occurred to me that I was completely at ease, joking, laughing, and talking with the other musicians as though I'd known them all my life. My usual discomfort in social situations was absent, and it was because none of them knew—or cared—that I was a preacher's wife, so I didn't have to play the role. I looked at Augusta, her lovely face flushed; then from her to Rich, who, even in an animated conversation with the guitarist next to him, had that sadness in his eyes. Godwin, with his usual elegant dignity, was observing everyone silently from his wheelchair, his dark eyes sparkling with interest. I could be myself with these people, and they'd still love me.

Godwin and Rich went back to Crystal Springs after dinner, so Augusta and I walked leisurely through the brick streets of Seaside, peeking in the windows of the tin-roofed Victorian homes. "It's all beautiful," I said to her as we paused before a pink three-storied gingerbread house with a white picket fence, "but too picture-perfect for me."

Augusta tilted her head and looked up at the bay window of the house, where a family of four sat around a table, eating supper. The pretty blond mother stood over the children, pouring milk into their glasses; the handsome young father, looking like he had stepped off the pages of an investment magazine, passed a platter their way.

"They seem so safe, don't they?" she said, her voice soft. "So untouched by life."

"Don't you think someone looking in the window of Mimosa Grove would say the same about your family?"

Her face was pensive in the dull yellow of a street light. "Yeah. But they'd be wrong."

"Why is that?"

She shrugged, staring at the family showcased in the bay

window. "It's an illusion. That big old house . . . it's sucking the life out of us. But, it's the old home place, you know, so Maddox will hang on to it. We struggle financially, Dean, just like everyone else. A couple of times, Maddox has come close to closing the plant. The only reason he hasn't is what it'd do to the town, so he keeps plowing on, barely keeping his head above the water."

We walked off, leaving the beautiful family to their supper. "That just makes the Holderfields more human," I said. "Everybody struggles with financial stuff. What I meant was the security of your family. You and Maddox and Gus."

"Another illusion," she said.

"What do you mean?" I'd suspected as much, of course, since Labor Day.

She was quiet as we walked along, then said, "I want to talk to you about . . . some things, Dean, I really do. But I can't now, because here we are at Modaci's." When she raised her face, her mask was in place again. "Let's splurge and get one of their giant cinnamon rolls for breakfast, what do you say?"

We'd gotten our cinnamon rolls, plus extras for Maddox, Gus, and Ben, and were filling up a shopping cart with all the exotic items you couldn't get at Crystal Springs's Piggly Wiggly, when we heard a familiar voice behind us. "Augusta, Dean—what are you two doing here?" Turning from a display of capers imported from Spain, we were astonished to see Libby Legere and a young man standing next to us.

The young man was obviously Libby's son. Fortunately for him, he looked like his mother, with the same golden coloring and creamy-rich skin. Both of them were dressed casually, in khakis and cotton sweaters. As though nothing had happened the last time we saw each other, Augusta, Libby, and I greeted one another cordially. Libby put her hand on her son's shoulder proudly. "Dean, this is our oldest son, Branscomb."

"Where are your girls?" Augusta asked her.

"Oh," Libby replied, her pride unmistakable, "Cramer's rowing team had a meet, and Caldwell's visiting her fiancé's parents on Martha's Vineyard. They'll be home for Christmas."

As I shook Branscomb's hand, I wondered if rich people ever named their kids things like Joe or Sue. "You're in law school now, aren't you?" Augusta asked Branscomb.

"Yes, ma'am," he answered politely, with no trace of a Southern accent. "My first year."

"He's at Harvard," Libby told me, then turned to Augusta, her voice like the purring of a cat. "Pray you never need Branscomb's services; he's specializing in divorce cases."

Augusta didn't miss a beat. "How convenient for you to have one in-house. I'm surprised you two didn't go to Tallahassee for the big game."

It was hard to tell who turned up their noses higher, mother or son. "Spending a whole day with a crowd of drunks painted like Indians or gators is not my idea of fun." Libby sniffed. "Simms took some of his business associates who like to play redneck when they come south. Then they were going out on our boat, deep-sea fishing, tomorrow. Actually, that's what Branscomb and I are doing here. We're going to surprise them. We're loading up with goodies and going to the boat for a midnight supper."

Augusta smiled politely. "Sounds like fun. Y'all still keep the boat docked in Destin?"

Libby nodded. "Simms took Gus and Maddox out last year, remember?"

"Of course," Augusta said, then turned to me. "We need

to get a move on, Dean. It was nice seeing you again, Libby, Branscomb. Good luck with school."

I was surprised when Augusta abruptly whirled the cart around and pushed it to the checkout counter, knowing she had not finished shopping. She flung the groceries on the counter at breakneck speed and drummed her fingers impatiently as the clerk rang us up. When we went out the door, carrying two bags of groceries each, she looked over her shoulder and saw Libby and her son still shopping. "Hurry," Augusta said.

"She's not going to follow us," I sighed. "Slow down."

Ignoring me, she scurried down the sidewalk toward the B&B, a block behind the deli. When we got to her station wagon parked in front, she popped the back open and flung her two bags in, then grabbed for mine. "I want to keep my cinnamon roll out," I protested, but she took the bags from my hand.

"Come on, baby girl," she said. "Hop in." I got in the passenger seat as she cranked up.

"Augusta? Why are we in the car? Where're we going?"

"I have a bad feeling about this," she muttered, backing out. When we passed Modaci's, she craned her neck, trying to see inside.

"Augusta?" I said, fastening my seat belt. "The bad feeling you have is someone calling your name, trying to get your attention, trying to find out what's going on."

She turned right on the highway, looking in the rearview mirror as though expecting Libby to follow us. "Okay," I said, "we turned right. Which means we aren't going back to Crystal Springs. Which is good, I guess. If we were going back to Crystal Springs, we'd not only be leaving without checking out, we'd be leaving our luggage at the Seahorse. That's the only overnight bag I own. Not to mention my makeup, my face cream, the Estée Lauder you made me buy, which cost me a month of piano students, and—"

"Dean, please! You're making me nervous." Again, Augusta looked to see if anyone was following us. We whizzed past the turn to Grayton Beach.

"We just passed Highway 283, which means we're not going to Grayton. And listen, Augusta, don't worry about making me nervous, okay?"

"Jesus, we're just going for a ride. Bet you haven't ridden this far up the coast, have you?"

"Can't say as I have. Not at night, anyway, when I can't see a thing. Now we're back on the Emerald Coast Parkway." As soon as we pulled onto the four-lane, Augusta hit the gas pedal and we were going seventy-five in a matter of seconds. When we passed a road sign, *Destin, 26 miles*, I nodded. "Okay, I know now where we're going. Destin, right? We're flying along, risking life and limb, to make it to Destin, Florida, ten o'clock at night, so we can have the good fortune to run into your dear friend Libby and her cloned son again. Meeting up with them at Seaside wasn't enough for you."

"Just hope I remember where Simms keeps his boat," Augusta muttered. "Thank goodness Libby didn't remember that I came with Maddox and Gus last year."

I laid my head back on the seat, looking out at the sawgrass and scrub pines on either side of the highway, rolling past us in the moonlight as we sped down the dark highway. "Ah-ha. At least I understand it now," I said. "It's Simms's heart you're worrying about. He has a heart condition that he's told no one but you about. So, you want to beat Libby and her son to the boat, warn Simms about the surprise supper—"

"He has a heart condition, all right," Augusta interrupted, smiling in the darkness of the car.

"Celeste, you mean. His little fling with Celeste. Okay, it's making more sense now. You don't want her to be heartbroken when Simms croaks after Libby shows up and surprises him and the Yankee businessmen."

"Don't be so naive," Augusta sighed. "Jesus, you drive me crazy! There *are* no Yankee businessmen."

I stared at her, blinking. "But—who'd Simms go to the game with, then?"

"Oh, Lord, you poor sheltered preacher's wife, unwise in the ways of the world. He didn't go to the game, but there's a TV on the boat so he can say he did. The *Rebel Yell*, I believe it's called."

I nodded slowly, turning and staring straight ahead. We were going over a huge bridge, and the moonlight sparkled as though riding on the ripples of the black waves. "I think it's at the first marina past this bridge," Augusta muttered.

"Celeste is there," I said, "on that boat, with Simms. A repeat of Halloween night. A rerun, with Simms's britches down to his knees and his tallywhacker hanging out. Except this time, Simms's nice young son will get to see his daddy like that. I guess that's only fair—everybody else in town got to. Too bad their daughters aren't with them, make it a family affair."

"The son's going to be a divorce lawyer, Dean, didn't you hear that? That could only mean bad news for Celeste."

"Not as bad as for Simms, I'd think. But tell me why you said that, Augusta, just for curiosity."

"Why do you think? Libby said if she catches him with another woman again, she'll take his ass to the cleaners. Celeste deserves to have something for once in her life, don't you think? Simms is worth a fortune and could give her anything. But not if Libby gets it first."

"Let me get this straight. I'm the naive one, the innocent preacher's wife who knows nothing about these things. Yet you, the worldly one, actually expect Simms Legere to *marry* Celeste?"

"It's not unreasonable to think he'll marry her, once he dumps Libby. I just don't want her to get the goods on him and do it first."

"Augusta! If you think Simms is in love with Celeste, then you don't know jack about men. He's sleeping with her, is all. That's not the same as being in love."

"For a man it is. Especially a man married all these years to the Snow Queen."

"I really appreciate you and Celeste letting me in on this. Celeste said she wouldn't lie to me, then gave me all that bull about going to Grayton Beach to commune with the power within. I didn't realize she was referring to Simms Legere's pecker."

"She did go to Grayton, but she's been meeting up with Simms at the boat when he could get away. I'm not even sure they're here, actually, but there's a good chance of it. I just remembered something about Branscomb Legere that's scary. His hobby is photography. I've never seen him without his camera."

"Handy for a divorce lawyer," I said dryly.

"Exactly. Ah, here we are."

"What if you can't find the boat?"

Augusta ignored me, turning the car off the highway to a marina hidden in moss-draped oak trees. Hundreds of boats were docked there, bobbing in the dark waters of the Choctawhatchee Bay. Augusta pulled into the oyster-shell-paved parking lot and parked the car under the canopy of a giant oak tree. "Okay. I'm going to look for them, tell them to get the boat to the ocean and stay out there until the coast is clear, so to speak. You've got to stay here, Dean, and be on the lookout for Libby and Branscomb."

"Oh, no, I'm not! I'll be damned if I will. That's the stupidest thing I've ever heard. What would I do if I saw them, pray tell?"

"Stall them. You'll think of something." Augusta got out of the car and headed toward the marina, her boots clicking on the wooden sidewalk. I caught up with her, grabbing her arm. She sighed mightily and stopped, her hands on her hips. "Dammit, Dean, could you for once show just a little bit of courage? Go back to the car and look out for Libby and Branscomb."

"I can't. I'd mess up because I can't think of a single reason to be here."

She ran her fingers through her hair. "Okay, okay, you probably would mess us all up. I'll tell you what—just hide in the car and blow the horn if you see them. Can you do that?"

I nodded miserably. "All right. What kind of car does she have?"

"How the hell should I know? They might be in Branscomb's car. Just blow the car horn if anybody drives up, how about that?" She gave me a push, and I turned and stumbled back to her car, muttering to myself, swearing I'd never go anywhere with her again. I looked over my shoulder and saw Augusta jump down onto the swaying dock where boats were lined up on each side, bobbing like corks. Lightbulbs were strung along the posts of the wooden dock, and although their light was feeble in the blackness of the night and the water, it was possible to see the boats well enough to read the names. The *Rebel Yell*. A cold wind blew off the water and I pulled my sweater closer, buttoning it all the way to my neck. I'd changed from the crushed-velvet dress when we went to dinner, putting on slacks and a turtleneck and a cotton cardigan, which had been perfectly comfortable until now. Now I was cold, shivering, wishing I'd worn a heavier sweater.

When I spotted the big oak where the station wagon was parked, I hurried to it and grabbed for the door. When it didn't open, I ran around to the other side, my knees suddenly weak, my throat dry. It was locked. Too late I remembered Augusta complaining about the car's safety feature, how she'd locked herself out several times until she remembered to set the switch on the driver's door. In her haste to find Celeste and Simms, she'd forgotten to set it.

I stood stupefied. Should I stay there and wait for Augusta? Surely it wouldn't take her long to find them, tell them to crank up the boat and head for the high seas. I knew she wouldn't linger, but if I stood waiting for her, they could see me if they drove up, since the oyster-shell parking area was not that big. No matter what Augusta might say, I refused to crouch down behind the car. Even under the big oak . . . I sighed and walked over to the tree, my arms folded against my chest. It was even colder under the tree because it was closer to the water, and the wind was blowing strong. But I could stand in the shadow and not be seen if someone drove up.

No sooner had that thought entered my head than I saw a car turn off the highway, its headlights cutting through the darkness, moving down the graveled road. I flattened myself against the tree, feeling like an idiot, and watched as the car pulled into the parking lot. It was a low-slung black Jaguar, and there was no question about it: Even in the darkness I could see the golden-blond head of Branscomb Legere in the driver's seat, his mother next to him. Without stopping to think, I slipped behind the mammoth trunk of the oak and crept to the dock, bent over like an old beggar. I jumped down onto the pier, and my feet slid out from under me, but I righted myself before hitting hard. Running like a fool, I hurried down the swaying pier as quietly as I could. Looking over my shoulder, I saw the Jag pull into a parking place and the headlights go off.

I didn't have to look for the *Rebel Yell*; when I got almost to the end of the pier, I saw Augusta. She had just jumped off the deck of a big white boat and was unwinding one of its ropes from a dock post. Simms Legere was in the captain's chair, idling the boat, and Celeste was standing on the deck, her arms outflung, waiting for Augusta to throw the rope to her. Celeste looked like a fool, barefoot in a skimpy gown, the wind blowing her hair like a tempest, but not as much so as Simms, who I could tell from here was in his underwear, his fat butt shaking in the cold wind. I ran up to Augusta, grabbed her arm and shook her, hard. "They're here," I yelled so she could hear me over the boat's engine. "Hurry!"

"Oh, shit," Augusta yelled back, still tugging on the rope. "Are they coming this way?"

"Yeah—they just parked the car. Hurry!"

"Help me with this rope. Why didn't you blow the horn like I told you?"

I bent over and we loosened the rope and threw it to Celeste. She grabbed it and the boat floated away from the pier. "I couldn't get in," I told her. "The car doors were locked."

"What?" Augusta screeched, then looked over my shoulder. She grabbed my arm and pulled me forward. "Oh, Jesus—I see them coming! Quick, jump on the boat." Motioning for Celeste to help us, Augusta deftly grabbed Celeste's hand and jumped the two feet between the boat and the pier, barely making it. Then she and Celeste both reached over the side for me.

"I can't," I cried. "My shoes are too slippery."

"Take them off," Augusta commanded. I looked back over my shoulder and could see two dark figures at the other end of the dock, jumping down to the swaying pier. "You have no choice," she yelled. "What could you say to Libby and Branscomb now?"

I took my shoes off and crouched down, getting into position to leap toward the boat, tucking my new shoes under my arm. As soon as I jumped, Augusta grabbed one arm and

Celeste the other, and my shoes fell into the water with a loud splash. I fell forward, plunging head-first onto the deck of the boat. When I landed, Augusta and Celeste pulled me down the hatch and closed the door with a slam. I felt the boat move away from the dock in a powerful burst of motion, and we were off.

"Did you hurt your head when you fell?" Augusta asked as she pulled me to my feet and sat me on a bench.

"Not nearly enough," I moaned, my head in my hands. "Not enough to knock some sense into it."

Celeste was standing at a porthole, peering out. "They see the boat is leaving," she cried.

"Let me look," Augusta said, standing beside her and pressing her face to the glass. "They can't see in here, can they? Quick, Celeste, cut that lamp out."

"What they'll probably see is your car when they go back to theirs," I said. "Everybody in Crystal Springs knows your Volvo station wagon."

"Oh, bull, there's a hundred white Volvo wagons around. Libby'll be too mad to look at anybody's car, her little party spoiled."

"What do you imagine she'll think about the boat pulling out just as they get here?" I asked. "She'll know that Simms saw them coming and took off, and she'll put two and two together."

"Maybe. But she can't prove anything," she said. "Celeste, I hear Simms calling you. Look and see if we're far enough out for you to go up there."

"They cannot see us," she said, peering out the porthole. She was still in her leopard-print gown, her feet bare. "The boat's turning the bend in the bay. It's very dark with the moon behind the clouds." She looked around and her eyes fell on a hooded sweatshirt on the floor. "Simms is cold, is why he calls me. I will take him the stuffed shirt."

"Sweatshirt. And from what I saw," I told her, "you'd better take him the britches, too."

Augusta giggled and I glared at her. "Augusta Holderfield, if you start laughing now, so help me God, I'll throw you overboard. This is not funny, not one bit. I'm not only freezing, I'm barefooted as a yard dog. I lost my shoes when I jumped on the boat."

"I'll buy you some more shoes," she said, eyes twinkling. "Those were tacky, anyway. I didn't want to hurt your feelings, but I'm glad you lost them."

"God forbid that you hurt my feelings," I said grumpily, putting my head back down in my hands.

"Put on a robe before you go out there, Celeste," Augusta said when Celeste opened the door. The salty wind that blew in was freezing cold, and I tucked my feet under me for warmth. My stockings were soaking wet, and I pulled them off in disgust.

"Don't you love this boat?" Augusta asked me when Celeste left. "It's adorable the way it's fixed up."

I raised my head and looked around. It was more like a yacht than a fishing boat, certainly swankier than any boat I'd ever been on. We were in a sitting area that had built-in upholstered seats and backrests all around, except for the kitchen galley. "Oh, yeah. Great little love nest," I said, looking at all the food on the teak counters. There were champagne bottles and dirty fluted glasses, along with mounds of strawberries, peaches, mangoes, and grapes. The tiny countertop held a half-eaten honey-baked ham, its sugary spiral slices pink and glistening, and stacks of cheeses, brie and gouda and strong-smelling gorgonzola. Godiva chocolate wrappers littered the floor.

"Want a glass of wine?" Augusta asked, but I shook my head.

"No. I want something stronger."

Augusta chuckled as she went to the teakwood bar and poured the two of us an amber-colored drink. She brought mine to me and I sniffed it, frowning. "What is it?"

"Brandy and soda." She raised her glass in a toast. "Mud in your eye."

"In the movies they always drink brandy in a crisis, but I've never had it." I made a face and shuddered when I tasted it. "God almighty. Like everything else in life, it's overrated."

"Feels good on the way down, though."

The second glass was better, and Augusta was right. It did feel good on the way down. "How about going up to the cabin and telling Simms that I don't know when I've had more fun, but I'm ready to go back now?" I said.

Augusta shook her head. "Can't go back yet. Libby's bound to hang around, waiting for Simms to reappear."

"Augusta, I'm tired. I'm ready to go to bed. I have no intention of staying on this boat all night."

"Why not?" she asked nonchalantly. "We're safe from Libby out here, and there're plenty of beds. We can dock at daylight, slip back over to Seaside then."

"I refuse to do any such thing," I yelled, holding out my glass for her to refill. The third brandy was even better than the other two. "I want to go to bed," I whined. "I'm exhausted."

"Lay down where you are," she said. "That seat's like a couch, and there's a cotton throw behind you. Just stretch out for a minute, rest your eyes. You'll feel better."

By the time I finished the third brandy, my eyelids were so heavy, I couldn't hold them open. Mumbling and grumbling, I put my glass down on the floor and stretched out on the upholstered seat. Augusta threw the blanket over me, and its warmth covered me like a cocoon. "I'm not going to sleep," I told her. "I'm just going to rest my eyes for a minute. Then you've got to make Simms turn around and go back. I mean it, Augusta. I'll never speak to you again if you don't. . . . I cannot miss church tomorrow!"

"Shh . . . just close your eyes and quit worrying. Trust me," she whispered. "There's no way you're going to miss church tomorrow."

But of course I did. Unbeknownst to me, Simms anchored the boat and we all slept the night away, rocking gently in the watery cradle of the Choctawhatchee Bay. We were awakened by the sun when it rose high enough to shine through the portholes and send its golden rays over us. Once my initial panic was over, I resigned myself to having to return to Crystal Springs and face the consequences. That I'd left my Sunday school class of young children without a teacher and the choir without one of its members was bad enough. But it was the first Sunday in December, and Ben and I were scheduled to light the advent candle, as was the tradition. I almost hoped we'd see Libby and her son lurking with their cameras as we pulled into the marina at high noon, hungover and groggy. At that moment, I'd much, much rather face them than Ben.

Nine

FORTUNATELY, THE ILL-FATED Sunday I missed church because we were on the *Rebel Yell* was the first one in December; otherwise, the consequences might've been worse. The onset of the holiday season saved me. By not showing up, I disgraced myself with the congregation and made Ben furious, but my transgressions were soon lost in the rush of activities celebrating Christmas. Ben was so incoherently angry, it scared me. I'd told him only that we overslept, nothing else. If I'd told him what really happened, Branscomb Legere would have had his first client.

Celeste reopened Celestial Things as though nothing had happened, telling us that Simms swore to Libby that it was sheer coincidence the boat took off just as they appeared; that his Yankee buddies had wanted an early start fishing. Evidently Simms and Celeste were now hiding their affair more carefully, but I didn't know for sure. I told Augusta I didn't want to hear anything about it, and I meant it. By sticking to a policy of see no evil, speak no evil, hear no evil for the holiday season, I managed to appease Ben and the congregation, and to redeem some of the damage I'd done. I was so pleased with my new deaf-mute image that I kept it up throughout the new year, even though Augusta nicknamed me Helen Keller. Things settled back into a familiar routine, and I became once again content with life in Crystal Springs.

My second summer in Crystal Springs, Augusta and I again volunteered with the migrant children, even though Julio's family hadn't returned. We suspected, but never found out for sure, that their working elsewhere had to do with Augusta's encounter with them last summer. After one of our volunteer sessions in June, we left the church to have lunch with Godwin and Rich, our last one before they left for Maine. Since the first of the year, I'd become a regular visitor to the St. Clair house. That spring I'd taken to lugging my dulcimer over almost every evening, playing my music on the twilight coolness of the sunporch. It had started when Rich found an old folksong book among Godwin's antiques and asked me to play some of the songs. After the first night, when the three of us sang every song in the book, we were hooked, our songfest quickly becoming a twilight ritual. Augusta and Maddox joined us and brought Gus, who sat on the rug by Godwin's wheelchair, watching the adults of his life sing and carry on like the family Von Trapp.

Because of the heat, Augusta and I drove to Godwin's house that Thursday in mid-June rather than walk from the church. "I've got a bone to pick with God when I get to heaven," she grumbled as she turned off the car. "How come it's so hot down here you can roast your wienie without a campfire?"

"If you get to heaven, God'll pass out from shock," I said.

"That's not very Christian of you," she laughed, opening the wrought-iron gate. "In my new church, everybody goes to heaven."

Augusta'd taken to teasing me about First Methodist's—

and Ben's—latest woe. She and Maddox had decided Gus needed biblical education and the fellowship of a church. I'd been delighted, knowing Ben would be beside himself, until she said in spite of our friendship, she wouldn't go back to First Methodist. So this past Easter, the Holderfields shocked everyone in town except me by appearing at All Saints' Episcopal. For some reason, Ben blamed me for their defection.

"Rich is in his studio," Augusta said, closing the gate. Rich's studio was behind the house, hidden in a clump of sweet gum trees, and we walked through the gardens with drooping brown leaves hanging pitifully from parched shrubbery. Because of the heat, restrictions had been placed on water consumption. Until it rained, we couldn't wash our cars or water our lawns. Folks who had prized flower beds sneaked around to water them, after dark.

It was still and airless, the sun overhead like an angry god glaring down at us. "Rich got so pissed with Godwin the other day," Augusta told me. Through the bank of windows in the studio, we could see Rich at work. "He was working, and Godwin sneaked out to water the flowers. He almost fell out of the chair trying to unwind the garden hose." She opened the door to the studio, which was a big room with watercolors in various stages of completion standing everywhere. Rich was bent over a canvas in the back, a smudge of blue paint on his cheek. "Excuse me, Rich baby," Augusta said, "but will you cut off your ear for me?"

Rich put his brush in a jar of murky blue water before turning to us. "Let's go to the house before Godwin sees y'all and tries to come out here."

"Surely he wouldn't," I said. "It's high noon, heat index one hundred twenty."

Rich shook his head as he arranged a stack of paper. "Even after I raised hell about him watering the flowers, he came outside the very next day, looking for me. This time, I left Ollie guarding him on the porch and made him promise to bark his fat ass off if Godwin leaves."

"Oh, dear," I said, looking out the bank of windows. "Ollie's barking and here comes Godwin!" He was wheeling across the lawn toward us, his white hair glistening like ice in the sunlight, his arms strong and able, muscular from maneuvering the wheelchair. He'd come down the wooden ramp and was a few feet from the house. The backyard was huge, a difficult terrain from the house to the studio, with many hedges and flower beds to circumvent.

"Shit," Rich muttered. "Could you two help me get this stuff in order? It'll take him ten minutes to get here."

I went to the back reluctantly and began cleaning the paint off the sink, trying to hurry, feeling uneasy about Godwin. When I finished the sink, I looked out the window. "Rich, I don't see Godwin," I said, arching my neck to see beyond the roses. Ollie had stopped barking and was baying now, like a werewolf.

"There's a bend in the path, behind the azaleas," Rich said, washing his hands. "You can't see him when he gets there. God, Ollie sounds like the Hound of the Baskervilles, doesn't he?" We turned out the lights as Rich held the door open for us. We'd just started down the pathway to the house when we saw Godwin. The wheelchair was at an odd angle behind the azalea beds, and Godwin lay facedown on the ground, his hands thrown out as though he'd tried to catch his fall.

"Oh, Jesus Christ—Godwin!" Augusta screamed, stopping in her tracks. Rich and I pushed her aside and ran to where Godwin lay sprawled on the sunlit path. Rich reached him first, whimpering and falling to his knees.

"Oh, no, oh, no . . ." he cried, turning Godwin over. There was blood from a gash on his forehead, blood on the front of his blue shirt, blood on the ground. His face was white, like the underbelly of a fish; his eyes were closed, and his head lolled to the side when Rich lifted him.

I felt for a pulse while Rich began to weep. "Is he dead?" Augusta whispered, kneeling beside me. From the back porch, Ollie's mournful cries floated over the yard like the waves of the oppressive heat.

"There's a pulse," I said, "but barely. Hurry—go call an ambulance!" Augusta stumbled to her feet and ran toward the house. "Rich, run to your studio and get some water. Bring a towel, too." But Rich didn't hear me, sitting in the path with Godwin cradled in his arms, sobbing like a child. "Rich!" When he looked at me, his look was so anguished that I stood up instead. "Okay. Okay," I said, trying to quell my panic. "You stay here, wait for the ambulance. I'll go."

In the studio I couldn't find anything to put water in. Grabbing a towel instead, I ran water over it until it was soaking wet, then ran out, hurrying down the path, praying. "Oh, dear God, please, please don't let him die!"

Augusta knelt sobbing beside Rich, rocking back and forth in distress, her face red and contorted. I knelt beside them and wiped Godwin's face with the wet towel, sloshing water everywhere. The blood was washed away from the wound on his forehead, which didn't appear to be as bad as it looked. Even though his skin was pale, it was hot to the touch, and I was afraid he'd had a heatstroke. "He's dead, isn't he?" Rich asked me, gasping for breath. "He's dead, and it's my fault," he wailed. "I should've stopped what I was doing, taken him back into the house. It's all my fault . . ."

He was still wailing when the ambulance came, the siren piercing through the heavy stillness of the morning. Augusta ran to bring the attendants, two burly black men dressed in white, bearing a stretcher. Both of them knelt by Godwin and pushed us aside. "Heatstroke," one of them said to us. "That towel might've saved his life. We'll get him in the ambulance, get some fluids started," he said, looking at me. Evidently he'd correctly determined that Rich and Augusta were too undone to respond. "How old is he?" he asked as they put Godwin on the stretcher.

I looked toward Rich expectantly. "S-sixty-two," he stammered, getting to his feet and following along beside the two attendants as they pushed the stretcher toward the ambulance.

"Looks older," the attendant said. "He crippled?"

"Stroke," Rich muttered. "Just tell me if he's going to be all right. Please!"

The attendant whistled, shaking his head. "Stroke, huh? It's going to be touch and go, then. Y'all follow us, we'll take him to Southwest Memorial."

"I'm riding with you," Rich said as they hoisted the stretcher in the back of the ambulance. One of them jumped in and placed an oxygen mask over Godwin's face while the other stood and shook his head at Rich. We saw then there was a driver in front, a woman.

"Follow us in the car," the older of the two attendants said sternly, pushing Rich aside to close the door. "Against regulations to ride in here."

"Goddamn your regulations," Rich screamed. "I'm riding with him!"

The attendant turned to me and jerked his head toward Rich. "Take him in the car with you. Meet us in the emergency room. We'll call ahead for the doctor."

I nodded and grabbed Rich's arm. "Come on, Rich, honey. Let's go."

Just before he closed the door, the ambulance attendant took pity on Rich and his dark eyes softened. "Go on now, son," he said gruffly. "We'll take good care of your daddy."

· · ·

Had Dr. Brandon been on duty, things might have turned out differently. As it happened, the receptionist in the emergency room was a member of our church who knew Godwin. She took it on herself to call Dr. Perkins, a family friend who'd treated Godwin on and off for years, and he came out to talk with us in the waiting room.

"Appears to be a heatstroke," Dr. Perkins said abruptly, looking from Rich to Augusta and me. "He's in pretty bad shape. Being taken to ICU now."

Rich let out a cry, and Augusta put her arms around him. "Is he going to be all right?" I asked Dr. Perkins, who scowled at me, his face guarded. It was a good thing he was familiar with Godwin's health, since his bedside manner left something to be desired.

"We'll do everything we can," he said tersely, "but the next twenty-four hours are critical." He turned then to Rich. "You want to call Eunice and Esther, or want us to?"

"Eunice and Esther?" Rich gasped, his eyes wild. "Surely it's not that serious."

Eunice and Esther were Godwin's two older sisters; one lived in Clearwater and one in Myers Beach. Augusta'd told me they didn't approve of their brother or his companion. As I watched Dr. Perkins, I saw with a sinking heart that the sisters were not the only ones. What I'd taken for a gruff bedside manner was the doctor's disapproval of Rich. Dr. Perkins shrugged. "Someone will have to make decisions about his care, and Eunice and Esther are his next of kin."

"I—I can make decisions concerning Godwin," Rich said, swallowing.

Again, Dr. Perkins shrugged. "Can't do that, Mr. Kingsley. Long as Godwin's unconscious, all forms have to be signed by next of kin."

"But—" Rich began, looking bewildered. We were interrupted by the appearance of Ben, turning the corner of the corridor and hurrying toward us.

"I was visiting a church member upstairs," he said, "when Faye had me paged. Said they'd just brought Godwin in."

Rich grabbed Ben's arm. "Thank God you're here, Dr. Lynch," he said, then his voice broke and he began weeping again.

Startled, Ben looked up at Dr. Perkins. "How's Godwin doing?" he asked, shaking the older man's hand. He stayed in good graces with all the doctors and nurses because of his frequent visits to the hospital.

"How're you, Reverend Lynch?" Dr. Perkins said, instantly less hostile. "We'll know more in the next twenty-four hours. His condition is delicate at this point. A heatstroke at his age isn't good."

"Heatstroke, huh?" Ben shook his head and whistled. "What was he doing outside?"

Rich hung his head, wiping his eyes on his sleeve. "My fault, Dr. Lynch. I—was in my studio with Dean and Augusta, and Godwin tried to come across the yard and join us. I don't know if he got overheated and fell out of the wheelchair, or if the chair tripped up first . . ." His voice broke, and he buried his face in his hands.

Ben nodded as he again patted Rich heartily on the shoulder. "Hey, now, don't look so worried, Rich. He couldn't be in better hands. Anything ever happens to me, I want y'all to call Dr. Perkins here." I'd heard him say the same thing to Dr. Brandon. One thing you could say for him, Ben knew how to butter folks up.

Dr. Perkins directed his remarks to Ben. "Judy Anderson still secretary at your church?" When Ben nodded, Dr. Perkins continued. "How about getting her to call Godwin's sisters, Esther and Eunice? You know them?"

"No, but I knew he had sisters."

"Judy'll get in touch with them. So they get here soon as they can," the doctor said, and Ben's eyebrows shot up.

"Oh! It's that serious then?"

"It's not that. I was telling Mr. Kingsley and the ladies, any medical decisions have to made by next of kin. You know that, Reverend."

Ben nodded. "We'll get in touch with them, then."

"But, can I see Godwin?" Rich asked, looking from Ben to Dr. Perkins.

Dr. Perkins shook his head. "Not in ICU, you can't. Y'all might as well go home, get some rest." We all stood there, staring at him, unable to move. "Reverend Lynch," he said finally, "come with me and you can see him for one minute. But one minute only."

Augusta gasped. "He can see Godwin but Rich can't?"

"Hospital policy," Dr. Perkins snapped. "We had to let priests in to give unction, so the Protestants raised hell. Excuse me, Preacher. Now we just let them all in."

Augusta glared at him. "Rich has to go to theology school to visit his friend, huh?"

I tugged on Ben's sleeve. "Couldn't you take Rich in with you, Ben?"

"How about it, Dr. Perkins?" Ben said. "Just to see that Godwin's okay."

With a mighty sigh, Dr. Perkins shrugged and relented. "All right, all right. One minute only, you hear? When Esther and Eunice get here, they decide, not me."

I was scared to death of Godwin's sisters when they arrived the next day. They were forbidding-looking women of the old school, dressed in dark dresses with cameos and pearls, wearing heavy shoes and thick stockings. Eunice, smelling of rose-scented talcum powder, had a tight gray

perm and a tighter mouth. Square little glasses perched on
her nose, and she stared down at everyone, squinting. Esther,
a retired librarian, wore her white hair in a bun and her face
in a scowl. She walked heavily with a cane and could be
heard thumping a mile away. They called Godwin "Brother"
in accents thick as sorghum syrup. Augusta dubbed them the
Wicked Witches of the West and swore Esther's cane turned
into a broom, which she'd ridden up from Myers Beach. The
sisters' hatred of Rich was a palpable thing. They moved their
heavy suitcases into the upstairs bedrooms of the St. Clair
house, their old bedrooms, and proceeded to make life miserable for Rich, without Godwin to defend him. Rich was too
gentlemanly—as well as too gentle—to go against them. He
cowered in the ICU waiting room, going home only to sleep.
When they turned Ollie out in the heat, Augusta rescued him
by taking him home to Gus.

The first thing the sisters did was to ban Rich from the
ICU unit, whose visiting hours were as strict as an army
camp. Ben refused to sneak Rich in again once he met the
fierce St. Clair sisters, since he was scared of them, too. Not
only were they were staunch Methodists, they were longtime
friends of the bishop's. He came home grumpy and exhausted, irritated that he had to spend time with the St. Clair
sisters each day.

The heat wave hadn't broken, making everyone's temper
short. In the four days Godwin was in ICU, I spent every
spare moment sitting with Rich in the waiting room, Augusta
and I taking turns. On the fifth day, I arrived at ten in the
morning to find Maddox pacing outside the waiting room,
and my heart leaped to my throat.

"Maddox," I cried, running to him, "why are you here?
Is Godwin—"

"No, no, no," he said, "Augusta took Gus to camp today, remember?"

"Oh! Yes, of course," I sighed, relaxing. "But—you didn't need to wait for me—"

"Oh, but I did, too, because I want to show you something." He took my arm and began leading me down the hall. We passed the chapel and the cardiac unit, turning down a long hallway. "Here we are," he said, stopping in front of a room on the west wing.

"Godwin got moved to a room," I squealed, then remembering where I was, put my hand over my mouth. "They moved him to a room?" I whispered, and Maddox chuckled.

"Yep. And look in there."

The door was slightly open and I peeked around it to see Rich sitting close by the bed, holding Godwin's hand and speaking in a low voice. Godwin was paper-white and frail-looking, with oxygen tubes coming out of his nose and a bandage on his forehead, but he was alert and listening to Rich. His dark eyes, watching Rich over the oxygen tubes, were as lively as ever. Tears stung my eyes as I squeezed Maddox's hand.

"Want to go in?" he asked me, but I shook my head.

"No, no. Rich has had to wait four days for this."

"Let's go get some coffee, then. Believe it or not, the cafeteria makes a pretty decent cup."

We drank our coffee in a corner of the noisy cafeteria, both of us looking up occasionally to speak to people we knew. Dr. Brandon stopped by the table and chatted a moment, asking after Godwin, and when he left, I told Maddox how much I wished he was Godwin's doctor instead of Dr. Perkins.

"Oh, Joe Perkins's not a bad guy," he said, stirring sweetener into his coffee. "I've known him forever. He took care of my mama and daddy."

"Well, he seems like a jerk to me. You gonna eat that muffin?"

"I told you to get one. Here, take half of it. Got dates

and walnuts in it." He broke the brown muffin in two halves and handed one to me. "You've got to realize Godwin and Rich's—ah—situation is something most people aren't comfortable with."

"But they've lived in this town for twenty years, and nobody's bothered them. People surely know what's what, don't they?"

Maddox shrugged. "Godwin and Rich aren't in Crystal Springs that much, remember. Normally they're in Maine by now, at their summer place. Weren't they planning on going up there in a few days?" I nodded and he continued, his gray eyes thoughtful. He wore a dress shirt the same shade of gray, with the sleeves rolled up, and a darker color tie, patterned with deep red. I realized he was taking time off from the plant to be here. "Godwin and Rich keep to themselves, don't rock the boat. Always have. Good churchgoers, contribute to every charity in town. Godwin's plenty smart; he knows how to make it in a town like this."

"I've always wanted to ask them but it seemed too rude," I said. "Why do you think they've stayed here? Looks like Sarasota, Winter Haven, places like that would be more receptive to them. Or Maine, if they lived there year-round."

Maddox laughed as he took his glasses off and wiped them clean with a paper napkin. He held them up to the light, squinting. "Strike Maine. Godwin couldn't survive one of their winters. Actually, I asked him that after his mama died. I mean, I understood it when she was alive, Godwin was so devoted to her."

"So, why'd they stay after she died?"

"Godwin's such a gentleman of the old school. It has to do with his love of the St. Clair place, this being his home, having roots, Rich not having a hometown anymore, things like that. Plus, all the folks who adored Godwin's saintly mother adore Godwin, too."

"Too bad the two sisters didn't take after their mother," I said dryly.

Maddox chuckled. "Want some more coffee?" I nodded, and he left to refill our cups. "Dean, what we have is a perfect example of the downside of Rich and Godwin's lifestyle," he said when he returned, passing my coffee to me. "Rich has no say whatsoever in Godwin's life. Joe Perkins told me this morning that Esther has taken out a power of attorney."

"Oh, Jesus. Isn't that something Rich could've done?"

"Not while Godwin was unconscious, he couldn't. Sure, Godwin can sign it over to him when he gets well, but if he's unconscious again, has another stroke, the next of kin can contest it." Maddox sighed and looked at me pointedly, running his hands through his gray-streaked hair.

"Oh, Lord. I didn't know that, Maddox. This isn't a good situation, then."

"Not at all. I'm afraid there's nothing but trouble coming from it, either. Nothing but trouble."

Maddox proved to be as prophetic as Celeste. Once the sisters arrived that morning and found Godwin in a room, they ran Rich out as soon as Godwin dozed off. Rich found Maddox and me in the cafeteria, and I knew by the expression on his face what'd happened.

"Sit down, Rich," Maddox said. "Looks like you can use a shot of caffeine." Rich's golden-hued skin had a grayish tinge, and his shoulders slumped.

While Maddox was getting the coffee, Rich buried his face in his hands and I reached over and rubbed his back. He hadn't shaved this morning, and the fine blond stubble of a beard shone in the sun streaming in the window behind us.

"I talked to Dr. Perkins," Maddox said, sitting down. "He thinks Godwin can go home by the end of the week."

Rich nodded. "I know. I've got to pull myself together."

"You need to get some rest, Rich, get things ready for

Godwin," I said. "You're going to need all your strength to take care of him." Maddox's eyes were on me, and I realized with a shock what he was thinking: Good luck with the Wicked Witches of the West there.

By the Fourth of July, all hell had broken loose in the St. Clair house. The heat wave of mid-June dissipated with the first heavy rain of the summer, only to reappear again with a vengeance the first of July. Temperatures rose to the high nineties, topping a hundred on the Fourth; and everyone sweltered in the festivities—the parade downtown, the watermelon cuttings, the softball games in the dusty park, the boat races on the lake. The Wicked Witches of the West had returned to their homes after they'd hired a sitter for "Brother" in an effort to keep Rich from caring for him. In spite of his weakness and the possibility of another stroke, Godwin'd had a hissy fit and chased after the sisters in his wheelchair, waving one of Esther's spare canes over his head, Rich told us, like a Wild West cowboy. Ollie had run along the side of the wheelchair, barking and adding to the confusion. It would have been funny if it weren't so sad. Rich and Godwin couldn't go to Maine until Godwin recovered, so Augusta and I began to visit daily, helping Rich with Godwin until he regained his strength.

It was on one of those visits to Godwin that I had my first hint of what was to come. Rich was running errands, and I had some time alone with Godwin. I parked him at the round table and tied a napkin around his neck, as I'd seen Rich do.

"Your puny appetite's about to take a nosedive, my good man," I said to him, opening a plastic container of ice cream.

"Fresh peach," Godwin sighed. His eyes, though sunken and ringed by purplish smudges, shone like dark stones underwater. With a trembling, fine-boned hand, he raised the spoon to his mouth, and I watched as he swallowed, then scooped out another spoonful. "Umm . . . this is wonderful." I sat back in my chair, relieved, and Godwin looked up. "Being sick, I've missed out on the gossip lately, Dean. Is Simms's fling with Madame Celeste still going on?"

I nodded. "Last time I talked to her, it was, even though the Knight of Spades was beating the Queen of Cups over the head with the Page of Swords, or something."

Godwin shook his head. "Poor Celeste. Nothing's going to come of that, you know. Simms has had countless mistresses over the years, always flamboyant types; cocktail waitresses, go-go dancers, strippers. I hear he's good to them, taking them on trips, giving expensive gifts, and so forth. So Celeste'll get something out of it, if not a permanent arrangement. I can't see him and Libby ever divorcing, even though she's a rather cold woman, I suspect."

"You wouldn't think so if you could see her hot on the trail of Simms."

He chuckled. "My theory is, it's a game she and Simms have played since they married. His affairs, her fits of jealousy—it's the stuff that holds them together."

"What do you think Maddox saw in Libby?"

"Oh, she's a lovely woman. Quite charming, in spite of her snootiness. But when Maddox kept putting off setting a date for their marriage, I suspected they weren't right for each other. Which was proven to me when he fell for Augusta. She was exactly what he needed, I thought. Back then, Maddox was a rather despondent young man, in spite of everything he had going for him. Augusta's brought a spark to his life and saved him from himself, I suspect."

"That's been my observation, too."

"And it works both ways. Maddox provided the stability Augusta needed. You know, Dean, sometimes the gifts the gods give us turn out to be curses. I've observed that too much beauty is not good for a woman."

"I wouldn't know," I said, smiling.

"You're quite lovely, but you should be grateful not to be as beautiful as Augusta. Any woman should. I know that sounds strange, but it's true."

"No, I think you're right."

"Augusta was so beautiful, even as an adolescent, that every man she met fell for her. But that sort of power is overwhelming for a young girl, and she had a difficult time with it. She was a wild child in her youth, running around with all sorts of unsuitable men. I always suspected she was trying to escape a broken heart."

I leaned toward him. "She said something like that to me once! Do you know anything about it?"

Godwin shook his head thoughtfully. "Not a thing. She's never told me or Rich about it."

"Well, whatever it was, she obviously did the right thing by marrying Maddox and having Gus, don't you think?"

"Absolutely," Godwin said, handing me his empty bowl with a contented sigh. "That was delicious. It's been a while since I've enjoyed food."

"Let me put it in the freezer and you and Rich can have some later on." When I came back from the kitchen, Godwin motioned for me to move my chair closer.

"Dean, I'm glad you came over today," he said, his eyes clouded, "and that I've had a chance to talk to you with no one else around. As much as I've enjoyed our gossiping, I'd like to discuss something rather—ah—delicate with you now."

"With me?"

With his elbows rested on the wheelchair, he formed a steeple with his fingers as he stared out the window. He looked much better now. There was a flush of color in his cheeks and he appeared stronger. Again, I admired his classic good looks, his perfectly shaped face and thick, snow-white hair combed back from his high, noble forehead. "Yes, with you, my dear Dean," he said. "You don't realize what a compassionate listener you are. In the short time we've known each other, I've come to feel very close to you."

I took his hand in mine and smiled. "Thank you for that, Godwin."

"Nothing to thank me for—it's simply the truth. For one thing, you were privy to the problems Rich and I experienced with Eunice and Esther. They're not bad people, Dean. They just don't care for, or understand, my . . . situation with Rich."

"I know that, and I understand that about them. We all do."

He frowned, his dark eyes still troubled. "I'm not sure what's the best way anymore, the way things are for people like Rich and myself nowadays, or the way they used to be. The younger ones, they're all for openness and honesty. Coming out, they call it. I can't see that it causes any less heartache than the way people did it in my day, tell you the truth. But—that's not what I want to talk to you about." Again, he was silent as he stared out the window. "I had quite a scare with the heatstroke, Dean. So if anything happens to me, I want you to help Rich. Will you promise me that?"

I nodded. "You know I will."

"I'm all Rich has, Dean. His parents have pretty much disowned him. My sisters will, as you know, make things difficult for him. I have to do something to protect him when I'm gone."

"Surely there are things you can do, Godwin. Legally, I mean. Your will—"

He held up his hand to silence me. "Ah, yes, I've already done all that. Even though I can see Esther and Eunice challenging any legal document, I've covered every possible angle legally."

I'd already thought of the same thing; that his sisters would surely contest any will that left his share of the St. Clair property to Rich. Godwin was too intelligent not to appreciate the hazards involved in his providing for Rich after he'd gone.

"There's something else I can do, Dean. I haven't mentioned it to Rich yet. Ever since my heatstroke, I've thought of nothing else." Godwin studied me before continuing, as though to gauge my reaction to what he was about to say. "There's a minister I've heard about, a Methodist minister. A young man named Luke Shepherd," he continued. "He's in Port St. Joe, directing a church-related camp there."

"Great name for a minster," I smiled. "I've heard of him."

"Listen to me very carefully," Godwin said, squeezing my hand, and something in his tone startled me. "Luke Shepherd, Dean, is a very compassionate young man."

"Compassionate?" I echoed.

"Compassionate," he said, his voice firm. "Luke Shepherd, an ordained Methodist minister, will perform a marriage ceremony for Rich and me."

I stared at him, unable to believe what I was hearing. "Oh, Lord," I whispered, swallowing hard, and Godwin chuckled.

"You look like you've seen a ghost," he said, but there was no reproach in his voice.

"I—I don't know what to say. I'm totally surprised. I mean, I've heard of things like that, but in places like New York, or California . . ."

Godwin nodded, but didn't take his eyes from mine. "I called Reverend Shepherd, and we had a long talk. I had to make sure he'd do this before I mentioned it to Rich, or anyone."

I stared at him, dumbfounded. "Dean, it's important, very important, that you understand this: Luke Shepherd won't do this without talking to Ben first. I'm a member of Ben's church, and in spite of his unorthodox approach to our denomination, the Reverend Shepherd is very much a Methodist. His father and both grandfathers were Methodist ministers. And you'll like this: His mother's a Methodist minister as well, recently ordained. So, he knows the protocol."

"Surely the . . . ceremony you mentioned isn't protocol," I said, my throat dry.

"Not protocol at all. But, according to Luke Shepherd, there's a matter of interpretation, a way of being joined in the eyes of the church when you can't be by law. I've thought a lot about this, Dean. Talk about protocol! This is very unorthodox for me, a sixty-two-year-old man who's lived a life in the same house as my parents, among people I've known all my life."

I looked at him for a long time before I nodded. "Not only unorthodox, Godwin," I said finally, understanding. "But something that a man like you would not do in most circumstances. You're doing this for Rich, not for yourself."

He smiled at me. "That's why I told you first. I knew you'd understand."

Oh, yes, I understood Godwin, but I couldn't imagine how his unorthodox idea would play out. The only thing I knew was this: My escapades with Augusta, the problems with Celeste and Celestial Things, the Eagle Forum, Simms and Celeste, the Holderfields' defection to the Episcopal church—all of those things would pale in comparison to the controversy that would hit Ben's ministry if the Reverend Luke Shepherd came to town to marry Rich and Godwin.

But come to town he did, one hot day in the middle of

August. Ben was distraught, aghast, and appalled when Luke Shepherd walked into his office and told him what he proposed to do. I'd never seen him so unnerved. It had taken all I could do not to prepare him when Ben had told me, with some smugness, that the Reverend Shepherd had called and asked to come talk with him. We were eating breakfast a few days after my conversation with Godwin, Ben sopping up the runny yellow of his fried eggs.

"Oh, did I tell you who's coming to see me this afternoon?" he asked. I poured coffee into his cup, unprepared.

"The pope?"

"Ha ha. No, that young minister who runs Camp Wacahoochee, Luke Shepherd. Called and said he wants to talk with me. Pass me a piece of bacon."

My knees gave out on me and I sank to my chair, almost dropping the coffee pot. "What does he want?"

"I assume he's going to ask me to be a resource speaker for the big centennial wing-ding in the planning stage for Wacahoochee couple of years from now. I've been halfway expecting someone from the committee to ask me, just didn't expect the director himself to pay me a visit."

"That—may not be what he wants," I said, avoiding his eyes.

"Oh, thanks a lot." His look was cold. "Now why say something like that? Don't think I'm important enough, is that it? My new book's coming out next year, both the membership and the stewardship have increased twenty percent since I've been here, and I serve on some of the most influential committees in the conference—I've really gotten the bishop's attention since being sent to Crystal Springs."

Not like you're about to, I thought as I lowered my head, taking a deep breath.

• • •

Ben didn't call me after Luke Shepherd left his office; he stormed into the house instead. It was four-thirty in the afternoon and I was in the music room, sitting on the piano bench with chubby little Courtney Harris, Noreen's granddaughter, trying not to flinch as she banged out the chords of "Wonderful Words of Life." The first hymn chosen for my pupils because it had only one flat, it was a dull and repetitive song that I'd come to detest. When the door flew open and Ben stood there, breathing like he'd just run a marathon, Courtney and I both jumped.

"Hey, Brother Lynch," Courtney cried. "You wanna hear me play my hymn?"

Ben stared at her as though he'd never seen her before. When he realized who she was, he forced a tight smile. "N-not right now, Courtney. I need to talk to Mrs. Lynch. Isn't it time for your lesson to be over?"

Not waiting for my protest, Courtney jumped to her feet, her ponytail bobbing. "I'll betcha it is! Me-maw told me to come get her when I got through—she's over at the Fellowship Hall, fixing something for her circle meeting tonight." Remembering her manners, she turned to me, wrinkling up her pudgy face. "We're through, ain't we, Miss Dean?"

"Aren't we," I corrected automatically.

"I don't know, that's how come I'm asking you," she said, her face blank.

"We'll stop early today," I mumbled. "Go on and find your grandmother, okay?" She grabbed her lesson book and was out the door before I could change my mind. Her footsteps sounded down the hallway, then the back door slammed.

Ben's stare was so unfocused that it scared me. "Ben? You okay?" I asked. He shook his head, his eyes glazed.

"You knew, didn't you?" he said finally. "You knew why Luke Shepherd came to see me."

I put my head in my hands. "Oh, God, Ben . . . I've been dreading this moment."

"For good reason. Do you know what this kind of thing could do to my career?" He sank into a chair as though he could no longer stand.

I sighed, loud. "Just once—once—I wish that your first reaction to every single thing wasn't how it might affect your career!"

"I'm going to pretend you didn't say that, because I'm too upset to deal with it." He looked heavenward, as though seeking divine guidance. "Everything I've worked so hard for could blow up, just like that." He banged his hand on the arm of the chair and I jumped. "Just like that! Let the media get hold of this, it'll blow like a bomb." He put his head down in his hands as I looked on, helpless. When he raised his head, he was furious. "Rich cooked this up, didn't he? Godwin'd never come up with something so outrageous."

"I don't think Rich knows about this," I murmured, stunned at the force of his anger. When Ben got mad, he could be scary.

"Oh, Godwin's such a gentleman, he might try to pretend it's his idea, keep people from thinking bad of Rich. But I don't buy it, not for one minute."

"I don't know why you don't like Rich," I said. "He's every bit as nice as Godwin."

"Yeah, I've noticed how you think he pure hung the moon," he said. "I don't know why women carry on over gay guys like they do. Beats anything I've ever seen."

"Ben," I said, leaving the bench and going to kneel beside him. "Listen to me. Casting blame, flinging a fit . . . none of that's going to do you any good. The question is, what are you going to do?"

He looked down at me as though I'd lost my mind. "What

do you mean, what am I going to do? What do you think? I absolutely will not allow any such thing in my church. Absolutely not."

"Silly me—and all this time I've thought it was God's church," I said.

"I'm God's steward of this church, as you well know, the shepherd of my flock, responsible for the souls of my congregation."

I shook my head. "That kind of thinking will get you in an early grave. Each of us is responsible for our own soul, Ben. You can't possibly take that on."

Again he banged the arm of the chair with such force that I jumped back. "I'll tell you what I'm going to do!" he yelled. "I have no intention of dealing with something of this magnitude myself. I'm calling the bishop. The Book of Discipline states the position of the Methodist church clearly. We believe in ministering to the homosexual's spiritual needs, which is not the same as condoning homosexuality. We do not—repeat—do not sanction same-sex marriages. Disciplinary action needs to be taken against Luke Shepherd, and it needs to be done right now."

"Disciplinary action? For talking with you about a same-sex marriage? For merely *talking* . . ."

Ben glared at me. "It's gone way beyond that. Luke was raised in the church, both his parents are ministers, so he did the right thing by coming to me. You never go into another minister's congregation and perform a marriage ceremony, or do a funeral, or baptism, without the permission of the person's minister. You know that. When I told him I absolutely opposed him, wouldn't give him permission or my blessing, and would go so far as trying to stop him, he got mad, showed his tail. Said he'd prefer me in their corner, but if I wasn't, it didn't matter. Under the special circumstances Godwin and Rich find themselves in, he said, he'd do it regardless."

"I had a feeling he would," I murmured.

"The plans are to do the . . . ah . . . ceremony at the St. Clair house," Ben continued, his voice ragged. "Since I won't give it my blessing, Reverend Shepherd asked me to look the other way. He promised he wouldn't say anything about coming to see me beforehand."

I let out a sigh. "That's your out, then. You don't approve, can't go along with it—well, you don't have to. You don't even need to know when it takes place—" The look on Ben's face stopped me.

"After twenty years of marriage, Dean, you don't know me. You don't know me if you think I'm going to let something like this take place right under my nose."

"But, Ben! Please, listen to me—"

"I know Godwin, know his kind. I've had old maids in every church, sissies, men who never cut the apron strings. Mama's boys. Godwin won't go against the town his mama's so revered in, I guarantee. I can stop this with just a few well-placed phone calls."

I sank back on my heels. "Oh, no, Ben. I beg you . . . please don't do this. Please, please don't do this . . ." My voice broke and I began crying.

Ben rose to his feet, his face closed against me, his eyes devoid of feeling. "I'm not going to let everything I've worked so hard for blow up in my face." He stepped out the door before turning back and pointing a finger at me. "And you'd better listen to me, Willodean. Whatever you do, don't even think about being a part of this, you hear? If you want to stay married to me, you'd better stay out of this. Stay out of it, or so help me God, you'll regret it!"

Ten

SINCE WE'D BEEN IN Crystal Springs and I'd come under
the influence of Augusta, I'd done things that Ben wasn't
happy about. Although he'd made his displeasure known by
rolling his eyes, making sarcastic remarks disguised as jests,
or complaining outright, he'd never ordered me not to do
something. If he had, I'd've obeyed. I might grumble and
snap back, but I always caved in. It was my nature to be the
appeaser, the peacemaker who survived the instability of her
childhood by being compliant. This time, however, I risked
everything to stand by Godwin and Rich. When Sunday afternoon came and Ben took the paper and went to his room,
I waited for his snores, then left. Unbeknownst to Ben, this
was the day chosen by Rich and Godwin for Luke Shepherd
to return to their house for the marriage, where I'd play the
music, and Augusta and Maddox would sign their names as
witnesses.

In spite of the heat, I walked to the St. Clair house. Next
to our parsonage with its trimmed boxwoods and azalea

bushes drooping in the sun, I paused and looked up at the church with something akin to grief. The white steeple pointing to heaven in a cloudless blue sky, the stately columns, the brick facade beckoned to me, and I fought the urge to slip inside the cool darkness of the sanctuary and fall to my knees. Sanctuary. What an appealing word, with its connotations of safety and refuge! The church had always offered sanctuary for tortured souls, for those of us who sought shelter inside its cloistering walls. But what about people like Rich and Godwin, or Celeste—outside the norm, different from the rest of us? Hadn't I retreated to the church myself because of my own shame? I'd always identified with Matthew the tax collector, the hated Zaccheus, the Samaritan woman at the well, and the harlot Mary Magdalene—all the outcasts whom Jesus sought out. The altar inside was engraved with words that gave me comfort: *Come to me all ye who labor and are heavy-laden, and I will give you rest.*

Rich answered my timid knock and led me to the sunroom, where all the shades were closed so that no light came in. It was cooler but strange, like being in a cave. Sanctuary, I thought. They've created their own.

On the porch, I hugged Augusta and Maddox, standing silently next to Godwin, who was elegant in a dark suit and a blue shirt with his initials on the pocket. His white hair showed the marks of much combing, and his goatee was perky and debonair. I kissed him, then turned to the young man standing on the other side of the wheelchair. "Luke Shepherd." I smiled, taking his hand. "I'm Dean Lynch."

"I know," he said simply. "A pleasure to meet you." Dressed in a gray clerical shirt and collar with jeans, he was rather ordinary-looking—a slight young man with pale skin and reddish-gold hair—until you saw his eyes. They were alight with a strange fire, unsettling in their intensity. The eyes of an anarchist, I realized. Maybe the kind of eyes Mary Magdalene saw when she looked at the young carpenter from Nazareth.

Because of the atmosphere created by the pulled shades, a pall settled over the occupants of the sun porch, in spite of what should have been a festive occasion. I looked around nervously. "Augusta's been at work," I said inanely. Gardenias perfumed the air; candles burned on the round table in the corner, which she'd covered with an embroidered cloth; and a bottle of champagne stuck out of a silver bucket of ice. Luke Shepherd cleared his throat. "Why don't we get started?" Rich put a hand on Godwin's shoulder, and Godwin grasped his hand, smiling. Luke looked at each of us intently before taking his place in front of Godwin and Rich, a *Book of Worship* held close to his chest.

"Dean, Augusta, and Maddox," Luke Shepherd said, "your presence here took remarkable courage, and I commend you. By your presence, you have demonstrated your love for Godwin and Rich. Because we know God is love, love is never wrong. You cannot love too much or give too much love. *Beloved, let us love one another: for love is of God.* Now, we are here to join Rich and Godwin together in marriage, which should always be entered into reverently, but never so much as the union we are witnessing—and by our presence, sanctioning—today. Because Godwin and Rich cannot be joined by law, we are joining them in spirit and offering them our blessings. That is all we can do. We will dispense with the usual ritual and use one I've modified for this occasion." He then turned to face Rich and Godwin, saying, "Rich Kingsley, do you take this man to be your life's companion, to live together in the estate of marriage as provided by the church? Will you love, comfort, honor, and keep him in sickness and in health; and forsaking all others, keep you only unto him, so long as you both shall live?"

"I will," Rich said. The vows were repeated to Godwin, who answered, "With God's help, I will." Then Reverend Shepherd asked that Godwin and Rich join hands. "Rich, repeat the vows after me, then likewise, Godwin," he said. Rich and Godwin dutifully repeated the vows, Godwin's voice stronger than it'd been in weeks. Reverend Shepherd continued, "Forasmuch as Godwin and Rich have consented to be married and have given and pledged their love to each other, and have declared the same in front of witnesses, I declare by the power vested in me by Christ's holy church that they are duly joined in spirit and in love. What God has joined together, let no one put asunder." Maddox and Augusta burst into applause, but I sat with tears rolling down my cheeks. Luke said to me, "Dean, will you offer your song as both a blessing and a benediction?"

I played the song that we'd closed our songfests with, a tune that had become our theme song, and we sang together, "Drifting Too Far from Shore."

Once the ceremony was over, the tension lifted from the darkened room like the blinds Maddox raised to let the sunlight in. "A metaphor," he said, and all of us hugged one another and danced around Godwin's wheelchair. Augusta grabbed Luke and kissed him square on the mouth. "O aptly named one, you're an angel," she proclaimed. Ollie came out from hiding under the table and barked at us, thumping his tail on the floor. Maddox popped the cork on the bottle of champagne, the pale gold liquid like bubbling sunlight in Godwin's antique crystal stems.

"In honor of the occasion, a vintage Bollinger, 1988," Maddox said, to the appreciative applause of Rich and Godwin, as he held his glass high. "To Rich and Godwin," he said. "Today you have shown us what love, commitment, and courage are. For that, I salute you."

Augusta cut the wedding cake she'd made, a masterpiece

of half a dozen pale chocolate layers piled with dark chocolate frosting. She served Rich and Godwin, then forced me to
take one even though I groaned in dismay when I saw the
serving size. "Shut up," she commanded. "It took me a
whole day to make this, and by God—whoops, excuse me,
Reverend—by George, we're gonna eat it. And save room for
the ice cream." She gave Ollie a bowl of ice cream, too. He
gobbled it up, then licked the bowl noisily, sliding it around
the wooden floor with his nose. "Exactly what I feel like doing," Rich laughed.

"Tell me about the songfests you folks had this spring,"
Luke said as he sat down with his bowl of ice cream.

"You would've loved them," Godwin replied, spooning
ice cream into his mouth with trembling hands. "Dean and
Augusta have great voices, but Maddox, Rich, and myself
sound like a chorus of bullfrogs."

Luke Shepherd turned his intense blue eyes on me. "Actually, I'd heard about Dean's music. I'd like to invite you to
perform for us at Camp Wacahoochee for our centennial celebration summer after next. We don't pay much, but
Methodists from all over the southeast will be there, so it'll be
good exposure."

I blinked, startled. Ben would never get over it if I were
on the program instead of him. "I-if I can," I stammered.

"What do you mean, if you can?" Augusta scoffed. "I'm
her manager, and of course she can. Her social calendar ain't
filled up through summer after next, believe me."

I concentrated on my bowl of ice cream, now half-
melted, the consistency of a watery milk shake. Maybe I
could work out a deal, agree to come if they let Ben speak. Of
course I could never tell Augusta that. Or Ben.

I was the first one to leave, since I was playing the piano
that night for evening church services, old Sylvia Whiney-
Hiney being on vacation. Augusta pushed me toward the door,

groaning. "Run along, since First Methodist can't start without you. And tell His Holiness he was missed this afternoon!"

I didn't play the piano for church that evening. I heard later that Lorraine Bullock had to do it, conducting the choir sullenly from the piano bench.

It happened in Bible study. August was traditionally a slack month in the church, with a lot of families on vacation, so Ben was trying something new, conducting a Bible study in the hour before church. I got there late, the discussion well under way, and I took a seat near the back of the church. There was a slim crowd of about fifty tonight, including Ben's cheering section: Bob and Noreen Harris, Collie Ruth, Vanna Faye, A.H. and Lorraine, Dr. Brandon and Elise, Janice and Mike Johnson, all seated in the front rows. Ben stood facing them in front of the pews, a podium set up for his notes.

As soon as I sat in the cushioned pew, I saw that something was wrong. In the second pew on Ben's left, Miss Lottie Mae Brickman was standing, banging her cane on the floor. The tension in the air was thick as a thundercloud.

"You people better listen to me," Miss Lottie Mae was saying. "We're talking about a Methodist preacher, not one of those Anglicans or what you call them?—Utilitarians—but a *Methodist* preacher right here in our conference. This is not only going to affect our town, it's going to involve our church!"

My heart leaped to my throat when I realized what was going on; it was obvious from the stricken look on Ben's white face as he stood clutching the podium. Miss Lottie Mae, a notorious gossip and busybody, was a friend of Godwin's sisters, Eunice and Esther. Ben's call to them about Luke Shepherd had worked, and now he was facing the consequences.

Angry whispers swept over the congregation, and Miss Lottie Mae banged on the floor with her cane to shut them up. Ben's eyes jumped around nervously, desperate to get control of the meeting as Miss Lottie Mae said, "This preacher is not only willing to perform marriages between two men or two women, but he is coming to our church to do so!" When the congregation gasped in shock, Miss Lottie Mae pointed a finger at Ben. "And you, Brother Lynch, know this is true."

"I'll be glad to talk with any of you about this issue after church tonight," Ben said, swallowing hard, his face so red I was afraid he'd have a heart attack, "but for now, let's . . . ah . . . get back to our scripture reading."

It didn't work. The congregation burst out in an angry clamor, and my heart sank as A. H. Bullock stood up.

"Our church?" he repeated incredulously. "We've got to find a way to stop this. Never heard of anything so disgusting." He then sat down, his red face puffed up like a toad's. People all around me were nodding and whispering their agreement.

Dr. Brandon raised his hand. "Dr. Lynch, it's my personal belief that a person's sexual orientation is his or her own business. But what's the official position of the Methodist church regarding same-sex marriages?" His voice rang out clearly over the clamor, which quieted immediately. Ordinarily a doctor would be an authority figure they'd listen to, but it wasn't just his youth that he had going against him. African American and a Yankee to boot, Dr. Brandon was not totally accepted by the congregation, in spite of his position in town.

"Thanks for asking, Chuck," Ben said with relief. "We love the sinner but hate the sin," he said. "In an official statement from the most recent Council of Bishops, the Methodist church does not condone same-sex marriages. Now, let's get back to our discussion of Romans—"

But it was no use. Someone in the back of the room

called out that the Bible stated clearly that homosexuality was an abomination to the Lord. Feeling sick to my stomach, I gathered up my purse and my Bible, planning to slip out so I'd have some time to pull myself together before the service started. As I slid to the end of the pew, Ben tapped on the microphone. "People, people, please," he pleaded. "Let's stand now for the benediction." But even with the microphone on, Ben's voice was drowned out by the clamor. If only I hadn't looked back at him when I started out of the church, I'd have made it. Spotting me, Ben gestured frantically. "Dean? Will you come forward and play the benediction?"

I went to the front of the church reluctantly, sick at heart at the venom and hostility of the angry voices. But playing the benediction would end it. Ben would never let the evening church services get as out of hand as this meeting had. I'd just crossed the front of the church, heading toward the piano, when A.H.'s voice sang out over the sanctuary, and we all heard him say, "I tell you what I think—any queers in this church pull something like that, I say we kick them out."

I don't know what came over me, the bona fide coward. I stopped just as I reached the podium and stared at A.H., then the congregation, my hand trembling as I reached for the microphone.

"Since the rest of you have had your say, I'd like to have mine," I said, and the room fell silent. "The song we sing for our benediction is 'Bind Us Together.' To me, that song says that the church welcomes us and binds us with love, regardless of who we are or what we are. That thought has always given me great comfort. Because of what I've witnessed here tonight, it looks like I've been wrong. Music means too much to me to play that song as though it had no meaning. You'll have to find someone else to do it." My eyes filled with tears, and I hurried out of the church, not caring that the heavy doors slammed behind me, as loud as a thunderbolt.

• • •

Ben came to sit on the side of my bed after the evening service. When I'd gotten home, I'd put my gown on, taken two aspirins, and crawled into bed. When Ben flung my door open, I'd jumped up, startled. He crossed the room, turned my lamp on, and sat down heavily on the bed.

"Oh, God," he sighed, "I'm bound to get a call from the bishop first thing in the morning, if not tonight. I'm tempted not to answer the phone."

He was too distraught for me to remind him that he'd brought it on himself. If he'd not flown off the handle, called Godwin's sisters . . . but Ben never listened to me, always thinking he knew more than I did about handling people. He wrote the book on it. He had to be terribly upset not to jump on me for running out of the Bible study, not showing up to play for church. I'd assumed that was why he came into my room, to chew me out. Instead, he raised his head and looked at me, staring so intently that I pulled my knees up and hugged them to me. "What?" I said finally.

"Dean, it's hard for me to ask this, but . . . you've got to go to Godwin and Rich and beg them not to do this. Tell them . . . tell them how much it'll hurt the church, how it'll divide the town. Tell them they've got to call their ceremony off."

When I didn't say anything, Ben grabbed my shoulder, his hand rough on my bare skin. "You've got to do this for me. My career—"

"Stop it, Ben," I said, pulling away from him. "That hurts."

"Eunice and Esther . . . I realize that was a mistake, calling them. But you might be able to stop this."

I sank down in the bed and pulled the sheets around me. "Let's talk about this in the morning, okay?"

"I can't believe it! After all I've done for you, taking up for you when everyone told me you weren't suitable, that I should've married someone from a better background, and one thing—one thing!—I ask you to do for me, and you refuse. You don't know how that damages our relationship."

"Oh, you want to talk about damaging our relationship? What about me begging, pleading with you not to tell anyone about Luke Shepherd's visit? Take a page out of your own book, Preacher. You reap what you sow."

"Okay, I made a mistake. And now I need your help. That's all I'm asking for, Dean—your help."

I sank back on the pillow. "Then you might as well go, Ben, because it's too late."

"Too late?" He repeated dumbly. "You mean, Luke Shepherd—came back to town? He actually did this . . . thing . . ."

"You can say it," I snapped. "Not saying it won't make it go away. Yes, Luke Shepherd performed a marriage ceremony for Rich and Godwin."

"When?" he gasped.

"This afternoon."

Ben was so stunned that he struggled to his feet in a daze then began to back out of the room, stricken. Turning around jerkily like a puppet, he opened the door, not looking at me. "Ben?" I called out. "Ben—wait!" But instead, he went out the door without another word to me.

None of us ever knew exactly how the word got around about the marriage ceremony, but it only took a couple of days for it to spread throughout the Panhandle area. By midweek, it ran not just in the local papers, but was picked up by the *Pensacola Press-Register* and the *Mobile Times*. Moving quickly, the Eagle Forum took out another of their infamous full-page ads, denouncing the Methodist church for its lax interpretation of Scripture. Luke Shepherd was called the antichrist, and a boycott of Camp Wacahoochee was urged. By the weekend, a steady stream of the curious began to ride by the St. Clair house. They craned their necks out the windows, trying to catch a glimpse of the "queers" who'd dared do such an outrageous thing in their God-fearing community.

It became a sign of solidarity for the angry protestors to ride by the St. Clair house and blow their car horns, day or night. Only when the neighbors complained did the sheriff put a deputy on the corner. It was a halfhearted endeavor, though, the deputy coming by when he finished his other jobs, for the horn-blowing went on. In addition, the protestors began throwing things through the gate or over the hedges into the yard; mostly trash, Coca-Cola and beer bottles, wadded-up papers and such. Late Friday afternoon, I went to Godwin and Rich's house, again on foot. I was afraid to drive over. Augusta had left her station wagon parked in front of the house, and someone driving by had thrown something that cracked her windshield. She'd tried to get Godwin and Rich to come out to Mimosa Grove until this blew over, but they'd refused. We were taking turns checking up on them, Maddox going by at night and Augusta or me in the daytime.

After hugging Rich, I went to Godwin and knelt in front of his wheelchair. "How are you doing?" I asked, squeezing his hand.

He smiled at me, as composed and unperturbed as ever. His face was grayish and his eyes sunken, but the old sparkle remained. "Question is, how are you? Dr. Brandon told us about your little escapade last Sunday night. At Bible study, right?"

"You've got supporters," Rich told me. "Dr. Brandon said he was quite proud of you. Said he wished he and Elise had walked out with you."

I smiled weakly, wishing they had, too, and held my hand out to Ollie when I saw him peeking from under a cloth-covered table in the corner. "Come on out, boy," I said, snapping my fingers. "You know me."

Rich laughed. "Since we've become a tourist attraction, Ollie hides under everything. He gets up his nerve to come out, a car horn blows, and he runs for cover."

I looked up at Rich, frowning. "I'd feel so much better about you two if you'd go out to Mimosa Grove—"

But Godwin cut me off. "We've thought about going even farther. Good friends just bought a winter place in Sarasota, and they're begging us to stay in their guest house."

"Godwin's not quite up for a plane ride yet," Rich said, "so we're staying put."

"This will all blow over soon," Godwin said philosophically.

"But—"

"So don't worry about us," Rich insisted, tugging at his ponytail. "It's inconvenient now, hiding in the house like fugitives, but things'll be back to normal soon."

I turned to Ollie, who inched toward me, nose down and long ears dragging on the wooden floor, and scratched his big old head. Maybe I was overreacting. After all, Godwin and Rich knew this town better than I did.

"Poor old Ollie. I've been sneaking him out in the backyard to do his business, then quickly back in the house," Rich said. "He doesn't like that, since he's used to coming and going as he pleases. But I don't let him roam around chasing his imaginary rabbits, even after it gets dark. I'm afraid he'll get scared and try to get under the house, get stuck."

"It's almost dark now," I said, "so I've got to go. Maddox'll be dropping in for his guard duty."

"Rich, give Maddox a call and tell him not to come," Godwin said firmly. "Dean, you, Augusta, and Maddox are wearing yourselves out, and I'm not going to have it, you hear?"

"Stay and eat, Dean?" Rich called out from the kitchen as he picked up the phone, but I declined, having a home-coming planning meeting to attend shortly.

"Oh, Godwin, I forgot to tell you!" I said. "Guess who will be our guest speaker for homecoming next month."

"Jesus Christ?" Rich called out from the kitchen.

"Close," I smiled. "None other than the famous Dr. John Marcus Vickery."

Godwin tilted his head to the side. "Really? That must be quite a feather in your husband's cap. The congregation's been begging Dr. Vickery to come back for years, but he's not honored us with his presence since he left here."

"Ben's beside himself," I agreed. I didn't tell him that Dr. Vickery's letter of acceptance had arrived just this morn-ing, express mail, and Ben suspected that the bishop had urged him to come as a way of distracting the congregation from the controversy under way, the charges pending against Luke Shepherd, the media coverage Crystal Springs First Methodist would get as a result. "Tonight I'm going to the first of the homecoming planning meetings." I was actually grateful for the homecoming plans, wishing the festivities were happening sooner. The bishop was right; nothing could be more distracting at this crucial time.

Godwin smiled. "First Sunday in October, isn't it? We always miss it, just getting in from Maine. But I hope I'll feel up to it this year."

My head jerked up, but I looked away before Godwin saw my surprise. I couldn't imagine him and Rich coming to First Methodist for homecoming, as though nothing had hap-pened! In spite of the cars of protestors throwing trash, the horns blowing, and newspaper articles, Godwin and Rich had no idea how their marriage had thrown the town into a turmoil.

•   •   •

It was ten o'clock when I got home from the meeting that night. After dumping my purse and kicking off my shoes, I got the tea kettle and filled it with water. My hands were trembling and I felt nauseated. I'd just put a chamomile tea bag in a mug when Ben came in, throwing his briefcase and papers on the table without looking my way. Since the night he came into my bedroom and discovered Luke Shepherd had performed the marriage ceremony, we'd barely spoken to each other.

He loosened his tie wearily. "We've got a mess on our hands like nothing I've ever seen. The shit's about to hit the fan."

I dunked the tea bag up and down, watching it diffuse into the hot water, turning it a pale brown color. The homecoming committee meeting, the one I'd counted on to distract the congregation, had erupted in discord. In spite of the excitement over Dr. Vickery's return, the congregation could talk of nothing else but the marriage between Godwin and Rich, and things had quickly gotten out of Ben's control. As I stirred honey into my tea, sighing, Ben turned on me. "You know, Dean, people are talking about you almost as bad as Rich and Godwin. Word's gotten out that you were present when Luke . . . did what he did."

The shrill ringing of the phone interrupted his accusations. It was hard to imagine things getting much worse between Ben and me, me and the congregation, than they already were. I'd been ostracized tonight; everyone at the supper had deliberately sat at the opposite end of the table from me, leaving me to eat alone until Dr. Brandon and his wife had taken their plates and moved to sit with me.

Ben reached for the phone as I washed out my cup. I dried my hands, surprised, when he held the phone out. "Don't know who's calling you this late," he snapped.

I watched Ben go to the den, unsnap his briefcase, and

rummage through the papers there, frowning. "Yes?" I said into the receiver.

Someone was breathing ragged, then a muffled voice, male, rough and harsh. "You know what they call women like you, preacher's wife?"

"Beg your pardon?" I said.

"Fag hags," the voice said. "What they do, let you watch? You get off watching men hump each other?"

"Who is this?" I asked, my heart pounding. Ben raised his head and looked my way.

"Them queers stay in town, they both gonna need a wheelchair. But you decide you want a real man, preacher's wife, meet me at their house tonight. Got a nice big one waiting for you."

I slammed the receiver down, my face burning. Ben stood still, his hands on the papers in his briefcase. "Dean?"

"It was . . . nothing. Some pervert." To my shame, my voice broke.

Ben came back into the kitchen and, pushing me aside, picked up the receiver and punched three buttons. He frowned and slammed the phone down. "The last number to call your line is unavailable," he intoned, mimicking a recorded message. "Must've called from a phone booth. What'd they say?"

"Nothing," I whispered, shaking so that I sank into a kitchen chair.

"Bull," Ben snapped. "Whoever it was scared you to death." He gave a martyred sigh and glared at me. "Did it have anything to do with Rich and Godwin?"

I looked up at him as the horrid words of the caller registered with me. "Oh, God! I'd better go over there, see if anything's going on."

"Go where?"

"To—Godwin's. That man said . . ." But I was unable to repeat the ugly words. Ben grabbed my arm when I got to my feet, pushing the kitchen chair aside.

"You are not going anywhere. Don't be ridiculous. It's ten-thirty at night."

"I'm scared, Ben. That voice—"

"I'm glad you got scared," he said, his eyes cold. "Maybe now you'll realize what an explosive situation this is."

When the phone rang again, both of us stared like it was some kind of evil spirit. Ben picked it up, motioning for me to stop my whimpering. "Yes?" he said sharply, then relaxed. "Oh, hello, Augusta. No, we hadn't gone to bed yet." He listened a minute, avoiding my eyes. "Could I take a message? Dean can't come to the phone now." I reached for the phone but Ben backed away. "I'll tell her."

"Why didn't you let me speak to her?"

"She said she didn't need to talk to you, just to tell you that Maddox called her from his office, that he was working late filling out some reports, but he'd gone by the St. Clair house a few minutes ago and everything was fine."

I nodded, then reached for my purse, looking for my car keys. Ben grabbed my arm, hard. "What do you think you're doing?"

"I told you, I'm going to Godwin's. I won't even get out—just ride by, see if anything's going on. If you're so worried, come with me."

Ben stared at me as though I'd lost my mind. "Absolutely not. Suppose a bunch of rednecks are over there, blowing their horns and throwing stuff? You and me drive up, they've got a target."

"Listen to me! That man on the phone," I cried, "he sounded . . . deranged or something. This is different, I can feel it."

Ben rubbed his eyes and reached for the phone. "No!" I said, grabbing for his arm, "don't call Godwin. The phone'll wake him up—"

"Give me credit for having some sense," he snapped, punching in a number. "I'm not calling Godwin." I waited, holding my breath, until he spoke into the receiver. "Maxine, Reverend Lynch here. Fine, thank you. Listen, ask Buddy if he'll send his deputy over to the St. Clair house, okay?" He listened, then said, "Yeah. Thanks, Maxine. See you in church Sunday."

I slumped against the table, exhausted and nauseated. Ben started out of the kitchen, then turned before going to his bedroom. "Might as well go to bed. I've taken care of it."

I didn't turn the light on in my room; instead, I pulled my dress over my head and hung it on a hanger in the dark. The curtains were parted to reveal a full white moon, hanging high and heavy in the black sky. The anonymous phone call had so unnerved me that I sank onto my bed weakly, sitting in the dark in my bra and panties. The ugliness in the caller's voice haunted me, and I'd never sleep with it echoing in my ears. I picked up the phone on my bedside table to call Augusta, but stopped myself. What could she do? She was there by herself, Maddox working late. No point in scaring her, too. The deputy sheriff could take care of things, surely. If only I could see for myself. . . . I dialed Maddox's office number.

He answered it on the first ring, and my eyes fell on my alarm clock. Almost eleven. "Maddox?" I said in a small voice.

"Dean? What is it? What's happened?" His voice echoed my fears.

"It's—I'm probably being silly, but I got this phone call tonight and I've been worried about Rich and Godwin ever since. Some man, he called and said—"

"Said what?"

I couldn't tell him. "Just that Rich and Godwin better get out of town, or they'd both need a wheelchair. Then he said for me to meet him over there tonight if I wanted a real man, or something like that."

Maddox was silent, then said, "I'll call the sheriff. I was there just a few minutes ago and everything was fine. Augusta made Rich leave me a beacon. The lamplight in the backyard stays on all night now, signaling that everything's okay. I saw Ollie out there sniffing for rabbits, so they're fine."

I smiled in spite of my state. "Oh. Sounds okay, then."

"I'll call the sheriff anyway. Or better yet—I'm about to leave here, I'll go by again."

"No, no." I let out a trembling breath. "No point in you driving all the way into town. Maybe I'm overreacting. That phone call shook me up."

"Wonder why they called you."

"Because word's gotten around town that I was at the ceremony."

"Uh-oh. That's not going to make you the most popular member of First Methodist, is it?" he chuckled. "Listen, Dean, bet it's the full moon that's got you spooked. I can see it out my office window, and it's pretty awesome."

I looked out my window and smiled into the phone. "Yeah. You're right. That's probably it."

"You going to be all right?"

"Yeah. Sorry I bothered you."

"No problem. I'm going home now, make sure Augusta's not up worrying, too. Go to sleep, Dean. Sounds like they were trying to lure you over, so whatever you do, don't go over there, you hear? Let the sheriff take care of this one."

I sat for a minute before getting my gown from the foot of the bed. I leaned over and looked out the window at the moon shadows of the dogwood trees. The air-conditioning was turned up so high that I shivered. I admonished myself for overreacting, bothering Maddox at his office, scaring him with a late phone call. But . . . something he said was gnawing at the back of my mind. I fingered my gown until it hit me, and the silky gown slid through my fingers to the floor. Wait a minute—Maddox said he saw Ollie outside, chasing rabbits! Hadn't Rich told me just this afternoon that he didn't let Ollie out at night anymore? I stumbled over to my closet in the darkness, crying out as I stubbed my toe. Didn't mean a thing, I told myself; Ollie probably needed to relieve himself, so Rich'd let him out. I was overreacting again. But even as I thought it, I opened the closet door and got the shirt and shorts I'd discarded earlier today. Dressing quickly, I snapped on my sandals, fumbled for my car keys, then crept down the dark hallway. Ben's light was off. Good.

The moonlight was bright as I drove the four blocks to the St. Clair house. No one was on the streets, and the oaks lining the streets cast heavy black shadows on the sidewalk. All the houses were dark, their occupants asleep. The deputy's car was nowhere to be seen, although there was a suspicious-looking old pickup parked in the alleyway behind Godwin's house. I rode by it cautiously but it was empty, seemingly deserted. I circled the block, then parked in front of Godwin's house.

The house was peaceful, silent as a tomb, with all the lights out and the trees surrounding it casting long shadows in the white moonlight. The grounds were undisturbed, too, no beer bottles or litter tonight. I saw what Maddox meant; the lamplight in the back, which was mounted on a tall pole, was on, illuminating the rose garden. I couldn't tell if Ollie was there or not.

I went to the side gate, the one by the garage that we'd carried Godwin through on the stretcher. Rich had taken to locking this gate, too, so I pressed up against it, looking for

Ollie. Craning my neck to look at Rich's studio, I saw a movement in the azalea bushes in front of it. Ollie! If he were all the way to the studio, though, it was more confusing than before. Why wouldn't Rich just let him out the back door to do his business then let him back in? Rich had told me he often got up in the night and worked in his studio, but there were no lights on out there. I had to go into the backyard and see if Rich was with Ollie; otherwise, I'd worry myself sick.

The back gate wasn't locked, after all. Even though Rich and Godwin were taking precautions, they shouldn't be careless. I moved through the moonlit bushes, creeping down the stone path to Rich's studio. As soon as I got closer, I saw what was going on. A light was on in the studio, and Ollie was scratching at the door, whining, begging to be let in. Evidently Rich had gotten Godwin settled for the night, came out here to work, but hadn't realized Ollie'd followed him. Rich didn't let Ollie into his studio because once he'd chewed up some brushes. Might as well tell Rich I was here, and see if he wanted me to put Ollie back on the porch.

At the front door of the studio, I knelt down and patted Ollie, speaking low to him, but he ignored me and continued to whine, scratching harder at the door. "Come on, boy," I whispered, pulling at his collar. "This place is off limits to you." He weighed a ton; no way I was going to move him from the doorstep. I'd have to climb over him. He looked up at me with his droopy brown eyes as though just recognizing me, then tried to leap on me with his short little front legs. He turned back around to whine and scratch the door again, as though I'd let him in now that I was here. I eased the studio door open, backing in as I patted him on the head. Bless his heart, he was none too bright, and it was easy to outsmart him. "Stay, boy," I said. "I'll take you to the porch in a minute." Although he tried to push past me, I managed to slip in and close the door behind me, leaning on it with a sigh.

I blinked in the semidarkness of the studio stupidly, standing against the door frozen with shock. Rich wasn't in here—instead there were two men with flashlights, moving around in the darkness. From the mess, it was obvious they'd been throwing things around as they vandalized the studio and destroyed Rich's paintings. Another man was crouched on the floor behind them. The phone call had been a trap, and I'd walked straight into it.

They both spotted me at the same moment that I gasped and turned back to the door. "Hey, there she is!" one of them cried, and I recognized the voice from the phone call. Just as I reached the doorknob, the one closest to me made a lunge and grabbed me from behind. His hand went over my mouth, cutting off my screams, and his other arm went around my waist, almost knocking my breath away. He smelled like motor oil, and the hand on my mouth was grimy and tasted of dirt. Outside the door, Ollie had stopped scratching and was now barking mournfully.

"Look what my phone call brought me," the man who held me said, his breath hot in my ear as he dragged me over to his companions. One of them shone a flashlight so close in my face that I closed my eyes and turned my head. "Pretty boy's girlfriend, the preacher's wife."

"Preacher's wives don't look like her. Betcha she's one of them drag queens," the man who held the flashlight grunted.

My eyes flew open and I struggled when the one holding me moved his arm from around my waist and put a hand on my breasts. His laugh was coarse. "This ain't no drag queen," he said. "She's got real titties. Nice ones, too."

"Let me see," the other one said, and I struggled helplessly as his hand went to my blouse. The fabric of my shirt was ripped as he snarled at his companion, "Goddammit, Junior, hold her still. Wooweeee. . . . Give her here to me."

"The hell you say, man," the one holding me, Junior,

said, his arm around me so tight, I could hardly breathe. He
was strong and big as a bull. His smelly hand was pressed
against my nose, blocking off the air, and I was losing con-
sciousness. Ollie had stopped barking outside and was baying
instead, and I prayed it was loud enough to rouse somebody.
"You got pretty boy, so this one's mine. I'm the one who got
her over here."

"Aw, com'on, Junior. Ain't no fight left in his faggy ass.
But this little gal, she's moving good. Let me have her."

"Awright," Junior grunted. "After I get through with
her, I'll hold her for you, down there by pretty boy."

The figure I'd thought was another one of them crouch-
ing low was Rich, in a crumpled heap on the floor. Red
stuff—blood!—was all over him, and I called his name as
they pushed me to the floor. "Keep your hand over her
mouth, goddammit," the one called Junior snarled. "That
deputy keeps riding by's gonna hear her yelling if you don't."
The vile hand clamped over my mouth again.

Somewhere in my delirium of fear I remembered being
in a youth group years ago when a policeman came and
demonstrated self-defense. The only thing I recalled was to
go limp, then move quickly, catching your assailant off
guard. I forced myself to relax all the muscles of my body
while the man called Junior pinned me down on the floor,
next to Rich, and sure enough, his grip on me loosened. I
made myself lie still while the other man put his flashlight on
the floor beside me and began to unzip his pants while Junior
held my hands. Just as he bent over and reached for the waistband of my shorts I sprang up, fighting and clawing like a
wildcat. Junior was caught off guard and lost his balance.
Then I heard a sound that propelled me even further: Rich
stirred and moaned. He was alive after all! As I flung my
arms and kicked my feet, I saw that he was moving, as
though trying to raise himself. Terrified that they'd start beat-

ing him again, I kicked and screamed at the two men who held me between them, trying to get me on the floor, grunting and cursing me. I ducked when Junior's arm flung back to hit me, but not in time, and his blow knocked me to the floor so hard that I stayed down, the breath knocked out of me.

What happened next will always be a blur to me, a confusing blur of sounds and sensations. The flashlight must have rolled away because suddenly it was dark except for the moonlight coming through the bank of windows. Rich called my name, and I tried to raise my head to tell him to shut up, to play dead. At the same time, both men jumped on top of me and began pulling and pounding me, and I put my arms up to cover my head. One of them unzipped my shorts, but I kicked out and heard a loud grunt and a curse when my foot landed on his crotch.

The strange noise reverberating in my ears was the sound of Ollie's baying, so loud, he seemed to be in the dark room with us. Suddenly Ollie was in the room, in the blackness, but it was no longer dark because someone else had a flashlight, so bright it hurt my eyes and I covered my face with my hands. There were shuffling noises and loud shouts, cries of some kind, doors banging. I was free, the heavy bodies of the two men no longer on me, but I couldn't move. Someone was calling my name again, over and over—Rich!—but I couldn't take my hands from my face. Another voice joined Rich's, shouting, the sheriff and his deputies, and I knew that they'd pulled the men off me; that Rich and I had been saved. But I couldn't move from where I'd fallen on the floor, huddled with my head in my hands, covering my eyes.

Then someone else was calling my name, lifting me to my feet. It was a voice I knew, a voice I trusted, but I couldn't let go, couldn't look. I could still smell the oily hand over my mouth, could feel the blows that knocked me off my feet. My knees were too weak to hold me up, and I sank to the floor again.

"Dean, Dean, listen to me," the voice spoke in my ear. "Can you walk? Can you come with me?" Strong hands grasped my wrists, pulling my hands away, and I started to sob. Once I started crying I couldn't stop, and began to scream instead. "Dean?" the gentle voice said. "Stop screaming and look at me. Look at me. We've got you now—you're going to be all right, you hear? Look at me!"

I opened my eyes and looked at Maddox, holding me. It was his voice I'd heard in the darkness. "Maddox," I cried, throwing my arms around him. "Thank God you're here!"

"Come on, Dean," he said. "I've got you and you're okay now."

"But Rich—he's not dead, is he?" I cried. Maddox held on tight as he led me toward the open door where moonlight poured in. I stumbled and began to sob again, loud.

"No, he's not dead, sweetheart. He's going to be okay," Maddox said gently, holding me up and making me walk. My knees were weak and my head was swimming, throbbing. "The deputy has already gotten him into the car, and I'm taking you there, too. We're taking the two of you to the hospital, okay?" He spoke slowly and carefully, as though to a young child.

"Those men—those horrible men . . ." I said, shuddering, leaning now into Maddox as he led me out the door. Ollie was barking now, running around in circles at our heels as we left the studio and began the walk down the pathway.

"The sheriff has taken them away. He's taking them to jail; you won't have to see them."

I stared up at him in the moonlight. "Oh God, Maddox—they hurt Rich and they tried—Oh, God . . ."

"Shhh. Don't think about it now. We've got to get you

and Rich to the hospital. Don't think about anything now. You can tell us about it once we get you two to the hospital."

"How did you know to come to the studio?"

"Shhh. We'll talk later. Let's just get you to the car, okay?"

"Ollie's going to wake Godwin up," I cried out, almost stumbling over Ollie as he barked around my feet, and Maddox chuckled.

"Rich told me that Godwin's medication makes him sleep through all the horn blowing and noise lately, so a hurricane couldn't wake him. Godwin'll be fine. Here we are. Careful now, I'm putting you in the backseat beside me."

I crawled in obediently and Maddox slid in next to me. Rich was in the front with a deputy sheriff at the wheel. I raised up to look at Rich, who was lying back in the seat with his hands over his face, but Maddox pulled me back and put his arm around me firmly, forcing my head against his shoulder. "Don't look at Rich now, Dean. They worked him over good, so he's not a pretty sight."

"Call an ambulance for him," I cried out, struggling as he held me back. "My God, look at him!"

"We're taking him straight to the hospital. We can get him there quicker than an ambulance can get here," Maddox told me.

"He has blood all over him!" I cried out, but Maddox shook his head.

"There's some blood, but what you see is paint. Evidently Junior and Billy thought it was funny to throw paint on him after they beat the shit out of him."

"You know them?" I sobbed.

"Oh, yeah. Sorry as hell, both of them. Out on parole. This'll keep them locked up for a long time, thank God."

The deputy at the wheel, a muscular young man with a trim mustache, looked at Maddox in the rearview mirror.

"Mr. Holderfield, I'm not going to turn on the siren and stir up the neighborhood, but hold on because we're going to haul ass to the hospital. I've already radioed in and they're waiting for us."

Another blur, the ride to the hospital, stopping at red lights, then speeding through them as Rich stirred and moaned in the front seat. I cried all the way, and Maddox kept his arms around me, shutting me up when I tried to talk. When we pulled up to the emergency room entrance, people in white uniforms swarmed around us, and put Rich on a stretcher. He seemed only half-conscious, but before I could get a better look, they wheeled him away. Maddox got me in a waiting wheelchair and a nurse pushed me into the lobby. I blinked my eyes against the bright lights and put my hands over my face when the nurse pushed me through swinging doors into an examination room in the back. When she opened the door to push me in, I cried out and reached my hand back for Maddox, but the nurse closed the door on him. "We'll let your husband in after the doctor sees you," she said briskly.

"Oh, no, don't call my husband," I cried. "Please don't wake him up."

The nurse looked startled, then ordered me on the examination table. As soon as I got shakily to my feet, the door burst open and a team of doctors and nurses came in. Outside the door, I could see the sheriff and two deputies talking to Maddox.

It was only when I was examined that I realized my shirt was torn in the front, my shorts were half off, and there was blood all over me. My clothes were removed and I was dressed in a hospital gown. I didn't know I had a cut on my head, wetting my hair with blood, until one of the doctors touched it and I cried out. The exam was frightening, penlights shining into my eyes as I was prodded and pulled on and poked at. Looking down at my uncovered body during the exam, I gasped to see big ugly bruises like birthmarks. There was a bleeding cut on my knee, and nicks and bruises all over my hands. They applied stinging ointments as they bandaged me in all the cut and swollen and bleeding places. Suddenly the exam was over, and everyone left the room except for two of the women doctors. One of them, a pretty black woman with skin like coffee and cream, pulled up a stool and took my hand.

"Mrs. Lynch," she said, "I'm Dr. Moore and this is Dr. Sanders. We're a part of the rape crisis team, and we'll do the rest of your examination."

"I wasn't raped," I told them, and started to cry again. "They—tried to, but I fought them off. Then the sheriff and his deputies got there." It was only when I said it aloud that I realized what I'd escaped.

The two doctors exchanged glances. "We need to examine you anyway, for two reasons. One, sometimes rape victims block things out. And two, those men can be charged with attempted rape."

"Does that mean I'll have to testify in court, tell everybody what they did to me?"

Dr. Moore shook her head as she pulled on a rubber glove while the other doctor began opening sealed packets marked "Evidence." "You might. Sometimes if they enter a guilty plea, your statement's enough. But don't think about that now. The sheriff's waiting to talk to you when we get through."

"Oh, no, please," I sobbed, my head throbbing. "Don't make me go through it again now. My head hurts too bad. Can't I just go home?"

Dr. Moore smiled at me. "You've had a rough night. You have a slight concussion, so we're going to keep you overnight. But if our exam is negative, we'll ask the sheriff to wait and talk to you in the morning."

When they'd finished, they put me in a dimly lit hospital room, propped up on a pillow, all bandaged and cleaned up, then Maddox finally got to come in and tell me what had happened. The sheriff, he told me, was with Rich, and would wait until tomorrow to take my statement. "Oh, God—how is Rich?" I said. They'd given me a sedative and I lay back on the pillows, suddenly feeling awful. I'd noticed on the clock in the examining room downstairs that it was almost one o'clock.

Maddox pulled up a chair and leaned on the bed rail. "He's a mess. Black eyes, busted lip, some cracked ribs, eyes swollen almost shut. Not a pretty picture. But they're going to keep him good and doped up so he won't suffer."

"What happened, do you know?"

He shrugged and rubbed his eyes. "Don't know anything yet, really, not until Rich is able to tell us. Just the sheriff and me speculating. Guess Rich went out to his studio to work and the goons jumped him. They'd probably been laying low for several days, watching the house, trying to catch him or Godwin alone. Frankly, I can't help but be glad it was Rich they found instead of Godwin."

I shook my head. "I can't even think of that."

Maddox took my bandaged hand. "How about you, Dean? You scared the hell out of me, you know."

I tried to smile, but it hurt too much. "The doctors tell me I'll be horribly sore for several days, but I'm not seriously injured. A mild concussion, but it could've been a lot worse."

"I can't tell you how glad I was to hear that . . . they didn't . . ."

"If you and the deputies hadn't gotten there when you did . . ." I shuddered and squeezed his hand. "How'd it happen that you came then?"

"After we hung up, I went home. Augusta and Gus were asleep, so I was sitting downstairs, having a nightcap. I don't know, Dean. There was something in your voice . . . all of a sudden I had to go back into town, ride by Godwin's house before I could sleep. Then, when I got there, I saw your car, which told me something was wrong. That, and the strange pickup in the alley. When I got to the back gate, that damn fool dog started jumping on me. That's when I knew something was bad wrong. The sheriff and his deputies came then, and Ollie led us to the studio."

I shook my head in amazement. "It seems like some kind of weird nightmare now. Or maybe a horror movie. I only remember bits and pieces of it."

"You're probably lucky then. But listen, Dean. I need to call Ben, don't I? I would've earlier, but the nurse said you'd begged her not to. Think that's smart?"

My lips were getting numb and my eyelids were heavy from the sedative. I struggled to keep them open as I grabbed for Maddox's hand. "Please, please don't call him. I swear I'll get them to call him first thing in the morning. No point in him losing a night's sleep, not with all that's going on in the church now."

"But what if he wakes up and sees that you're gone?"

"He won't. I mean, he wakes up a lot, but he stays in his room, working on his sermon and stuff. He never comes to my room. I promise it'll be okay, Maddox. Really."

Maddox raised his eyebrows in surprise, then said, "Okay. If you think that's best."

"I know it is. But what about Augusta? You'd better get home before she wakes up and sees you're not there."

He patted my hand, his eyes darkening. "God, she's going to be frantic over this. But, like you said about Ben, she needs her sleep. You know how she is, she'll be running back and forth trying to take care of you and Rich and Godwin."

"You're right. So you'd better go now, Maddox. Go home and get some rest."

He nodded solemnly. "I will. But I'm not leaving you until you go to sleep."

I shook my head. "Don't be silly. Go on, see about Augusta." But I couldn't hold my eyes open any longer. When I closed them and began drifting off, Maddox leaned over and brushed his lips to my forehead.

"Rest well," he said. "Augusta and I will be in to see you in the morning."

"Maddox," I managed to call out as he opened the hospital door. "Wait a minute." I was able to open my eyes long enough to see him standing by the door, his hand on the handle.

"Dean?" he said. "Did you call me?"

"I just wanted to say thank you," I whispered. But I don't think he heard me.

Eleven

RICH AND I RECOVERED from the attack that night, me
of course much quicker than Rich. As soon as I was able, I
went into the darkened hospital room where Rich slept,
studying him before he woke up. I cried as I looked at him,
battered and bandaged, stitched back together, black and
blue and purple. I remembered his telling me about being
picked on by the bullies of his hometown, of the ridicule and
torment he'd suffered all his life, and wondered, not for the
first time, where the intolerance and hatred that put him here
sprang from. What had Rich ever done to hurt anyone, to
bring about so much malevolence? It made no sense to me,
none at all.

I hoped and prayed that things would return to normal
for Rich and Godwin. People were feeling bad about what
had happened to me and Rich; our church members forgot
their anger at me and sent me flowers, cakes, and casseroles,
sweet little get-well notes. When Rich came home from the
hospital, Augusta, Celeste, and I sprang into action, taking

turns helping out. We each did our own thing: Augusta cooked, Celeste entertained with her cards and crystal ball, and I played my music, going over as soon as Ben left for his nightly meetings, reestablishing a form of our songfests. It was at the end of September, when the nights had cooled enough to sit on the porch in the early evening, that Sheriff Coleman paid us a visit.

I'd gotten there late because Ben was home for supper, and I'd fried fresh catfish for him. Even though things had been bad between us lately, and he'd been so furious at me about my attack that he was unsympathetic to my injuries, he was completely wrapped up in the homecoming plans and his good humor spread to include me. He sopped a hushpuppy into a mound of tartar sauce and said, "This homecoming will be talked about for years! Exactly what we need now to get our minds off—the other thing. Smart of the bishop to send Dr. Vickery here now."

I'd lucked out; because of my hospital stay, I'd been re-placed on the planning committee. Dr. Vickery was staying with us, and my new job was official hostess for the great man. Good thing I'd had a full recovery and was up to it. It would never have occurred to anyone in the church that the trauma of the attack would excuse me from my duties.

"I've been on the phone with Dr. Vickery every day this week," Ben told me. "He thinks Beth will be able to come on Sunday, after all."

I nodded. The congregation had been disappointed that Dr. Vickery's sainted wife wouldn't be with him, since she was almost as revered as he was. A dean of something at FSU, she had some kind of workshop that weekend. I was relieved not to have to entertain her, too.

Ben surprised me by patting me on the top of my head when he rose to leave. He hadn't touched me for weeks, and I hadn't wanted him to. "This morning, Dr. Vickery said he couldn't wait to hear your dulcimer music. Well, gotta run to the meeting now!" And with that, he was gone.

As I cleaned the kitchen, I struggled again with the conflicting emotions of the last few months, the resentment I'd felt for Ben so often lately. I sat staring out the bay window of the kitchen, looking over the backyard in the fading light of day. There was a brick patio we never used, with black wrought-iron furniture, uncomfortable and useless, and a small slope of green yard, bordered with azalea bushes pruned to even-shaped mounds. Impeccable and pristine as a golf course, all for show. It hit me why Ben was being nice to me, and I felt like an idiot. Homecoming, of course, in the company of his idol, John Marcus Vickery. Ben was hell-bent on presenting himself as a dedicated minister with an adoring helpmate at his side, cheering him along.

That night on the sunporch of the St. Clair house, Sheriff Coleman demanded that everyone sit and listen to him, even Maddox.

"I'm glad the two of you weren't any more seriously injured than you were," Sheriff Coleman said, looking from Rich and me to Godwin, Maddox, and Augusta. He was a big man, grizzled and gruff, but since the night of the attack, I'd come to trust him. He'd been abrupt in his treatment of Rich and me, but thorough and professional. "Even though it's over now, and the judge has sent the perpetrators to the pen, I can't guarantee your safety. Mr. St. Clair," he said, turning to Godwin, narrowing his eyes, "I'm advising that you and Mr. Kingsley go away for a while. Let this thing die down."

"I agree one hundred percent," Maddox said emphatically.

Rich hung his head. "Godwin and I don't want to leave our home, Sheriff Coleman. Couldn't we stay here if we keep a low profile?"

The sheriff shook his head and repeated, "I can't guarantee your safety if you do. Don't y'all have someplace you could go?"

Before they could answer, Maddox stood up, his hands on his hips. "Actually, Sheriff Coleman, I've been thinking about this since Rich was released from the hospital, and I think I have come up with a plan." He turned to Godwin and Rich. "Your friends in Sarasota, didn't you tell me they've invited you down?"

Godwin nodded. "Many times. We could go there for a visit, but neither of us have been up to the trip."

Maddox looked at the sheriff. "Here's my plan. Augusta and I will drive them down, me driving Rich's van, Augusta following in my car. Then we'll return, leaving the van so they'll have it with them. That will work out for all concerned, won't it?"

Rich looked forlorn, but Godwin looked at Maddox with gratitude. "Thank you, Maddox," he said. "If you and Augusta can make the trip next weekend, then Rich and I will go."

Celeste once told me that we could never escape our fate because it always waited for us, around the next bend in the road. On the day the caravan for Sarasota was leaving, with Maddox driving Rich's van down, Augusta, Gus, and Godwin following in the Mercedes, Celeste's words proved to be true. I'd been surprised to hear that Celeste was going with them, until Augusta told me about a rendezvous with Simms, who had a business meeting there. I was distracted, hardly listening to Augusta's litany when I went by the St. Clair house to tell everyone good-bye. My mind was elsewhere, because in addition to tomorrow being the departure date for Sarasota, it was also the beginning of the homecoming weekend.

Fortunately, I'd said my good-byes to Godwin and Rich

rather than waiting until the following day, since it was much busier than I'd counted on. All day, people from the church were running over to the parsonage to see if they could borrow this, that, or the other as they decorated for the centennial festivities on Saturday. By four o'clock in the afternoon, I longed for a good long soak in the tub before Dr. Vickery got there. He was arriving late that afternoon but had insisted that we not plan anything special for him, even dinner, Ben told me. The only problem with this plan was Ben. He'd been horrified when I said, "I'll fix us some vegetable soup for supper, with corn muffins, then he can turn in and be all set for a full day Saturday."

Ben had looked at me as though I'd lost my mind. "What are you thinking? Any preacher's wife would be foaming at the mouth to fix an impressive meal for John Marcus Vickery, and you're talking about *soup*?"

"But," I'd argued foolishly, "you said that he asked us not to go to any trouble!"

"What'd you expect him to say, fix me a nice meal?"

"No, but if he wanted that, he'd not say anything. Everybody fixes him a fancy meal. He asked us specifically not to."

Ben had thrown up his hands dramatically. "If you don't want to do this, I'll ask Collie Ruth and the UMW to do it."

"No, you won't, either," I'd snapped. Augusta was right. She'd teased me that entertaining Dr. Vickery was like preparing for the second coming.

"That shrimp dish you do," Ben said, "is perfect. Just the right touch. With that frozen lemon stuff for dessert."

Oh, great, I thought, you mean the one that takes me all day? I'd given in, of course, and spent all day cooking and resenting it. It was late in the afternoon of the big day when I realized that Ben had forgotten to pick up the arrangement for the dining room table as he promised. Nothing now but for me to do it; there was no telling where Ben was. I still had a couple of hours before Dr. Vickery got here, so I'd get back in time to take a long bath.

When I returned from the florist, so many cars were at the church, some of them in front of our house, as everyone made final preparations for the homecoming event, that I didn't notice a strange car parked closer than the others. The first weekend in October had arrived much cooler than any of us had dared hope. For the last few days, the skies had been impossibly blue and cloudless, and the temperatures pleasant. After some cooling rains, the air was clear and sweet-scented. This time of day, the late afternoon sun poured across the green grass of my lawn like melted butter. It was with a light step that I hurried into the house, closing the back door behind me.

As soon as I went into the kitchen, I knew instinctively that I was not alone in the house. "Ben?" I called out, putting the arrangement of flowers and my purse on the kitchen table. I'd left the stereo playing bluegrass music, so my voice was lost in the foot-stomping sounds of fiddles and banjos.

As I stepped into the den, I saw him before he saw me, and I knew immediately who he was. Dressed in a dark suit, he was standing and looking out the bank of windows at the backyard, his hands on his hips. It seemed fitting that he was bathed in yellow light from the late sun coming in the windows, turning his perfect profile pure gold. Tall and broad-shouldered, he was as handsome as I'd heard, but I wasn't prepared for the sheer magnetism of his presence. When he turned to me, his face lit up and he held out both hands.

"You've got to be Dean," he said, his booming voice like an organ, as though made to reverberate through huge sanctuaries of worshipers. "I'm John Marcus Vickery."

Twelve

I FIND MASCULINE BEAUTY an interesting thing. I'll never forget the first time I saw Rich Kingsley, when I looked up on the dance floor at Mimosa Grove at one of the most gorgeous men I'd ever seen. Ben was good-looking in a classic, square-jawed way, with his thick dark hair and even features. But the evenness of Ben's features made them less interesting, in some way. Beauty has more to do with animation, fire, and sensuality than perfection. John Marcus Vickery had it all, and I was unable to take my eyes off him. His magnetism captivated me. At least six foot four, he had the build and wide shoulders of a professional athlete. His eyes—his most outstanding feature—were large and golden, so luminous, they glowed. I'd never thought a man's hair could curl about his head as his did, yet look so right. In his younger days, his hair must have been blond, but now it was platinum, like the patina of coined silver. I'd gotten so sick of hearing everyone rave about John Marcus Vickery, thinking no one could be so wonderful, so handsome, so charismatic. Now that I'd met him, I thought they'd not even come close.

He and I were walking around the parsonage, me staring at him like an idiot, when the phone rang. "Rich?" I answered in surprise as I watched Dr. Vickery study the pictures hanging in the hallway. "I thought the caravan to Sarasota would've been long gone by now." It was five o'clock; they were to have left at three.

"Oh, some problem at the plant has delayed Maddox," Rich said. "So he's modified our route, gotten us rooms in Apalachicola, which we can make by nightfall."

"That's good, because this trip is going to be rougher on you than you think. And it's got to be hard on Godwin." Dr. Vickery paused outside the door and I smiled at him. He smiled back, and my heart fluttered.

"That's why I'm calling," Rich continued. "Those pain pills you told me about? I want to get the name of them so I can call for a prescription before we leave."

"Just take mine. I don't need them anymore."

"Oh, great—thanks! I'll run over and get them."

"Haven't you just gotten your cast off? And the van's packed full of stuff? Don't try to drive. I'll bring them to you."

"No, no, I can't let you do that—" he began, but I cut him off.

"Rich, I can be over there and back by the time you maneuver the van out of the garage. I'm on my way." And I hung up before he could argue.

Dr. Vickery had wandered to the music room, so I got the headache pills and put them in my jeans pocket. I hadn't had a chance for the leisurely bath and primping I'd hoped for. When Ben got here, I'd let him entertain our guest while I got dressed. Dinner was all ready, the table set, everything waiting to be reheated and served.

"Dr. Vickery?" I said, stepping inside the music room where he stood thumbing through the lesson books on the piano. "I've got to step out, but won't be gone but a minute."

He leaned against the piano, arms folded, and looked at me thoughtfully. When I showed him to the guest room, he'd taken off his coat and tie, unbuttoned the top button of his crisp white shirt and rolled up his sleeves. "Please call me John Marcus, Dean," he said. "And, can I ask you something?"

"Sure," I said.

"I overheard your phone conversation and two names I know, Rich and Godwin. You were talking to Rich Kingsley, weren't you?"

I nodded. Now he'd chastise me for championing Rich and Godwin, my estrangement from the church as a result. Instead, his face lit up. "And you're going to the St. Clair house?"

"Just briefly. They're going to Sarasota in a little while."

"Could I go with you? I haven't seen them in years, and I'd love to say hello."

"Oh! You want to go with me? Well, ah, sure—of course." Before I could think of a way to sneak back to my room and let Rich know, John Marcus Vickery took my elbow and ushered me down the hall.

"I hadn't planned on visiting anyone while I was here because you know how that goes; you see one family, others get their feelings hurt," he said as he steered me into the kitchen, his hand holding my elbow. "But Godwin and Rich—I need to see them, considering what they've been through lately."

"I'm sorry," I said when we got to my Toyota, "but my car's real small."

"No problem," John Marcus said, folding his long-limbed body into the passenger seat, turning his broad shoulders sideways. I winced as he tossed a handful of crumpled-up papers aside. The backseat was piled with newspapers for the recycling center that I'd been driving around for weeks.

When we pulled into the street, he looked at the church.

Everyone had cleared out now. "Does it seem strange coming back to a church you served—what?—twenty years ago?" I asked him.

"So you knew about my being here?" he asked, which surprised me. I always assumed well-known people knew how talked-about they were.

"Folks talk about you a lot. I've heard about you for a long time."

He laughed his magic laugh. "I hope you didn't believe half of it."

I smiled, then pointed to a Victorian house in the block next to the church. "Augusta's old house is a bed-and-breakfast now."

"Collie Ruth told me that you and Augusta had become friends. How nice for Augusta."

Again, he surprised me, and I glanced at him. I would've expected him to see it the other way, that my friendship with Maddox's wife would be good for Ben's career. I looked back to the street quickly before I ran into a tree. "Ah—yes. Augusta and I are good friends."

"She's a lovely young woman," he said. "What did they have, a boy or girl? I'm sure I heard but have forgotten."

"A boy, Gus. A perfect blend of Augusta and Maddox. He's adorable."

"He'd have to be, with two such attractive parents. Maddox is a fine man. His stability's a perfect balance for Augusta's . . . vivacity."

I smiled. "Vivacity, huh? What a diplomat you are. I've never met anyone as wild as Augusta. She and I have had some adventures."

He chuckled, shaking his head. "I can imagine. She's so full of life."

"I've never known anyone like her. Oh—I heard she baby-sat for your children when you lived here."

His eyes were on me as I turned onto Godwin and Rich's street. "Did she say that she earned her keep, since the kids were typical preachers' kids?"

"Actually, Augusta's never mentioned it to me. Babysitting for your kids, I mean."

"Really?" It was obvious he was taken aback. "They must've been worse than I thought! Now I'll wonder what they did. Ah, here we are, and I haven't had a chance to ask you about Rich and Godwin. You've recovered well after your attack, Dean, but what about Rich?"

"He's still pretty banged up; he has a neck brace, though the cast is off his arm. It was an awful thing."

"I'm sure it was. I'm anxious to get the inside story from you." We pulled up in front of the house, and I turned off the car. "The house looks the same," he said as he unfolded his long legs.

As usual, Rich and Godwin were in the back of the house, so I yelled out to Rich once we were inside the hallway. John Marcus tapped on the plain glass pane replacing the antique stained glass in the front door. "I heard a brick was thrown through here by a passing car," he said, shaking his head. "They've had it bad, haven't they?"

Before I could answer, Rich yelled for me to come on back, they were on the sunporch. When we walked on the porch and they saw who was with me, both Rich's and Godwin's mouths fell open. "Surprise," I said. "I brought you a visitor."

"Dr. Vickery!" Rich stammered, "I—I had no idea you were here."

Godwin rolled the wheelchair over to join them, his face alight. "John Marcus," he cried. "What a marvelous surprise!"

John Marcus hugged both men exuberantly, as though he weren't part of the establishment bringing charges against

Luke Shepherd for performing their unorthodox marriage. I
watched them as they talked, reminiscing about the old days
when Godwin's mother was alive and Dr. Vickery was a regular visitor. From their enthusiastic smiles, I could tell that,
like me, Godwin and Rich were under John Marcus Vickery's spell.

"Rich, get us a glass of wine. Let's toast the homecoming
and John Marcus's return," Godwin said after I'd given Rich
the pills I'd brought.

"Oh, no, no, Godwin," John Marcus said, holding up
his hands in protest, "you folks are trying to get on the road.
Dean and I aren't going to stay."

"Nonsense," Godwin insisted. "I refuse to leave till we
have one for the road."

Rich brought out a bottle of wine and four crystal
glasses, and we held our glasses high as Godwin toasted: "To
our dear friend John Marcus Vickery, who is back among
those who love him."

John Marcus added his own. "And to your trip to Sarasota. After all you've been through, may you find peace and
happiness there."

We were sitting and sipping our wine when the front
door opened, and Augusta called out to us. Rich answered,
"Augusta—come on back, girlfriend. Have we got a surprise
for you!"

When Augusta came on the porch, she couldn't see John
Marcus, sitting by Godwin, his chair blocked off from her
view. She was her old bohemian self today in tight jeans, high
black boots, and an Indian-print tunic.

"Look who's here," Rich said, getting up to greet her.
Thinking he meant me, Augusta looked my way and tossed
her head.

Grinning, she said to me, "So you're not going to wait at
home to kiss your esteemed visitor's royal ass, huh?"

Rich's eyes widened, and Godwin gasped when John Marcus Vickery stood and stepped forward so she could see him. "Augusta?" he said. "Is it really you?"

Since I'd known Augusta, I'd never seen her caught off guard and at a loss for words. Her face turned white and she stepped backward. If John Marcus had not caught her up in a bear hug, I think she would've fallen over. Unable to stop ourselves, Rich and I looked at each other and smirked at Augusta's blunder. Godwin's eyes twinkled but he pressed his lips together, too polite to laugh at her expense.

"What a pleasure to see you, Augusta—it's been such a long time," John Marcus said as he hugged her. Her arms hung limply by her side, her eyes stricken. "Dean and I were talking about you on the way over here," he continued, oblivious to her mortification.

"Talking about me?" Augusta repeated, turning her head my way. I met her gaze, grinning at her discomfort. Do her good to suffer for once from her foot-in-mouth disease.

Rich came to her rescue, pouring her a glass of wine. "Here you go," he said, guiding her to the wicker swing. John Marcus sat beside her and put his arm on the back of the swing. With wide blue eyes, she looked at him and downed the glass of wine like it was a shot of whiskey.

"I don't have any more wine chilled, Augusta," Rich said, struggling to keep his face expressionless. "Only thing I've got is sherry in the decanter."

"That'll do," Augusta said weakly.

"We've been reminiscing about the old days, Augusta," Godwin said as Rich poured everyone a round of sherry, "when Mother was alive and we enjoyed visits with our beloved minister here. You could count on John Marcus to be up on the latest art and books, as well as all the cultural events in the area. He treated Mother like an intelligent person with a master's degree, rather than a sick old lady."

"Back then we had a local theater group, Dean," John Marcus said, turning his head to me, "and Augusta made a perfect Annie-Get-Your-Gun. Weren't you a senior in high school then?" he continued, and Augusta knitted her brow. "You stole the show with 'Doing What Comes Naturally.' You two remember that?" he asked Rich and Godwin.

"Yes, of course," they both said, and I tilted my head, looking at Augusta reproachfully.

"You stinker," I said, "as much singing as we've done, you never told me that! Augusta has a great voice, John Marcus."

"Marvelous stage presence, too. I always told her she'd have made a good actress," he said.

We heard the front door slam and footsteps running down the hall, then Gus came in, breathless, his glasses askew. His knees were dirty and his jeans grass-stained. He'd been climbing the magnolia tree in front, one of his favorite ways to entertain himself at the St. Clair house.

"I didn't know Gus was with you, Augusta," Godwin said, raising his eyebrows. Ever since my and Rich's attack, Augusta had not let Gus play by himself in the yard. Evidently her gaffe had thrown her off so badly, she'd forgotten him.

"This is Gus?" John Marcus said, rising to his feet. "Come here, young man, and let me get a good look at you."

Gus ducked his head shyly, but he walked over to stand in front of his mother and John Marcus. "Gus," John Marcus said, "I'm a friend of Godwin's and Rich's and your mother's. My name is John Marcus Vickery." Holding his large hand out, he smiled down at Gus. Gus looked up at him, putting a small hand out. John Marcus shook it formally, then tousled Gus's hair.

"Oh, Lord, Gus," Augusta cried, "look at your hands. They're filthy! John Marcus, I'm so sorry."

"No problem." He grinned, brushing his hands together to shake the dirt off. "I know how little boys are, having had two myself. Tell me about yourself, Gus. What grade are you in?"

Augusta rose to her feet. "Let me get a washcloth for Gus's hands."

I watched as Gus basked in the attention he was getting from John Marcus, loving the way he kept looking over at Godwin and Rich for approval. He'd come out a lot from the supersensitive little boy I'd met two years ago. Godwin and Rich both laughed at Gus's description of his teacher. "She's *real* old," he said, "at least forty. And mean as a snake. Here's the way she looks at you." And he scowled, scrunching his face up and crossing his eyes, enjoying the laughs his performance was getting.

Augusta paused at the door before entering the sunporch, the washcloth in her hand. A tall plant was on my side of the door, so she didn't see me look her way. All of a sudden, I was glad the plant was there. Augusta froze and watched the scene, her face caught in a look I'd never seen before. Her eyes dark, she looked at John Marcus Vickery in such a way that a veil lifted from my eyes. A night came back to me, many months ago, when Augusta and I sat out under the stars and drank margaritas. I'd asked her suddenly, catching her off guard, if Maddox was the only man she'd ever loved. "No," she'd said dreamily, surprising me. "A high school boy?" I'd asked. "High school," she'd replied, "but no boy. A married man." "A teacher?" And she'd answered, "No. But, you're close. Someone like that."

I knew then, knew why Augusta had never told me about her relationship with the Vickerys; why she'd turned away when Godwin asked about it. Rich, too, had noticed, had tried to tell me that Augusta was hiding something, but I'd not listened. Now I knew why. It wasn't her faux pas that had her so flustered after all; it was the surprise of seeing John Marcus Vickery here. She'd been in love with him once, as only a young girl can yearn for a man so much older, so unattainable. Watching her, I wondered why she'd not told me about it. She'd had ample opportunity. Having met him, it was easy to see how anyone could fall for him. Good Lord, how he must have been back then, in his prime! Incredibly attractive now, in his late fifties, as a younger man he must've been a hunk. I'd've probably been in love with him, too.

Augusta went to Gus, taking his hands and washing them with the washcloth as he squirmed and protested. John Marcus tousled Gus's hair, then stood up, saying that he and I had to get back. Tall as Augusta was, John Marcus towered over her. She looked up at him, still holding Gus's hand in the wet washcloth. Her eyes moved over his face as though memorizing his features, the gold-flecked eyes, the curly hair, the full-lipped mouth. I drew my breath in and released it slowly. In a flash of insight, I realized what I'd seen on Augusta's face as she stood in the door frame, watching her son and this man. A blind man could see it—Rich and Godwin could, Gus could, and John Marcus could, if only he'd look down. It was as obvious as sunlight. And it wasn't what I'd thought a minute ago. Not that at all. By the way Augusta was looking at John Marcus, I knew for sure that she was still in love with him.

My discovery of Augusta's secret so unnerved me that it colored the rest of the evening. On the ride back to the parsonage, I was distracted and could barely drive. John Marcus had to repeat a question twice, asking me about Godwin and Rich's trip to Sarasota. When I felt his curious eyes on me, I pulled myself together. He was too sharp not to notice my state of mind. I needed time alone, a chance to mull over the shock of Augusta's love for this man, to think back over the things she'd said to me, bits and pieces of our talks. When I parked the car in the garage, John Marcus put a hand on my arm.

"Dean? What is it?"

"W-what do you mean?" I looked his way but turned my head, quickly.

"Did I do something to upset you?"

"You do something to upset me—oh! Oh, no, nothing like that," I gasped.

He looked at me reproachfully, turning his head sideways. "Come on. I thought we'd become friends. You can trust me, Dean. Didn't I just prove that to you?"

"Prove it to me?" I sounded like an idiot, but couldn't help it.

"You were nervous about taking me to Godwin's, afraid I'd say something about their marriage. But I wouldn't have done that, you know."

"Oh! I know."

"I want us to talk about all that, sometime this weekend. We'll have to find some time alone, okay?"

"Fat chance of that."

"I'll make the time. I want to explain my viewpoint to you, Dean. There are people in a position to help Luke Shepherd and Godwin and Rich, believe it or not."

I looked at him, and he returned my gaze calmly. No wonder Augusta loved this man! If I wasn't careful, I'd fall in love with him myself.

I needn't have worried about the rest of the evening; Ben took over. He wouldn't have noticed if I'd been stark naked and hanging from the chandelier. He was so taken with the idea of entertaining the great man that he fell all over himself, embarrassing me with his fawning. I gloated when John Marcus chided Ben for the elaborate dinner, the linen and china and candlelight. "Ben Lynch, I asked you specifically not to do this," he said, obviously distressed. "I wouldn't have had Dean go to this much trouble for anything!"

I threw Ben an I-told-you-so smirk but he outsmarted me, knowing I wouldn't dare contradict him in front of his superior. "I gave Dean your message," he said, rubbing his hands together as though equally distressed, "but you know how women are; no one tells them how to run their kitchen or entertain their guests."

When Ben turned, I gave him the finger behind his back. I detested his good-old-boy, you-know-how-the-little-woman-is act. Plus, he'd said just enough, as usual, so I couldn't call him a liar later. I could hear him: "Now, Dean, I said you didn't like anyone telling you how to run your kitchen, that's all." How would he like it if I'd told our guest the truth, that Ben had blackmailed me into the fancy dinner by threatening to have the church ladies do it? One of these days, his silver tongue would catch him in a trap of his own making.

The dinner offered a perfect time for me to study my guest and muse about Augusta's feelings for him. He and Ben talked church politics, although John Marcus often turned to me and begged my forgiveness. I ended the meal with my only claim to culinary fame, a multilayered lemon dessert I'd learned to make in home ec class. Since Augusta had taken me under her wing and educated me, I'd added new touches to my repertoire. The salad dressing with mixed baby greens was a balsamic and walnut vinaigrette; the dark-grain bread homemade; the coffee, freshly ground beans.

"I'm surprised that you're a gourmet cook in addition to your many other talents." John Marcus smiled at me when I poured him a cup of coffee from a brass French press. "I've heard not only about your music, but also your involvement in the church," he continued. "I wonder how you find time to do so much."

"Unlike your wife, Dr. Vickery, Dean doesn't work," Ben told him, holding his cup up. I resisted the urge to ask if he wanted the hot coffee in his cup or down his back.

John Marcus raised his eyebrows. "Really? Then I've been misinformed. I heard that you taught piano, as well as played for weddings and parties."

"You weren't misinformed," I said, stirring cream and sugar into my coffee.

Ben quickly corrected himself. "I meant, Dean doesn't work outside the home." Seeing the way the wind was blowing, he patted my shoulder. "Dean's very much in demand as a piano teacher. And as an entertainer, too."

John Marcus winked at me. "Miss Dean's quite an asset to you, Ben. I'm sure you realize that."

Was it my imagination, or was his voice reproachful? Ben's face flushed. "Oh, certainly!" he said, his voice loud and jovial.

"We don't give our wives enough credit. It's a lot to ask of a woman, the lives we lead."

"Absolutely," Ben agreed, sipping his coffee. "Matter of fact, I'm speaking at the South Alabama Ministers and Spouses Association next month. My topic is the challenge of being the wife—I mean, spouse—of a minister."

John Marcus tilted his head. "Looks like Dean would be more qualified to speak on that subject, doesn't it?"

Ben laughed, too heartily, I thought, then John Marcus asked, "Have you done a lot of research in that area, Ben?"

I lowered my eyes to my coffee cup. The question was perfectly innocent, but the implication seemed clear to me. Why was Ben, of all people, asked to speak on such a topic? Oblivious, Ben beamed, looking up from his second piece of dessert. "Oh, no, no, not at all. I assumed it's because of my book, the chapter on marriage," he said. "Did I mention that the publication date of my next book has been set?"

Dr. Vickery had written religious books as well, so the two of them went off on a discussion of publishing while I cleared the dishes. At first, Ben offered to help me, knowing I'd insist he entertain our guest while I cleaned up. It was a ruse; Ben wouldn't know the dishwasher from the disposal, and had never once cleaned up the kitchen.

When I finished, I went to turn the lights off in the dining room. Ben and Dr. Vickery were sitting in the stiff chairs in the living room, facing each other under the light of a marble-footed lamp on a table between them. Talking church politics, I assumed from Ben's rapt gaze as he stared up at his idol. John Marcus was telling some story, moving his large hands grandly as he did, and like Augusta earlier, I stood in the door frame watching. He threw his head back and laughed his golden laugh, and I marveled at the way he lit up a room. His voice boomed and I watched, mesmerized, unable to move.

Oh, dear God, Augusta, why couldn't you tell me about your love for this man? I wondered, with a jolt, if Maddox suspected. One bit of gossip that I'd dismissed scornfully was that Augusta had married Maddox on the rebound from a broken heart. How the tongues would wag if they knew the truth; that she'd loved a man as unattainable as God! It explained a lot, I realized—Augusta's underlying restlessness, her evasiveness, that wild part of her nature. Since I'd known her, it'd always seemed as though she were running from something, and now I knew what it was.

Since the guest room was taken, I slept in Ben's bed. In the darkness I snuggled up to him and he responded, obviously surprised. Since our falling-out over the marriage of Godwin and Rich, we'd been cold and distant; it had been weeks since we'd made love. But for some reason tonight, I drew him to me, my fingers over his lips to silence him before undoing his pajama bottoms. Lately I'd wondered if I loved Ben; if I felt anything but anger toward him anymore. As we came together, quickly and silently, our sounds muffled because of the presence of someone sleeping in the room next to us, I vowed that I'd be a better helpmate. Somehow, I'd put the hostility and resentment of these last few months behind me. Spent, I went to sleep, repeating that vow like a mantra.

Homecoming at First Methodist couldn't have been a clearer, more beautiful day, much to everyone's surprise, since a tropical storm was building to hurricane force in the Gulf. October was often as hot as the dog days of August here, but today a hint of autumn was in the crisp blue air. Although not cool, it was pleasant, with wispy fragments of clouds that held the bright sun at bay. A festive atmosphere put a smile on my face, in spite of my hurt pride. My vow to put my resentment of Ben behind me hadn't lasted out the morning.

After our lovemaking, I'd slept the sleep of the dead. When the watery sunlight woke me, I'd gotten up and bathed, singing as I splashed in the shower, feeling happy for the first time in months. I'd walked in from the bathroom, my hair tangled and wet on my shoulders, to find Ben dressed in his centennial costume. "You're looking good, Reverend," I'd said as he preened in front of the full-length mirror, tying a string tie and admiring himself in the black circuit-rider outfit Vanna Faye Bell had made him. He looked like he'd just stepped out of the sepia pages of the centennial scrapbook on display in the church's vestibule.

Draped in a towel, I stepped over to Ben's dressing table, where I'd put my brush, comb, and makeup. Ben's eyes met mine in the mirror, and I saw the look on his face. "Good

God almighty, Dean!" he gasped and I froze, expecting to see a huge hairy spider suspended over my head. Instead, Ben stumbled to the bedroom door so fast, I thought he was leaving. "Our door is not closed all the way and you're practically naked as a jaybird!"

I laughed as he pushed against the door. "Oh, for God's sake—you scared me to death. The door's closed, silly."

"It is now," he said, his jaw clenched. "What if Dr. Vickery had walked by?"

I stared at him in disbelief. "He wouldn't see anything he's not seen before." When his eyes widened, horrified, I sighed mightily. "Come on, Ben, he's got two kids. You think Beth Vickery conceived by the Holy Spirit?"

"Just hurry up and get your clothes on," he snapped.

"Ben," I laughed, "because you're so in awe of John Marcus Vickery, you can't see that he's very much a man. You've got him on a pedestal."

"Well, of course he's very much a man. He's very down-to-earth."

"That's not what I meant. He's one of the sexiest men I've ever seen."

Ben looked as though I'd blasphemed. "How can you say such a thing about a man of God?"

I smiled. "Bet half the women in his congregation say the same."

Swallowing convulsively, Ben grabbed my robe off the foot of the bed and threw it at me. I caught it, startled by his reaction. "Get your clothes on," he hissed. "Every time I think I've gotten you away from your raising, you prove me wrong. I would never make love with a guest in the house, but last night you gave me no choice. And now, talking dirty like some kind of—you-know-what!" And with that, he'd stormed out of the room, slamming the door behind him.

"It's not closed all the way," I'd yelled after him, then

muttered, "you pious bastard." Tears of humiliation stung my eyes, and I stumbled to a chair in the corner, where I'd laid out my homecoming costume. My hands shook as I picked up my underclothes, but I took a deep breath, determined not to let Ben rattle me. The vintage dress of ivory-colored muslin and lace that I'd borrowed from Augusta was lovelier than anything I'd ever worn, even my wedding dress, and I was going to wear it with pride, Ben be damned. I fixed my hair as Augusta had instructed, modeled after a painting that hung in the library of Mimosa Grove. She'd insisted I wear the heirloom featured in the painting: two silver-tipped Spanish hair combs, which I'd used to pull my hair back before twisting it high on my head. John Marcus bowed over my hand and complimented my appearance when I joined him and Ben for the walk over to the church, and I threw Ben an eat-your-heart-out look.

Although dressed casually in a denim shirt and khakis instead of a costume, John Marcus stood out in the crowd on the church grounds, head and shoulders above everyone there. As soon as he appeared, he was swarmed by admirers, and his booming voice and hearty laugh floated over the grounds like the woodsmoke in the air. The Methodist Men's Club had dug pits to barbecue whole pigs under the big oak trees. Music had been added to the day because Dr. Vickery had asked to hear me play, doing little to enhance my popularity with some of the church ladies. Although she grumbled and whined, Lorraine Bullock finally got off her rear and lined up performances all day. The handbell choir was playing on the front portico of the church, fifty bells caroling out "Onward Christian Soldiers" high over the crowded church grounds.

For the homecoming visitors who didn't like barbecued pig, my UMW Circle, the Lilies of the Field, had set up a hot-dog booth. Before taking my scheduled time working there, I wandered around the transformed church grounds and wished Augusta were there. In spite of her cynicism, she'd have to admit it was impressive, and Gus would have loved it. With a pang, I knew Godwin and Rich would have, too, though their presence would have caused an uproar. I spotted Eunice and Esther with Ben, hanging on to his every word. They saw me and nudged each other, turning up their noses. Eunice—or was it Esther?—hobbled on her cane, her hand like a claw clutching Ben's sleeve. I had a childish urge to stick my tongue out at them, the sour-faced old biddies.

One of our members had a white carriage pulled by two horses, offering rides through town, and people stood in a long line for a ride. Costumed members of our youth group were serving as guides, standing beside the driver and reciting the town's history. I waved at the teenaged guides waiting for their turn and they waved back, smiling. I'd been so rejected and snubbed by the church lately that any show of acceptance touched me.

The booths and demonstrations were set up under the branches of the big oaks on the church grounds. For the children, there were pony rides and old-timey games, croquet and horseshoes and badminton. The demonstrations featured skills and crafts employed in making things for the church: candle making, weaving the altar cloths, carving the altar rails. One section of the church yard was roped off for the making of cane syrup, with stacks of purple sugarcane, a boiling vat of syrup that smelled heavenly, and a mule-drawn mill, where the blindered mule walked round and round in a circle, hooked up to a contraption that extracted the juice from the cane, once it was peeled and tossed in by costume-clad members of the men's club. Other food booths offered molasses cookies, saltwater taffy, fried apple and shoofly pies. Reluctantly, I made my way to the Lilies of the Field hot-dog booth.

Janice and her crew had fixed up a booth from some

past event, decorated to look like an old ballpark cart. I was in the serving line between my nemeses Sylvia Whiney-Hiney and Vanna Faye Bell. As usual, Vanna Faye stood out, looking like a Madame Alexander Doll in a costume of pink satin, all bustled and beribboned and beaded. Perched sideways on her head was a little hat tied with pink ribbons under her chin and topped with ostrich feathers that fluttered in the breeze. Sylvia, her usual tacky self in a brown calico dress, plucked wieners off a smoking grill with a pair of tongs. I closed my eyes and let out a deep breath. This was going to be a long hour.

"Oh, hello, Dean," Vanna Faye said. "You look real pretty in that dress," she added, sounding surprised. "Family heirloom?"

"Nope. Borrowed from Augusta," I muttered, tying on my apron.

"I guess Augusta'll be here today," she breathed, fluttering her eyelashes. "I saw her a little while ago, headed this way."

I shook my head as I unwrapped a stack of buns from foil. "Wasn't her. She's out of town."

"But . . ." Vanna Faye frowned. "I know it was Augusta! In that white station wagon of hers."

"It's out of town, too," I told her, rather shortly.

Sylvia Whiney-Hiney actually seemed happy to see me, which surprised me until I saw that she was waiting to get in a dig. "Oh, there you are, Dean," she whined. "I told everybody not to worry, that you'd surely not let us down again."

I smiled sweetly at her. "I wouldn't miss this, Sylvia. Someone's gotta make sure you don't roast the wrong wienie."

We were so busy at the booth that the time flew by. Working feverishly and mindlessly was what I craved before my upcoming performance so I wouldn't get nervous. I wished this part of the centennial would go on forever, and I could stand here until the last trumpet blew for judgment day. Then I wouldn't have to think about my performance, especially about singing with John Marcus in the audience.

John Marcus Vickery. As though my thoughts conjured him, I looked up and into his golden-brown eyes. For a moment I blinked stupidly through the smoke from the grill.

"Even the entertainment has to sell hot dogs, huh?" he said, eyes shining.

I smiled. "No rest for the weary. How about a hot dog?"

"Sure. Burn me one."

"Dr. Vickery!" Vanna Faye and Sylvia cried at the same time. "What are you doing at *our* booth?" Sylvia yelped, leaning over, almost knocking me out of the way.

He eyed her calmly. "Getting a hot dog, same as everybody else."

"Surely you'd rather have some of our good barbecue, Dr. Vickery," Vanna Faye said, trying to elbow in front of Sylvia.

"Oh, don't worry, I'll get some barbecue, too." He laughed his booming laugh. "You ladies going to sell me a hot dog or not?"

Sylvia rejected several burnt wieners before finding the largest one just for him, then Vanna Faye double-doused it with mustard. I rolled my eyes, and John Marcus winked at me. "About time for you to perform, isn't it?" he asked me.

Before I could answer, Vanna Faye leaned toward him. "Oh, no, Dr. Vickery. I don't sing until later this afternoon. You'll be there, won't you? Because I'm singing 'I'll Fly Away' especially for you."

John Marcus met my eyes, and I looked away before I laughed out loud. A brisk breeze had blown up and the feathers in Vanna Faye's hat were fluttering wildly, making it look like she was about to take off.

"I wouldn't miss it, Vanna Faye," he said. "When did

you say you were scheduled to perform, Dean?" he tried again.

"When I finish my shift," I told him.

"Leave your post now, let these sweet ladies finish for you," he said, biting into the hot dog, then jumping back when a stream of mustard shot out.

"You got carried away with the mustard, Vanna Faye," I said wryly, and John Marcus laughed.

"Either that, or I didn't jump far enough," he said, motioning to a big glob of mustard on the leg of his khakis. Vanna Faye gasped, and Sylvia glared at her. Both of them almost pushed each other over grabbing a paper towel, but John Marcus winked at me again.

"Since I've got to wear these all day, maybe you'd better take me to your laundry room, Dean, to see if we can get it out," he said. Vanna Faye and Sylvia began tugging at their aprons, telling me to stay right there, that they'd be happy to help dear Dr. Vickery get the mustard stain out of his britches. But I outsmarted them, ducking out of the booth quickly, my apron still on.

"I'm sure you two can manage without me," I called back to them, safely outside the booth, and hurried away with John Marcus as they stood watching me, openmouthed. He tossed the mustard-soaked hot dog into the first trash can we came to, and I took off my apron.

"Thank you for rescuing me," I said when we escaped to the parsonage, closing the door behind us. "Even though you ruined your pants. Mustard won't come out, you know. Not that cheap yellow stuff."

"I have another pair of khakis with me. I'll change, and no one will know the difference."

I sank into a large stuffed chair in the den while John Marcus changed. When he returned, he walked past me to the laundry room and I watched in amazement as he searched my laundry bottles until he found the stain-remover. He squirted some on the mustard stain, laid the pants on the sink, and returned to the den, smiling. "What?" he asked, seeing the look I gave him.

"I can't believe you did that. Ben doesn't even know where the washing machine is."

He chuckled and sat across from me, in Ben's leather recliner. "Dean, my wife's either been in school or working our entire married life, so I've had to do for myself. Besides, I don't see why Beth should do something for me that I'm perfectly capable of doing myself."

"You're a remarkable man," I said boldly, thinking to myself, No wonder, Augusta.

"And you are perfectly delightful, Dean. It's been a pleasure getting to know you."

I blushed, tilting my head. "I can't wait to meet Beth. She must be a wonderful woman." As well as a lucky one, I thought.

He nodded. "Beth's great. I couldn't get along without her. I'm sure Ben feels the same way about you."

I forced a smile, but didn't tell him that I doubted it. "Dean?" John Marcus said. "I conspired to get you away so we could have our talk—" Both of us jumped when the shrill ring of the phone interrupted him. Automatically, I stood and started toward the kitchen. "Somebody wanting to know what time the barbecue's served, I'll bet," I said over my shoulder. John Marcus held up his hand to stop me.

"Let your answering machine pick it up," he said. "You need to learn the tricks of the trade. It's the only way to survive this crazy life you got yourself into."

We were quiet as the recorder came on, then I looked at him in surprise. "That's Maddox," I gasped. All he'd said was my name, but I'd know that honeyed voice of his anywhere. "Oh, God, something's happened to Rich or Godwin!" I said.

I ran into the kitchen and grabbed the receiver, cutting Maddox off in mid-sentence. John Marcus came and stood beside me, frowning in concern, his hands on his hips. "Maddox," I cried. "What is it?"

"Playing hooky from homecoming, huh?" he said.

"No, no," I said, breathless, "I just came over for . . . something. What's going on?"

"Calm down," he chuckled. "Nothing's wrong. Unless you count both Ollie and Gus getting carsick and puking from Apalachicola to Sarasota."

"Oh, Lord." I smiled, and John Marcus relaxed, smiling back at me.

"If it weren't both boy and dog, I'd think that Gus got his mother's bug, but seems to be just car sickness. We're here now; everyone's fine, safely at Godwin and Rich's friends' guest house. Which is absolutely perfect, by the way. Great situation for them."

"Tell them Eunice and Esther are at their place, so be glad they're not. But wait a minute—Gus got Augusta's bug? She throw up the whole trip, too?"

"That's why I'm calling, Dean. To leave a message, ask you to check on her."

"Check on her? Where is she?"

"She hasn't called you?"

"No. Well, not that I know of. I see the message light blinking, so maybe she has."

"She's at Mimosa Grove. We started to leave yesterday afternoon, and Augusta had to stay home. Some kind of twenty-four-hour puke bug; she spent last night doing just that."

"Oh, no," I groaned. "She must be even sicker with disappointment, missing the trip. But—who drove her car?"

"Carl Hernandez, my foreman. He and Theresa have relatives in Sarasota, so I bribed them into going for a visit. He drove my car down, and Rich and Celeste rode with them.

Me, Gus, and Godwin went in the van. Worked out fine, except for Celeste trying to convert Carl and Theresa to her New Age bullshit."

"Bet that was a hoot. Does that mean you ride back with her Monday?"

"Thank God for adultery—she's coming back with Simms," he chuckled. "It'll just be Gus and me with Carl and Theresa, who's teaching Gus Spanish, so guess they'll be *hablo*ing *español* all the way."

"Sounds like it's all worked out in spite of everything. Tell everyone hello, and I'll check on Augusta."

"Knew I could count on you, Miss Bean. See you Monday."

I looked at John Marcus as I hung up and pressed the Play button for the messages. "Guess you got the gist of that," I said, and he nodded. None of the messages were from Augusta. Frowning, I dialed her number and sighed with relief when she answered, her voice weak and shaky. "Augusta? You sound like pure-tee hell."

"Just a barf bug." She sighed, loud. "I told Maddox not to call you."

"I'm glad he did. Soon as I get through here, I'll come see about you."

"Oh, no, you won't," she said emphatically. "All you need is to throw up before the big homecoming service tomorrow, though that might be appropriate. Aren't you playing your dulcimer at church?"

"Nope. This afternoon. Matter of fact, in about five minutes."

"Then get on over there and don't worry about me. I'm okay now. Matter of fact, I'm actually enjoying having time alone to recuperate."

"I'll come see about you later. Bring you some broth or something."

"Don't you dare come out here! I wouldn't wish this bug on Saddam Hussein, much less my best friend."

"Guess you're right. But I'll call and check on you, okay?"

"No way. About the time I get off to sleep, you'll call. I'll call if I need you, okay? You've got your own thing going on, and I'm wrapped in a quilt and loving having some quiet time. So let's just leave it that way."

"Well, okay," I said. "If you're sure."

"John Marcus isn't there, is he?" she said, and I looked over at him. He was leaning against the kitchen cabinet watching me, following my conversation with Augusta.

"Yeah, he's right here," I said, and he raised his eyebrows in surprise.

"Why don't you go to the church, get ready for your thing, and let me talk to him?" Augusta said. "I need to apologize for acting like such a fool when I saw him yesterday."

"Uh-huh," I agreed. "And me and you need to talk as soon as all this is over."

She sighed. "Yeah, I know. You're on to me, right?"

"Hmmm . . . I've figured some stuff out." I couldn't say anything with John Marcus listening.

There was a silence on her end of the line. "I should've told you, Dean. And I will. I'll tell you all about it. But for now, go on to the church and let me talk to him, okay?"

"Okay. But call me if you need me." I held the phone out to John Marcus and he took it, puzzled.

"Augusta!" he said, his voice filling the room. "What's this about you being sick?" He listened for a minute, then held the receiver down. "Sorry, Dean. Augusta says I have to demand that you go while she apologizes to me. For what, I don't know." I nodded and started toward the door. "Don't you start without me—I won't be but a minute," he called out, and I waved good-bye. I had no idea what Augusta would say to him, but I'd bet the ranch on one thing. She wouldn't reveal what she'd just acknowledged to me: her long-secret love for him.

Augusta's feelings for John Marcus Vickery haunted me as I played the old songs, plaintive with heartbreak and loss. Set up on the front portico of the church, I started out with "Down in the Valley," marveling at the words of the second verse, which described the lover in a castle, forty feet high, watching her loved one ride by. Augusta on the top floor of Mimosa Grove, looking out over the vista of the old plantation, Holderfield land as far as the eye could see. All of it hers, yet empty without the man she truly loved. No doubt I was overly romanticizing the whole thing, Augusta's love for the man of God. Why I'd suddenly turned into such a romantic was beyond me, the realist whom life had taught better. Every time I'd looked at life through rose-colored glasses, reality had come along and snatched them away.

I spotted John Marcus in the crowd, hair gleaming like moon-glow in the afternoon sun. Ben was on one side of his idol, then Vanna Faye pushed through the crowd to get to his other side, her ostrich feathers fluttering in the wind. Some mischief made me lean to the microphone and say, "I'd like to dedicate my next song to our honored guest, Dr. John Marcus Vickery." I should've included Ben and would have, had he not humiliated me this morning. Let him suffer a little, be embarrassed that he was excluded. I'd grown tired of his endless taunts about my background. Where was the disgrace, being born into a situation I had no control over?

After I finished "Precious Memories," I read a prepared announcement. "I've been asked to remind everyone of the special service coming up. At four today, we will close our celebration here. Then all of you are invited to join us at Lake Crystal, by the new pavilion. At sunset, Dr. Vickery will honor us with one of his famous Galilean messages by the water's edge, in the tradition of Jesus' sermons on the Sea of Galilee." I paused as the enthusiastic applause died down. "Afterward, stay for an old-fashioned picnic. We'll finish up before dark so everyone can rest up for our special service tomorrow at eleven." I looked out over the audience, meeting John Marcus's eye. "In honor of the Galilean service, how about joining me in singing 'Shall We Gather at the River?'"

At Lake Crystal, the approaching storm was evident. A wind rippled the dark water and caused the fronds of the palm trees and the willows fringing the lake to dip and sway. I was surprised to see so many people at the water's edge, sitting on blankets or lawn chairs or standing in clusters of threes and fours. Ben was under the pavilion with his usual flock of admirers, Bob and Noreen Harris, Janice and Mike Johnson, Vanna Faye and Collie Ruth, and I went to join them. Everyone had changed from costumes to picnic clothes, jeans and T-shirts and windbreakers. After greeting them I tugged at Ben's sleeve. "Did everything work out?" I whispered. Setting up the Galilean service had been a pain; he'd had to find someone not only willing to row John Marcus, but also skilled enough to manage the rowboat while he stood in it.

Ben grinned jovially for the benefit of his admirers. "You don't have to whisper, Dean, all these folks are in on the plans." Part of the appeal of the Galilean service was the element of surprise; the sudden appearance of the wooden boat with two costumed characters in it. Most of the people here had never attended a Galilean service, but they'd heard that Dr. Vickery was famous for them, and anticipation crackled like the ozone in the heavy air.

"Dr. Brandon is playing the role of Simon Peter," Janice Johnson told me. Janice was one of the church ladies whose

attitude toward me hadn't changed in spite of the controversy, which I suspected had more to do with self-absorption
than tolerance. "He was a coxswain at Tulane," she added.

Noreen Harris gasped. "Surely not Dr. Brandon! He
seems like such a nice young man."

Bob Harris laughed sheepishly. "Honey, Janice means he
was the steersman of the rowing team, so he can manage the
boat."

"Oh," Noreen said lamely.

"Think the wind'll be a problem?" Mike Johnson
asked Ben.

Ben wagged his head, frowning. "Most certainly. But
Chuck swears he won't let the boat topple, no matter how
rough it gets."

When Ben left to take his place, I joined the crowds
down at the water's edge. The Galilean service was more
moving and impressive than I'd expected. Speaking into a
hand mike, Ben set the scene, describing the Sea of Galilee
and the crucial part it played in the ministry of Jesus, for it
was beside the Galilean Sea that He called His disciples to be
fishers of men. It was the Sea of Galilee that He commanded
to be still, when a tempest blew up and frightened the disciples. It was on that same sea that He walked toward them on
the turbulent waters, the night after the miracle of the loaves
and fishes. "The multitudes following Jesus were so great,"
he said, "that it was necessary for Jesus to speak to them
from a boat, as they gathered on the shore. From there he
taught some of his most memorable parables, among them
the parable of the sower and the seed, the hidden treasure,
and the pearl of great price."

A murmur swept over the crowd when a boat carrying
two men, one in a dark robe and the other in white, could be
seen coming around the bend in the lake, heading our way.
The small dark-robed man in front was rowing, and the

larger man clothed in white sat behind him, bathed in the glorious light of the setting sun. Even though I knew they were coming, I still got goose bumps. Dr. Brandon, in the role of the fisherman Simon Peter, rowed to the edge of the shore and jumped out to hold the boat still while Dr. Vickery stood up and held his hand high in greeting. As Chuck Brandon stood in the heavy robe, the cold water up to his waist, I understood why they'd had trouble persuading someone to play Simon Peter.

The white hood of the loosely draped robe fell from Dr. Vickery's head, and a sigh went up from the women in the crowd. With his thick curly hair tossed by the wind and the sunset bathing him in golden-red light, he was magnificent. I was thankful for the virus that had laid Augusta low, for if she'd seen him like this, she might have jumped in after him. Soon I forgot Augusta; forgot my surroundings as I lost myself in the magnetism of John Marcus Vickery as he told Jesus' parable of the mustard seed.

When the stories were over, John Marcus held his hand high and said, "All of you who have ears to hear, hear the words of the parables." Chuck Brandon, soaked with lake water, climbed back into the boat, causing it to lurch to one side, but John Marcus stood firm. Even more surprising, he stood as Chuck rowed the boat away from the shore, when the only sound breaking the hushed silence was the soft swishing of the oars through the dark waters. He didn't sit until the boat began to turn the bend in the lake, and Ben clicked on the microphone to pronounce the benediction. The sun had set and darkness was enveloping the lake, even though I'd not noticed it until now.

The spell lasted as the crowd broke up, people speaking to one another in hushed whispers as they made their way to the pavilion. The plan was that Dr. Vickery wouldn't return to the picnic. He'd go back to the parsonage and rest up for the big sermon tomorrow. The church ladies had left him a picnic basket on my kitchen table.

The planning committee outdid themselves when it came to serving up supper for so many, almost like the miracle of the loaves and fishes. Mammoth-sized coolers of ice held soft drinks, and a booth had been added to hand out the picnic suppers. It went so smoothly that spirits were high, everyone laughing and talking and stuffing themselves on barbecue sandwiches. Such a large crowd was squeezed around the picnic table where Ben was eating his supper that I couldn't have found a place if I'd wanted to. Even so, I felt absurdly slighted when I went for a Diet Coke, then stood next to the table, and no one there, including Ben, suggested I join them. All eyes on Ben, the church members surrounding him continued to laugh and talk, pointedly ignoring me.

My face burning, I slipped away from the pavilion without telling anyone I was leaving. If Ben were to miss me, I hoped he'd think I fell in the lake. I'd slip back to the house and have some quiet time. I wouldn't go to the master bedroom, but to the music room, sleeping on a pallet on the floor. Ben would be furious, but I was still hurting from his humiliating words this morning and couldn't face him.

The wind had really whipped up now, and the smell of rain was in the dark night air. The church's worst fear for tomorrow was bad weather, but it was obvious that we were in for it. As I pulled my car onto the highway leading back to town, I turned the radio on to catch the weather. Sure enough, the tropical storm was building to hurricane force, heading our way through the night. I thought about Augusta, sick and alone in that big old house, and wondered if I should go see about her. Turning my car to the left, I told myself I'd just ride by, see if any lights were on. If she was up, I'd stop by and ask if she needed anything. I didn't want her bug, but neither did I want to worry about her all night.

The road to Mimosa Grove led me past Carl and
Theresa Hernandez's place, about half a mile from the main
gates. For the first time, it hit me that Augusta'd been truly
alone without Theresa and Carl nearby. As I passed their
house, I craned my neck to look at it, a historic house that
had been part of the Holderfield plantation at one time. Slowing down and looking, I almost missed seeing a car pull out
of the driveway of Mimosa Grove. The car turned to the
right, onto the highway that led back to town, its headlights
cutting through the darkness of the blustery night.

I knew immediately whose car it was, for it had been
parked in my driveway since yesterday. John Marcus Vickery's black Lincoln, with its Leon County license plate! I
speeded up as I turned into the driveway to Mimosa Grove,
my hands trembling on the wheel. Obviously, he'd been at
our house alone and Augusta had called, needing me. She
must have gotten really sick—you could get dehydrated
quickly with a stomach virus. I could kick myself for listening to her, not checking on her sooner.

No lights were on when I pulled in front of the house, so
I turned my car around to follow the Lincoln back to town,
truly alarmed now. What if John Marcus had Augusta in the
car with him, taking her to the emergency room? But as I drove
through the circular drive, I saw a light on after all. Maybe
Augusta was still here and John Marcus was going back to get
me or something. It wouldn't take but a minute to find out.

I heard footsteps when I rang the doorbell and stood
waiting in the cold wind, pulling my light sweater closer. The
door flew open and Augusta stood there, dressed in a long
white nightgown and robe. She was barefoot and her hair
was tousled, but her eyes were bright and shining. As soon as
she saw it was me, her face froze. "Dean! What are you doing
here?" She looked past me, out into the gloom of the night.

"What am I doing here? Checking up on you," I said.

"And you can stop looking down the driveway. John Marcus has already gone."

"You met his car as you came in?" she asked, looking stricken.

"Of course. How'd you lure him out here, tell him you were deathly ill? Even though it was obviously effective, it's not very romantic. And you half-dressed, nothing but a night-gown on? As my granny used to say, in your shimmy-tail?"

When she shrugged nonchalantly, I sighed. "God, you're so transparent, Augusta! How'd you get him to come in? He was standing right there by the phone when you *insisted* I not come out here because I might catch your bug. Guess he thought you didn't care if he did or not."

"He knows better than that."

"Oh, really? What'd you do, lure him out here to profess your undying love? Tell him you've carried a torch for him since you were—what?—sixteen, seventeen years old?"

"Even younger than that," she said simply.

"You *didn't* tell him, did you? Surely you didn't tell him how you feel about him!" I cried, and Augusta reached out for my hand.

"Why don't you come in, Dean? We need to talk."

"Oh, no," I said. "I'm not exposing myself to your nasty bug. John Marcus can puke if he wants to from gallantly rushing out here, but I'm not."

She smiled calmly. "You're not going to catch anything. Not from me you're not."

"How do you know? You don't know for sure that you're over it. When's the last time you threw up?"

"About ten years ago, when I was pregnant with Gus."

I stared at her, stunned, as it hit me. "You made it up? You were faking being sick?"

She nodded and I watched, dumbfounded. "But—why? Why'd you do that, after planning the trip to Sarasota?"

"I hated that, I really did. Until I remembered the Hernandezes' having relatives there, then it worked out beautifully. Once I saw John Marcus, I couldn't leave here, don't you see? It had been such a long time since I'd seen him."

I put my hands over my eyes. "You're right," I whispered. "I'd better come in."

Augusta led me back to the sun room, where the lights were out but candles flickered on the rattan coffee table. "The electricity's off?" I asked, stumbling to the sofa and sitting down. "That's how you got John Marcus out here, pretending you were scared of the dark?"

"The power's on; I just like candlelight better. More romantic. Let me get you a glass of wine. I just opened a new bottle," Augusta said.

I blinked as I looked at the coffee table. Next to the candles were two wineglasses and one empty wine bottle. The antique wine cooler of heavy silver, engraved with the Holderfield crest, held a bottle of chilled wine, water beaded on the dark green sides. When I saw Augusta getting a wineglass from the corner cabinet, I motioned to the glasses on the table. "No need. There are two glasses here."

"Those have been used," she said, pouring wine into the glass she'd just brought over, handing it to me.

I nodded. "Ah! You lured him out here and got him drunk, huh?"

Augusta sipped her wine before answering me. "I didn't lure anyone. Wake up and smell the coffee. John Marcus and I arranged this when we talked on the phone. Drink your wine. You're going to need it."

Obeying her blindly, I turned up the wineglass. Smiling mysteriously, Augusta refilled her glass, and sat beside me.

"Okay, I can accept that," I said. "When we talked this morning, you asked John Marcus to come out here after he left the lake, right?" She nodded, and I thought about it. "Just tell me this, Augusta. Did you tell him that you're in love with him?"

Her eyes met mine and didn't waver. "I didn't have to tell him; he knows it. He's known it for years. Since I was fourteen years old."

I drank more of my wine, slower this time. "I'm so stupid," I admitted, "thinking he didn't know. He's too perceptive for that, isn't he?"

"You're not stupid," she said softly. "Just unworldly. In spite of a rough beginning, your life's been sheltered. You pride yourself on your backwoods savvy, but you're naive when it comes to men and women. Isn't Ben the only man you've ever slept with?"

I looked at her sheepishly. "Well . . . there was the guy I was pinned to all through college. Though Ben doesn't know."

"You've never told me about him, either," Augusta said. "Why didn't you marry him?"

"We were going to, but I went back to my hometown to direct the music for my church. And there I met Ben."

"It's unbelievable that we never talked about any of this, isn't it?"

"Yeah," I said. "I had no idea that you loved someone else, Augusta. Though I always felt you were hiding something from me."

Augusta stared at a flickering candle. It gave off the scent of sweet oranges, the fragrance floating in the air like smoke. "I'll confess, Dean. The reason I came to the reception for you and Ben your first Sunday afternoon? I'd heard about you and made up my mind to meet you. If things had been different and I'd married John Marcus, you were how it would have been for me."

"No way I can ever imagine you as a preacher's wife," I said with a smile. "But I have to tell you something that came to me after I realized you loved him."

Augusta poured herself another glass of wine and watched me as she sipped it. She was more serious than I'd ever seen her, her eyes dark and solemn in the yellow glow of the candles. "Okay," she said simply.

"Even though you loved a man who was unattainable, you didn't let it ruin your life. I admired the way you'd never acted on that secret love."

Augusta put her head down in her hands and closed her eyes. "Jesus Christ, Dean. Jesus H. Christ!"

"*What?*"

She raised her head, her eyes darker now, with something in them that I couldn't understand, that scared me. "You just don't get it, do you?"

"Don't get what?"

"John Marcus and me. Me and John Marcus. We're not talking about a schoolgirl crush here, we're talking about the only man I've ever loved! Ever. I love him so much I can't even tell you. I'd die for him, Dean, I swear to God. I wouldn't die for Maddox, but I'd die for John Marcus. Right now, if I had to."

I stared at her in alarm, knowing then what the strange light in her eye was. It was obsession. "Don't say that, Augusta."

"I mean it. So help me, God, I do."

"But . . . Maddox, Augusta! What about Maddox?"

She shrugged. "I *do* love Maddox, in a lot of ways. Not like John Marcus, but a really deep affection. If I could've loved anyone else, it'd have been Maddox Holderfield. God knows I've tried. I've convinced myself at times that I did; that I'd gotten over John Marcus and loved Maddox instead. I wanted to have his child, thinking that would do it. But nothing—nothing, I tell you—that I've done has made me stop loving John Marcus. If I could've taken a knife and carved him out of my heart, I would have." She smiled wryly. "Hey, that'd make a good country song, wouldn't it?"

"Maddox doesn't know this, does he?"

Again she shrugged. "Oh, he's suspected there was someone, but . . . no. I've never told him anything specific. Men tend to believe what they want to believe."

"You sure fooled me," I told her. "Since I've known you, I've envied your relationship with Maddox."

"Next to my daddy, Maddox's the best man I've ever known. I've tried so hard to love him, to be happy with him."

I was saddened for Maddox, a man I'd come to appreciate as a good friend. I couldn't stand the thought of him being hurt, loving Augusta all these years when she couldn't love him back. "It explains a lot, of course," I said, my voice low. "Like you leaving him at Seaside that time."

She nodded, her eyes lowered. "There have been many times when I've tried to run away from my feelings for John Marcus—run away from Maddox, from Gus, from everything, I've been so miserable. And other times, I've run from Maddox to John Marcus, times when I couldn't go another day without seeing him."

I felt as though my breath had been knocked out of me. "You had an *affair* with John Marcus Vickery?"

Augusta stared at me. "An *affair*? An affair is cheap and tawdry. What we have is not anything like that."

"What you have—"

"What do you think? That I've had a schoolgirl fucking crush on him all these years, that I've pined away for him in secret?"

"Actually, that's . . . exactly what I thought," I admitted.

"Then you're much, much more naive than I imagined!"

"I—I—guess I am," I stammered.

"Listen to me," Augusta said. "John Marcus Vickery was my first. The first man I ever had."

"The first? When you were in high school? Please tell me you weren't a high school girl, Augusta."

"No. I wasn't in high school."

"Thank God. I was afraid—"

"I was fourteen, Dean—fourteen years old. Barely."

"Oh, no. Oh, Jesus, no."

"I baby-sat for his children, and his wife was getting her doctorate, so she was gone half the time. The first time we made love, I'd turned fourteen the week before."

"Augusta, no!" I cried out. "Then . . . that wasn't love, that was just sex! Screwing, fucking, fornicating, whatever you call it, but not *love*. He molested you! No wonder you're obsessed with him. Did he force you?"

Augusta hooted. "Hardly."

"Even so, he was an adult and you were a child. A *child*! I've been thinking he's so wonderful, but I've been wrong. Completely, utterly, totally wrong. What you're telling me makes me sick!"

"Don't say that. Please don't say that."

"Augusta—listen to yourself!" I shouted. "You've got a child now. Do you want someone taking advantage of Gus like that? John Marcus should be reported. I've got a good mind to tell everyone—"

"You can't do that," she wailed. "It'd kill me if you did. I should never have told you."

I stared at her, trying to control myself. "Maybe you shouldn't have."

"Promise me you won't say anything. Please! Promise me."

I shook my head, glaring at her. "I can't make a promise like that. All those people, thinking he's God or something. If only they knew!"

Augusta began to cry and grabbed my arm, her nails digging in through my sweater. "Okay, I'll tell you something I hadn't planned on telling you. So you'll know it's not—like that, like you said. Come on, sit back down." But I shook my head stubbornly and folded my arms. "Listen to me, Dean. You love me, don't you? You love me and want me to be happy, don't you?"

I sighed, closing my eyes. "You know I do."

"John Marcus and I have stayed away from each other for years. I swear it. Since Gus came, I've been determined to be a good mother, to work things out with Maddox. John Marcus has his precious calling to God, which he wouldn't give up for me. He was willing to give up his wife for me, but not God, and I sure as hell can't compete with Him. But when I saw him again, I knew I still loved him; that I couldn't live without him. I made him come out tonight, Dean, to see if he feels the same way. And he does! So, we're going to find a way to be together, finally. We can't be apart anymore."

I shook my head. "That's really rich, Augusta. He's going to be a bishop, and somehow I can't see you as a bishop's wife. Though actually, that's something you won't have to worry about, because he won't get elected if he's involved in a scandal. If he were to leave his wife for another woman, his career would be over in the Methodist church."

"None of that means anything to him anymore," Augusta said, and her face glowed. "We're going away together. We'll leave Florida, go to Mexico or somewhere, and finally, we'll be together. Like we should've been all along."

I shook my head, softening toward her. "Oh, Augusta, honey. I saw him at sunset tonight, giving the most unbelievable sermon. I wish I could believe that, that he'd give it all up for love of you. But I don't. I don't believe it for a minute."

But she smiled at me, her face aglow and her eyes shining in the candlelight. "I want you to go on home now. Then I want you to get up in the morning and go to church and listen to John Marcus's homecoming sermon. I'll be there, too. I told him tonight that I'm going to slip in, sit in the very back, and listen to it, too. I want to hear it, and I want you to, Dean. You know why? Because it'll be the last sermon anyone will ever hear John Marcus Vickery, the most famous preacher in Florida, preach."

Thirteen

I DON'T KNOW HOW I got through the homecoming service the next day. I got home late from Augusta's, driving carefully in the misty rain and blowing wind, my mind in a turmoil. I parked my car and stumbled out. John Marcus's sleek black Lincoln was parked next to Ben's blue Buick, with clergy stickers on both cars, and I stared at them before making my way into the dark house. Spent and exhausted, I was too tired to understand what had happened tonight. Augusta's confession about her affair—which was all it was, no matter what she said—with John Marcus had shaken me to the core. I felt disillusioned and cynical, bitter about my naivete. When I'd joined the church at age twelve, I'd thought it was my salvation, a refuge from the turmoil of my sorry childhood. Now it was tarnished, as sordid as everything else in my life. The rose-colored glasses had been yanked from my eyes once again.

The light was out in the guest room, but I stood outside the door, fighting an urge to bang on it and yell at John Marcus, to tell him that I knew the truth about him. He was nothing but a child molester, even if Augusta at fourteen was precocious and irresistible. He'd not only been an adult but also a man of God, and I was bitterly hurt and disappointed in him.

Homecoming Sunday was a nasty one, weatherwise. The tropical storm had been upgraded to Hurricane Nancy, off the coast of Louisiana, and the wind blew like a tempest, tossing the trees all around, swaying and dipping like frenzied dancers. It rained all day, and everyone but me grumbled and groaned. The storm suited my mood.

I avoided both Ben and John Marcus getting ready for church. I put out breakfast and was making coffee when Ben came in, followed by John Marcus. I kept my back turned, fiddling with the coffeemaker. Ben went to the bay windows and pulled back the curtains. "Good Lord, Dr. Vickery," he groaned. "Take a look at this storm!"

John Marcus laughed his big laugh, and I stole a glance at him. He had on a stiff white shirt and dark pants, his curly hair wet from the shower. Even this early in the morning, his eyes glowed brightly. I lowered my eyes before he caught me staring at him.

"Looks like we'd better build an ark, Brother Ben," he said, slapping Ben on the shoulder so heartily that Ben jumped. Good, I thought, still smarting from my humiliation yesterday. Knock the hell out of Ben while you're at it.

"Had the radio on, Dean?" Ben asked.

"Tropical Storm Nancy is now Hurricane Nancy, moving eight miles an hour off the coast of Louisiana," I said to the coffeepot. "She's a grade three, so no evacuation orders, just a lot of wind and rain."

"Mmm, your coffee smells good," John Marcus said, and he came up behind me, getting a mug.

I turned to leave the kitchen without looking his way. "Y'all help yourself," I said over my shoulder.

"Oh, Dean?" Ben called, and I stopped. "Just wanted to tell you, Mrs. Vickery—Beth—called and said the rain's delayed her. She'll meet us at the church."

I nodded, and John Marcus said, "Not joining us for breakfast, Dean?"

I glanced at him and faked a laugh. "No, since it's raining I've got to pin my hair up and it takes forever," I lied. I could do it in two minutes flat.

"You've got me there," he smiled, looking up from pouring a cup of coffee. "What does rain have to do with putting your hair up?"

"Unlike yours and mine, Dean's hair's straight as a stick, Dr. Vickery," Ben answered for me. "When it rains, it gets even straighter. Won't hold a hairpin or anything."

"Speaking of which, those antique combs you wore in your hair yesterday were exquisite," John Marcus said. "Heirlooms?"

Ben frowned, wanting to answer for me, but I knew he hadn't even noticed them. I took a perverse delight in looking straight at John Marcus, watching his reaction. "They're Augusta's now," I said. "They belonged to an ancestor of Maddox's." Maybe she'll take them along when you two run away together, I wanted to add.

Had Augusta not told me everything, I'd never have suspected that John Marcus was anything but the godly man he appeared to be. His face composed, he raised the coffee cup to his lips. "I hope you'll wear them today," he said. "I'd like Beth to see them."

"I will. And I'll make a point of showing them to your *wife*, telling her they're Augusta's," I said pointedly.

"That'd be great," he said, unruffled. "Beth was just

crazy about Augusta when she baby-sat for us. She'll be disappointed not to see her today."

"You never know," I said, my voice neutral. "She might show up."

"Naw, she won't," Ben said, buttering a blueberry muffin. "I tell you, Dr. Vickery, losing the Holderfields has been the biggest disappointment of my ministry here. They're attending All Saints now."

"From what I've heard, Ben," John Marcus replied, "you did everything you could. You've done such a great job here that it's caught the bishop's attention."

I watched Ben glow like a quarterback being praised by his coach, then turned to go back to the bedroom. With Ben's next question to John Marcus, though, I paused in the hallway. "What I hear, Dr. Vickery," Ben said, "is you're our next nominated bishop. You'll let them put your name up, won't you?"

There was a silence before John Marcus answered. "I don't know, Ben. I've thought about early retirement instead."

I hurried back to the room, my mind spinning. Early retirement! Did that mean skipping the country with Augusta? And with Gus, too, of course—God, I'd forgotten about Gus! Could Augusta do that, take Gus if she left Maddox and ran off with John Marcus? I had no idea what the legalities were, but I knew she wouldn't go without her son. And poor Maddox, he doted on Gus. How could they bear living so far away from each other? I forced myself to stop this line of thinking. It was giving me a sick headache, which I didn't need. My heartache was enough.

In wine-colored robes decked with gold satin vestments, I stood in line with the rest of the choir members waiting to go into the sanctuary for the processional, and a hand touched my shoulder. It was Collie Ruth, and I knew why she'd singled me out. A woman was with her, smiling broadly, greeting everyone with handshakes or whispered hellos.

"Dean," Collie Ruth said, beaming, "Beth wanted to meet you before you went to the choir loft. Beth Vickery, this is Dean Lynch."

Instead of taking my hand, Beth Vickery hugged me. Like her husband, she was stunning; tall, poised, and lovely. She had short silver hair, sharp brown eyes, and a lively look of interest on her face. Dressed in an elegant black-and-white suit, she was a woman at ease with herself, confident in her place in the world. She could be a stateswoman, a president of a college, or an ambassador to some faraway land. She and her husband made an impressive couple.

"I can't wait to spend more time with you, Dean," she said smoothly, her bright eyes shining. "John Marcus raved about you." Then she leaned forward and whispered in my ear, "And he doesn't rave about many people, so you've made an impression."

"Thank you," I replied, and she patted my shoulder.

"I'll see you after the service, at the luncheon. We'll be seated together at the head table, Collie Ruth told me."

The church service was hard to get through. The choir loft was high behind the pulpit area, giving us a bird's-eye view of the congregation. In spite of the rain, the sanctuary was packed today, the crowd as big as on Easter or Christmas. I searched the faces for Augusta's as soon as the first song and prayer were over and the choir sat down. During the reading of the scripture, I spotted her, just as she'd said, in the back row. She'd evidently tried to dress so she wouldn't call attention to herself, which was difficult with her height and coloring. She was in all black, her golden hair in a knot at the nape of her neck, small dark sunglasses on top of her head. If she saw me, she gave no indication, motionless with her face reposed. Ben was making announcements, so I turned my attention back to the pulpit. The overhead lights highlighting her silver hair, Beth Vickery stood and bowed her head at Ben's introduction, and the congregation burst into spontaneous applause. I couldn't resist looking at John Marcus, in an ornate pulpit chair like a king on a throne. It was hard to resist the temptation to stand and point an accusing finger at him; tell everyone that he was not what he seemed.

It was even harder when John Marcus took the pulpit and delivered the sermon. I looked over the rapt faces of the congregation, their undisguised adoration. Had I not gone to Augusta's last night, I would have been one of them, with the same look on my face. I wondered what Augusta was thinking, if she was looking at his large, graceful hands and imagining them on her body. His powerful voice, reverberating over the large sanctuary—was she hearing his moans instead? Did she smile to herself, knowing that the passion he brought to delivering God's word was equaled only by the intensity of his lovemaking?

The stirring sermon over, the silence was broken only by the sniffling and sobs of the congregation. John Marcus returned to the chair by the pulpit and sat down, his head bowed in prayer. Ben looked his way, then stumbled to the pulpit, wiping his own eyes. He picked up the hymnal, and in a hushed voice said, "Let's close by standing and singing together that great hymn of homecoming, 'Softly and Tenderly Jesus Is Calling.' "

The luncheon was difficult. The choir loft had removed me from the adoring worshipers, but in their midst I was surrounded by both Ben's and the Vickerys' fan club. Disheartened, I made my way toward the head table where the church officials sat, Ben and the Vickerys waiting. The camaraderie of the homecoming festivities yesterday had buffered the hostility the congregation felt toward me, but if I thought all was forgiven, I was dead wrong. Although my detractors were careful not to show their feelings in front of the Vickerys, I was shunned in ways both subtle and obvious. I sat in my chair straight as an arrow, not daring to look their way, to see the malice shining in their eyes.

The luncheon and ceremonies afterward went on and on, into the afternoon. When everything finally came to an end, Ben and I were called forward and presented with a small silver tray, engraved with the date and occasion. Then Bob Harris called the Vickerys forward and presented them with a silver tray as well. But theirs was huge and heavy, so much bigger than mine and Ben's that it was embarrassing. I hid my smile behind a cough when I saw Ben staring at it in dismay. The message couldn't have been clearer: As much as they liked Ben, he was still way behind Dr. Vickery. That was mainly my fault, which Ben wouldn't hesitate to point out to me as soon as he had a chance.

Back in the parsonage while the crowd lingered in the Fellowship Hall, I changed out of my toffee-brown silk suit and suede heels—a stylish new addition to my wardrobe—and slipped into a sweatsuit. I'd gotten home early under the pretext of walking Beth Vickery to her car. Once the ceremonies were over, Beth whispered to those of us at the head table that she was going to sneak out, get on the road so she could get back to Tallahassee before dark. I lowered my eyes when she kissed her husband on the cheek before she left, saying she'd see him Tuesday. Ben had already told me, much to my relief, that John Marcus wouldn't be staying with us tonight; that as soon as homecoming was over, he was driving to Pensacola, where he was scheduled to give a speech at a ministers' meeting on Monday. I'd walked Beth to her car.

Once outside, Beth encouraged me to go home. "Don't go back over to the Fellowship Hall, Dean. Learn the tricks of the trade," she'd said, hugging me good-bye, echoing her husband's words to me.

Padding around in my warm socks, I opened the curtains to the dreary day outside, listening to the sound of the blowing rain against the windows and the sight of the trees in the backyard, especially the moss-draped oaks, flapping around in the strong wind. I sat in the den and looked out at the rain, trying to quiet my tumultuous thoughts. Haunted by Augusta's confession, I'd longed for some time alone to do exactly what I was doing: sitting and thinking, replaying conversations, analyzing and agonizing over this latest development in Augusta's tempestuous life. I needed to talk to her; to try and make her see reason. Maddox was a much better man than John Marcus would ever be, and Augusta should see that. She had too much to throw it all away for a love that seemed more like obsession to me. Surely real love wasn't that addictive. I couldn't imagine throwing away everything in my life for a man, especially a hypocrite and liar like John Marcus. I put my cup down and went to Ben's bedroom to call her.

Augusta answered on the first ring, breathless. "It's just me," I told her.

"Thank God it's you," she said. "I'm in such a mess, baby girl."

"I know you are," I said, closing my eyes and rubbing my temples with my free hand. The headache that had been lurking all day was still there. "Please tell me that you love Maddox and Gus, Augusta, and that you have no intention of ruining your life."

"Ruining my life? I've already done that. You've never loved anyone this much, have you, Dean?"

"No. And I hope to God I never do."

"Me, too. I wouldn't wish this hell on you, baby girl. I've never been more miserable."

We were silent, then Augusta said, "Dean, could you do something for me? I hate to ask you, but . . . will you give John Marcus a message? Here's all you have to do. Somehow, mention Crystal River in your good-bye. It's a code and he'll know what it means."

"Gladly. Instead of good-bye, I'll say this: John Marcus Vickery, go jump in Crystal Lake, you low-down lying hypocritical son of a bitch."

"Not Lake—Crystal *River*. This is important."

Crystal River, about five miles from Mimosa Grove, was a wide and beautiful river that, in the past, was the main site for picnics and water sports. "What about Crystal River?" I asked.

"Work it into the conversation," Augusta pleaded. "Say something like, 'Be careful when you drive over Crystal River; the road gets real slick.' It's a signal to meet me out there in our old place, a secluded spot on the riverbank."

"Augusta, look out the window. It's pouring down rain. A hurricane is heading our way, and you're talking about meeting at the river?"

"He can't come to Mimosa Grove in the daytime."

"Oh, excuse me for not thinking of that."

"Don't turn against me, Dean—I need you now."

"I'm *not* turning against you," I said, my voice louder than I intended. "But—I cannot watch you do this without trying to stop you."

"Please, baby girl. You're the only woman friend I've ever had."

"Only because you're a crazy woman, and this latest thing—it's the craziest yet. Just tell me you won't do anything stupid!"

"Define stupid."

Again, a long silence as I rubbed my throbbing temple. "Listen, I'm getting the headache from hell. Let me go take some medicine, catch this headache before it lays me low, then call you later."

I hung up the phone and sat for a minute on the side of the bed, trying to remember where the Tylenol was. I started down the hall, but when I passed the guest room, someone grabbed my arm.

"I need to talk to you," John Marcus said, pulling me into the guest room. Before I could protest, he closed the door and leaned against it. I hadn't heard him come in. His suitcase was on the bed, closed and ready to go.

"What about?" I said, my voice cold. I didn't want to confront him now.

"What have I done to offend you?" he asked me gently, his eyes puzzled.

"To offend me? Why . . . nothing." I shrugged elaborately. I had to fake it, get him out of here, or I'd give myself away. "I—I just have a headache, so I'm not myself. Actually, I was heading to the kitchen to get the Tylenol. Ben always leaves it in there on the windowsill," I babbled.

"Look at me." I kept my eyes down until he gave me a gentle shake. "Dean Lynch, look at me. What have I done?"

I looked up at him, into those unbelievable eyes, then let my breath out slowly. "I can't talk about it."

"It's Augusta, isn't it?" he said, leaning down, his face next to mine. "Isn't it?" he repeated, and I nodded. "When did you talk to her?"

"I saw your car leaving Mimosa Grove last night. Augusta thought I was you when I knocked on the door."

"I can explain it," he said, his voice calm.

"I know everything," I said, my voice breaking. "And it makes me sick." Unable to stop myself, I started crying, and buried my face in my hands.

"Oh, Dean. Please don't cry." John Marcus put an arm around my shoulder, and I pushed it off as though he were a coral snake. For a long moment he stared at me in surprise, then he put his hand over his eyes. "Oh, dear God," he sighed.

"You've ruined Augusta's life, John Marcus," I cried. "She has a loving husband, a great kid, and everything anyone could want, yet she's obsessed with having you. But I don't really blame Augusta, because it's not her fault."

I didn't think John Marcus was going to say anything else. It was as though he'd been struck dumb by my knowledge. "Don't look so devastated, *Reverend* Vickery," I said scornfully. "You don't have anything to fear from me, the biggest chicken that's ever lived. Even if I try to expose you, I've lost every battle I've fought lately, so you're probably safe."

"I doubt anyone would believe you, anyway," he said, his eyes closed.

"Yeah," I said. "No one would believe me, would they?"

He turned from me and looked out the window, rubbing his neck wearily. It was gray outside, dark and dreary, even though it was only four o'clock. The rain beat against the window and the limb of a dogwood tree scraped forlornly on the screen. "Oh, God. I was hoping Augusta wouldn't tell you," he said, finally.

"I'll just bet you were." I moved over to a chair and sat down, my knees weak.

"I loved Augusta, Dean, and I still do," he continued, almost dreamily. "As a young girl, she was so sweet, so appealing, and the kids simply adored her. We took her on family trips, she stayed here a great deal, but I certainly never—intended for anything to happen! I never intended to . . . become involved with her. I have plenty of weaknesses and imperfections, and I simply wasn't able to keep myself from

falling in love with her." He rubbed his neck again, still looking out the window. "I think Augusta fell for me for one reason only; because of our age difference and my position, I
was unattainable to her. When she wanted a man, she got
him. You know that she broke up Maddox's engagement."
He sighed and closed his eyes. "I would've done anything for
Augusta except give up my calling, and I finally made her see
that. That's when she . . . became involved with Maddox.
She told me that she loved Maddox, that she was over me,
and I believed her. I believed her, and everything seemed fine.
Time and distance took its toll on us until last night." He
stopped and glanced over at me.

I raised my head to look at him long and hard. "She says
she's giving it all up for you. But I intend to do everything in
my power to get her to come to her senses."

"You'll be doing both Augusta and me a favor if you do,
believe me."

"Guess what, John Marcus," I said, standing to face
him. "I don't give a good goddamn about doing you a favor.
I hope that there's a special place in hell for people like you.
But I love Augusta, and I'm not going to let her throw her life
away."

He flinched. "I admire you, I want you to know, for
standing up for Augusta."

"I don't want your admiration, either," I said in a loud
voice, and he held up his hand to silence me.

"Well, too bad, because you've got it. Let me tell you
something that will surprise you, Dean. Ben thinks the bishop
sent me here to distract everyone from the marriage of Godwin and Rich. But that's not entirely true; I *asked* to come. I
wanted to meet the woman with guts enough to defy not only
her husband but his whole congregation. And now that I've
met you, I find you not only a courageous woman, but an in-

credibly lovely one as well. If things were different, I'd have to be careful not to fall in love with you myself."

"That kind of talk has kept Augusta on the hook all these years," I said in disgust, "but it's wasted on me."

John Marcus turned from me, his hands hanging limply at his side. After a long silence, he sighed. "I can't blame you for your anger. But here's what I think we should do now: I'll go on to Pensacola and leave you to channel that anger in a positive way. If you can convince Augusta that she needs to stay with Maddox and Gus, you'll be doing both of us a favor. Then I want you and me to talk again. Let's get together after you've talked to Augusta, okay?" Reaching into his pocket, he took a card out and put it in my hand. "My private number," he said. "There are very few people I give that to."

I put the card in my pocket, my anger suddenly turning to exhaustion. All the fight had gone out of me, and I just wanted him to leave. "You should get on your way before the rain gets any worse," I said, walking to the door and opening it. "And Augusta says if I say 'Crystal River' to you, it'll mean something."

He frowned as though searching his memory, then nodded. "Crystal River! Yes, I know what that means."

Not wanting to listen to any more, to hear about their rendezvous spot, I walked out into the hall, leaving the door open behind me. I went to the kitchen and took three Tylenol. As I was standing at the sink washing them down with a glass of water, John Marcus came through, raincoat on and suitcase in hand. He paused at the back door.

"I've already told Ben good-bye. I invited him to come to my speech in Pensacola tomorrow. It'll give you some time to spend with Augusta."

I nodded. "That's what I plan to do, before Maddox and Gus return. And it'll do Ben good to get away."

To my surprise, John Marcus tilted his head to the side and said simply, as though commenting on the weather, "Ben's going to lose you, Dean. But you know that, don't you?"

"I—don't know what's going to happen," I stammered, shocked.

I wasn't sure what he said as he went out the door, closing it behind him. It was either, "He doesn't deserve to," or "He doesn't deserve you."

I didn't realize how exhausted I was until I lay down on the couch in the den. I lay facing the windows, watching the rain, my thoughts like the branches of the trees outside, tossing and twisting, blown one way and then the other. I don't know when I fell asleep, but I woke to darkness and a crick in my neck. I struggled to my feet, blinking, and turned on the floor lamp. Then I stumbled into the kitchen and squinted at the clock. Seven o'clock. I'd been asleep for two hours. I had no idea where Ben was, since we weren't having church services tonight. Then I remembered, the homecoming committee was meeting for an evaluation.

While drinking a cup of tea, I pressed the button on the blinking answering machine. Three messages, all from Augusta, begging me to pick up the phone. The last one, though, grabbed me by the throat. "Dean, please come out here! I need you, bad. The lights are flickering like the power's about to go off, and I hate the thought of being in the dark. Bring your gown and stay with me tonight."

The door opened with a bang, blowing rain in, and I shivered. Ben came in, his brow furrowed, looking tired and cranky and bleary-eyed. Although he wasn't wet, having walked under the covered walkway from the church, his hair was ruffled and his dark suit crumpled. He was barely in the door before he jumped me. "I can't believe you don't have the weather channel on," he snapped. "Looks like the hurricane's right outside our door."

I looked up from my tea. "By the time it gets here, it'll be downgraded enough so that all we'll get will be a lot of wind and rain."

"I hope that's right," he said, dumping his stack of papers on the table. He nodded his head toward the answering machine. "What was that all about?"

"What?"

"Augusta's hysteria. I thought they'd gone to Sarasota, taking Godwin and Rich."

"She got sick and didn't go with them," I said, hoping he wouldn't ask me more questions.

"Why don't you go?" he said, crossing over to the refrigerator. He opened the door and stood looking inside, still frowning. "I want something but don't know what."

"Why don't I go to Sarasota?" I echoed.

"Oh, God, Dean, not tonight. Please don't question everything I say tonight," Ben said, sighing mightily. "I heard your message from Augusta, begging you to come and stay with her." He spoke as though to a child, dragging each word out slowly. "All I'm saying is, if she's sick and by herself, you ought to go stay with her, is all."

"You must be a lot tireder than you look," I said.

"What's that crack supposed to mean? You got any chocolate syrup? Think I'd like a cup of hot cocoa."

"Move and I'll fix you one," I said, going to the cabinet and getting out the Hershey's. Ben couldn't fix hot chocolate if his life depended on it. "Funny, you encouraging me to go to Augusta's; you usually pitch a fit when I do."

"I do no such thing," he declared. If I wasn't so tired, I'd argue with him, overwhelm him with a hundred examples. Make it a real good shouting match. "Reason I'm suggesting it is because me and you are taking the day off tomorrow," he continued. "I'm going to Pensacola to the ministers' meeting there, personal invitation from Dr. Vickery, so you can do what you want."

"Oh, goodness, your royal highness. Thank you for granting me permission to have a day of my own." I stuck the mug of hot chocolate in the microwave and punched the numbers in angrily.

"I can't win, can I, Dean? You get mad at me if I say Augusta's not a good influence on you but—"

"You've never put it that way! It's always that she takes up too much time from you and my church work," I interrupted him.

Ignoring me, Ben continued, raising his voice. "But when I suggest you go out to Mimosa Grove, spend the night with her, you jump down my throat. Fine. Do what you please. You always do anyway."

"Yeah, I wear the pants in this family, don't I?'

"You said it, I didn't. Well, I'm going to bed now. I'm meeting Dr. Vickery at the Old World Inn at nine."

"They're having a preachers' meeting there?"

"No, it's a retreat at some lake—I'm meeting him at the inn so he can show me how to get there. If you need any of your stuff out of my room, you'd better get it now."

The phone rang as Ben left the kitchen, and he paused to see if it was for him when I answered it. I was surprised to hear Celeste's voice on the other end, and I motioned to Ben to go on, it was for me.

"Celeste?" I said, soon as Ben went into his room and closed the door. "What it is?"

"Augusta is well now?"

"She's fine, Celeste. She's over her . . . uh . . . stomach virus now."

There was a long silence on the phone, and I thought Celeste had hung up. "No, Dean," she said finally. "I don't think she is fine. No."

"W-what do you mean?" My heart thudded and I felt weak and dizzy.

"You must be a friend to her now. I do not think Augusta had the vomits. Something is very strange about this."

"I don't know what you're talking about," I lied.

"Last night, I dreamt of Augusta," Celeste said. "A very disturbing dream. You must go to her, Dean. You must be her friend now."

At Mimosa Grove, a candle burned in a hurricane lamp in the kitchen. "Augusta!" I called out, walking to the swinging kitchen door, which was propped open. "It's me, Dean."

The house was so still and scary in the darkness that I was afraid Augusta wasn't here. Even if she'd gone to Crystal River for a tryst with John Marcus, she should be back by now. Putting down my overnight bag and dulcimer, I picked up the hurricane lamp and walked out in the hall. "Augusta!" I called.

I stopped before the wide curving staircase and looked up. With the candle flame sending long shadows up the stairs, the entrance hall looked like a setting out of a scary movie. "Dean!" Augusta cried as she appeared on the landing, looking down at me. Wearing her long white nightgown, she looked like a ghost. Running down the stairs barefoot, she flung herself in my arms, almost causing me to drop the hurricane lamp. "Thank God you came," she said. "Ever since the lights went out, I've been scared shitless."

"You're cold as ice," I said. "Let's get a couple of blankets and go sit somewhere, get you warm."

"The fireplace in the library? I tried to light a fire but couldn't." Her face was drawn and white, her eyes red. She was jumpy, talking too fast, and I needed to get her warm and calm before she lost it.

I wasn't much better than Augusta at making a fire but eventually I got a pitiful one going. I took a fleece throw off the back of a chair and wrapped it around Augusta, and she looked up gratefully, the flames from the fireplace reflected in the pupils of her eyes. I took the candle to her bedroom and found her a warm sweatsuit and a pair of socks. After I'd helped her change, she seemed so fragile in the beige throw that my heart went out to her, in spite of my anger about her stupid plan to run off with John Marcus. We wouldn't talk about it tonight. She was too emotionally shaky to confront. It would wait until we had lights and warmth, and a hurricane wasn't knocking at the door like the big bad wolf.

Taking the candle to the kitchen, I filled a tray, then went back into the library. "Are you going to be surprised at my inventiveness," I said, pushing the door open with my foot, then kneeling before the black marble fireplace. I melted butter in a griddle propped on top of the grate and placed two pieces of bread and cheese on it. Once the cheese melted and oozed over the sides of the bread, I fished it out and put it on a plate. "Cheese toast, only slightly burned on the bottom," I said, handing Augusta one. "And a glass of merlot. Then I'll bring a pan to heat up some lemonade, make you a hot toddy that'll put you right to sleep."

"I'm not hungry," she said, but by the time I poured our wine, she'd eaten the toast and licked her fingers. "Didn't think I was, anyway."

"Haven't eaten all weekend, have you?" I said, taking the other piece of toast after she refused it, shaking her head.

"I don't think so. The whole weekend's gone by in a haze. Oh—I talked to Rich and Godwin a few minutes ago, told them I was over the bug now," she said. Her voice had gotten heavy, drowsy with the warmth of the fire.

"They okay?"

"Doing great. They love Sarasota."

"The power's off but you spoke on the phone?"

"My cellular phone's upstairs. How about that toddy now?"

We settled back on the leather sofa, Augusta on one end, me on the other, with the hot mugs of whiskey-spiked lemonade cradled in our hands. The fire flared, its flickering flames sending our shadows on the shelves of books surrounding us. Augusta looked over at me as she sipped her steaming toddy. "Dean? We going to pretend nothing's happened, not talk about it?"

I was silent, watching the flames, sipping the fiery lemonade. It burned going down but warmed me all the way to my toenails. "When I went upstairs to get your sweatsuit?" I said. "Your room looked like Hurricane Nancy'd come through, stuff scattered everywhere. What were you doing up there, stumbling around in the dark?"

"Deciding what to take with me when I leave with John Marcus."

"Oh, God, I don't want to talk about him!" I groaned.

"I think we're going to have to."

"Let me fix us some more lemonade, then."

Even though my eyelids were heavy and my movements like moving through water, I fixed us another toddy. I sat cross-legged on the rug in front of the fireplace, a plaid throw around my shoulders like a squaw, then turned my head to look at Augusta. To my surprise, tears trickled down her cheeks, and she made no move to wipe them away. The firelight burnished her face and turned her pale hair coppery. "Oh, Augusta, don't," I said, tears burning my eyes, too.

She put her head down and wept, great racking sobs that shook her body, and I went to her and put my arms around her. "I can't stand to see you like this."

"I wish he'd never come back here! I was doing fine until I saw him again, after all these years. It hurts so bad," she sobbed, "so horribly bad."

The only thing I could do was hold her and let it run its course, which it did finally. "Oh, baby girl," I murmured, echoing her pet name for me, "you've got it bad."

"He didn't show up this afternoon," she said, blowing her nose. "If he had, I could've talked him into taking me with him to Pensacola."

"You expected him to take you to *Pensacola*, to a preachers' meeting?"

"I could've talked him into it," she said. Her body grew limp, and she sank down in the beige throw. Even now, tear-ravaged and red-eyed, she looked lovely. If I'd cried that hard, my face would be wet and snotty, my eyes would be swollen, and I'd look like Rudolph the Red-Nosed Reindeer.

"You don't believe that we're going away together, do you?" Augusta said.

"I didn't say that, but . . . it's difficult for me, is all."

"He loves me, and he's going to prove it."

I sighed. "Let's don't talk about this tonight. You're too wiped out emotionally. But I want to say one thing before we close the book on it. It's not that I think John Marcus doesn't love you. But I watched him this weekend, Augusta. He feeds on the adoration of the crowd—and he's not giving that up for anyone. Trust me on this one. He ain't giving God up."

"You don't know what's between us," she whispered.

"Then why don't you tell me? But I warn you, I'm going to do everything I can to get this man out of your system. We're going to exorcise him, like Jesus exorcised demons."

Augusta smiled dreamily and shook her head. "It won't happen. Not ever."

"You were just a child who became obsessed with a very charismatic man. I blame him, not you."

"I was more of a child than you think. I'll bet you have this picture of me as a young Lolita, wise in the ways of men. Come on, admit it," she said.

"Well, something like that . . ."

"Not so. I'd been my daddy's little princess, as sheltered as could be. When my mother died, Daddy doted on me, wanted me to stay his little girl. Not only that, I was a late bloomer, almost thirteen before starting my periods, no boobs, all braces and pigtails. But just before I turned fourteen, something happened. I blossomed and ripened and all that stuff; even high school boys started calling me."

She sighed, looking into the fire. "Okay, here's the way it happened. I started baby-sitting for the Vickerys when I was twelve, and John Marcus treated me like any other kid in the church. I had a crush on him; we all did. But when my appearance changed, so did he. At first I didn't think anything about the way he started staring at me, or his casual touches. Until one night when everything changed. I went to sleep on the twin bed with little Marcus Jr., and John Marcus picked me up to move me to the other bed. He'd done it before, but this time when he wrapped a quilt around me and put me on the bed, it was different. He started out by rubbing my back through my T-shirt. Dean, I was so naive, I thought he was just trying to get me to sleep. So I laid still, loving the feel of his hands. I'll never forget, I was wearing shorts and he moved his hands to my bare legs. He knew I was faking sleep, and that I liked his touch. He waited for my reaction before he did anything else."

"Oh, Jesus Christ," I whispered.

"Those nights went on for a while," she continued, "with me as willing accomplice. Just him rubbing my back and legs. That was all, until I sent him a signal that I was ready to do more."

"A signal? What'd you do, leer at him or something?"

"More subtle than that. See, I'll never know if that's all we would've done," she said thoughtfully, staring into the fire. "Neither one of us acknowledged those forbidden nights in any way. Remember, I pretended to be asleep, and when I'd see him at church, I never let on that I was any different than the other kids. But when I baby-sat, I got the kids to sleep, then pretended to fall asleep with little Marcus Jr. And without fail, when John Marcus got in from his church meetings, he'd come to the room, move me to the bed across from where his son slept, and caress my back and legs, as though to get me back to sleep."

"You spent the night when his wife wasn't there?"

Augusta nodded. "All the time. If the legislature was in session, Daddy'd be in Tallahassee, leaving me in the care of my old-maid aunt, who lived with us after Mama died. I stayed at the parsonage with her blessings because she thought her niece being so close to their adored preacher was sweet."

"She didn't know how close," I said in disgust.

"She could've never imagined what went on," Augusta agreed. "After a few weeks like that, having John Marcus's hands on my back and legs wasn't enough, and I let him know. Instead of my usual shorts, I wore a miniskirt the next time, and pretended to fall asleep again. He didn't stop with rubbing my legs; his hands went places they'd not been before. When he wrapped me in the quilt, he took me to his bed. Things changed totally then. The first time his hands went in my panties, Dean, I was terrified. But I won't lie, I was on fire, too."

"I remember making out as a teenager, that strange mixture of terror and excitement. But I was way too scared to go all the way at that age."

"I'd have been, too, if it hadn't been John Marcus. He

was so gentle with me, so sweet and tender. We'd go a little further each time, but always stopped at a crucial point, which of course kept us both incredibly turned on. After that kind of build-up, our eventual lovemaking was so passionate, it was terrifying. He kept his hand over my mouth so I couldn't cry out and wake up the children."

"Oh, God," I said, closing my eyes in revulsion.

"The risk was part of the thrill, and I was fifteen when I got pregnant."

I gasped and stared at her. "By John Marcus?"

Augusta rolled her eyes. "Who'd you think, the Holy Spirit? I didn't sleep with anyone else until college, though I had the reputation for being fast. Only because I dated frantically so no one would guess what was really going on."

"W-what happened about the pregnancy?"

"A secret abortion, which, oddly enough, made us closer; made John Marcus more loving toward me. But, it was messed up and it seemed I wouldn't be able to have children as a result. After that, we tried to stay away from each other. My daddy suspected something and sent me to a boarding school, but it didn't keep us apart. The first weekend I came home, both Beth Vickery and the kids begged me to baby-sit, and it started up again, every weekend I'd get home. This went on all my high school years, and I never made any demands. John Marcus was so many years older than me, a man of God, and I was a besotted teenager. I was so much in love, I didn't ask anything of him; never asked him to leave his wife or God or anything. Of course I didn't know enough about men to know those very things kept him devoted to me, too."

"How long did it go on?"

"Until Maddox. In college, I dated a lot of boys, slept with some, trying to break John Marcus's hold on me, but through it all, we continued our affair. Until I rediscovered Maddox that holiday weekend, I thought I'd never be able to love anyone else. But Maddox was different. Not only was he so sweet, unlike the college boys I'd shunned, he was older and mature. Maybe I have an Electra complex or something."

"No, subconsciously you knew you needed his stability," I said. "Think about it—those two men are polar opposites. Maddox is quiet and thoughtful, while John Marcus is so intense, it's scary."

She shrugged. "All I knew was, my feelings for John Marcus had totally consumed me for years. After the emotional roller coaster I'd been on, Maddox seemed like a life raft. John Marcus shook me to the core, but Maddox made me laugh, and I felt *safe* with him. Does that make sense?"

"Maddox was what you needed, and at some level, you knew that."

"So I convinced myself I truly loved him, that my obsession with John Marcus was finally over," she said, sighing. "I concentrated on being a good wife, having a baby. But a few years afterward, John Marcus called me, and that's all it took. Just hearing that incredible voice did me in, and I sneaked off to meet him. I knew then he was the only man I'd ever love. If I wasn't able to love a man like Maddox Holderfield, then I wasn't likely to get over John Marcus, ever."

I closed my eyes and rubbed my forehead. I was so tired and drained that I couldn't think clearly. It made sense when Augusta told it, made the whole sordid thing clearer. "Augusta?" I said finally. "Let's put this to rest now, get some sleep. Things will look clearer in the morning."

She surprised me by moving fast, since she'd been so languid after her paroxysm of crying. She lunged toward me and grabbed my hands. "I can't go to sleep until I find out what happened to John Marcus; why he didn't come by this afternoon. He promised he wouldn't leave without seeing me.

Did you see him go this afternoon? Do you know what time it was?"

"I—I think it was about five," I stammered, taken aback by her sudden intensity. The gleam in her eyes that had scared me earlier was back.

"Oh, my God, no wonder he didn't come to the river!" she cried, her face lighting up. "I was back here by then—he told me he was leaving the church at three."

"It—everything went on so much later than we'd planned," I said.

"Where is he? Tell me where he's staying."

"I don't know, honestly. Some kind of retreat on a lake out from Pensacola—" I stopped myself, staring at her. "No, wait! Ben's meeting him at the Old World Inn, downtown, in the morning—"

I didn't finish before Augusta had thrown off the blanket and scrambled to her feet. Without a word, she grabbed the hurricane lamp and headed for the door, almost slipping in her socks.

"Augusta, wait! Where are you going?"

"I'll be back in a minute," she cried over her shoulder. "Just stay right there."

I heard her run down the hall then to the stairs, knowing she was going upstairs to call the Old World Inn. I stood, the library lit now only by the dying fire, and started after her. Stopping at the door, I hesitated. Maybe he wouldn't be there, wouldn't be anywhere she could reach him. I built up the fire, then took a candle in a heavy brass stand, went into the kitchen, and got my dulcimer. Sitting by the fire, I picked out a song, "All Good Times Are Past and Gone," an old song about loving a lying man, ironic now in light of Augusta's dilemma.

I took the candle and went up the stairs and down the hall, to Maddox and Augusta's bedroom, where I stood outside the door, trying to decide whether to go in or not. I could tell Augusta was on the phone; could hear her talking, then silent. Suddenly she began to cry, loud and uncontrolled as she had in the library earlier. She was quiet then, as though he were comforting her. Her sobs broke my heart. I wanted to shake her, to tell her he wasn't worth it. I turned around and went back downstairs.

I sat on the floor in front of the sofa and played my dulcimer in the yellow firelight, all the songs of pain and love that I knew. When I raised my head, I was startled to see Augusta standing there, her arms hanging at her side. She stared at me like a zombie, tear tracks on her cheeks. I stopped playing and struggled to rise to my feet. "Please don't stop," she said, holding up a hand.

"What do you want to hear?" I asked her. She looked so distraught that it scared me.

She shook her head lifelessly. "Anything. What were you playing when I came in?"

" 'Hard Times Come Again No More,' " I told her, then flinched when she laughed, bitter and harsh. She sank on the sofa and reached for her mug.

"Pass me that Jack Daniel's," she said.

"You're not going to Pensacola, then?"

"If I could just see him, I could change his mind. Even though he loves me, he can't give up his calling, he says. All this time, I've known I wasn't a match for God. Now God's making sure I pay for daring to think I could be."

"So John Marcus's not running off with you, is that it?"

"One question. That's all you get. I'm sorry to hog the sofa, but I'm so tired."

I played another song, singing softly, and I thought Augusta'd gone to sleep. When her voice came from deep in the bundle on the sofa, I jumped in surprise. "Dean?"

"Yes?"

"I love you. You know that, don't you? Whatever happens, I want you to know that."

"I love you, too, Augusta. I always will." I played another tune, glancing over at her, listening to her even breathing. She was asleep now.

"I want to prove it to you," she murmured, and again I jumped at the sound of her voice.

"You don't have to prove it. I know you love me."

"Not that. About John Marcus and me. I know how I can prove he loves me. My trump card."

"You don't have to prove anything, so shut up."

"Okay. Put your dulcimer away and go to sleep now."

She didn't have to talk me into it; my eyelids had gotten so heavy sitting by the warm fire that I could barely hold them open. Without putting my dulcimer in the case, I laid it on the floor and crawled over to the window seat, grabbing the blanket on the way. I tossed all the pillows off but one, which I plopped my head on, snuggling under the warmth. The fire had died down and was almost out. Lying next to the window, I could hear the sound of the falling rain, and I closed my eyes.

"I can prove it to you, Dean." Augusta's voice floated over the darkness of the room.

The only sound was the rain outside, beating against the window. I sank into darkness until Augusta's voice jerked me awake. Her voice was so low, I wasn't sure I heard her right. "Think about it, Dean. Gus has his eyes, but John Marcus is so goddamn stupid he doesn't even know." Her laugh was bitter and sad.

"What did you say?" I whispered, sure I'd heard her wrong. Had she laughed, or was that the wind? I waited a long time, but she didn't answer me. "It sounded like you said something about Gus, but maybe I didn't hear you right. Augusta? Augusta, answer me, you hear?" Again, there was a long silence, then her even breathing floated across the room. She was asleep. That cup of Jack Daniel's had knocked her out.

I called out to her again and again, but she didn't answer me, and finally sleep overtook me.

Fourteen

WHEN I FIRST WOKE up the next morning, I didn't realize that Augusta had gone. The rain was still falling steadily but more gently now, the wind no longer howling like a were-wolf. I arose stiffly and made my way across the floor, going to the kitchen to see if the power had been restored. I tried to step lightly so that the old heart-of-pine floor wouldn't creak, since last thing I wanted was to wake Augusta. Thank God we had a whole day to get her pulled together before Maddox and Gus got home tonight. Gus! I couldn't think about that now, or what I thought Augusta said as she was falling to sleep last night. My dreams had been haunted with eyes: Maddox's gray, Augusta's blue, and tiger eyes, a luminescent mixture of gold and brown.

Augusta wasn't on the sofa, and I figured she'd gone to the bathroom. In the kitchen, I almost let out a cheer when the lights came on. By the time I found the coffee grinder and got the coffee brewing, I wondered if Augusta had gone back to sleep. I went to the library and peeked in. The sofa was still empty. Surprised, I walked down the dark hall to the slate-floored entranceway and looked up the stairs. No noise came from the second floor, but maybe she was in the shower.

At the kitchen counter, I sat on an antique wooden stool and drank a cup of coffee while looking out the windows. Before pouring myself a second cup of coffee, I went upstairs to see if Augusta had fallen asleep under the shower. She'd had plenty of time to bathe and dress, even if she changed clothes fifty times. Maybe she was cleaning up the mess she'd made throwing stuff around like a crazy woman last night.

Nope. The room was still a mess. Sidestepping the scattered clothes, shoes, and papers, I went to her bathroom. She'd taken a shower. The sweatsuit I'd helped her dress in last night lay crumbled on the floor, in a puddle of water. The light was on and the bathroom was a bigger mess than her room. Where could she be? Had we missed each other when I was sitting in the kitchen, my back to the door? It made no sense. I went to the sunporch and looked around. Not finding her, back to the library again. Back in the kitchen. I went to both bathrooms downstairs, the one next to the sitting room, and the smaller one under the stairwell, calling, "Augusta!" The only answer was the stillness of the house.

I started back up the stairs after looking through each room on the ground floor. I'd reached the landing when there was a loud banging on the front door. Startled, I froze in my tracks, my heart beating in my throat. Who could be at the front door this time of the morning? Had Augusta gotten up early, gone for a walk in the rain to clear her head, and locked herself out of the house? All along I'd been purposely blocking out the other possibility, that she'd gone to Pensacola to John Marcus. Maybe she'd started to Pensacola, realized she was in no condition to drive, and had returned without her house key.

When I opened the door, I stared in bewilderment into the eyes of the man standing there. It was one of those disconcerting times when I couldn't think who he was, though I knew him. "It's Sheriff Coleman, ma'am," he said, taking off his hat, wet with the rain.

I must have motioned for him to come in, for the next thing I knew, he was standing in the slate-floored hall next to me, wet and dripping rainwater, and I'd closed the front door. I looked at him as if for the first time, even though several weeks ago when I was attacked, I'd come to know him rather well. "Morning, Mrs. Lynch," he said politely, showing no surprise at my opening the door this early in the morning at a house other than my own.

"Good morning, Sheriff Coleman," I said, shaking as though I were freezing. "Sorry it took me so long to get to the door; I didn't want to open it until I saw who was out there."

"Always a good idea," he said, glancing around him.

"What are you doing out so early?" I felt suddenly sick to my stomach, the coffee I'd had earlier boiling like acid in my throat.

Again, he glanced around the entranceway. "I'm looking for Mr. Holderfield, Mrs. Lynch. Is he up yet?"

I shook my head. "I don't know if he is or not," I said stupidly. "I mean, he's not here, so I don't know . . ."

He nodded, his face impassive. "Do you know how I can get in touch with him?"

I stared at him. "Is something going on at the plant?" That was it, of course; a problem at the tomato plant. Must be bad, for them to call the sheriff.

Instead of answering me he said, "You know Mr. Hernandez, don't you? Cuban fellow, lives down the road?"

"Of course, Carl Hernandez. He's Maddox's right-hand man. Has—something happened to Mr. Hernandez, Sheriff?"

"No, ma'am. Not that. Just thought Mr. Hernandez might know where Mr. Holderfield is. I can go over to his place, find out from him."

"Oh! No, he's *with* Mr. Holderfield. He's out of town . . . I mean, they're out of town. Both of them, together."

"Business trip, huh?" He nodded. "And you don't know how I can get ahold of him?"

"Who? Maddox or Carl?" I asked.

"I need to talk to Mr. Holderfield, Mrs. Lynch."

I ran my fingers through my hair, which had come out of the neat bun I'd pinned it in yesterday and was tangled on my shoulders. "I—I can't ask Augusta, Sheriff, because I don't know exactly where she is. It's crazy, I know." I laughed halfheartedly and looked up at him. Why hadn't he asked for Mrs. Holderfield; asked if she knew where her husband was? She'd be the logical one. "I stayed here last night because the electricity was off and Augusta was afraid being alone with everyone out of town. I mean, her husband and Gus and the Hernandezes. Then this morning, when I got up she'd gone out . . . for a walk or something . . ." My voice trailed off at the look on his face.

"Mrs. Lynch, could me and you sit down for a minute?"

I have no idea why I led him back to the kitchen instead of the living room, right next to where we stood in the hallway. I don't recall asking for his wet slicker, but he handed it over and I hung it on a wooden peg by the back door. I motioned for him to have a seat at the kitchen table, and without asking, I brought him a cup of coffee, then refilled my cup.

"When did you see Mrs. Holderfield last?" the sheriff asked me, picking up his coffee cup as I sat down across from him. He held the cup in his large, rough hand but didn't drink from it.

"I—that is, we went to bed late. Real late. The power was out, so we built a fire in the library and slept in there. She fell asleep on the sofa, and I slept on the window seat."

"About what time you reckon that was?"

"Uh, gosh, I don't know. Way after midnight, I'm sure."

I took a swallow of my coffee and choked, coughing and gasping. My eyes watered, and I wiped them with my fingers as I looked up at the sheriff.

"Augusta's not missing, is she?" I said, coughing. "I mean, is that why you're here? Because she was asleep in the library last night—I know she was!—so she hasn't been gone long."

His eyes held mine. "Mrs. Lynch, I'm sorry to be the one to tell you this. I'm afraid Mrs. Holderfield's been in an accident."

"An accident? W-what do you mean, an accident? Not a—not an automobile accident?"

"Yes, ma'am. A fatal one. I'm really sorry, but I'm afraid that Mrs. Holderfield, well, she's been—"

I didn't let him finish. I'd known since I opened the door and saw him standing out there. "Oh, no," I cried out, putting my hands over my face and looking at him through my fingers. "Oh, dear God, no—please, no!" I shook my head and couldn't seem to stop. Shaking, shaking my head in protest—no no no no.

"I'm really sorry to be the one to tell you," he said. "Can I do anything for you? Need a glass of water or anything?"

I ignored his clumsy but well-meaning questions and pushed my hair back from my face with trembling hands. "Tell me what happened," I said.

"It was one of the deputies found her car and called me to the scene."

"Her car? No—her car's in the garage." And fruitlessly, I stumbled to my feet, knocking over my coffee cup, going to the window. Her car was gone, the space next to my car dark, its emptiness mocking me in the early morning gloom.

Sheriff Coleman took two white linen napkins from a basket on the table and laid them on the spilled coffee, stopping the flow. No, I wanted to say to him. Don't do that—

coffee will stain those old napkins and Augusta will be upset. You can't get coffee stains out of antique linen, you know. Augusta had taught me that. Sinking down into my chair, I watched wordlessly as the coffee soaked through the fine old lace of the napkins, turning them from white to brown.

The sheriff regarded me gravely before continuing. Even though his face was composed, his eyes were sad and I knew this was the part of his job he hated most. "A motorist called us as soon as it began to get light this morning," he said, "reporting a suspicious sight at Crystal River. The top of the guard rail, he said, just before you come off the bridge traveling east, was missing, the bottom rail demolished. Looks like someone's gone over it, he says, wrecked their car on the bank or even gone into the river. See, car going off the bridge at that point, it'd be more likely to land on the bank than in the water. So Deputy Glover goes out to the river to see what's going on. You know him, Mrs. Lynch, Larry Glover? I believe he belongs to your church."

I shook my head.

"Oh. Maybe it's that Methodist church outside town he goes to," he said, scratching his head, then patting his thinning hair back into place. "Well, Deputy Glover, he finds the car and sees a woman in it, calls the ambulance. Radios in, finds out who the car's registered to, then calls me. By the time I get there, it's light. Raining pretty bad, but good visibility. Deputy Glover, he don't know Mrs. Holderfield, but I do, so I knew it was not only her car but her driving, soon as I get to the scene. The ambulance'd come but too late for her—she must have died on impact, Mrs. Lynch."

There. He'd said it, said the dreaded word. I blinked at him but didn't move, felt nothing. The feelings would come later, I guessed. *Died on impact. She must have died on impact.*

I cleared my throat. "Impact? With—the bridge?"

"No'm. The car flew off the bridge, over that guard rail,

knocking off the top rail. I been saying for years that guard rail's too low, somebody's going to go over it. Lucky her car didn't land in the river, otherwise might be a while before we'd found her. But the car landing on the bank like that . . . well, made it easier to find her. We got a wrecker out there now."

"And where's Aug—Mrs. Holderfield now?"

"Oh, don't worry, ma'am. We got her out of the car, ambulance took her on to the morgue." He shook his head. "Car's as bad as any I've ever seen. And Mrs. Holderfield was banged up bad, Mrs. Lynch. Real bad. She must've hit that bridge going a hundred miles an hour."

I closed my eyes tight, so tight, they hurt. "Can I go out there, Sheriff Coleman, see what happened?"

He nodded, his face grim. "Well, you can if you want to, Mrs. Lynch. Reckon that'd be okay, if that's what you feel like you need to do. But first, we got to get ahold of Mr. Holderfield."

I opened my eyes and stared at him, wide and startled. Oh, my God, Maddox! "We've got to tell him, Sheriff Coleman," I cried. "He's—supposed to drive back today with Gus and Carl and Theresa, and they might hear it on the radio—"

"Exactly where are they, Mrs. Lynch?"

"Sarasota! Remember, Sheriff Coleman, you said Godwin and Rich needed to go away for a while? Maddox took them to Sarasota. Augusta was supposed to go . . ." My throat closed up and I swallowed painfully. If only she'd gone, not faked a sickness in order to stay home! "Wait. I've got that number in my purse somewhere."

I'd left my purse in the kitchen, next to my overnight bag, when I came in last night. Unzipping a pouch, I fumbled through a stack of papers stuffed inside. I'd put the address and phone number of Godwin and Rich's friends there until I could move it to my address book; I knew it was there. Crying out in frustration, I dumped the papers out on the table and scattered them around, my hands shaking. "I can't find the number but I know how to get in touch with them. Could you hand me that phone on the cabinet behind you?"

Looking up her number, I dialed Libby Legere's house. She answered after several rings, her voice muffled, barely awake. I cleared my throat and forced myself to say it: "Libby, this is Dean Lynch. Sorry to wake you, but it's urgent that I get in touch with Simms in Sarasota. Do you have a number there?"

Silence at the end of the phone, then her voice was cold. "Does this have anything to do with that Gypsy woman?"

I couldn't tell her before anyone else; couldn't have her, Augusta's old enemy, know before Maddox did. Without hesitation I answered, "Yes. It's an emergency."

"Tough shit," she said, and I could hear her rustling in the bed, moving across it to hang up the phone.

"Libby—wait! Please, this is urgent. All I need's his number."

Something in my voice must've stopped her, and even though she sighed heavily, she told me. "He's staying at the Sarasota Hilton, the rotten son of a bitch. If you talk to him, tell him I'll see his ass in divorce court." And she hung up.

Simms answered the phone jauntily, either a cheerful morning person or in a good mood after a weekend with Celeste. His voice sobered up quickly when I told him that I had to get in touch with Maddox, that I couldn't find the number. "What's happened, Dean?"

I hesitated only a minute. Celeste was with him, and Augusta had loved her. "A car accident, Simms. It's Augusta."

"Augusta?" he repeated, and I heard Celeste's gasp. "Is it bad?"

"Yeah. Real bad."

"She's—not gone, is she?"

"Yeah. She's gone, Simms." None of us could say it yet. *Died on impact.*

"Oh, Jesus Christ, no," he moaned. Celeste's scream was in my ear, as though she were standing next to me. I wanted to talk to her, to comfort her, but I couldn't. Not now. There was a long silence, then Simms said, "Listen. Don't call over there, tell him over the phone. Let me go tell him, okay?"

I let my breath out, ragged and trembling. Simms, Maddox's childhood friend. "That'd be much better," I said faintly.

A heavy silence, then he spoke again. "I have two tickets to the Panama City Airport, leaving in a couple of hours. Why don't I give them to Maddox and Gus, put them on the plane instead of me and Celeste? My car's at the airport, so Maddox could be back in Crystal Springs by three, four o'clock. What do you think?"

"Oh, God—that's a great idea." I looked over at the sheriff and told him what was going on, and he nodded. "Simms? I'm at Mimosa Grove, and I'll stay here for Maddox to call me when you tell him, okay?" Poor Simms, having to be the one. But someone had to, and the news couldn't be softened, no matter who told it.

"You know the details of the accident, then?"

"The sheriff's here," I said. "He can talk to Maddox, too, I guess." I looked at the sheriff, raising my eyebrows, and he nodded.

Again, a long silence, Celeste's weeping the only sound on the line. "Oh, Jesus Christ," Simms repeated.

"Oh—Simms, I just thought of this. What about you getting on the plane with Maddox and let Celeste and Gus come with Carl and Theresa? That way, Maddox will have time to get here, get some things . . . ah . . . taken care of before Gus gets home. He might not want to tell Gus anything yet."

"Poor little Gus," Simms sighed.

"Gus loves Theresa and Celeste," I said, "so it would be good for him to be with them. Celeste can keep him entertained. But for God's sake, tell them not to play the radio."

"That's a great plan. Okay. Let me get over there before Maddox and them leave, then."

Sheriff Coleman poured me another cup of coffee, motioning for me to sit down again. I could tell by his face that there was something else, something I didn't want to hear. Stalling, I fiddled with my coffee, pouring in half-and-half, dousing it with sugar, sipping it carefully. Nauseated, I sank into the chair I'd vacated during the call and faced the sheriff reluctantly.

"Mrs. Lynch," he said, "I need to ask you a few questions. I hate to do it now, but there's some things we need to discuss before Mr. Holderfield gets here."

I nodded, but didn't say anything. I didn't trust my voice.

He took a notebook and pen from his jacket pocket. "Now, first thing is where Mrs. Holderfield might have been going that early in the morning."

I didn't answer, watching him scribble the question on the notepad. Pretty handwriting, for a man like him. "Mrs. Lynch?"

"I wondered that myself," I said finally. "When I got up this morning and couldn't find her, I thought she'd gone for a walk or something."

"In the rain? Was that something she was likely to do?"

"Not really." He waited, looking at me, and I cleared my throat. "Ah, I thought about this. Could she have been going into town to get us some doughnuts, maybe? Sometimes she and I, we'd go to Jean's place, get her doughnuts soon as she took them out of the oven."

"Here's a problem with that. I wondered why Mrs. Holderfield would go into town by way of the bridge, which is out of the way from Mimosa Grove. Was she in the habit of going to town that way?"

I shook my head, but I didn't want to tell him that Augusta had never gone that way, not that I knew of. That road, if you stayed on it, eventually took you to Pensacola.

The sheriff continued. "Even more of a problem: way the car hit the bridge, she was heading out of town, not in."

I nodded, looking down at the coffee cup I held in my hands. I tried to raise the cup to my lips, but my hands were shaking too bad, so I put it back down. Would it come out, then? Was it inevitable that everyone find out Augusta was leaving? I knew what she'd done—she'd gotten up early and set out for Pensacola, determined to make John Marcus change his mind. When I didn't say anything for several minutes, Sheriff Coleman got up and poured himself another cup of coffee, then sat back down across from me.

"There's something else I have to ask that's gonna be hard." He cleared his throat, looking uncomfortable. "You and Mrs. Holderfield were real close friends, weren't you?" When I nodded, he continued. "She confided in you?"

He had no way of knowing the irony of that question. If Augusta were here, she'd laugh. "Well," I hedged, "we became real good friends, but had just begun to confide in each other. You know how that goes . . . takes a while to trust each other, I guess." It sounded lame, so I gulped the sickening coffee to stop my babbling.

"Was anything going on in Mrs. Holderfield's life that had her upset lately, or depressed, or . . ." He shrugged, as though not sure how to best express it. "You know, troubled?"

I raised my head sharply. "Troubled?"

The sheriff frowned, then scratched his head. "She was

traveling so fast, it was like she was—I don't know, running away from something. Couldn't figure out why anyone would be going so fast in the rain, dark as it was."

Avoiding his eye, I took a deep breath and forced myself to ask him, "Will you ask Maddox these same questions?"

"Yes, ma'am. A full accident report has to be filed. That's partly why I wondered if there was anything you wanted to tell us before Mr. Holderfield got here."

I swallowed and turned my head from him. "No. There's nothing. When Augusta and I went to sleep last night, she was fine. Her usual carefree self. We sang songs, talked and laughed like always. So she wasn't leaving, I'm sure of that." It wasn't so hard to lie when I turned my head, looked out the window at the rain.

"Seems strange to me—"

The ringing of the phone was sharp and insistent, like the pain in my heart, cutting him off. I stared at it, knowing it was Maddox. When I didn't move, Sheriff Coleman cocked his head to the side. "Mrs. Lynch? You need me to get that? I expect it's Mr. Holderfield."

"I'll get it," I said faintly, rising slowly. It didn't matter how many times it rang; he wasn't going to hang up until I answered. I picked up the phone and sank back into my chair.

"Dean?"

"Yeah, it's me, Maddox."

"Simms caught me as I was packing the car, me and Carl, about to leave. He said—" His voice broke, and he cleared his throat before continuing. "He said Augusta had been killed in an automobile accident."

"That's right."

"When did it happen?" There was nothing in his voice, not shock or surprise or grief. He might have been talking about the weather, or the day of the week, or anything but the loss of his wife. The sound of weeping was in the background, another voice joining Celeste's wailing, and I figured it was Rich. Possibly Godwin, but more likely Rich, the more emotional of the two. Or maybe it wasn't either of them. They were probably trying to hold up, keep from breaking down. More likely it was Theresa's sobs I heard. Only women were allowed to be emotional at times like these, in the stupid codes of our society.

"I'm not sure. Sometime early this morning," I said. He couldn't hear me over the wails in the background and I had to repeat it, louder this time.

"Early?" he echoed.

"I think. I spent the night out here, and we stayed up pretty late. When I got up this morning, she wasn't here. Sheriff Coleman came to tell me about the accident then."

He took a deep breath. "So Augusta is dead," he said. It wasn't a question. The starkness of the sentence hit me like a slap in the face, and I closed my eyes.

"The sheriff said she died on impact."

He asked the same question I'd asked earlier. "Impact with what? She hit another car?"

"Her car went over the bridge, Maddox."

"The bridge? The Crystal River bridge? What the hell was she doing out there?"

"I think . . . going into town to get doughnuts. You know Jean's bakery, how we liked the fresh doughnuts first thing Monday morning?"

"Going into town that way? She's never done that before—it's three or four miles out of the way."

"I know, but I was thinking, maybe it was earlier than she thought, and she realized the bakery wouldn't be open until six, so she was just driving around until then."

"That doesn't make a damn bit of sense."

I hurried on, before he could pursue that line of thinking. "And, it was raining pretty hard, so the bridge was slick. The sheriff said the visibility was poor. She was going too fast, too."

"She always drove too fast." There was a long silence as he digested this, then he said, "Guess you'd better let me speak to Buddy now."

I blinked, startled, not knowing who he was talking about. Then it hit me. Sheriff Coleman. Buddy. I hadn't thought of him having a first name.

I handed the phone to the sheriff—Buddy—but walked out of the room so I wouldn't have to hear him repeat what he'd told me earlier. I stood in the hall until the sheriff brought the phone to me. "Mr. Holderfield needs to talk to you again."

"Dean?" Maddox's voice was still lifeless, with no inflection, no emotion. "I don't think I should tell Gus yet, do you? He's still asleep, so I was thinking, I'll fly home with Simms, get there a few hours before Gus does. Tonight, when Carl gets to Mimosa Grove with Gus, I'll tell him then. What do you think?"

"That you're absolutely right," I said. "I can't stand the idea of him riding in the car all day knowing what's waiting for him when he gets home. There'll be time enough to face it then."

"Are you going to stay there?"

I hadn't thought about it; hadn't thought beyond the present moment. "I'll be here when you arrive."

"Thank God." Without another word, he hung up.

"You'll stay at Mimosa Grove until he gets here?" Sheriff Coleman asked when I turned back to face him.

When I nodded, he continued, "You don't need to be by yourself. Brother Lynch going to come stay with you?"

Ben! Guiltily, I realized I hadn't thought about Ben once since I'd gotten up this morning. "He's in Pensacola," I said.

"Gone to a preachers' meeting." With John Marcus Vickery, but I couldn't go there now; couldn't let myself think about him and his responsibility in all this.

"When you expecting him back?"

I shrugged. "Late this afternoon, I imagine."

"Reckon you can get in touch with him?"

"I'll leave a message on our answering machine, tell him to come out here when he gets in."

"You got a woman friend who can come stay with you till Mr. Holderfield gets here?"

I glanced over at him, opening my mouth to tell him there was no one. No one now that Augusta was gone. But I didn't. If I told him the truth, that I didn't want anyone, he'd think I wasn't thinking straight; probably send someone out to keep me company. "Don't worry, I'll call someone, Sheriff, thanks."

"You'll be getting calls all day, reporters, people like that. Folks may come out here, too. If I were you, I'd turn the answering machine on, screen the calls. Nobody needs to be broadcasting anything till Mr. Holderfield gets here. Don't tell anybody anything. You know what I mean?"

Oh, yeah, I knew exactly what he meant.

Sheriff Coleman rose and put his jacket on. "I told Mr. Holderfield to call me when he gets in so we can make some arrangements," he said. "He's got to come in, identify the body, sign some things. If he forgets, would you remind him? People don't think straight in times like these."

Identify the body—oh, God! Poor Maddox. How could anyone be expected to do something like that and continue to live? How could you see such a sight and ever close your eyes again to sleep? I thanked the sheriff as I walked him to the front door and let him out of the house, though not sure what I was thanking him for. I went back into the house, which was utterly empty now; emptier than it had ever been or would ever be again. Maybe the sheriff was right; maybe I should call someone to come out here, stay with me. The emptiness of the house without Augusta was devastating. My knees gave out on me, and I sank down on the bottom step of the staircase. Flinging my arms up helplessly to cover my head, I fell on the slate floor and wept, sobs that shook my body like convulsions. I wept so hard, I began retching and ran to the nearest bathroom, under the stairs. After throwing up for what seemed like an hour, I was so weak that I had to lie on the cold bathroom floor until I was able to pull myself up, wash my face, and do what had to be done.

Grateful for Augusta's sloppiness, I spent the day cleaning her huge house like a madwoman. I wore myself out polishing, scrubbing, waxing, washing clothes, drying and folding, even linens that weren't dirty. The phone began ringing mid-morning, but I only answered it once: Rich, so upset, he was incoherent, so I told him I'd call them back tonight when I knew more. About two o'clock, cars began pulling into the driveway, I assumed to see if Maddox was here yet. One car parked, and the driver got out and banged on the front door. From my vantage point behind the living room curtains, I saw the Episcopal priest Father Bush, black umbrella over his head, his dark-green raincoat dripping rain. Awful as it was to see the poor old fellow turn around and walk back to his car, bent over against the steadily falling rain, I didn't go to the door. When Maddox got here, all these people would come, and I wouldn't be able to stop them. But for now, I didn't want to see anyone; didn't want to talk or hear their shocked condolences. It would only take one word of condolence to push me over the edge.

Preparing Mimosa Grove for the return of Maddox and Gus was the best antidote I could have for my grief. I'd put clean sheets on Maddox and Augusta's bed and was tossing the pillows back in place when I saw the note. Augusta must have left it on Maddox's pillow, and not seeing it, I'd knocked it to the floor when I stripped the bed this morning. With trembling hands, I picked it up.

It was a sealed ivory-colored envelope with Mimosa Grove's return address in the corner, "Maddox" written on the front and underlined. Augusta's handwriting. I sank on the bed and sat for a moment, the envelope in my hand. It had to be her Dear John letter to him, where she told him she was leaving him for another man. Oh, God!—my denials to the sheriff, my frenzied efforts to get everything in order were all in vain now. They'd know; Maddox would know that his wife had loved someone else so much that she'd run after him, and it had cost her her life. What if she told him about the possibility that Gus was not his son? How could Maddox stand that, losing not only his wife but also his child? And Gus, losing both his mother and father? I hesitated, then put the note in my pocket. Not today. Later, when the initial shock was over.

After I showered and changed, I went to the lemon-oil-scented library. On the sofa, I pulled the plaid throw over me—the one I'd wrapped myself in last night—and huddled in the corner. I don't know when I fell asleep, or how long I slept. A hand on my face, touching my cheek, woke me, and I opened my eyes to see Maddox kneeling beside me, Simms Legere next to him. Coming out of a deep sleep, I dissolved into tears at the sight of Maddox's anguished face. I collapsed into his arms while poor Simms paced, shaking his head and wiping his eyes as he, too, sobbed.

After exhausting ourselves weeping, Simms made coffee and Maddox sank onto the sofa next to me, shaky and dazed. Simms sat on the edge of a leather chair, watching Maddox anxiously.

"My God, Dean," Maddox said hoarsely, "what are we going to do without her?"

"I can't even imagine it," I said.

"Such a shock," Simms said. I knew what he was referring to: not just the shock of the call this morning, but the reality of returning to Mimosa Grove. I imagined when their plane was aloft, and on the hour and a half drive from Panama City, he and Maddox had talked little, if at all. Or it had been small talk; the upcoming storm, the rain, the condition of the roads. But once they got here, there was nothing to do but face what awaited them.

"What has to be done?" Maddox asked me, putting his empty cup down, and Simms jumped to his feet and went to get more coffee.

"You're supposed to call the sheriff. I think—you've got to go to town."

"To town?" he repeated, and I looked up at Simms helplessly when he returned with the coffee.

"I imagine you have to identify the body, Maddox," Simms said gently. Maddox flinched but nodded, his eyes closed. "Let me call Buddy for you," Simms added, leaving as Maddox asked me, "How am I going to tell Gus? How can I tell him such a thing?"

"When do you think they'll be here?"

"Late, thank God. I'd say ten o'clock at least. It's a long drive, and they didn't get off until mid-morning."

"Did you tell him anything?"

He shook his head. His shoulders were slumped, and his gray eyes bleary. "He was still asleep. Theresa was to tell him I had to go back with Simms to take care of some business. When I left, everybody was composing themselves so he wouldn't suspect anything. Rich was so undone, he was staying in the guest house rather than facing Gus. He's taking it hard."

I nodded, then looked up when Simms came back in the room. "I'll take you into town now, Maddox," he said.

"Sheriff'll meet us at the morgue, then take us to the site of the accident."

Maddox rose unsteadily, like an old man. At the front door, he turned to me. "Dean? Could you stay? I hate to ask you, but—"

"Of course I'll stay," I said.

He nodded, then turned to the car without looking back.

The only thing I could think to do was fix supper. In the fridge I found a container of oysters, fresh from Apalachicola Bay. The simplest thing to make, and one of the most nourishing, was oyster stew. After it was ready, I covered it and set it aside. Pouring myself a glass of wine, I made my way back to the library and sat on the sofa. I'd put it off all afternoon, but I had to call Ben. In spite of Ben's and Augusta's animosity toward each other, she'd been my best friend and he was my husband. I didn't know why I was reluctant to call him; somewhere in the back of my mind I associated him with John Marcus Vickery, illogical as it was. Ben had spent the day with John Marcus, most likely following him around like a puppy. I'd never hear the man's name again without reliving last night, Augusta's last night with me, and the awful anguish her love for that man had brought her. I went to the kitchen and left a message for Ben to call me at Mimosa Grove, that it was an emergency.

Simms didn't stay when he and Maddox returned, but when he left, I didn't want to be alone with Maddox. He was bound to ask me questions I couldn't answer. "I found oysters in the fridge, made some oyster stew," I told him.

"Comfort food," he said. "Though I'm not sure I can eat anything."

"Me neither, but we can't survive this without nourishment," I said, ladling up a bowl and handing it to him.

We sat at the kitchen table wearily, spooning in the stew

without talking. The phone rang constantly, but like me, Maddox ignored it, letting it switch to the answering machine. Finally he said, "I can't tell you how much I dread Gus coming home. He worshiped his mother. God! How can I tell him that she's gone?"

I pushed aside my half-eaten bowl of stew, suddenly nauseated. If only Augusta could have looked beyond Vickery and focused on Gus, I thought, tears stinging my eyes.

Maddox laid his spoon down. He took off his glasses and rubbed his eyes, then ran his fingers through his hair. "I don't know what I'd have done if you hadn't been here today, Dean," he said. "I'm fighting an urge to ask you to stay until Gus gets here. I'll have to tell him about his mama first, of course, but then if people he loves, like you and Theresa and Carl, could be here afterward—"

"Of course I'll stay. Ben's out of town today, so it's no problem."

"So Ben doesn't know yet?"

"Not unless he hears it when he gets in. Or on the radio . . ."

"I forgot about the local radio station," Maddox moaned. "Simms reminded me to call my sister, Kathryn, but I haven't even thought about calling other relatives."

"Maddox, the most important person now is Gus. Worry about him first, then the others. Kathryn'll call the relatives, won't she?"

"Yeah, you're right. I'm not thinking straight."

I looked at him helplessly. "I'm afraid it hasn't even hit us yet," I said. "The next few days are going to be tough."

We sat looking at each other bleakly, trying to imagine what lay ahead. "Dean?" Maddox said finally. "There's something about this that doesn't make sense to me, something I need to ask you about."

Stalling, I took a saltine and crumbled it into my soup.

Suddenly there was a banging on the back door, then it was thrown open. It was Ben, his dark head wet with rain. When he stepped inside the kitchen, brushing the rain from his suit jacket, I knew he'd come straight from Pensacola, still dressed in his brown tweed suit, wrinkled from a day's ride. He saw Maddox before he saw me. "Maddox!" he cried. "I just got into town and heard about Augusta."

Maddox got to his feet and held out his hand to Ben, but Ben ignored it and put an arm around him instead. "Oh, man, I cannot tell you how sorry I am," he said, shaking his head sorrowfully, hugging Maddox to him, although he almost had to stand on his tiptoes to do so. "Is there anything I can do for you?"

Maddox's face was expressionless as he shook his head. "I can't think of anything, but thanks for asking."

Ben's eyes fell on me, and he came over to my chair, holding his arms out. I got up awkwardly, banging my leg on the chair, as he hugged me, too, then stood with an arm around me, patting my back. "I am so sorry, Dean," he repeated, still shaking his head back and forth. "Such a shock. Such a shock."

"An awful shock," I agreed, lowering my eyes.

"Sit down, Ben," Maddox said, gesturing to the chair at the other end of the table. Augusta's chair. I was in Gus's usual chair, between the two of them.

Ben sat down heavily and I did, too, but Maddox motioned toward the stove top. "Why don't you have some stew, Ben? It's nasty out there, and you're pretty wet," he said.

"Oyster stew?" Ben asked, raising his eyebrows. "You bet. One of my favorites." He struggled out of his wet jacket and hung it on the back of the chair. "Of all days to go off without my raincoat," he muttered.

Maddox filled a bowl, stuck a spoon in it, then put it in front of Ben. "Need anything else?"

Ben looked around the kitchen until his eyes fell on the coffeemaker. "Got coffee?" I jumped up to get it for him so Maddox could sit down, stop waiting on Ben.

Ben took a handful of crackers and crumbled them into his bowl of soup. "Umm . . . this stew's great. Perfect." He ate gustily before turning to look at Maddox, who was sitting slumped in his chair, staring at nothing. "Ah, Maddox? Does Gus know about his mother yet?"

He flinched. "No. I flew back from Sarasota this afternoon with Simms Legere."

"Good you had a friend with you. I haven't seen Simms since . . . ah . . . last year." Ben said. His brow wrinkled as he spooned up the stew, and I remembered: almost a year ago now, the infamous scene here at Mimosa Grove, when Libby caught Simms in bed with Celeste, Augusta laughing like a hyena.

"Gus is coming back with Carl and Theresa, who drove my car down," Maddox continued. "They have relatives there and we traveled together." He didn't mention Celeste being with them, and I was glad, because Ben was so nosy, he was sure to ask why she was with the Hernandezes, what the connection was. I assumed Carl would drop Celeste off at her place when they came through town, on the way to Mimosa Grove.

"When will they be back, tomorrow?" Ben asked Maddox. He finished the stew and eyed the bowl wistfully, so Maddox got the pot off the stove and poured the rest of it into his bowl.

"No, tonight." Maddox glanced at the clock as he sat down. "About an hour now."

"Then you'll tell Gus? Or you'll wait until tomorrow?" Ben persisted.

Maddox shrugged. "Wish I could wait until tomorrow, let Gus come in and make up some story to explain his mother's absence. But I'm afraid that wouldn't work. My sister and her husband are flying in tomorrow, as well as a lot of others, I'm sure, and he'd wake up to chaos. No, I have to tell him tonight."

"It's not going to be easy any time you do it," Ben said, and Maddox nodded agreement. Finally Ben asked the question I knew was coming. When had I reached the point of being able to read him like a book?

"Ah, Maddox?" Ben said, clearing his throat, shuffling in the chair. "What about the arrangements?"

Maddox raised his head and looked at him, puzzled. Watching his face, I saw the exact moment of recoil when he understood what Ben was asking. "They took her to Johnson's after I—identified the body," he said. "So they'll handle the arrangements."

Ben nodded solemnly. "O. C. Johnson's in my church. He may be the finest funeral home director I've ever known."

There was an awkward silence, then Maddox said, "I've got to meet with him tomorrow afternoon at two. My sister, Kathryn, will go with me."

"So let's see," Ben continued, "that means visitation won't be until Wednesday night, then, and maybe the service Thursday. That what you're thinking?"

"Ben," I said, "I don't imagine Maddox wants to think about that tonight. When his sister gets here—"

"No, it's okay," Maddox interrupted. "It's got to be done. O.C. will ask me these sorts of questions tomorrow, and I should give some thought to them before I meet with him."

"Yes, but you'll have Kathryn with you," I said. "In times like these, it's important to have another person to help you look at things."

"Dean's right," Ben agreed, throwing me a pleased look. "So I'll be glad to meet you at O.C.'s office tomorrow, if you like."

Maddox looked startled. "Oh, no, Ben, no point in your doing that."

Instead of being rebuffed, Ben leaned forward and put a hand on Maddox's arm. "It's entirely up to you. Sometimes my church members want me there from the beginning, others wait and call me in after they've worked out the arrangements with the funeral home. Just know that I'm available whenever."

Maddox stared at him as understanding dawned in his eyes. At a time like this, Augusta was Ben's. She was a member of First Methodist, albeit an inactive one. Ben would be a vital player in the funeral service, regardless. Over the years, I'd seen Ben do countless funerals for people unknown to him; church members who attended other churches for years but had neglected to move their memberships.

Before anything else could be said, a voice over the answering machine caught our attention. All evening the phone had rung and we could hear the caller leaving his or her message, which we'd ignored, talking over them. This time we heard Carl's heavily accented voice loud and clear, calling from the car phone to say they were a few miles outside of Crystal Springs and should be arriving at Mimosa Grove shortly.

Ben took his coffee cup to the sink as I got up, too, and stuck the few dishes we'd used in the dishwasher. Ben came back to the table and put a hand on Maddox's shoulder. "Well, Dean and I will be on our way now," he said, "so you can get yourself prepared for the conversation with your son. Know that you will be in my prayers, you and Gus both."

I looked over at Ben as he took his jacket off the back of the chair, shook it out, and put it on. "Maddox asked me to stay, to be here for Gus after he talks to him," I said.

"Oh!" Ben said, pausing as he buttoned the suit jacket on. "Well, sure. I just assumed they'd want to be alone, but of course, we'll be glad to stay." He began taking the jacket off again, but Maddox stood, holding his hand up to stop him.

"No, no," he said, shaking his head. "Y'all get on home before the storm gets any worse."

"Of course I'll stay, Maddox," I said, coming to stand by him, throwing Ben a look. Surely he'd understand that since he wasn't close to Gus, the invitation wasn't meant for him. "I want to be here for Gus, I really do."

"We'll be glad to stay," Ben said, as though I hadn't spoken.

Maddox shook his head. "I appreciate the offer from both of you, but I'm thinking now I'll send Carl and Theresa home, too, then talk to Gus, just me and him."

"Sounds like an excellent plan," Ben said. "Why don't we have a word of prayer before I go?" As I bowed my head for the prayer, I knew there was nothing to do now but go home. Even though I resented Ben butting in, I felt a great relief. I'd never forgive myself if I went to pieces in Gus's presence.

If I hadn't gone back to the kitchen to get a glass of water before going to bed, I would have made it without having to talk to Ben. He beat me home by a couple of minutes, long enough for him to be in his room when I got in. The first thing I'd done was take Augusta's note and put it in my jewelry case. When the funeral was over, when everyone went back home and things settled down, I'd give it to Maddox. After washing my face and getting out of my clothes into my old flannel gown, I went to the kitchen for a drink of water, my throat dry from the raw weeping of today. Just as I turned to go back to my room, Ben was there, in his pj's, heading toward the fridge.

"Did you remember to get more ice cream?" he said, opening the freezer at the top and peering in.

I nodded wearily. My exhaustion had caught up with me, and all I wanted to do was collapse on my bed. "Yeah. I got the real stuff this time." He'd flung a fit because I'd tried to switch him to frozen yogurt.

He fished it out and began searching for a spoon. I started out of the kitchen with my water glass when his voice stopped me. "Dean?" He stuck the ice cream carton in the microwave and punched in sixty seconds. "I called Pensacola, told Dr. Vickery about Augusta. He was devastated, and said for me to express his sympathy. Said he'd stop by here on his way back to Tallahassee tomorrow."

I reeled and reached out for support, grabbing the door frame. Oh, God! If John Marcus Vickery showed up tomorrow, how would I face him? I turned my head so Ben wouldn't see my face. He spooned the half-melted ice cream from the carton, dispensing with the nicety of putting it in a glass.

"Have you thought about what could've happened if you'd been in the car with Augusta this morning?" he said, his eyes on me curiously.

"I can't talk about it tonight," I said.

"Seventeen messages on the answering machine when I got home this afternoon," he continued, oblivious. "Every one of them someone calling about Augusta. I've never been so shocked in my life."

"It was a shock," I muttered inanely. "I'm going to bed now. I can't stay up any longer."

"One of the messages was from Maxine Scoggins, dispatcher at the sheriff's office. You know her, don't you?"

"When I see her, is all," I replied.

"Maxine said there'd been a terrible accident, that Augusta'd been killed on her way out of town," Ben said, his voice puzzled. "All the other messages said she was going into town from Mimosa Grove. Said she lost control of the car on the old Crystal River bridge. Course, it makes no sense why she was going that way, except Augusta always did things that made no sense. But why do you think Maxine got it mixed up? I mean, if it'd been anyone else, I wouldn't think anything about it. But being the dispatcher, she ought to know better, wouldn't you think?"

I shrugged, wary. "Maybe that's what they thought at first. I think the car flipped around a few times, or something. There are always crazy rumors when things like this happen." There, I'd said it. Plant the idea in Ben's mind, and the way he talked with everyone in town, he was bound to spread it. Hopefully when suspicious ideas were brought up, he'd be the one to say, "Oh, you know how rumors go around." As I stumbled back to my room, I thought about facing John Marcus tomorrow. I'd have to watch him fooling people with his charisma and slick charm, playing the role of Augusta's beloved former pastor, extending his sympathy to her grieving family. I couldn't stop him from coming to the funeral. But, somehow, I'd get him alone and tell him if he ever came around here again, I'd expose him.

Fifteen

IT WAS LATE WHEN I got to Mimosa Grove, carrying a Red Velvet cake in a Tupperware container. The wide grounds were full of cars, many on the edge of the driveway, muddy now from the rains. Groups of men stood outside under moss-hung oaks as they smoked and talked. The Hernandezes' youngest son, Joe, being groomed by Maddox to help Carl manage the place, was cleaning up debris from the storm last night, fallen palm fronds and broken tree limbs and brown oak leaves scattered by the winds.

People everywhere in the house, standing in groups, were speaking in hushed whispers. Ben was here somewhere but I didn't look for him, afraid John Marcus would be with him. Simms Legere was with Father Bush, and the couple with them I recognized from family photos, Maddox's sister, Kathryn, and her husband, Bill. Kathryn was between Augusta's age and mine, and although Augusta had liked her sister-in-law, they hadn't been close. Two women couldn't be more different. Kathryn, sandy-haired and freckled, had an open, engaging face with none of Augusta's complexities.

Her husband, Bill, a basketball coach, was as wholesome and uncomplicated as his wife, and Gus adored him.

In the kitchen I expected to see Augusta standing over her copper pots, but it held only Theresa Hernandez, dressed in black, her back to me as she fixed coffee.

"Theresa?"

When she saw me, her placid face crumbled and she burst into tears. I caught her in my arms, both of us weeping, the cake in the Tupperware container pressed between us. The kitchen was full of food: platters of hams and cheese, potato salad, casseroles, pimento-cheese sandwiches, cakes and pies, the usual funeral fare. "Are things okay here?" I asked. Exhausted, I'd slept all morning, until Maddox had called to find out when I was coming to Mimosa Grove. When I'd asked how Gus took it, he answered in one word. "Bad," he said curtly, hanging up.

"Maddox is holding up well," Theresa answered, dark eyes grave. "Men always do, times like these."

"But Gus isn't, is he?"

Theresa shook her head. "Gus is very bad. Last night was terrible. He screamed for his mother for so long that Maddox called me and Carl to return. Finally, Maddox had to call Dr. Brandon, who came out and gave the boy a shot. He slept all morning. His uncle Bill played computer games with him, and now he's sleeping again."

I sighed. "At least Maddox and Kathryn have the funeral home visit behind them." What a ghastly ordeal that was, hearing the undertakers talk about waterproof vaults and steel-enforced caskets, as though any of that mattered. And then, walking through the display of satin-lined caskets and picking one out, as though shopping for a new appliance at Wal-Mart.

"Maddox said to let him know when you got here. He wants to ask you something about the service tomorrow," Theresa said.

"So they've decided to have it tomorrow?" While I baked the cake, Ben had told me talk was going around that Maddox would have a graveside service tomorrow, no church service and no visitation. Folks were scandalized at the haste and briefness of the service, but I'd understood. No point in dragging the pain out, just to appease the proprieties of the town.

"Yes." Theresa nodded, and though her face remained expressionless, it was obvious that she didn't understand, either. Of the old school, she'd be more comfortable with visitation at the funeral home, a service at the church, a graveside service afterward. "Let me get Maddox. It's good you're here for them," she added. Oh, God, what did she mean by that? Surely no one expected me to offer much consolation.

The kitchen door swung open and Maddox walked in. "Dean? Theresa told me you were here," he said briskly, crossing the room to where I stood. I held him to me for a moment, but neither of us cried again. He was composed and together today, not pale and shaky like yesterday. Theresa was right; he was holding up because he was a man and expected to.

"I brought the Red Velvet cake that Gus likes, remember?" I told him, patting his shoulder. "Gus called it Beanie's church-lady cake because I got the recipe from Noreen."

Maddox nodded grimly. "Maybe you could get him to eat something. I'm worried, Dean. I knew he'd take it hard, but . . ." His voice faltered and he turned away, took a step toward the cabinet. "Ah, fresh coffee. Let's sit down and have a cup. I need to ask you a couple of things."

"You sit, I'll get the coffee."

"About Gus," Maddox said when we sat across from each other with coffee cups in hand. "Bad as I feel sedating him, he's so high-strung, I'm afraid he'll come apart. Do you think I'm doing the right thing?"

"What does Dr. Brandon think?"

"That sedation's preferable to Gus going catatonic on us."

"Then I'd listen to him. If that's what it takes to get Gus through this, do it."

"Gus adores Kathryn, but he's having nothing to do with any of us. Bill played some computer games with him, then Gus ordered him out of his room. I wish now they'd brought the kids, but Kathryn thought they were too young. Oh—you won't believe what Gus did after running Bill out."

"I'm afraid to ask."

"When we got back from the funeral home, Ben was here, said he'd go up and see Gus." He stopped, trying not to smile. "Gus yelled at him through the door, told Ben to go to hell."

I put my hand over my mouth in surprise. "He's never done anything like that, has he?" Augusta had always made sure Gus's manners were flawless.

Maddox shook his head, then ran his fingers through his hair. "Never. I told Ben I'd make him apologize immediately, but Ben said he understood. Anyway, you can figure out what I'm asking you, if you'll be the next one to work on Gus, even knowing what might happen."

"I'll try to lure him down with a piece of cake."

He nodded. "Here's the other thing. Guess you've heard about the graveside service tomorrow at eleven? In lieu of visitation, everyone will be invited here for lunch afterward. Visitation would be too hard on Gus, and there's—ah—no question of having an open casket." He paused when I flinched and closed my eyes. "You know, Dean, Augusta was so young that we never talked about anything like this." He took his glasses off and wiped them clean, peering through them absently before putting them back on. "I have a feeling she might've preferred cremation, having her ashes scattered at sea or something romantic, but she'll be buried in the

Holderfield family plot. . . ." He shrugged, then got up abruptly. "More coffee?"

After refilling our cups, Maddox continued. "I'm finally getting to the big question. I was thinking about our theme song for the songfests, 'Drifting Too Far from Shore,' the one Augusta loved so much." His voice broke and he cleared his throat, not looking at me. "I wondered, could you . . . at the graveside service . . ."

I covered my face with my hands. "Oh, God, no. Please don't ask me. I couldn't do it."

Suddenly he was on his feet, walking to the sink, putting the cup in with a loud clank. "No, of course not. I shouldn't have asked."

"It's okay," I whispered, taking a big gulp of coffee and burning my mouth.

"What was her favorite Scripture?" he asked suddenly, coming back to stand in front of me.

"Ecclesiastes. You know, to everything there's a season."

He frowned, his eyes troubled. "I don't know if that's appropriate. Do you?"

"You mean, for tomorrow?" I thought a minute, then shrugged. "I don't know."

"I don't think this happened because it was Augusta's time to go, do you?"

I shook my head adamantly. "No. I don't think that way. Maybe Celeste does, but not me."

"Does Ben?"

I looked at him, surprised. "I don't think so. Why?"

"Ben's going to do the service, he and Father Bush. Dr. Vickery called and offered, but I didn't think we needed that many for a graveside."

"Thank God," I murmured, but he didn't hear me.

"Dr. Vickery's coming for the funeral, said he was coming here today but something came up, so he and Beth will arrive tomorrow," Maddox continued, unaware of my reaction. If Beth was with him, I wouldn't get a chance to speak to him alone. But I would, eventually. I'd not rest until I did. "Rich is flying in, but Godwin's not able to," he added.

"I'm glad Rich is coming," I said. But poor Godwin, how could he stand it? He loved Augusta as much as any of us, and for a man like him, not being able to pay his last respects would be an awful indignity.

"When you get a chance, Dean, I wish you'd call Celeste. She doesn't want to come out here . . ." Maddox paused and lowered his voice, even though we were the only ones in the kitchen, "because of Simms and Libby. I volunteered Rich to take her to the funeral tomorrow."

"Good idea. I'll go by and see her when I leave."

The kitchen door swung open and Maddox's sister, Kathryn, came in, arms outstretched. "You've got to be Dean," she said as we hugged. She was prettier up close, with Maddox's gray eyes and fair springy hair, cut short and close to her head.

"Dean's going to work on Gus next," Maddox told her.

"Great," Kathryn said, studying me. Apparently I passed her scrutiny, for she kept an arm around my waist as she turned to her brother. "Maddox, Dr. Brandon's here."

"You go talk to Chuck, Maddox, and I'll go upstairs and see if Gus'll talk to me," I said, taking my cup to the sink.

"Good plan," he said, nodding solemnly. With his arm around Kathryn's waist, they walked toward the door together. Maddox's shoulders were slumped as he leaned on his sister for support; only on the surface was he holding up well. He and Kathryn were almost out the door when I stopped them.

"Maddox!" Blinking back tears, I watched him stop at the door and turn to me. "That, ah, song for the service tomorrow? I'll do it."

"Thank you, Dean," he said, then went out the kitchen with his sister, the door swinging behind them.

When Gus didn't answer my knock on his bedroom door, I turned the knob and found it locked. "Gus?" I called out. "It's me, Beanie."

There was a rustling behind the door, then Gus's voice. "I want my mama, Beanie," he sobbed.

"I know you do," I said. "Let me in, and we can talk about it, okay?"

"I don't want to talk about it," he said. "And I want all those people downstairs to go home."

"They're here because they love you and your daddy. And they're sad about what happened to your mama, too." He still sobbed but didn't open the door. "Gus, I made church-lady cake. If you'll open the door, I'll get you a piece."

"I don't want your stupid old cake."

"Gus, remember how your mama taught you good manners? Do you think that was a nice thing to say?"

Again, silence, then he said, "I'm sorry, Beanie. I wouldn't care for a piece of your stupid old cake, thank you."

"That's better, I guess. If I'm standing outside your door with a piece of cake, you'll open up and see if you want it, okay?"

"Okay," he said reluctantly, and I hurried away before he could change his mind. As I made my way down the stairs, I had a flash of anger toward Augusta. Why hadn't she thought of the lost little boy she'd leave behind when she ran off?

The cemetery out from Crystal Springs was a pretty one, with honeysuckle on the wrought-iron fence, heavy magnolias shading tombstones, and tall oaks draped in Spanish moss like mourners in long veils. The Holderfield family was seated under the funeral home tent, and a crowd stood huddled behind them, pulling hats and scarves closer against the morning chill. A strong breeze cut through the trees, fluttering the edge of the dark-green canvas tent. Ben, decked out in his black flowing robe and white shawl embroidered with a gold cross and flame, stood next to Father Bush, who was dressed in a white robe with gold trimmings. Ben met my eyes as I approached the tent, and I looked away quickly. We'd argued last night after returning from the Holderfields' and had barely spoken this morning. He'd been angry because Maddox had turned down Dr. Vickery's offer to help with the service, and I'd turned on him furiously. He'd been so astonished that I had to backpedal quickly. The argument with Ben on top of my grief had left me feeling raw, torn apart in all the places of my life.

Standing at the head of the casket with Father Bush, Ben looked over the crowd until the whispers and shuffling of feet quieted, then held his hand high. After he did his part of the service, Father Bush, his face reposed and sweet, sparse white hair blowing about his head, stepped forward. When he began the eulogy, Gus started to weep in convulsive shudders. Although Maddox drew his son close, his eyes were vacant as he stared at his wife's casket. The funeral ritual with its majestic ceremony had brought me comfort in the past, but today it seemed hollow. I met Father Bush's eyes as he finished the eulogy, crossed himself, then motioned for me to come forward. Sitting in a small chair, I got out my dulcimer as someone whispered, "What a funny-looking guitar." A smile tugging at my lips, I felt Maddox's eyes on me and looked up. Our eyes met, and my smile died as my fingers strummed the cold strings, and my voice moved like the icy breeze over the suddenly stilled crowd as I sang my and Augusta's song, "Drifting Too Far from Shore."

As soon as the last note floated over the funeral tent, the service was over. People around me began to surge forward to greet the family members. It was over. Augusta was dead and soon would be buried in the dark earth.

Back at Mimosa Grove, I helped the church ladies serve lunch to the crowd that arrived like a flock of blackbirds in their dark funeral clothes. Not up to standing around and making small talk in the crowded kitchen, I slipped out the back door and headed for the rose arbor behind the house. There I found a wrought-iron bench that had dried out enough to sit on. As soon as I sat down, John Marcus Vickery appeared and, without asking, sat down next to me. He must have seen me leave the house and followed me. I'd avoided him at lunch, but here, I wouldn't have to be civil. "I thought Beth was coming with you," I said when he sat down, my voice cold.

"A crisis with a student detained her," John Marcus said, eyeing me warily.

"Guess it'd be awkward for her, anyway," I said.

"How so?" he asked, frowning.

I shrugged, turning my back to him and looking out over the rosebushes, stark and brown-leafed in the early afternoon sun. "Bet you can figure that one out all by yourself."

"You blame me for Augusta's death," he said with a heavy sigh.

"Must be how you've gotten to such a high position." My laugh was hard and bitter; bitter as my heart. "Your powers of observation."

"I couldn't leave here without seeing you, Dean; tell you how very sorry I am."

"I can't imagine why you'd want to see me," I said. "I can ruin you, you know. What I'd love to do is go inside right now and tell everyone the part you played in Augusta's death. I want to do that so bad, I can hardly stand it, but for Maddox's sake, and Gus's, I won't."

He sat slumped over, his hands held loosely together. "I don't care if you do. None of that matters now. I'm devastated." His voice broke in a hoarse sob. "I loved her, Dean."

I turned on him in fury, ready to call him a liar. But I was wrong. Devastation was written all over him, and it had taken a toll. He looked sick, weak, and frail. His hands trembled as he buried his face in his hands. "Oh, God," he moaned, sobbing. "Oh, my God!"

I closed my eyes and threw my head back, my face to the sun. Of course he'd loved her; how could he not? In spite of the fact that he seduced a girl-child and ruined her life, inadvertently caused her death, he'd loved her. His grief was too raw, otherwise. "She was coming to Pensacola when it happened, wasn't she?" he said finally, attempting to regain his composure. Pulling out his handkerchief, he wiped his eyes before glancing my way.

"Yeah. She was coming to you," I replied.

He let out a ragged breath, his shoulders slumped, and wiped his eyes again. "If only she'd listened to me! She pleaded, but I told her to wait. Wait until I got through in Pensacola, I said, then—we'd meet someplace. But she wouldn't listen. She never listened to me."

"Oh, really? If she'd not listened to you in the first place, she'd still be alive." I wanted him to suffer; wanted him to pay for what he'd done to her, when the only thing she'd ever done was love him too much.

"What am I going to do?" he sighed.

"I'm tempted to say that I don't really give a damn what you do, but I have to admit that I'm curious. Why are you asking me?"

He looked at me wearily. "I don't know. Because I have nobody to grieve with, I guess. I can't even let anyone know that I loved her."

"Oh, and that's supposed to break my heart? I'm supposed to feel sorry for you, grieving in secret over a woman whose life you ruined? Hey—maybe you'll come to her grave draped in a long black veil, like the song. I could play it in the background, standing behind the cypress tree. We could work out a routine."

"Oh, Dean," he said, "don't let this turn you bitter."

"I'd rather deal with my bitterness than your guilt." I took a deep breath and said, "John Marcus?"

He raised his head and looked at me, blinking like someone who'd been in the dark and suddenly found the sunlight in his eyes. I stared at him, unable to help myself. Although Gus's eyes may not be the exact color, that odd shade of burnished gold, there was no question of the similarity. There was something about the shape, too; elongated, almost slanted, like a cat half-asleep. Oh, God, I'd hoped that it wasn't true! Uneasy at my narrow-eyed stare, he asked, "What? What is it?"

"Until the other day, you'd not seen Augusta for what? Ten, eleven years?" Gus was ten now.

He nodded. "It was my fault. I wish to God I'd left her alone, but I was in Highlands, North Carolina, working on one of my books, and . . . I just wanted to hear her voice, make sure she was still happy with Maddox . . . but I shouldn't have called her! She left Maddox, came to Highlands, until I could convince her to return to Crystal Springs, try to work things out."

"Highlands! That's where she went another time . . ." My voice trailed off, and I swallowed painfully. Is that where Gus was conceived, and is that why she went back there?

"Didn't Augusta tell you about that time?" John Marcus asked.

I shook my head. "She never told me. I'm just trying to figure some things out." I stopped myself, taking a deep breath. The last thing I wanted was for anyone, especially him, to know that Gus might be his. I wondered if Augusta had proof, like blood tests or something, or had just fantasized because of Gus's eyes, so different in color and shape from hers and Maddox's. I remembered that she once told me it was the Spanish genes, and I'd believed her, having no reason to think otherwise.

"Nothing will bring Augusta back, but I'm going to give it all up," John Marcus said. "I'm leaving the pulpit, not letting them put my name up for bishop. That's the only way I can live with myself now."

I got to my feet, looking over the flowerless gardens. "I don't believe it," I told him. "Oh, you're full of remorse now, because Augusta's dead, but I don't think you can stay away from the adoration of the crowd. It's become a drug to you, one you're addicted to."

John Marcus rose unsteadily next to me. "Then I'll have to prove you wrong, won't I?" he said. "You know, you're quite a remarkable woman, Dean. You're so strong, so sure of what's right and wrong. No wonder Augusta loved you."

I stared at him, unblinking. "You don't know me, John Marcus. You can't even begin to know someone like me, coming from my background."

His smile was ironic. "No doubt you're right."

"Let me tell you who I am, so we can clear up any misconceptions. I was a scrappy backwoods kid who never had a single break, who made the choice to take my life and make something out of it rather than go back to the squalor I came from. In digging myself out of that dung heap, I found God, and I'll always be grateful. People like you and Ben—even Ben in his moments of piety—won't take that away from me. I won't be taken in by you and your kind again, and I hope that you leave the pulpit so no one else will be, either. Now do you know who I am, John Marcus?"

"Dean—" he began, reaching out to take my arm, but I

turned away from him. Coming toward us on the path, startled expressions on their faces, were Rich and Celeste.

"Here you are!" Rich said. "We've been looking everywhere for you."

"Rich must go to the airport," Celeste said, tilting her head as she looked at us.

Glancing over at John Marcus, I saw that he was trembling, a film of perspiration on his face.

"Dr. Vickery!" Rich cried. "Are you okay?"

"I—I'm fine, Rich, thank you," he muttered, putting a hand to his forehead. "Just got a little faint out here in the sun . . ."

"Let me help you back to the house," Rich said, but John Marcus shrugged him off.

"No, no, I'll be fine. I, too, have to leave, so I'll go inside and say good-bye to everyone now," he said. Perfunctorily, John Marcus hugged Rich, shook hands with Celeste, and turned to me. "Dean and I have already said our good-byes." And with a little wave to us, he turned and walked toward the house.

I turned to Rich as tears welled up in my eyes. "You're leaving now, Rich?" I cried, collapsing against him, wishing he could stay, or I could go with him. With Rich's departure, another part of Augusta would be gone from me.

Rich kept his arm tight around me as I buried my face in his chest, but there was no consolation for either of us. "I don't want you to go," I said finally, wiping my eyes.

"I dread going back," he whispered. "Godwin's in such bad shape."

"I've purposefully not thought of him all day, alone and grieving," I said, raising my head. "I take it back. Hurry home and see about Godwin, okay? And tell him I love him. Tell him how much he was missed today."

"I will," he said, kissing my cheek. "And come see us soon, okay?"

"Soon as things settle down here." It would be hard for me to make the trip that Augusta and I had planned together. So much so that I might never be able to do it, but I didn't tell Rich.

"Maddox won't ever come back to Sarasota," Rich stated, and I knew he was right. Not to the place where he'd heard about Augusta. It would always be spoiled for him, and I knew that Rich and Godwin would never return to Crystal Springs. Suddenly, everything had changed, for all of us.

When I returned home later that evening, Ben was sitting at the kitchen table eating a bowl of soup. I looked at him, surprised, as I put my purse on the kitchen chair.

"Ben?" I said, looking from where he sat hunched over his bowl to the cabinet, where an empty can of Campbell's soup stood beside the can opener. "I thought I saw you eating supper at Mimosa Grove." A few relatives had stayed for supper, along with Ben and Father Bush and myself. Gus clung to me, and I didn't leave until I'd gotten him to sleep.

Ben looked up at me guiltily, as though I'd caught him with his hand in the cookie jar. "Oh, yeah," he replied, "but it didn't fill me up. Did you eat?"

I shook my head, bone-weary.

"Looks like Gus got better today," Ben remarked, and I nodded absently. "Folks were saying Chuck had him pretty well doped up. As many situations as I've witnessed like this," he continued, "I've never seen a kid go to pieces like Gus did."

"He was very close to Augusta, and he's going to have a hard time with her death," I conceded.

"Too bad Augusta didn't think of that," Ben said.

"Oh, Ben, you know that none of us think we're going to be killed when we drive too fast in bad weather."

"There's plenty of talk going around," he said, cutting his eyes at me.

I sat across from him, feeling sick. "Folks say all sorts of things when something like this happens."

"I expected you to say that, but Augusta was heading out of town, evidently leaving Maddox again."

"That's ridiculous," I snapped. "She most certainly was not."

"I tell you," Ben continued, "I didn't approve of your getting so close to Augusta, but even so, I never dreamed she was so crazy. Like everyone else, I thought she was just kind of, you know, high-strung. Flighty." He sighed as I got to my feet, blinded by my tears. I almost fell over my chair. "I—Dean?"

I ran out of the kitchen, running to the darkness of my room, my hands over my ears like a child.

The long difficult day was not over for me yet. After I went to bed that night, I tossed and turned. I tried to pray, tried to ask God for comfort, but couldn't form a prayer on my frozen lips, couldn't make myself believe that God was even out there, much less that He'd listen to me. As I dozed on and off, images of the day played over and over. I saw the casket perched over the dark hole in the ground and smelled the sweet scent of roses. And, bigger than life, ballooning above everything like a cartoon character in a holiday parade, was John Marcus Vickery.

Finally I threw the covers back and left my room, making my way down the chilly hall to the master bedroom. Unlike me, Ben kept the curtains tightly pulled. His body was warm, snug in flannel pajamas, his feet in thick socks. Crawling into bed beside him, I huddled as close as I could without waking him. I closed my eyes to shut out the kaleidoscope of images from the day and instead saw Augusta, her eyes closed forever.

I slipped closer to Ben, not wanting to wake him, but longing for his warmth. I felt colder than I'd ever felt in my life, frozen to my very soul. In spite of my cautious moves, Ben turned over and jumped, startled awake. I was tempted to slip out before he could say anything, since all I'd wanted from him was his warmth.

"Dean?" he whispered hoarsely.

"Go back to sleep," I whispered. "I just didn't want to sleep by myself after . . . everything that took place today."

He sighed heavily, his irritation obvious. "Thanks a lot for waking me up," he muttered.

I didn't say anything, holding my breath, closing my eyes and willing him back to sleep. But instead he turned with another exaggerated sigh.

"Okay, Ben," I said, getting up. "I get the picture. You're going to hyperventilate if you don't stop sighing so loud."

"Oh, it's my fault I have insomnia? I'd expect some consideration instead of . . ."

But I didn't wait to hear the rest, leaving the room fast, hurrying back to my solitary bed and pulling the icy covers over me. I'd cried so much in the last few days that my eyes were swollen, my throat raw. I lay awake staring at the moonlight coming through the windows. There were no tears left for me to cry. For the first time in many years, I saw my life stretching before me like a windswept field. My path was an uncertain journey through a place as dark and frightening as a swamp. With Augusta gone from my life, gone was joy and laughter and friendship. Even with Ben sleeping down the hall from me, I was terribly, terribly alone.

Sixteen

I WAITED TWO WEEKS before returning to Mimosa Grove, weeks that passed for me in a blur of meaningless activity. Going through the motions of my life, I didn't even begin to mourn, I was so intent on simply doing the things necessary to make life go on without Augusta. I slept late after restless nights, I cooked and cleaned, attended church functions, and taught my piano students. But I didn't play my dulcimer again, and I didn't listen to the rumors that swept through Crystal Springs like tidal waves. Because I was the last one to see Augusta alive, I was questioned by everyone and contacted by reporters, but I didn't talk. Ben, too, kept his distance. We fell back into our perfunctory coexistence, polite to each other in public and as remote as distant planets in private. Consumed by a loss Ben couldn't begin to understand, I found absolutely nothing to say to him.

In Augusta's absence from my life, I sought out links to her. I called Gus often. He'd started back to school and was having such a difficult time that Kathryn extended her stay. I phoned Rich and Godwin, talking late into the night, and I visited Celeste in her store. I longed to ask Celeste what she knew of the rumors, but refrained, talking of other things instead. Libby Legere had pulled a surprise move and filed for divorce. Celeste would be subpoenaed in the case, and she was scared.

A few days after the funeral, I went to the St. Clair house and stared at it, as empty now as my life. In a tear-filled phone conversation the night before, Rich had given me the news: a great-nephew of Godwin's was buying the St. Clair place, and he and Godwin had decided not to return to Crystal Springs. I grieved anew, knowing Godwin was losing a home he'd loved with his heart and soul, leaving him as alienated from his roots as Rich was.

When I returned to Mimosa Grove for the first time since the funeral, Theresa Hernandez was outside with her son Joe, working the gardens. It was a perfect autumn day, the kind Augusta and I'd loved. I walked the pinestraw-strewn pathway to the back of the house and caught up with Theresa and Joe, in the beds next to the bench where I'd sat with John Marcus Vickery on the day of Augusta's funeral. Last night when I called Gus, Maddox took the phone and asked me to come to lunch today, discuss disposing of Augusta's things.

Wheelbarrow in hand, Joe waved, his crow-black hair gleaming in the sunlight. Theresa got nimbly to her feet when she saw me, brushing the dirt off her hands. "What are you and Joe doing?" I asked her.

She sighed. "Maddox wants Augusta's white roses gone before Gus gets home from school today."

"You're digging up her rosebushes?" Not the glorious white roses Augusta'd loved so much—I couldn't stand it. I walked to the ugly raw holes in the flower beds where the roses had once been. "How can Maddox do this?"

Joe lit a cigarette and blew the smoke my way. "Mr.

Maddox," he said, "said Gus had a nightmare, thought he saw his mother standing out here in the white roses."

"But—surely by the time they bloom again, Gus will be better . . ." I let my voice trail off. Despite my determination not to cry again, my eyes filled with tears, and the ruined rose gardens blurred and ran together in a watery tableau. Theresa took my arm and led me toward the house. "Come on, Dean," she said gently. "Let's you and me get lunch on the table."

I followed her, stumbling over the clods of loose dirt. Florida soil was not rich and earthy but sandy, insubstantial, slipping through your fingers like life itself. I pictured another dirt pile two weeks ago, a dark hole in the sandy soil. Suspended over it was Augusta's casket, holding her body, her fragile bones as delicate as a baby bird's.

As I helped Theresa set up our lunch on the sunporch, I waited for Maddox's arrival with trepidation, the thought of discussing Augusta's belongings painful. I was on edge after breakfast with Ben; when I'd said I was having lunch with Maddox to talk about disposing of Augusta's things, he'd perked up.

"So you're going to get first dibs at Augusta's stuff, huh?" he'd said as he poured cane syrup over his waffles.

I shrugged, my eyes glued to the thought for the day on the devotional calendar that hung over the kitchen table. *James 4:14. Whereas ye know not what shall be on the morrow. For what is your life? It is even a vapor, that appeareth for a little while, and then vanisheth away.*

Ben smiled like he'd just found the Holy Grail. "You'll be the best-dressed preacher's wife in Florida. Augusta had some great-looking clothes till she started dressing like a hippie."

"Her clothes wouldn't fit me, Ben. She was not only taller, but several pounds lighter."

"That's for sure. You've got some meat on your bones."
Ben studied me curiously. "I can't wait to see what you come
home with," he said, and I rose, turning away from him before he could see how his words stung.

Maddox looked terrible. Normally robust, he'd lost
weight, his skin slack, his tanned complexion ashen. His eyes
were red-rimmed, as though he wept long, lonely hours for
Augusta. He appeared much older than his forty-eight years,
and I could see how he'd look as an old man.

"Dean—so nice to see you," he said formally, holding
out his hand. I hid my surprise at his haggard appearance,
longing to comfort him, but he was distant, remote as a star.
"So you and Theresa decided it was warm enough for lunch
on the sunporch, huh?"

"That's right," I said, determinedly cheerful. "Augusta
and I loved eating out here . . ." I faltered at the look on his
face, but he moved to pull out a chair for me, and I sat down
with my face burning. I shouldn't have brought up Augusta's
name yet, so nonchalantly. And just this morning I was looking down my pious nose at Ben for his insensitivity!

After helping ourselves to the lobster bisque Theresa
brought in with a basket of her homemade rolls, we fell silent
until I said, "Joe and Theresa told me Gus has been having a
problem with nightmares."

Maddox nodded. "He retreats to his room after school,
comes out and eats dinner, then retreats again. Theresa stays
with him until I get home, which seems to be his worst time."

I thought for a minute, studying my plate. "Maybe I
could come out some, help him with his homework, or . . ." I
paused, shrugging. "Do some things with him, take him into
town for an ice cream or something."

"Sure," Maddox said. "But don't be surprised if he
doesn't respond much. I'd almost rather see him raising hell
like he did right after Augusta's death than like this. If this

keeps up, we'll try therapy, but for now, the school counselor says to give it more time."

I nodded. What else could he do?

"Dean?" Maddox wiped his mouth with his napkin and looked at me. I swallowed my soup nervously, waiting for him to bring up Augusta's things. Instead he surprised me. "Lot of rumors are going around about Augusta, you know."

I turned my head from him. Hidden away in my jewelry box was a note, addressed to him, that I *had* to hand over, soon. It wasn't fair that I keep it from him. I should tell him, at least prepare him for it, but I couldn't. Time, I'd said. I'd give him some time to get better. "I know," I said.

"How was she when you and she stayed out here that Sunday night? I'd talked to her earlier and she was fine."

I picked at my roll in order to avoid his eyes. "When I got here, she was scared because the lights were out. We built a fire and sat in the library; I played music until she went off to sleep. When I woke up the next morning, she was gone."

He took off his glasses and rubbed his eyes. "Then it makes even less sense, doesn't it? That she'd . . . ah . . . run away again. Doesn't add up, any way you look at it. You don't believe she was leaving town, do you?"

The question I'd hoped he wouldn't ask me. His eyes were on me, but before I could say anything, he sighed. "Well, I'll be goddamned. You're not sure, are you? The rumors have gotten to you, too, haven't they?"

"Absolutely not," I said, my face burning.

We were silent a minute as Maddox moved his wineglass around with both hands, dawdling absently, staring at nothing. "Augusta was never completely happy with me," he said finally.

"How can you say that? She never gave any indication of . . . of not being happy with you." Until the last time we were together, so my statement was at least half true.

"Remember I told you she only let you into her life a little bit? She never let me in. There was always a part of her I couldn't reach."

There was nothing I could say in response to that, knowing it was true. "But she did love you, Maddox," I insisted, and to my relief, he nodded, although halfheartedly.

"Oh, yeah, I think she came to love me, in her way. Never like I loved her. Not even close." His voice was bitter. "I never want to love that way again. I swear to God, I don't."

It shocked me how closely his words echoed Augusta's the weekend before she died. "I hope you never love anyone like that, Dean," she'd said. "It hurts too much."

Before we could say anything else, Theresa opened the door and stuck her head in. "Maddox? Your friend is here."

Maddox jumped, startled, and looked at his watch. "Damn, I lost track of time. Send her out here, Theresa, okay? And how about some of your coffee?" By the time Theresa had closed the door, it swung open again. His visitor must have been waiting right outside.

It was Libby Legere, sweeping onto the porch grandly, more elegant than ever in a beige suede suit with a long slit skirt and brown leather boots. Her smile was warm as melted butter. "Why, Dean—how nice to see you! I didn't get a chance to tell you how perfect your song was at the funeral."

"Thank you," I muttered. It made no sense that I'd been so comfortable with Augusta yet so awkward around Libby. So aristocratic was she that in her presence I felt gawky and tacky, like I had crossed eyes, buck teeth, and weighed three hundred pounds. Libby certainly hadn't let any grass grow under her feet in attaching herself to Maddox, I thought as I eyed her curiously. She'd kicked poor Simms out, and his lawyers had ordered him to have nothing to do with Celeste, she'd told me just yesterday, not even phone conversations.

"Sit down, Libby, have some coffee," Maddox said, pulling out another chair for her.

"Now I remember!" Libby said to Maddox, raising her eyes to him as she sipped her coffee. "You couldn't do lunch today because of meeting with Dean about Augusta's things. Y'all get everything disposed of?"

Maddox looked at me as he stirred his coffee. "Actually, we didn't get to it, did we? Kathryn got all of Augusta's things out of our room and boxed up stuff to store. Isn't there a keepsake of hers that you'd like, Dean?"

"Right offhand, I can't think of anything." I didn't need anything to remember Augusta by; she'd always be with me.

Libby's eyes traveled over me as she tucked a golden-brown lock of hair behind her ear. "Can't you wear her clothes? As a minister's wife, you have a lot of dressy functions to attend. Size four, Maddox?"

I snorted. "I couldn't get my big toe into a size four."

"Kathryn couldn't wear them, either," Libby sighed, and I felt like a hippopotamus.

Maddox looked my way. "Augusta'd liked you to have something, Dean. Why don't you think about it and let me know?"

I nodded glumly. Disposing of Augusta's stuff was like uprooting her roses. I hated to think of all that was left of her put out of sight forever. As though reading my mind, Maddox added, "Kathryn's stored everything in the attic so Gus can have it one day."

Libby beamed. "That will be so special to him." She glanced at her watch, then laid a hand on Maddox's arm. "I don't mean to rush you, but my agent's meeting us there in an hour."

I gulped down my coffee, and Maddox looked at me apologetically. "Sorry, Dean. I let the time slip up, and I'd promised Libby to look over some investment property this afternoon."

"Oh, no—please, go ahead—"

Libby leaned toward me. "You're welcome to come, too. Lake property, about fifty miles south, and quite a lovely ride."

"Thanks, b-but I've got to get back to my piano students," I stammered, getting to my feet and banging my knees on the table. Libby's eyes widened when I tripped pushing my chair back. I had to get out of her oh-so-elegant presence before I fell flat on my face.

I'd not lied about getting back to my piano students. They awaited me, demanding my attention, although my mind teemed with images of Mimosa Grove without Augusta, as gaping an absence as the rosebushes. The lessons seemed to go on forever today, the tedious running of the scales, then the simple tunes played over and over. My pupils' parents hoped they'd one day play for church, while I was sure most of them aspired to a rock band named something like the Acid Heads.

My pupils gone, I took my dulcimer out for the first time since Augusta's funeral. Touching the strings tentatively, I closed my eyes. The song I tried was a happy melody, "Ash Grove," an old British folk song, but I couldn't do it. My fingers froze, and I wondered if I'd ever play again. I sensed someone else in the room and turned, startled, to see Ben watching me, leaning on the door frame. Looking spiffy and handsome, he was dressed in his usual attire, a starched long-sleeved shirt with dark slacks and a tie. My hands fell from the strings, the music silenced.

"What's for supper?" he asked, shifting his weight impatiently from one foot to the other.

Supper! He'd told me he had a Council on Ministries meeting tonight and needed an early supper. I'd forgotten, but there were minute steaks in the freezer, and I could chop up some potatoes and onions with them, slice tomatoes. The thought of frying meat made me nauseous, but Ben would love it.

"Dean? I wondered about this," he said as I started past him, toward the kitchen. He was holding a letter in his hand.

I frowned, taking the envelope from him and turning it over. The return address was the University of Florida in Gainesville. "It's to me?" I asked, looking up from the envelope to Ben, who was squirming, his eyes lowered. "But—it's opened. You opened my mail?"

Ben shrugged. "Didn't think you had any secrets from me," he said defensively. I could feel his eyes on me as I took the letter out and scanned the contents. When I finished reading it, I looked up at him, astonished. "This is unbelievable," I murmured.

"What?"

It was too strange, this letter coming after my trip to Mimosa Grove, after seeing a part of Augusta destroyed and the rest of her packed away. "Since you read it," I said dryly, "you know it's from the chairman of Florida's music department, Dr. Zeanah. Maddox introduced me to him at the Halloween party." I looked back down at the letter. "It seems Augusta wrote and asked if they had a master's program with the dulcimer as the major instrument. Although they don't, he suggests I apply for a women's study project that's being offered next year, a grant having to do with discovering Florida heritage through folk music." I thumbed through the sheets of material and blinked in astonishment at the thick application. Then I tucked it under my arm and sighed, starting down the hall to the kitchen. Ben followed, plopping down at the kitchen table while I got out the frying pan.

"How about peeling the potatoes?" I asked, rather shortly. He looked up surprised.

"Where do you keep them?"

Sighing, I put a couple of potatoes in a bowl, laying the vegetable peeler on top, then went to the stove and threw two steaks into hot grease.

"How come Augusta sent that letter to Florida?" Ben asked as he struggled to peel the potatoes, grimacing as though I'd asked him to carve a marble statue. "First I've heard of you wanting to get a master's degree. What would you do with it, anyway?"

I didn't tell him that Augusta had often urged me to go back to school and teach at the community college; I'd earn more than the pocket money my piano students and occasional performances brought in. Ben had never wanted me to work outside the home, except for my piano students. He liked having me at his beck and call. "What does anybody do with one?" I said instead.

"No way you could go to Florida or FSU, either one," Ben said.

I looked up from the sizzling frying pan. "How come?"

"I'm not moving from Crystal Springs anytime soon. Not until the time's right." He held up his bowl. "What do I do with them?" He'd cut off more potato than peel. I took them from him, slicing them into the frying pan with the onions and steak.

I set the table, pouring us both a glass of tea. After dishing up Ben's plate and putting it in front of him, I sat down. "So, how'd it go today?" Ben asked as he stuffed steak and potatoes in his mouth and chewed happily. "Bring back a bunch of Augusta's stuff?"

I gazed out the window, longing for the leaves to turn, burst into glorious shades. The dogwood leaves had turned red, but that was about it. "Maddox had Joe and Theresa dig up Augusta's white roses," I said inanely.

"Huh?"

I shook my head. "Nothing."

"What'd you get of Augusta's?" he repeated.

"Her things are being packed away and I'll get something later," I said as Ben lustily wiped up the juices from his plate with a piece of bread. It occurred to me that he put all his passion into either eating or preaching. In all our years of married life, I'd gotten very little of it.

"How's Maddox doing?" he asked. A perfunctory question since Maddox had cast his lot with All Saints. The death of Augusta cut the final ties of the Holderfields with First Methodist.

"He's having a really rough time," I replied, and was surprised when Ben pushed his plate aside and nodded intently.

"He worshiped the ground Augusta walked on, didn't he?" he said. "Bet she lapped up his adoration, too. Only natural, don't you think? Anyone would." Ben's dark eyes met mine and held them for a moment, then he looked away quickly. "Look what time it is! Better run on to my meeting," he said. Rising to his feet, he left, pulling the door behind him.

I stared at the closed door. Oh, God, where had it gone? I'd once looked at Ben as Maddox looked at Augusta, eyes aglow. Had it worn away with the busyness, the endless church meetings, the mundane details of everyday life? In spite of his lack of passion, his streak of puritanism and piety, I'd fallen hard for Ben. But had I ever loved him as madly as Maddox had Augusta, as she had John Marcus? The thought shook me so badly that I began clearing off the table blindly. Fumbling, I banged Ben's glass against his plate, spilling it. The tea crept to the letter from Florida, and I watched the thick application form turn amber as the tea soaked into it. The rose garden, Augusta's things, now her surprise for me, all gone in one day. Unless . . . I grabbed the application, pressing it close, wiping it dry with a napkin. I might never go to Gainesville even if I could get into the program, but I wouldn't throw away Augusta's last gift. I'd send it off, at least. I owed her that much for bringing music back into my life.

A few weeks later, Maddox called and invited me to come out to Mimosa Grove for lunch again, as soon as I could arrange a time. When I told him that, because of the upcoming holiday season, I had a million things at the church I couldn't get out of attending, he suggested we meet for a drink instead. "Guess I just need someone to talk to," he told me. "But I know how busy you are now."

The loneliness in his voice moved me, and I reached for my calendar and pencil. "I'm not too busy to have a drink with you, Maddox; don't be silly," I said. "But you pick the place. I'm not too familiar with the bars of Crystal Springs."

He chuckled. "Me neither. Sometimes after work, Simms and I meet at the bar at the marina outside of town, if that's okay with you."

At the marina the following afternoon, Maddox and I sat in a booth and ordered beers. I nibbled peanuts and looked at him curiously. "In this divorce thing, you're torn between Libby and Simms, aren't you?" I said.

"Yeah," he replied. "But Simms knows I'll have to take Libby's side."

I didn't ask him why. It'd been less than two months since Augusta's death, so he wasn't actually going out with Libby, but I didn't feel comfortable discussing their relationship. After enough time passed, it'd be rather natural for them to get together again. Clint Black was on the jukebox now, singing with Wynonna, "A Bad Good-bye," one of my favorites. "Umm . . . love that song," I said.

"Haven't performed in a while, have you?" Maddox asked, looking at me over the rim of his glass.

I shook my head, not telling him I'd turned down several requests because I wasn't up to it. "Are you and Gus still going to Kathryn's for Thanksgiving?" I asked instead.

His face darkened. "Yeah," he said finally. "And back up there for Christmas, too. No way we could stay here. Christmas at Mimosa Grove without Augusta—I can't imagine it! I've already gotten permission to take Gus out of school a week early, so we'll be gone for three weeks, back after the new year."

"Guess that blows my Christmas present for Gus, then," I said. "I was going to ask you if I could get him a puppy."

Maddox raised his eyebrows. "A *puppy*? There are a hundred damn dogs at Mimosa Grove, always has been."

"Farm dogs. You and Carl and Joe have bird dogs and setters and retrievers. What about a puppy Gus can call his own? One he can take care of, cuddle and play with, like he did Ollie. I was thinking of an Ollie dog, actually, one of those long-eared whatchamacallits."

"A basset?" He thought about it, shaking his beer can to get more out. "Sounds like a good choice. You'd wait and bring it out after New Year's?"

I nodded eagerly, and he gave in. "Oh, all right." Then he smiled, his eyes softening. "More than all right. It's such a good idea, I'm kicking myself for not thinking of it first."

"Do you want to give it to him instead? I can get him something else."

"Naw. I'd have to take it to North Carolina, and Kathryn's kids already have a dozen dogs. He wants Santa to bring him a mountain bike. Tell you what. I'll tell Gus you have a special gift waiting for him so it won't be so hard to return home after Christmas."

I nodded, pleased, but then we grew quiet and gloomy

again, thinking of Gus's silent grief and the loneliness of the holiday season approaching. Always a bad time for mourners. "Guess what Gus and I get to do this afternoon?" Maddox said finally. "Matter of fact, gotta go now, before it gets any darker, and pick Gus up. Might as well come with me, Miss Bean. Suffer along with us."

"Dare I ask?" I said, standing up when he did.

"The headstone's here. I told Gus I'd take him to the cemetery to see it," he said grimly.

"Oh, God. Do you have to take him?"

"Believe it or not, he asked if he could go." On our way out, one of the men at the bar tipped his Florida Gators cap. "Afternoon, Mr. Holderfield," he muttered over his beer, and Maddox groaned as soon as we got outside. "Crap, now I know what they were staring at," he said, opening the Jeep door for me. "Didn't recognize J. T. Clark, who's worked for me for years. Guess he'll tell everyone at the plant that I'm running around with floozies and my wife barely in her grave."

"Floozies? Thanks a lot." Augusta would've gotten a kick out of the whole thing, the marina, Garth and Clint singing in the background, the men staring at us from under their caps. And now more gossip, all this town needed.

"I'll bet you, Miss Bean, it's those tight jeans of yours." Maddox grinned, cranking the Jeep. "Now on to Crystal Springs Cemetery. Never say you don't have a fun time with me."

The sun was setting when we got to the cemetery, almost beautiful enough to make our sad journey bearable, and we stood watching the pageantry over the dark tops of the cypress trees. Gus stood with his arms folded as though he were cold, his glasses reflecting the setting sun. "Mama loves sunsets," he said. "She can see them up close now."

"Out of the mouths of babes," Maddox said in a low voice as his eyes met mine.

" 'We see through a glass darkly, but then face to face,' " I quoted.

Theresa had sent an arrangement of smilax, hawthorn berries, and yellow mums, which I carried. "Want to put the arrangement on the grave?" I asked Gus, but he shook his head. Both he and Maddox averted their eyes from the new tombstone, although it was what we'd come to see. My eyes wandered to the inscription in an almost horrified fascination, but I immediately looked away. Augusta's name couldn't be there, on a tombstone—it wasn't possible! Kneeling, I anchored the heavy metal vase with gravel to keep it upright. Maddox and Gus shuffled around the other graves, reading the inscriptions of the Holderfields as though they'd never seen them before. Maddox had changed into jeans and a faded FSU sweatshirt, Gus was similarly dressed, and they looked so much alike standing together, their glasses glinting in the sun, that I whispered a prayer: "Don't let it be true. Please, dear God, don't let it be true."

They were next to Augusta's tomb now, having covered the whole plot. Nothing left to do but face it. Maddox went down on one knee in front of the headstone, his hand reaching out to touch the letters carved in the white marble. I couldn't stop myself from looking at him, his fingers tracing the engraved words like a blind man reading braille. Gus, too, stared at his father kneeling before the tombstone, new and white among the weathered ones around it.

"I wish Daddy wouldn't do that." Grimly he walked past me and tugged on Maddox's arm. "Daddy, stop it! Let's go home."

Maddox looked up at his son as though trying to remember who he was, then pulled himself to his feet and dusted the fine gravel off his knees. "Yeah, guess we should, son," he said in a dead voice. "It's about dark."

When Maddox moved, Gus was left facing the white headstone and the hated words were eye level, unavoidable: *Augusta Spencer Holderfield, beloved wife and mother, now with the angels.* Suddenly Gus reached for Maddox, his wails rising as he closed his thin arms around his father's waist. Maddox's shoulders began to shake with his own racking sobs as he gathered his son to him.

I longed to be brave and strong, to reach out and help both of them, but I couldn't. I buried my face in my hands and cried as well, weeping for the broken people Augusta had left behind, the sunset gilding us with a golden brush.

When I put my car in the garage, emotionally exhausted, I noticed a number of cars parked at the church, which meant Ben's meeting was still in progress. It was good and dark now, almost eight o'clock. I vaguely remembered something about a supper tonight, but couldn't recall what it was.

I heard voices as soon as I got in the house, then Ben's voice came from the living room, calling out: "Dean, is that you?" The kitchen was a disaster; Ben must have fixed dinner. Pushing open the swinging door to see what he was doing in the dining room, I stopped in my tracks, my mouth falling open as I looked at the crowd sitting around my dining room table at the same instant I remembered what Ben had said about supper tonight.

Everyone at the table, including Ben, jumped to their feet and began talking at once. Vanna Faye was the first one to reach me. "Dean!" she squealed, her hand to her throat. "Thank God you're all right. See, folks, here she is, all in one piece."

Ben was next, coming to my other side, his hands on his

hips. "We called the hospitals, the highway patrol, the sheriff's office . . . where on earth have you been?"

I looked around the table, my face flushed. Besides Ben and Vanna Faye, there were Lorraine Bullock, Sylvia Hinds, Collie Ruth Walker, Dickie Edwards, and Tom Farmer. The music committee of the church, whom I remembered exactly ten seconds ago Ben had invited here tonight for a potluck supper.

"I—I'm sorry I worried you," I stammered. Vanna Faye pulled up a chair for me as Collie Ruth went into the kitchen, pausing on her way to pat me on the back. I sank into the chair, horrified that I'd forgotten they were coming to plan the Christmas cantata. Ben returned to his seat, a worried frown on his face.

Collie Ruth reappeared with a glass of iced tea, which she placed in my hands. "Relax." She smiled. "We're having a real informal meeting, talking about the cantata while we eat our supper." Each of them had a plate piled high with food from their potluck dishes, the mess I saw in the kitchen.

"We did fine without any meat, Dean." Vanna Faye smiled vacuously at me. I blinked at her, puzzled, until I realized what she meant. At these potluck meetings, the hostess always provided the meat dish, and the others brought side dishes. I glared at Ben, who could have taken fifteen minutes to go to the deli and get a sliced ham, since he was the one who'd invited the committee here, not me.

"I'm so sorry," I muttered again, and Vanna Faye reached over and patted my hand. "Why don't you go fix yourself a plate?"

"Tell us where you've been first," Ben said, leaning forward. Beyond his concern was a look that said, And it had better be good.

I was too thrown off to even attempt to cover my tracks.

"I—I was at the cemetery," I said, my face burning. "I forgot the meeting here tonight."

"At the cemetery!" Ben cried. "All afternoon? We've called you, and Vanna Faye went out looking for you—"

"Don't you have a car phone?" Sylvia Whiney-Hiney squeaked.

"Of course not all day," I answered Ben, ignoring Sylvia. "I visited Celeste earlier, then . . . Maddox, and we took Gus to the cemetery . . ." It sounded so lame, I let my voice trail off, appalled.

"Celeste?" Dickie Edwards, a big fat man prissier than any woman in town, said. He was a marvelous tenor but his speaking voice bordered on falsetto. "Oh—you mean Miss Celestine Howell, out at the nursing home? Good for you, Dean. And how's she doing, poor old thing?" Although his face was sweet as a baby's, everyone in church feared Dickie's barbed tongue.

"That's not who she means, Dickie," Sylvia said gleefully. "You mean that fortune-telling woman who's a friend of yours, don't you, Dean?" She looked at me like a predatory animal.

Miss Celestine Howell, who didn't know she was in this world—it would be easy to pretend I'd visited her. Being both blind and deaf, she'd never tell on me, but I nodded weakly instead. "That's right. Celeste Cozma."

"Oh? Is she sick?" Collie Ruth said.

"No, I just paid her a—visit."

There was a dead silence until Dickie Edwards looked around the table, puzzled. "I don't believe I know who you're talking about," he said, wiping his lips with a napkin prissily.

Lorraine Bullock leaned forward, looking at Dickie over her half-glasses. She'd never pass up a chance to get me, and this one was ready-made. "Oh, yes, you do! The Gypsy woman who has that weird store on West Bay. The one who broke up Simms and Libby Legere's marriage!"

Dickie looked at me in horror. "She's a *friend* of yours, Dean? Surely not."

"She's a friend of mine," I said stiffly, and again, a dead silence fell around the table.

Ben cleared his throat and glared at me. "Well, I didn't apologize for you properly, Dean, because I was sure you'd had car trouble or been in an accident, or something, to keep you from being here for the supper."

"We're just relieved you're okay," Collie Ruth said quickly. "No need to keep apologizing. You took flowers to Augusta's grave, I'll bet?"

I nodded, grateful to her, as usual. "The headstone's in. I went with Maddox and Gus to see it for the first time."

Vanna Faye's face lit up. "Does Maddox have a black Jeep?"

When I nodded, puzzled, she wagged a finger at Ben, gurgling happily. "See, I told you that was her!" Laying a hand on my arm, she explained. "Brother Ben loses that bet. When he sent me looking for you, I went to the bank and the post office and everywhere, asking folks if you'd been in this afternoon. You know Nadine, at the Piggly Wiggly? She told me she saw you with Maddox Holderfield in a black Jeep! I told Brother Ben"—she looked at him, tilting her head prettily—"and he said Nadine didn't know what she was talking about because Maddox has a black Mercedes, not a Jeep!"

"The Jeep's black, too," I said lamely, but I dared not look at Ben. Last time I'd glanced his way, his eyes were like lasers, aimed right at me.

"Oh—y'all heard about the St. Clair house? A nephew's bought it and is moving in next year," Vanna Faye said.

"I hope he's not one of those you-know-what's, too," Lorraine said, moving her arms to suggest wings flapping.

"Oh, no," Vanna Faye said, big-eyed. "He's married."

"Well? So was the last couple who lived there," Dickie Edwards said, then poked skinny little Tom Farmer in the ribs, laughing at his own joke. "Get it? Ha-ha-ha-ha!"

"Go on and fix your plate, honey," Collie Ruth said to me, ignoring the others. "And why don't you put the coffee on while you're in there?"

I stumbled to my feet, glad for an excuse to get away from the accusatory stares. As I made the coffee, it was impossible not to hear the talk from the dining room, even with the swinging door closed.

"Let's get back to our discussion of the cantata," Collie Ruth the peacemaker said. "If we do 'Keep the Christ in Christmas,' we'll need both a piano and an organ. Okay with you, Sylvia?"

"I'm not sure now," Sylvia whined. "Who'll play the piano?"

"Why, Dean, of course," Collie Ruth said.

I held my breath as Sylvia said, "Ah . . . I don't know. Hundreds come to our cantata, Baptists, the 'Piscopals, everyone. Even the Catholics, since they got the new nun-lady to drive their van. We'd better make another choice."

"Why?" Tom Farmer asked, speaking up for the first time. Dickie's punch in the ribs must've given him courage.

Sylvia said in a loud whisper, "Forgive me for saying this, Brother Ben, but we can't count on Dean."

A long silence as I stood by the door, eavesdropping shamelessly. "After all," Sylvia continued, "tonight's not the only time she's let us down."

Finally Ben spoke up. "Everyone wants to do 'Keep the Christ in Christmas,' so I'll make sure that Dean plays the piano."

"Fair enough. I say we do it," Dickie Edwards said.

"Are you sure?" Sylvia said, her voice quivering. "You

told us she'd be here tonight, fix a meat dish. Don't know about y'all, but I'm not one of those saggitarians."

"Vegetarians, Sylvia," Dickie snorted.

"Sylvia's right," Lorraine put in, not bothering to lower her voice, even though everyone knew I was in the next room. "We need a commitment from Dean. It's not right to put Brother Ben on the spot."

Taking my cue, I walked into the dining room furiously, staring at Lorraine. "You're right, Lorraine," I said, my voice shaking. "*I'm* the one to make that commitment."

Smirking at me triumphantly, she pushed her glasses up on her nose. "I'm not one to talk about anybody behind their back," she said, and everyone squirmed. "So as the music director, I'll be the one to say it, Dean. Many times you haven't shown up to play—"

"Hold on. Once—not many times—I left during a heated meeting before church and didn't return to play. It was wrong to leave you without a pianist, and I apologized."

"Don't take but one time to be considered unreliable," she said. "Take tonight, for instance."

"This morning Ben told me y'all were meeting here; I let it slip my mind, and I've apologized."

"You didn't know until this morning?" Collie Ruth said, throwing a dismayed look at Ben.

Ben grinned easily. "I *reminded* Dean this morning," he said. "Of course I'd told her about it earlier." Of course he hadn't, but he trusted me not to contradict him in front of his church members.

"Let's resolve the cantata," Dickie Edwards said. "At this rate, we'll be here till midnight."

Lorraine shrugged. "It's up to Dean, whether she'll commit to playing the piano or not."

"What do you want me to say, Lorraine? I'll give you my word I'll be there."

"Good enough," Collie Ruth said.

But Sylvia Whiney-Hiney wasn't going to let me off the hook so easily. "You say that now, Dean, but what if you run out again before church starts?" she said. "Or, worse, run off somewhere with Maddox Holderfield?"

There was a sharp intake of breath both from Collie Ruth, sitting on Sylvia's left, and Ben, at the other end of the table. For a moment I couldn't see anything but a white blaze of anger.

"I *beg* your pardon, Sylvia. If I do what?" I said.

"I—I—didn't mean that like it sounded . . ." Sylvia stammered.

I turned my head from her to Lorraine. "Choose another cantata or get another pianist, Lorraine. As of tonight, I'm resigning from the choir." I turned to go out the door, but Collie Ruth jumped up.

"Oh, Dean, honey, please don't," she said.

"Don't pay any attention to Sylvia," Dickie Edwards chimed in. "Nobody else does." With a gasp, Sylvia jumped him, escalating the whole meeting into a fight.

"You shut up, Dickie," she snapped. "I'm not used to this kind of behavior from our preachers' wives—"

Collie Ruth's look shut her mouth in mid-sentence, but I turned toward the door, my eyes stinging with tears. Ben called after me, throwing his hands up in exasperation. "Oh, for heaven's sake, Dean, don't be so *sensitive*." Frozen at the door, I whirled around.

"You're right," I said, "I'm much too sensitive to stay here and be insulted in my own house. Except this isn't my house, is it?" I went through the door, letting it swing after me. But before I walked away, I pushed the door open again and stuck my head in. "By the way, *Reverend*. You know damn well that you didn't tell me about the meeting before this morning."

My exit this time was followed by the horrified gasps of everyone at the table. When the door swung to, it was Ben's voice that broke the silence. "I—I am so sorry, folks! I don't know what's gotten into Dean," he stammered. Leaving the messy kitchen behind, I went out the back door, walking as fast as I could away from the parsonage, hugging myself against the chill air.

Seventeen

IN THE MONTHS FOLLOWING Augusta's death, I found out how time passes when you're mourning: sometimes too fast, but more often, too slow. The good times go by swiftly, the bad ones like unwelcome guests. Over the next months, it was as though my heart had been cut out and I was expected to function without it; like being told, "Oh, don't worry; it's only your heart. A lot of people manage without one." Something funny would happen and I'd think, I can't wait to tell Augusta. In what had become almost daily phone calls, Maddox and I recounted similar dreams where she appeared to us and we'd say, "Augusta! I thought you were dead." And she'd laugh. "Me? Where'd you get such a crazy idea?"

Those were the bad times, more of them than the good ones. The best was Christmas, when I gave Gus the puppy. A magic time, the first since Augusta died. Later I blessed that charmed moment since it had to last so many months. As I grow older, I realize that's the way it is with happiness. That Christmas, Maddox gave me a framed copy of a Robert Frost poem, "Nothing Gold Can Stay," and I nodded as I read it.

Ben's family—his widowed mother as well as aunts and uncles and cousins whom we rarely saw—surprised us by their plan to spend the holidays with us, throwing me into a flurry of preparations; an excellent antidote for grief. Christmas with no one but Ben and me had always been depressing, since he didn't believe in the secular part of the season. With his family coming this year, he'd given in to my excitement over the decorating, baking, and shopping. It had made things more bearable between us. After that awful night of the choir meeting, the atmosphere at home had been so bad that I was relieved to have something—anything—to talk to him about.

Because of my falling out with the choir, I had some time on my hands and could finally play my music again. When asked to play for a Christmas party the first of December, I accepted, and afterward, I had more invitations than I could handle. Thrilled with the extra money to splurge on gifts, I accepted as many as possible, making sure none conflicted with church functions. Things were bad enough between me and Ben; if I had not appeared with him at holiday events, they would have been unbearable. Determined to put up a good front for his family's visit, I put off dealing with whatever it was between us. Another thing I couldn't handle.

Ben would have been furious if he'd known about my upcoming performance: playing in Crystal Springs's only night spot, the Crystal Cavern. A dark lounge on a back street, it was not the kind of place Ben and I'd ever go to. Not that it was disreputable; Maddox and Augusta had gone for drinks and dancing; Godwin and Rich often had dinner there. But it had the atmosphere of a nightclub, a place First Methodist wouldn't want its minister patronizing. On the night of my performance, I couldn't believe my luck when Ben announced that he'd be home late, since he was speaking at a meeting in Pensacola.

It was dark and smoky in the Crystal Cavern when I took my place on a small platform lit by candles. My audience sat on the barstools or at candlelit tables, drinking and laughing and dining as though I weren't there. It was after the dinner hour that they quieted down enough to request old favorites: "Jingle Bells," "The Christmas Song," "Winter Wonderland." They applauded unobtrusively, more intent on their drinks and conversations than my music, much to my relief. I was putting my dulcimer away when I heard a familiar voice from a table in the dark corner.

"One more request. Do you know 'Blue Christmas'?"

I turned and looked into Maddox's eyes. "Not as well as you do, I'll bet," I replied.

"Ha. You can say that again." He was slumped over the table, cradling a half-empty glass.

I put the dulcimer over my shoulder and went to his table. "What're you doing here, Maddox? Where's Gus?"

He squinted. "Who?"

"Very funny."

"What'd you think, Miss Bean, that I left the poor motherless kid alone to go out juking? He's spending the night at Theresa and Carl's." He motioned to the waitress and lifted his glass for a refill. "Which he's done the last two weekends, like it's a big adventure to go half a mile from his house. Packs his little suitcase and everything. Before Joe goes out on his hot dates, he teaches him soccer."

I smiled. "Learning a sport's just the thing for him now."

"The house is too quiet," Maddox said, "so I wander off. When I heard you were playing here tonight, I knew where I'd be."

I'd never seen him like this. "I thought you and Gus were leaving Sunday morning," I said. The plans were for me to come out tomorrow, Saturday, for good-byes before they took off for the holidays.

"Think I'll still be hungover Sunday? I've got all day to-morrow to recuperate." The waitress arrived with his refill, and he nodded toward me. "What will you have, m'lady?"

I hesitated, then shrugged. "Kahlúa on the rocks. With lots of cream." What the heck—just thinking about the holidays was enough to blow my diet. I pulled a chair up to the round table where Maddox sat. "Last time we had a drink together, we ended up in a dark corner, didn't we?" I said.

"A metaphor for our lives, maybe."

"Celeste would agree, I'm sure. She told my fortune not long ago. I'd gone to visit her, and she insisted on reading my cards."

"Oh, God almighty. Not you, too, Miss Bean," he groaned. "I thought you had good sense."

I laughed and stirred the Kahlúa, black and floating with thick cream. "Whatever gave you that idea?"

"Not the first thing I've been wrong about." He lifted his glass in a silent toast.

"Merry Christmas," I said, raising my glass.

"It's Christmas? Jesus Christ."

"That's the idea."

Maddox chuckled. "Tell me what your fortune is, Miss Bean. What did Celeste see in your cards?"

"Gloom and doom. A knight facedown, ten swords sticking in his back."

"If Madame Celeste can see into the future, how come she didn't tell Augusta to stay off bridges?"

I flinched, but I'd wondered the same thing. I sipped the creamy Kahlúa before replying, stirring it with my finger. "Actually, Celeste had a bad dream about Augusta before she died. And the first time we went to see her? She saw all sorts of bad things in Augusta's cards."

"No kidding? Maybe I should pay her a visit, then."

"You and every other man in town. The day I visited her

and she read my cards? A guy, a friend of Simms, was there when I arrived. Hitting on her. Can you believe that?"

Maddox studied me over the rim of his glass. "Of course. He's a man, and we're all untrustworthy shits. Or haven't you found that out yet?"

The image of John Marcus Vickery rose before me, in my mind's eye. If I'd ever had any doubts, he'd certainly made a believer out of me. Sneaking a glance at Maddox, I thought again of the note I had hidden from him. I couldn't give it to him before Christmas, but I would when he and Gus returned. I had to. This had gone on long enough. "You're looking awfully serious," he said, and I jumped, deep in thought. "Want another drink?"

When he motioned for the waitress, I looked at him in dismay. "You're having another one?" As soon as I said it, I grimaced.

Maddox smiled. "Don't think I need another one? Since I've got to drive home, you're right." He rose and pulled out my chair. "Come on. I'll walk you to your car."

Outside, he took the key from me and tried to unlock my car door. The struggle became a test of his sobriety, one he was failing. Throwing tact to the wind, I grabbed my key away and said, "I don't think you can drive home, do you?"

Maddox hung his head. "I can't go home without Augusta there. No matter how drunk I get, the house is so empty that I can't stand it. I can't stand it."

I sighed, unable to offer any consolation. "The house is going to be just as empty whether you're drunk or sober, right? So—"

"Why do this to myself? Is that what you're asking?" Taking off his glasses, which had fogged up in the cold air, Maddox wiped them on the sleeve of his cardigan sweater.

"I—guess," I muttered. "I mean, it's none of my business, but—"

"No, it's okay. You're right. Shit. You're right." He rubbed his eyes, put his glasses back on, and looked around the dimly lit parking lot. The Crystal Cavern was closing; festively dressed patrons were pouring out the door, heading toward their cars. When everyone had cleared out, I asked Maddox if he wanted me to drive him home.

"No," he said. "Let's go for a walk. That'll sober me up faster than you can say Jack Frost." Shivering in the cool night air, he buttoned his sweater, and I stuck my hands into the pockets of the velvet dress Augusta had given me last year when I performed at Seaside. For my birthday, she'd given me a matching cashmere shawl, light as goose down, and when I put the dulcimer up, I took the shawl from the backseat of my car and wrapped up in it.

"A walk? You mean in town?" I asked.

"Yeah. Let's go window-shopping."

"Maddox, it's midnight."

"So? Everything's still lit up, including me. Come on; this'll work wonders."

We walked the streets of Crystal Springs that night, a crazy, reckless thing to do, something Augusta and I might've done. Christmas lights lit up the shop windows, and we looked in the ones that caught our attention: gift shops and jewelry stores and even the Dollar Store, with its tacky display of plastic Santas and reindeer and snowmen, wreathed in gold tinsel. Maddox needed gifts for Theresa and Kathryn, and I made suggestions, pointing at displays. Lights flashed in the evergreen draped around the windows, lighting up our faces.

"I must be drunker than I thought," he smiled. "You're turning red and green, right before my eyes."

"Maybe Santa's flying overhead."

"More likely a UFO. Ever wondered what kind of taste aliens have? It seems they only like rednecks."

"I thought we were looking for Christmas presents."

We walked down the next block to an outdoor specialty shop and looked at the display of snorkeling and diving and waterskiing paraphernalia. "Kathryn's giving Gus a sled, by the way," Maddox said. "Like most kids who've never seen it, he's taken with the idea of snow, excited about a white Christmas."

I sighed and pulled my shawl closer. "I've never seen it, either."

"Libby's coming up to go skiing with us in a few days," he said as we strolled along slowly. "You ought to come with her, see your first snow."

I'm sure that would thrill her, I thought, but aloud said, "Sounds like fun, but Ben's family's spending the holidays with us. Want to look in the bookstore? I got Rich and Godwin's gifts there."

"Guess I should get Libby something," he said, both his hands in his pockets, his shoulders hunched against the cold night air. "But what do you give someone who has everything?"

A faithful husband? I thought, but said instead, "I know just the thing." Dragging him along, I led him to a touristy gift shop and pointed out the window display of pink plastic flamingos, stuck in AstroTurf. In the spirit of the season, the flamingos had plastic holly wreaths and red bows around their necks. "A half dozen of those would be perfect for her front yard."

"You have a mean streak, Dean Lynch, that has gone unnoticed until now."

Laughing, we went to the main drag, devoid of traffic except for an occasional car. Once a police car rode by, circled the block, then came back while the officer inside craned his neck. "Good thing I'm with the town's most prominent citizen," I said. "Otherwise I'd be locked up for vagrancy."

"Most prominent citizen, my ass," Maddox hooted. "I'm too zonked for that."

"Remember when me and Augusta went to that blues festival in Panama City?" We crossed the street again, heading back toward the Crystal Cavern. "A great singer was there, a skinny little black man, old as God, and he did a song that Augusta and I sang every time we overindulged. Remember that?"

Maddox stopped in the middle of the street. "Wait—don't tell me. 'I Can't Get Any Drunker,' right?"

"Close. 'I'm Drunk as I Can Be.'"

"How does it go?"

"It's crazy, but a great song. I think he made it up."

"Let's hear it."

"You want me to sing it? Right here, in the middle of town? You *really* want me to walk down the street at midnight singing 'I'm Drunk as I Can Be?'"

"Yeah."

I looked up and down the streets to make sure no one was around. Two cars came by, teenagers out cruising. One rolled down the window and yelled "Go Gators!" as he banged on the side of the car door. The boys in the other car honked their car horn and shot the passing car the finger, yelling "Go Seminoles!"

"Let's go to the middle of the street," I said, grabbing Maddox's arm. Main Street had a tree-lined esplanade, separating the two lanes. Although the palm trees were strung with Christmas lights, it was not as well-lit here as on the sidewalks with the bright lights coming from the store windows.

"You really expect me to do this?" I said. "If anyone sees me, I'll get put in jail."

"I'll bail you out. Come on, Miss Bean, let's hear it."

I took on the slouch of the elderly blues singer, pantomiming a guitar over my shoulder, as Augusta and I had done for our renditions. "The words are really complicated," I said. "I may not remember all of them."

"Quit stalling," Maddox said.

"Okay, okay—here goes." Closing my eyes, I strummed my pretend guitar and lolled my head from side to side. Mimicking the slurred voice of the old blues singer, I began singing: " 'I'm drunk as I can be. Yeah, yeah. I'm drunk as I can be, yeah, yeah. Oh, Lordy, yeah, yeah, I'm drunk as I can be.' "

I paused, waiting for Maddox's appreciative laughter. When I didn't get it, I opened my eyes, wondering if he'd sneaked off and left me standing in the street, singing like a fool. Instead, his head was turned and he stared down the street. When I followed his gaze, I saw why. A big blue Buick, screeching to a halt. Ben, on his way back from Pensacola!

"Oh, Lord," I moaned.

"Let me handle this," Maddox said as Ben slammed the car in reverse and began backing toward us. "I'll take the full blame."

"No, no," I said, pushing him behind a glittery palm tree. "You stay right here—don't come out of the shadows. He's going to be mad enough."

Maddox was doing everything he could to keep from laughing. "Don't you dare laugh!" I whispered. "Here he is. Let me handle this, and stay hidden, you hear? I mean it."

In the driver's seat, Ben looked as though his eyes would pop out. He couldn't comprehend what he had seen: his wife in a long velvet dress, standing in the middle of the street beneath a palm tree, swaying with her eyes closed, singing the blues with a pretend guitar. He didn't move a muscle, even when, red-faced and apologetic, I ran to his car, hurrying forward so he had to stop at a place where he couldn't see Maddox in the shadow of the palm tree. He rolled the window down, and I leaned over to speak to him.

"Hey, Ben," I said stupidly, as though he hadn't just caught me making a complete fool of myself. "You're getting home later than I expected."

"I certainly didn't expect to see you in the middle of the street when I turned this way, Willodean," he said icily. He only called me Willodean when he was beyond furious.

"I guess not," I said sheepishly.

"I'm afraid to ask you what you're doing," he said.

"Actually, there's a good explanation for this, crazy as it looks. It started off with me looking in the windows, you know, doing some shopping in my mind, and . . . ended up here, I guess."

I laughed weakly, but Ben continued to stare as if I'd just walked off a spaceship. "I'm on my way home," I said, breathless, "and I'll explain then."

Jaw clenched, Ben's eyes cut through me like lasers. "I don't understand what's going on. Where's your car?"

"Ah, at the Crystal Cavern," I said. The wind had whipped up, and I was freezing.

"You mean that *nightclub* on West Bay Street?"

I nodded, trying to decide whether to lie and say it was the only parking place I could find, or tell him the truth, that I'd played there tonight. Before I could decide, Ben hissed at me, "You're drunk, aren't you, Willodean?"

"It must look that way, but I'm not, I swear. I'm just acting silly. And please don't call me Willodean."

"Get in. I'm taking you home."

I shook my head, hugging my shawl tighter. "I'll go get my car."

"I said, get in the car!"

"I'm not, Ben. You're too mad, for one thing. I don't blame you, catching me acting the fool, but let's discuss it at home, rather than here."

Ben glared, but I watched with relief as he put the car in Drive. "This is the damnedest thing I've ever seen! I don't know what's gotten into you. I'm beginning to think you're having some kind of mental problems."

"I know it looks that way, but . . ." I began contritely. Then to my horror, a gasp turned into a guffaw and I laughed out loud. When I saw Ben reach for the door, I pushed against it to stop him. "No—no, Ben, please—ha, ha, ha—please don't get out. I'm coming home, I swear—oh, ha, ha, ha!" And, laughing and crying at the same time, I turned and hurried away from him before he could get out of the car and drag me into it. Leaving Maddox in the shadow of the palm tree, I crossed the street to the sidewalk on the other side, like Cinderella running away from the ball, glass slipper left behind. Looking over my shoulder, I saw Ben take off, tires spinning.

"Has anyone ever told you you'd make a preacher cuss, Willodean?" Maddox asked when he caught up with me.

"Ben's right—I must be losing my mind," I cried. "This reminds me of the first time I met you and Augusta, and I spilled punch. Remember? Augusta took me to the ladies' room at the church, and we started laughing and couldn't stop."

"I knew she was loony, but I didn't know until tonight that you were, too. I used to think you and Augusta were opposites." He grinned at me, shaking his head. "I've been wrong about you, Miss Bean. Miss Willo-Bean. You're a crazy woman in disguise."

"You know what?" I said. "I think you might be right."

The holidays I'd anticipated turned to ashes right before my eyes. Coal and ashes, what Santa Claus brings naughty children. Even though I apologized to Ben over and over, he wouldn't listen. I couldn't blame him; I'd been guilty of the ultimate sin, putting myself in a position to be the object of gossip again. Anyone could have ridden by and seen me acting like a drunk fool, he said, and I agreed, saying that I could not explain my moment of madness, except that it was the night air and the sparkling lights and the excitement of the holiday season.

I watched the relatives leave with great relief when the holidays were over. Christmas dinner, which should have been a joyous occasion, was a disaster. Ben snapped at me at the table, and I snapped back, red-faced, while the relatives squirmed. I'd had money to blow on gifts for the first time, and was as excited as a kid when we gathered around the tree afterward. Ben and I usually gave each other a devotional book or prayer calendar, and I'd mailed the relatives similar things over the years. But this year I'd gotten Ben a new suit, and fun gifts for the others, lavish baskets of gourmet goodies. I'd felt like King Midas, or Ebenezer Scrooge after his conversion, until Ben looked around at the ribbon and torn paper and scattered gifts scornfully. He stood and delivered a sermon on the commercialism of Christmas and the wastefulness of gift-giving when people in the world were starving. I hung my head guiltily, wishing I could take everything back. Everyone looked miserable, and shortly afterward gathered their loot and left. After that, I decided once the holidays were over and the new year rolled around, Ben and I *had* to go to the family-life counselor provided by the Methodist church.

A surprise came a few days after Christmas. I was putting away the Christmas stuff, although reluctantly. My reluctance was insane, as though leaving the decorations up would make the holidays happen again, this time the way I'd dreamed them. I'd never had a happy Christmas; when my parents were alive, they were drunk and fighting; holidays in my foster home were austere. We foster children got charity items from the townspeople, unbearable to me. No matter what I got, I gave it away to the other kids. Afterward, of course, I suffered when the others had crayons and roller skates and jump ropes, and I was left with nothing but my stupid pride.

As I wrapped the Christmas ornaments in tissue, I got a call from Maddox, asking if I could get Gus's puppy by tomorrow. "Tomorrow?" I'd squealed. "I thought y'all wouldn't be home till after the first of the year."

"We're home now."

"You're calling from Mimosa Grove?"

"Yep. A momentous decision's been made," he said. "We came back early to pack up."

"You're *moving*?" I sank into a nearby chair, too weak to stand. First losing Rich and Godwin, then Augusta, now Maddox and Gus. God was punishing me for my sins with impressive gusto.

"What a sad itty-bitty voice," Maddox mocked. "Will you miss us, Miss Bean?"

"I'll miss Gus," I said. "You can go to hell, far as I'm concerned."

He laughed, loud, and I wondered if he was having me on. "But what—what about Mimosa Grove?" I said.

"Tie a red ribbon around that stupid puppy's neck, come out tomorrow afternoon, and we'll tell you all about it."

"No way. I want to know now."

I pictured him at the other end of the line, running his hand through his hair like he did when exasperated. "Okay, okay. Gus is going to school in Chapel Hill next year, to the Episcopal school his cousins attend. He's been like a different kid up there with Kathryn's brood, playing in the snow—it's been great. The school's a couple of blocks from their house—"

"Not a boarding school, then?" I interrupted.

"Jesus, you think I'm so heartless, I'd send him off to a boarding school? It's a day school. We'll try it the rest of the year, see how it works."

I thought about it. For the past few months Gus had grieved every day, everything at Mimosa Grove a reminder of his mother. A change of scene would be good.

"You're awfully quiet," Maddox said. "What're you thinking?"

"That it's a good idea."

"You'll like this—his only reservations were how much he'd miss you and the Hernandez family."

Unexpectedly, my eyes filled up with tears. "And then," Maddox continued, "like the true mercenary he is, he made me call and have you bring his surprise."

Gus's basset puppy had reddish-brown spots, floppy ears, and droopy eyes, just like Ollie. He was three months old and clumsy, falling over his own feet, but affectionate and playful. When I picked him up from the breeder in Defuniak Springs, he settled into the passenger seat, peering out the window as though he knew where he was going. "You'd really be grinning, puppy," I told him, "if you knew what a gravy train you've landed in."

I called Theresa so we could time the arrival of the puppy. When my call came in, she assembled Maddox, Carl, and Joe on the sunporch. Then she pulled the bamboo blinds on the porch doors so I couldn't be seen, and I stood outside, hearing Gus whine. "Daddy, call Beanie and tell her to hurry up with my surprise."

I peeked in the door to see where everyone was situated. Theresa had trays of sandwiches and cookies and candy on the coffee table. Maddox and Carl sat on the sofa, Maddox leaning back, while Carl, a stocky man with a big laugh, watched Gus and his son, who knelt by the refreshment table, helping themselves.

"Guess what, Joe," Gus said. "You know in North Carolina, in the mountains? People ski on snow instead of water."

"What's snow?" Joe said, looking at his dad and winking.

"White stuff that's real cold," Gus answered seriously, his mouth full of cookies. "You can make ice cream out of it, too."

"You mean milk? People in North Carolina ski on milk?"

"Not milk, silly," Gus said. "S-n-o-w. Don't you know what that is?" Carl laughed as Gus jumped on Joe, trying to wrestle him to the floor. Good time to make my entrance. I stuck my head in the door and caught Gus's eye. Leaving his wrestling match, he jumped up when he saw me. "Beanie!" he cried. "Where's my surprise? Let go of me, Joe."

"What surprise?" I asked.

"Beanie! You said you'd bring me a surprise when I got home," Gus said.

"I did? Gosh, I must've forgotten."

"Miss Bean's getting old and senile, son," Maddox said. "She can't help it."

"You did not forget," Gus said, eyeing me suspiciously. "Did you?"

"Hmm, let me see." The puppy was scratching at my legs, so I unhooked his leash and opened the door wider. "Seems like I have a surprise somewhere."

The puppy couldn't have done better if I'd rehearsed him. As soon as I opened the door, he bounded into the room and headed straight for Gus. Maddox was ready with his camera, capturing the moment when Gus, openmouthed, caught the bounding puppy in his arms. In a frenzy, the puppy licked Gus so ecstatically that Gus's glasses fell off, and losing his balance, he fell on the floor, the puppy on top of him, wagging his tail and yapping.

"Now how did that damn dog know," Maddox murmured as he snapped away with the camera, "exactly who he belonged to in this room?"

Then we heard it, the sound we'd not heard for months, since before Augusta died: Gus laughing with all the happy abandonment of a boy with his first dog. Theresa and I looked at each other and blinked away tears, Maddox suddenly got busy fiddling with the camera, and Carl cleared his throat and wiped his eyes as Joe jumped in, rolling on the floor with the puppy and Gus like a ten-year-old himself. The sound of Gus's laughter brightened up the whole room, and I looked up to find Maddox regarding me, his gaze soft. I was sure he was remembering the day I'd first proposed getting the puppy, and the awful time afterward at the cemetery. We'd all come a long way since then.

Plenty of times in the lonely months after Gus returned to the mountains of North Carolina, I wondered if I'd imagined that healing moment on the sunporch. The winter months were difficult, dreary days of bare trees silhouetted against gray skies when I tormented myself with the letter hidden in my jewelry box. On Augusta's birthday in February, I'd taken it out and put it in another envelope, determined to drive out to Mimosa Grove and leave it for Maddox. I waited until I'd fixed Ben's supper, thinking I'd go before Maddox got home from work. However, Ben was running late, supper was late, and when I was cleaning up the kitchen, Maddox called me from Mimosa Grove, weeping because it was Augusta's birthday. After I hung up, I took the letter and put it back in my jewelry box. How could I even think of taking it to him on her birthday? Another time, I took the letter to the bathroom to tear up and flush away. But I couldn't do that, either. Like a demon lover, the letter tormented me, taunted me, but I couldn't destroy it, nor could I give it to its rightful owner. Desperate, I confided in Celeste and asked her to look at the cards.

"The cards are not needed," she said, wagging her finger. "Since Augusta's gone to the other side your friendship with Maddox has become very important, yes?"

Yes, I agreed. I'd not do anything to jeopardize the special bond we had.

"But you have done that by hiding the letter," Celeste warned. "Perhaps it is not too late. He will understand that you were trying to protect him and Gus, but give it to him now, or you will regret it one day."

But time went by and I did nothing. Another worry was competing for my attention: my and Ben's icy disregard of each other, our steely silences, our heart-slashing arguments. I swore that if we got into our comfortable rut again, I'd never complain about the lack of passion, our preoccupation with church activities, or the predictable deadliness of our routine. Anything was better than the hell we lived in.

Our time together—mostly meals—we spent in silence, Ben with the paper propped in front of him and me with a book. "What's on the agenda today?" I asked him at breakfast one Saturday in early March.

Ben read for a good five minutes before answering. "I've got a book signing this afternoon at Maylene's store. Be nice if you showed up for a change, pretended you cared."

"Why is she having another book signing?" I asked without thinking. "Everyone in town's bought your book."

Ben put down the paper long enough to regard me scornfully. "I asked her to. I'm trying to get my sales count up before sending the new manuscript to the publisher."

"Oh," I said, getting up to get another cup of coffee. "Want more coffee?"

"I'll get some at the office," he said. "Judy's coffee's better. She got a new coffeemaker for Christmas and it makes a difference."

"How selfish of her, with all the starving children in China," I said.

Ben got up to go. "Well? Will you come to the book-store?"

"Depends," I said. "Think Maylene's slimy husband, Frank, will be there?"

Ben stepped backward as though I'd slapped him. "*What?* Frank Herring couldn't be a better man. He's a dea-con in the Baptist church, president of the Lions Club, and one of the founders of the Promise Keepers."

"I never told you. First book signing you had, he cor-nered me in the hall and tried to feel me up."

Ben's eyes were cold. "Oh, come on. That's the most ridiculous thing I've ever heard."

I nodded. "Yeah, I made it up. I was the one who tried to feel him up. That toupee of his turns me on."

"You don't have to be so vulgar. All I meant was, that hall's narrow. He probably was just trying to let you pass, and it seemed he was getting too close intentionally."

"I'm sure that was it. The hall's so narrow that one of his hands went to my boob, and the other to my behind. You should tell Maylene, actually, because it could be dangerous. Somebody comes through with a real big butt, her precious husband's liable to get his hand caught, break a few bones."

Ben sighed mightily. "Just say that you don't want to go to the book signing. People will talk, but that doesn't seem to bother you anymore."

"You're right, and I thank God every day. I used to be scared to death, afraid they'd say something about me. Guess what? They did anyway. So I'm getting to where I don't care anymore."

I took refuge in my music, spending long hours practic-ing. I received a letter from the University of Florida, saying my application was one of twelve under consideration for next year's grant. The six finalists would be notified later in the spring, and asked to come for an audition. From those, the grant recipient would be chosen. When I told Ben I'd just been told I was one of the six finalists, he repeated tersely what he'd told me in the fall: I shouldn't get my heart set on going to Gainesville, that he wasn't moving. Neither of us dared put into words what hung in the air like a noxious poison: what I would do if I got the grant. I wasn't ready to think that far ahead. Too much in my life had been lost; I couldn't deal with losing my marriage, too.

But neither could I stand the hostility building up. I'd mentioned to Ben that we should see the family-life counselor in Pensacola, but he'd brushed the idea aside. "I'm a trained counselor," he reminded me. "Why would I go to someone else?"

"Because you can't be objective. Doctors don't treat their own families," I said. Late one afternoon, after another of our fights, I waited until my final piano student left, then took the bull by the horns.

"Ben, we've got to talk," I said, walking into his office at the church. Judy Anderson, his secretary, tried to stop me, looking up from the telephone in panic, as though I were interrupting a nuclear summit.

Ben put down the notepad he was scribbling on and frowned at me, sitting behind his mahogany desk like the Lord on judgment day. His office was impressive, the nicest one he'd ever had, spacious and dark-paneled, with Oriental rugs on the floor. There was a burgundy-colored leather sofa for visitors, a matching chair, and elegant tables and lamps. It was a mistake to come here, to face Ben on his turf. Surrounded by all his preacher materials, he looked righteous and secure sitting behind his desk. He was handsome, poised, and immaculate in a white shirt and expensive silk tie, and he looked at me like a king granting an audience.

"Of course we need to talk, Dean," he said, making his

fingers into a church steeple and looking across them at me. "Honest communication is important at this time." He was so into his ministerial stance that he sounded like a recording. See the nice preacher? Press One and he pontificates on honesty in communication. Press Two, and he sprouts platitudes about love and forgiveness. "Sit down, why don't you?" Press Three and he politely makes you feel welcome.

I sank into the upright chair across from him. "Ben, this thing that's been going on with us," I said, clearing my throat. "It's really gotten bad."

"I couldn't agree more," he said, his voice tight and unyielding.

I looked around the room desperately. "I hate it, Ben. I don't know what's happened . . . what to do . . ."

Instead of replying, Ben just watched me. I studied his face, this man I'd loved for so many years, searching for some softening, some warmth in his eyes, cold as stones. His mouth was set in a firm line, tight and compressed.

The phone rang, and to my surprise, Ben took the call, changing his demeanor, laughing and talking. At one point, he asked the caller to hold on a minute. Putting his hand over the receiver, he turned to me. "Dean, excuse me a minute. It's Jeff Stewart, you know, from the bishop's office? Got the latest goings-on in Tallahassee."

I sat with my hands clenched into tight fists while he chatted away as though nothing else was as important as what was going on at the Methodist headquarters in Tallahassee. Once his face lit up, and he said, "Dr. Vickery said that? No kidding? Wow, I'm really flattered." He listened for a minute but never looked my way. "Oh, absolutely. Please give him my regards." I tuned out, looking around at the stacks of books and materials on the desk, the coffee table, the bookshelves, everywhere. Bible commentaries, counseling texts, dictionaries, lectionaries, all seeming to hold the ancient mysteries of God and religion, of faith and worship, mighty words of power and prophecy. But nothing that could tell two people how to forgive and love each other again, to listen and understand and cherish each other, to overcome the petty squabbles and endless hurts of daily life.

"I shouldn't have come here, Ben, bothered you while you're at work," I said when he hung up. "I'll wait until you get home."

"I won't be home until late, then I've got to work on my sermon." Hesitating only a moment, he picked up the phone and pressed a button. "Judy? Hold my calls." Folding his arms, he regarded me from across the desk. "I'd planned on talking with you about all this later," he said, patting his hair down. I'd always loved his hair, dark and sleek as an otter, perfectly behaved, never unruly or out of place. "But since you're here, we might as well go on with it."

"Well, good," I said, not sure if it was or not.

"I'm not unaware of how things have deteriorated in our relationship," he said, and I sat forward in the stiff leather chair. "So I called Dr. Clark just the other day." Dr. Clark, the family-life counselor in Pensacola.

I sank back in the chair, closing my eyes. "Thank God," I whispered. "I'm so glad."

Pleased, Ben nodded. "Only thing is, I should've checked with you about the appointment date," he said, looking sheepish. "I took the first one open."

"Oh, no, that's fine," I said. "I'll change anything I have scheduled."

"Next week," he said, thumbing through his calendar. "Wednesday at eleven. That okay?"

"Next Wednesday at eleven. We can have lunch afterward."

"Ah—it's your appointment, Dean. Next Wednesday is your appointment."

"Oh!" I said, putting my hand to my face. "That's fine. I just assumed we'd go together first, but he wants us individually, huh?"

Ben tilted his head and regarded me. "I'm not going. You've been trying to get me to talk to Dr. Clark and I did. You're the one who's having the problems, not me."

It wasn't sinking in. "But—"

"I talked to Dr. Clark for a good hour about you. He says it sounds like menopause, maybe, or your depression coming back. I've been afraid it's much more serious, that you might be heading toward a nervous breakdown. But— I'm not going to try to diagnose this myself. You gave me good advice when you said a doctor didn't treat his own family." He sat back in his chair, making his fingers into a pyramid again.

"Wait a minute," I said, holding my hand up. "I'm missing something here. You and I need to talk to Dr. Clark together, about our marriage."

Ben's eyes hardened again. "I don't have time to run to a therapist, nor do I need to."

Frustrated, I hit the flat of my hand on his desk. "We both need to see Dr. Clark, can't you see that?"

Holding his hand up, he stopped me. "There's a reason I can't go to a marriage counselor now. I wasn't going to tell you yet, but guess I'll have to."

"Tell me," I said.

"It embarrasses me to say it," he said, trying to look humble, "but word is out that I'm being groomed for an important job in the bishop's cabinet if Dr. Vickery accepts the nomination for bishop and leaves a vacancy. I can't go running off to a counselor with that going on."

I said nothing about Dr. Vickery swearing to me that he'd turn down the nomination. Ben wouldn't have believed me anyway. Instead, I sat back in my chair in surprise. "I see.

That's what you've always wanted, isn't it?" A big church, a nice appointment, all that paled in comparison to being appointed to the bishop's cabinet, the select few men who ruled the conference. For years, Ben had dared not even long for such an appointment, although he'd wanted nothing else.

He glowed with pride, leaning back in his chair and putting his hands behind his head. "I never dreamed it would happen. To serve on the bishop's cabinet—I can't tell you what that would mean to me."

"You don't have to tell me," I said. "I hope it happens for you, I really do."

As though remembering me and what I'd come for, Ben studied me carefully. "Things are going to be good for us, Dean, if you can just get yourself straightened out. You'd like being a cabinet member's wife. Lots of prestige. We'd have a housing allowance instead of a parsonage, and we can get a nice place in Tallahassee. We'd go to First Church, which has thousands of members with more programs going on than you can imagine. Yep, if you'll just go see Dr. Clark and get yourself on the right track, things will look a lot different, you wait and see."

I sank back in the chair, suddenly too weary to fight him. "Yeah," I said finally. "Sounds great. Just peachy." Before I could stop myself, I burst into tears and buried my face in my hands.

Ben's voice, cold and full of disgust, rose over the sound of my sobs. "I just gave you the best news I've had in years, and this is your reaction?"

When I didn't answer, he pushed his chair back and came to me, fumbling in a drawer. I raised my head to see him opening a box of tissues. "Here," he said, thrusting the box at me. "Pull yourself together. If Judy hears you, she'll tell everybody in the church."

I wiped my eyes. Ben sat on the side of his desk and

folded his arms. "Maybe I'd better call Dr. Clark back," he said, "and see if he can see you before next Wednesday. These crying spells of yours are a bad sign."

"Yeah, why don't you do that." I stood up, tired beyond words. Ben regarded me as though I were a slobbering idiot, falling apart at his feet. Tossing the wad of damp tissues into his burgundy wastebasket, I turned to go. To my surprise, Ben followed me to the door and opened it for me, patting me on the shoulder as he did.

"I'm so glad you came by, Dean," he said, his hand on my shoulder and a big smile on his face for Judy's benefit. "Come back anytime—you can always talk to me about your little problems!"

Had I not been so astonished, I would have burst into laughter. I stumbled out of the church office in a daze, not bothering to look Judy's way, even though I could feel her eyes on me as I opened the door and went outside into a late afternoon sunset. Taking deep breaths, I looked around me, bewildered. For a moment, I didn't know where I was, didn't recognize anything familiar. I was lost, adrift in an unfamiliar landscape. All I knew was that everything was changed, torn apart like the bridge shattered by Augusta's car that awful day last October. As I stumbled forward on the covered walkway to my house, I could hear Celeste's warning in my ears, mocking me. Mysterious forces were at work, Celeste had said when she read my cards, and the old order of my life was falling apart.

Eighteen

AS THE NEW YEAR went by, all the unhappiness of my life was channeled into my music. I prepared for my upcoming audition at the University of Florida as though it were a concert in Carnegie Hall. I selected and discarded song after song, panicked that the audition, scheduled for June, would be upon me and I would not be ready. Because of the tension on the home front, I retreated into a shell erected of music. Even though I taught my piano students and Sunday school classes, attended church services and the usual meetings, my mind was elsewhere. As winter gave way to spring, I longed not only for Augusta, but also for everything familiar to me: my marriage, my livelihood, my everyday existence.

The bright spring passed me by as I buried myself in rehearsals. I played louder and louder when I heard Ben coming and going, to drown out the sounds of his presence. After I canceled the appointment with Dr. Clark, Ben didn't mention my going again, and neither did I. Over our miserable meals he'd update me on his climb up the career ladder, as his hopes for being named to the cabinet post became more of a reality.

Officially, Ben would be reappointed to Crystal Springs in June, but if Dr. Vickery was nominated for bishop, all the shifts to fill his position could involve Ben. Ben didn't know that John Marcus would turn down the nomination and give it all up, leaving the ministry. The plans were all hush-hush, and Ben spoke in whispers, as though spies were lurking behind our curtains. But he didn't ask about my audition, my music, or my depression. His eyes were distant, filled with visions of Tallahassee, himself seated in the bishop's cabinet.

The only brightness during this time was my developing relationship with Gus, and our weekly phone calls. When he came home for his spring break, he and I spent a day at Panama City Beach. Even though the water was still fairly cold, I introduced him to snorkeling, which became his new interest. I promised to take off for a whole week in the summer and spend it with him, snorkeling. I made the plans for that time without any hint that my life would once again be turned upside down, and everything I knew and believed in called to question.

My week at the beach with Gus evolved from what seemed like endless plans and details. My audition was scheduled for the first week in June, the week before the annual conference of the Methodist church, held at the church's headquarters in Tallahassee. For twenty years, I'd gone to the conference with Ben. Only the wives of the most ambitious preachers went, forming a tight little clique that I tagged along with, even though my heart wasn't in it and my mind wandered during the endless conversations about their husbands and churches, their lunches and coffees and dinners presided over by the bishop's wife. I'd assumed that this year, even though Ben and I were barely speaking, he'd insist I go. I came into the kitchen and found him writing on the wall calendar, filling in the week of conference, and moved beside him.

"Oh, good," I said. "Conference doesn't start until the twelfth. I'll be through with my audition then." I clicked a pen against my hand absently as Ben wrote down his endless meetings. "Busy week," I commented.

"No busier than usual," he said tersely. "For conference."

Excuse the hell out of me, I thought, but said nothing. I studied the calendar, frowning and chewing on the pen, until Ben looked my way. "What do you want?" he said.

"Just trying to decide the best time to take Gus snorkeling for a week."

"The week of conference." He thumped the calendar with his knuckle. "Be the best time since the church calendar's clear then."

I blinked at him, stepping away. "But—I always go to conference with you."

Avoiding my eyes, Ben closed the pocket calendar and put it in his shirt pocket with a gold pen that Vanna Faye had given him for Christmas, inscribed with his name and *WWJD,* for "What Would Jesus Do?" "No need for that," he said. "I've got so many responsibilities I'm not going to have time to squire you around Tallahassee."

"Have I ever asked you to squire me around?" I asked, my voice rising. "What a ridiculous way of putting it, anyway."

Ben stood with his hands on his hips. "There'll be so many caucus meetings this year," he said, "about Dr. Vickery's nomination. So if you want to take Gus to the beach, take him during conference, because I'm not going to have time for you then."

I opened and closed my mouth like a fish out of water. "You make it sound like I'm the one who's begged you to take me every year. You can't imagine how I've hated it."

"Oh, really?" He folded his arms, his dark eyes cold. "Wish I'd known, because I could've concentrated a lot more if I'd not had you tagging along."

"I see." I turned my back and stared out the window, the pain like acid in my stomach, roiling and burning. "This is how history gets retold, isn't it?"

Ben sighed, loud and dramatic. "Now you're pouting because I suggest you take Gus to the beach instead of going to conference? There's no pleasing you, Dean. No pleasing you at all."

Three weeks later, when I sat in a music room at the University of Florida and faced the committee, my fingers shook on the strings of my dulcimer, but once I began playing, I'd practiced so much and the music was so familiar that the shakes went away.

I owed my ease in performing to Maddox and Theresa and Carl, who had sat on the sunporch watching as I went through my audition again and again. Each of them offered suggestions that I found helpful. Carl, with a sharp ear for beat, suggested I speed up "Wildwood Flower," since the chorus seemed to drag a bit. Theresa insisted that my demeanor and appearance were crucial. "But I'm being judged by my musical ability," I protested. Carl agreed with his wife. "Everyone will have the ability, Dean, but not everyone will be the best person for their grant, the one they want to send out to do their programs," he said. So the next time, I brought over a selection of clothes. Each of us chose a different look, each for a different reason. "Wear the black silk dress," Maddox had said, pointing out a hand-me-down from one of the church ladies. "Pure class, what the University of Florida lacks."

Carl voted for a demure suit I wore to church almost every Sunday, saying that I looked scholarly and serious, but

Theresa and Maddox booed him. Theresa made the final decision, putting together a combination I wouldn't have considered, a long black skirt with a white T-shirt. Hurrying to her house, she returned with an embroidered shawl from Cuba, and my eyes filled with tears when I thanked her. Augusta would have approved.

It was Maddox who revised the fifteen-minute speech I had to give to the committee in order to convince them I was the best one for their program. "Sounds like you're reading from an instruction booklet," he'd scoffed. "Remember your audience. Why don't you talk about your passion for your dulcimer instead of being so technical?"

Hurt by his criticism at first, I'd had to admit that he was right when the audition committee perked up as I described my love for the dulcimer, how I valued it because it had been handed down from my grandmother, how she'd taught me to play it, and how I'd become the youngest member of my family's bluegrass band. The only thing I used from my research was the dulcimer's unique role as a private, handmade instrument, as opposed to the guitar and banjo and fiddle, now mass-produced and more public in their usage. I applied that to my granny's situation, telling them how she, like me, had originally taken to the dulcimer as a means of bringing music to a dreary life, not intending it for public entertainment.

The committee was made up of three people: the dean of the women's studies program, a smartly dressed older woman, and two young music professors, a man and a woman. The young woman looked like a prima ballerina, and the man had fuzzy hair that stuck out like Einstein's. The dean surprised me by asking me several questions after my presentation, wanting to hear more about music as a means of redemption. I hadn't realized that was what I said, but it sounded good, so I went with it.

Weak-kneed when the audition was over, I shook the

hands of the committee members as I tried to interpret their facial expressions. All were pleasant and smiling, but no one promised anything. When I left the room, I saw a woman filling out the audition forms and my heart sank. Young, she looked like a professional player, successful and confident. A guitar case was on the floor and a banjo slung over her shoulder. At that moment I felt like what I was: a tired, middle-aged woman with an outdated instrument, daring to think I had a chance of winning a lucrative grant. Ben had been right to discourage me. The last thing he'd said was for me not to get my hopes up; there were too many truly talented musicians out there. Hurrying to the door, I glanced back at the young woman, who was now spraying her throat with an atomizer. Oh, great, I thought, she's a singer, too. Probably sings like Allison Krause or Mary Chapin Carpenter, and auditioning right behind me will make me sound like Mother Maybelle Carter. Back in my dreary Motel Six room, I called Maddox as I'd promised, telling him about the young woman.

"And she was gorgeous, too," I told him, sniffing. "Think Faith Hill and Shania Twain. Young, confident, plays two instruments and sings."

"Bet she's back in her room, telling her friends that she didn't even bother to audition once she saw this poised, mature woman with a handmade dulcimer," he said.

"Seriously, I don't think it went well," I told him. "They asked me questions and seemed interested, but when I finished, they were kind of cool."

"Listen to me. You're dealing with academic types, veins running with ink instead of blood. The most deadly thing you can do as an academic is show emotion. If you do, somebody might mistake you for a human being instead of a walking, talking, grant-writing textbook. You can't expect them to throw roses at your feet. Speaking of which—"

"Hang on a minute, someone's at my door. Don't hang up in case it's a mad ax-murderer," I said, cradling the receiver under my chin as I stretched far enough to open the door. The young Asian man from the front desk handed me an arrangement of a dozen deep-red roses. "Oh, my God," I gasped.

"What—Charles Manson?" Maddox asked.

I sank to the bed weakly, pressing the roses to my face. They were fragrant, black-red and velvet-petaled. "Ben," I whispered.

"Ben's there?"

"No, but he sent roses, which is a surprise. He didn't even ask me to let him know how it went, so I didn't expect flowers."

"That was nice of him. To send the roses, I mean," Maddox said. "Speaking of which—"

"Oh, good heavens," I said, opening the card awkwardly with one hand.

"What now?"

"They're from *you*, not Ben."

"It insults me that you sound so shocked. I do nice things occasionally."

Unexpectedly, my eyes filled with tears, and I couldn't say anything. After a long moment of silence, Maddox cleared his throat. "Dean? You still there?"

"Yeah," I managed to say, wiping my eyes.

"What is it, allergic to roses?"

"Allergic to someone being so nice to me, I guess," I said, smiling through my tears.

"You're not crying, are you?"

"A little," I admitted.

"I didn't mean to overwhelm you, Miss Bean. It didn't occur to me that no one ever sent you flowers."

"Shut up," I laughed.

Maddox laughed, too, and I relaxed, lying back on the bed. "Maddox? Can I say something corny to you?"

"What—thank you? 'Thank you for the flowers, Maddox. You're such a sensitive guy. Although you look like Hulk Hogan, underneath you're all Mr. Rogers.' Is that it?"

"Something like that."

"Well, I'm waiting."

"Give me time. I couldn't say this to you in person, only over the phone."

"Oh, God, it must be cornier than hell, then."

"I just want to say—that—that your friendship means a lot to me. It really does." There was a long silence on the other end. "Maddox? You still there?"

"Yeah. I'm just choked up. No one's ever said anything that moving to me before. I'm overwhelmed."

"Kiss my ass," I said furiously, and he laughed, loud. "It's not funny," I snapped. "Saying things like that is hard for me, and then you make fun of me, throw it back in my face—"

"I did not. I'm overwhelmed. I'm prostrate on the floor, knee-deep in Kleenexes."

"I'm hanging up now. I'm too torn up from that horrible audition to listen to this." But when I put the phone on the receiver, I was laughing, my tears dried up and my spirits high.

For our week of snorkeling, Gus and I had researched the best places and picked out St. Joseph's Peninsula, so the day after my audition, Gus and the basset—whom he'd named Little Ollie and was calling Lollie—flew from Chapel Hill to Gainesville, where I picked them up and drove to the farthest tip of the peninsula. Our rented bungalow was on St. Joseph's Bay rather than the ocean, but the Gulf of Mexico was right across the road. The cabin was hidden in a dense foliage of sandpine scrub and pine flatwoods, so we'd be se-

cluded from the rest of the campers, a bonus with a boy and
a boisterous puppy. Gus ran in ahead of me, suitcase banging
against his skinny legs, Lollie under his feet barking in excitement. "Hey, Beanie, what a cool place. Daddy found it on
the Internet!"

"No TV or Internet here," I warned him. "The idea is to
escape civilization and enjoy nature."

I put my suitcase down on the wooden floor and looked
around. It had a certain charm, like a seagoing vessel the way
it was perched over the choppy gray waters of the bay. The
back was all glass with a panoramic view, the deck shaded
with the low-hanging limbs of a live oak. In the galley-like
kitchen, I dumped our supplies then opened the windows
looking out over the bay. "This is good," I called out to Gus.
"This is very good."

Gus's excitement was high. "What's wrong with you,
boy?" I'd teased him when we reached the peninsula, and he
shrieked upon seeing the ocean. "Go north for a few months
and you act like a Yankee seeing the Gulf for the first time."

"I missed it, Beanie," he'd said earnestly. "I had fun at
Aunt Kathryn's, but I missed here, too. Don't tell Daddy, but
sometimes I cried."

"I'm glad you're home now," I'd said. The rush of joy
I'd felt when I spotted him getting off the plane from Chapel
Hill surprised me. He'd looked so brave, so proud of himself
for his solo flight, yet so vulnerable, thin and pale as a turnip.
He'd grown two inches, his lanky body outgrowing his hands
and feet, reaching that preadolescent age where he stumbled
over himself awkwardly.

I stepped out onto the deck and a strong salt breeze
lifted my hair off my shoulders. As I leaned on the rail and
looked over the bay, waving at Gus and Lollie running on the
dock, I felt a lightening of the load I'd been carrying on my
back like a yoke: the pressure of the audition, and the tension

between Ben and me. From the dock came the laughter of
Gus and the baying of Lollie, and I called out for them to
come in before it got any darker. I looked up at the stars in
the darkening sky like tiny fireflies and focused on the brightest of them, far to the west: the evening star, which had
guided seafarers for countless ages. I prayed for the first time
in months. I prayed for God's help, that He'd guide me
through this week like the evening star had shown the way to
others like me, lost and uncertain but plunging forward,
however blindly.

Gus conked out right after our supper of tacos we'd
picked up in Port St. Joe. He'd explored all three bedrooms,
finally picking the one downstairs with windows opening to
the bay, leaving the one with the balcony upstairs for me. I
sat in a rocker on the back porch, breathing the heavy salt air
until my eyes drooped, exhausted after the audition yesterday and the long drive today. Looking in the downstairs bedroom, I saw that Gus was asleep with Lollie next to him,
sprawled out like a huge stuffed animal. I stopped by the
phone in the kitchen and left a message on the answering machine for Ben, then called Maddox's Tampa hotel to leave
him the number here. This week he was attending the annual
meeting of the Tomato Growers Association of America. Augusta had teased him about being vice president of the organization and taking his duties so seriously. Lord Mayor of the
Tomato, she'd called him.

I still had my hand on the receiver when the phone rang.
I stared at it stupidly for a minute, knowing it to be either
Ben or Maddox. Guiltily, I hoped it wasn't Ben.

"A phone? I'm not believing this," Maddox teased me.
"You chickened out, right?"

"Right," I admitted. "I owe you a dollar." Gus had insisted I bring his tent along so we could camp out at nights.

Maddox had hooted at the idea, telling me to pretend I forgot it. Why stay in a hot tent with a boy and a dog when I could be in an air-conditioned cottage? Piously I'd said that I loved the outdoors and would sleep in the tent every night if Gus wanted to. Maddox had bet me a dollar I wouldn't.

"Ha! I told you they wouldn't stay in the tent," I heard him say to someone.

"You talking to yourself?"

"Libby's here," he said. "Took a detour on her way to Palm Beach."

I twisted the cord around my finger, not saying what I was thinking; quite a detour for the old girl. But now that she was officially divorced from Simms, she could detour wherever and with whomever she wanted.

"What's the cottage like?" Maddox said. "It looked good on the Internet, but you can't always tell."

I sighed. "This so-called bungalow is about as rustic as the Hilton, where you're staying."

I held the phone away from my ear as he whooped and hollered, swearing I owed him much more than a measly dollar for selling out that badly. I hung up, promising to have Gus call him first thing in the morning. As I climbed the narrow wooden stairs, I wondered: When Gus called his daddy's room, would he wake up Miss Libby, as well?

I'd given Gus and me a day to relax before hiring a boat to take us snorkeling, so we spent the first day of our retreat sunning and swimming in the ocean. Here the Gulf was unspoiled, the water a clear emerald color and the sand white as sugar. I sat up on my towel and looked around me, searching for Gus. He'd found a playmate, a pale, skinny boy watched over by his father, sitting under an umbrella reading the *New York Times*. At this moment, Gus and his new friend were running in the white-tipped water, Lollie barking at their heels, and I waved at them. A sand castle Gus had built earlier in the day was deserted, now that he had a companion to romp with. Shading my eyes, I watched as the sand castle dissolved with every wave pounding against it until its shape was barely discernable. That's the way I'd felt ever since Augusta died; as though my life were that soggy, disintegrating sand castle.

Later that evening, Gus and I sat on the back porch, contented, stuffing ourselves with cold boiled shrimp as we listened to the slap of the waves on the shore and watched the shrimp boats in the distance, lights silhouetting their shapes so they looked like ghost-ships. Our plates in our laps, we propped our feet on the railing still warm with the day's sun. We'd stayed in the water until dusk, swimming until the sun sank and turned the water red. Then we'd floated on rafts, trailing fingers in the bobbing waves as they turned from red to pink in the setting sun. "It's like swimming in the sky," I said to Gus, when the color of the sea and sky merged on the horizon.

"Do you love shrimp, Beanie?" Gus asked me, cramming a big pink one in his mouth. He'd dipped it first in the spicy cocktail sauce I'd mixed up of ketchup, horseradish, and lemon juice, and more sauce landed on the front of his T-shirt than in his mouth.

"More than almost anything," I said. "Except maybe chocolate doughnuts."

"Wish I could eat a shrimp as big as a whale."

"Wish I had a chocolate doughnut as big as an inner tube."

Gus giggled so hysterically that I had to get up and bang him on the back when he choked on the shrimp. He held his glass up, his other hand around his throat as though he were dying, for a refill of iced tea to wash it down. When I came back with the tea, I brought out a plate of cookies.

"Look—Lollie's licking the floor," Gus cried after eating half a dozen cookies. Lollie was trying to catch the crumbs with his tongue before they fell through the cracks of the wooden deck.

"You know he shouldn't be eating sweets," I said.

"Yeah. He might get fat like Ollie. Sometimes having Lollie makes me not miss Ollie as much, then other times, it makes me miss him more." He threw out a couple more crumbs and Lollie chased them, his tail thumping. "It's the same with you, Beanie," he said. "When I'm with you, I don't miss my mama as much. But sometimes you remind me of her, and that makes me sad." Surprising me after his bout of giggles, Gus burst into tears.

I left my chair and knelt in front of him, waiting until he stopped crying. He took his glasses off and looked at me sheepishly. "I'm sorry, Beanie. I don't know what made me cry."

"Don't ever be ashamed of crying. You'll miss your mama your whole life. I still miss mine, and my granny, too. You'll be happy and having fun, and suddenly you'll miss your mama and want to cry. You don't have to apologize, you hear?"

He nodded, wiping his eyes with the backs of his hands. "Okay," he said, putting his glasses back on. "But I don't want to be sad this week."

"I don't want you to, either," I said. "So let's make a pact. It's okay to be sad and cry for your mama anytime, but we can take this week off, have nothing but fun thoughts. Okay?"

"Okay." A small smile of relief touched his lips. "Nothing but fun thoughts this week."

The days that followed were magical, everything I'd hoped for, with me and Gus spending every day in the sun, soaking up the healing rays like sponges. Gus took on a golden glow, and the sun burned highlights into his sand-colored hair. I told him that he looked more like his mother the older and blonder he got, and he smiled, pleased.

Gus took to the water like a fish. We snorkeled first in the Gulf, paddling our rafts past the waves on the shore to the calmer water farther out, where porpoises jumped around us. We took a charter boat out, surrounded by ocean as far as we could see. Once the boat anchored, we dived in and explored the wonders beneath, looking through our masks at the bright fish like flashes of jewels around us, brushing our legs with whispery touches. Later, we dropped anchor near a deserted beach for shelling. Gus saved everything we found: bits and pieces of shells as well as whole ones, and back in the cabin, he and his new friend, Mikey, looked them up in a book I'd bought, identifying triton, tripe, harpa, and clula.

That same night I was sitting cross-legged in bed, clad in my pj's, looking through a meditation book I'd gotten Celeste. When she testified in the divorce case, she got so nervous, she reverted to her native tongue, jabbering in her Slavic vernacular until the judge ordered her off the witness stand, which delighted Simms's lawyers but infuriated Libby's. Afterward, Simms took off for the Carribean, promising to send for her when the smoke cleared. When I left Crystal Springs, she was still awaiting his call.

Gus knocked on my door, then stuck his head in, frowning. "You awake, Beanie?"

"Come here and look at this." I patted a spot beside me on the bed and he hopped up, arranging himself cross-legged too, squinty-eyed without his glasses.

"I tried to sleep, but I couldn't," he said, blinking at me in the lamplight. "I thought about—scary things."

"What kind of scary things?" I asked, but he shook his head, picking at his fingernail.

"Why don't you try some of these meditations next time

you have scary thoughts?" I pointed to the one I was reading. "Like this one," I said, pointing to a picture of the sea. "Says here that meditating on the sea sedates the mind, easing the raging emotions, and calms the fears of the darkness."

Gus's look was skeptical. "Reckon it works?"

"Why don't you try it? Go back downstairs, open your windows so you can hear the ocean, and see if it works. Picture the sea and a breeze blowing the sea oats, and I'll bet you'll go right to sleep. Okay?"

Gus perked up and jumped off the bed. "Okay. I'll let you know if it works. If it doesn't, maybe you can get a refund."

I laughed. "You little businessman. You're getting more like your daddy every day."

Later I was sound asleep, lulled by the sound of the waves and the salt breeze billowing the sheer curtains on my open windows. A cry from downstairs woke me, causing me to jump up, my heart pounding. Slipping on my robe, I eased out of bed and went into the dark hallway, lit with moonlight coming from a skylight overhead. I pushed the door of Gus's room open and peeked inside. Lollie slept on, dreaming puppy dreams, but Gus was sitting up in the moonlight, huddled with his knees to his chest. I crossed the room and sat beside him. "Gus? Want me to turn the light on?"

He shook his head. "No. I'm afraid of what I might see. I had a bad dream."

"Can you tell me about it?"

He put his head down on his knees. "That meditation thing worked, Beanie, because I was thinking about the ocean when I went to sleep," he sobbed. "I dreamed we were in the ocean like this afternoon." He took a trembling breath. "It was real scary."

I bit my lip, wishing I hadn't taken him out, knowing how high-strung he was. It could be scary for experienced swimmers. "I shouldn't have taken you out yet."

He went on as though he hadn't heard me. "Fishes were all around us, darting like they do. They didn't scare me—it was what I saw in the water. . . ."

"Gus? Maybe it'd be better if you tried to forget it instead." I didn't want to hear what he dreamed, knew it was something unimaginable.

"I was looking for shells, and I saw something in the seaweed, something big and dark," he continued, ignoring me. "Caught in the seaweed and moving around like it was trying to get free. Daddy was swimming, too, but he was way up, near the surface of the water." He took a deep, ragged breath. "It was Mama—Mama was caught in the seaweed." I closed my eyes, shuddering. Oh, God in heaven, please. Not that.

"I saw Mama, plain as day," Gus continued. "Seaweed wrapped around her, and her hair was floating, and it kept getting in her face. Her eyes looked horrible, like she was scared of the water. She reached out her arms, wanting me to get the seaweed off her." His voice broke. "I couldn't get it off! I pulled and pulled, but it just got tighter around her neck. I kept yelling for Daddy, but he couldn't hear me. And I couldn't see you, either, Beanie. There was no one to help Mama but me, and I wasn't strong enough."

His cries broke my heart, but I could do nothing but hold him close, as I'd done so many times since Augusta died, trying to ease the pain of the child she left behind.

"I never want to go back in the ocean again," Gus sobbed against me, his tears wetting my knit pajama top. "I'm scared to. What if Mama's in there?"

"Gus, your mama's not in the ocean. That was just a bad dream. Very bad, but a dream."

"Where do you think Mama is, Beanie?"

Oh, God, Augusta. *Where are you?* I couldn't answer Gus because I didn't have the answer myself. At one time, I would have told him that she was in heaven, but I was no longer sure I believed that. I didn't know what I believed anymore, about anything. I looked out the open windows, to the darkness. "Come here, Gus," I said, taking his hand and pulling him to the window. We stood together, and I drew his shivering body close as we looked out over the bay and the dark sky beyond, studded with thousands of stars, as though God had flung a handful of diamonds on a black velvet cloth.

"Gus, I don't know where your mama is. But I know she's with God. I believe that. And I know something else, too." I knelt beside him and turned him to face me in the moonlight. "Your mama wouldn't want you to be scared, or to have scary dreams about her. She'd never want you scared of the ocean, as much as she loved it. And you loved it till now, right?"

He nodded, and I said, "Well, then. Let's think about the ocean again and what it feels like to be in it, but remember the good parts, the pretty little fishes and the seashells and the way the sun comes through the water. That's not scary, is it?" He shook his head, and I continued. "Can you do that, think about the good things and not be scared?"

Gus looked out the open window as I straightened up and stood beside him. "I'll try," he said in a small voice.

"Think you'll be able to go back in the ocean again?"

He reached for my hand. "If you'll go with me. I won't be scared if you promise you'll be with me."

"You can count on it," I said. And even though I knew it was foolish to make him a promise that I might not be able to keep, I repeated it. "I'm not going to let you go through this alone, Gus. That I promise you."

The next morning we went back into the ocean. Gus was pale and skittish, but bounced back more quickly than I dared hope, and I kept my promise by staying close. That afternoon Mikey Johnson appeared, and Gus ran to play with

him on the wave skimmer. After the sun went down, Mikey
invited Gus to go with him and his dad to Port St. Joe for a
pizza. When I met his father under the beach umbrella and
found out that he was a pediatrician, I readily agreed because
if anything happened to Gus, he'd be in good hands. After
they left and I had the house to myself, I sat on the porch
while Lollie slept at my feet, and I thought about Gus, the
way he'd handled the nightmare. I rocked on the dark porch,
feeling relieved. With the sun and the sea to heal him, Gus
would be all right.

Nineteen

❧❧

LATE THURSDAY AFTERNOON, GUS and I were stretched out on our towels, soaking up the last of the sun. Gus's even breathing told me he'd dozed off. Lollie slept beside him, curled in a ball and snoring like an old man. At the water's edge, a couple of women walked by briskly, swinging their arms and chatting. A browned jogger trotted by, and farther down the beach, a family swam, their gaggle of children squealing as the waves knocked them down. Although the umbrella that Mikey's dad sat under was empty, Mikey and Gus had planned a big camping trip tomorrow night, the Johnsons' last night.

Except for the steady rise and fall of his chest, Gus didn't move, so sound asleep was he. Lollie stirred and stretched his long fat body out, but he didn't wake up, either. They'd be fine sleeping here while I went back to the house and grabbed a cold bottle of water.

The white sand held enough of the day's heat to burn my feet as I walked back, sidestepping the sandspurs. A path behind our house went straight to the beach, skirting the bay's edge, so I scurried down it, coming up next to the dock. Approaching the back of the house, I groped in my beach bag for the key, then looked up in surprise, shielding my eyes with my hands. Someone was standing in the shadows of the back porch, watching my approach.

I froze, then edged up the steep back steps so I could peek in and see who was there. If I screamed loud enough, Gus would hear me and get help, surely. When I reached the top of the stairs, bent over like a spy, Maddox stepped out of the shadows and looked down at me, hands on his hips.

"Hello, Miss Bean." He grinned. "I was about to break in, till I saw you coming."

I sank against the porch rail weakly. "Maddox! You scared me to death." I was so unnerved, I dropped the key, and he reached over and picked it up, laughing. "It's not funny," I said. "What on earth are you doing here?"

"What kind of greeting's that? Having such a good time you forgot all about me, slaving my ass off with the tomato growers of the great southeast?" He was dressed in a dark business suit, and his briefcase was propped against the back door.

"What'd you expect, sneaking up on me like that?"

"Sneaking up on you? Bull. I was standing right here, in the broad open daylight," he said, unperturbed.

"Oh, well, excuse me for not expecting you. Just last night we talked, and you were going to be in Tampa until Saturday," I said. "How'd you get here?"

"Flew. Rented a car. The usual ways of getting around nowadays."

"You know what I mean."

"I got jealous of you and Gus here, having such a good time," he chuckled. "But I'll tell you all about it if you'll let me get out of this damned coat and tie first."

"Why wear a suit to a tomato growers' thing anyway?

You deserve to die of a heatstroke," I said, walking up on the porch and snatching the key from his hand. He laughed at me as I unlocked the door, and we walked into the dark coolness of the house.

He looked around curiously as he put his briefcase down. "Wow. You're right—nice place. The view's unbelievable." Pulling his jacket off and tugging on his tie, he tossed both over a kitchen chair with a proprietary air. "But first things first. Got anything to drink?"

I peered into the fridge, then back over my shoulder sheepishly. "Ah . . . wine coolers. I finished off the wine last night."

He came to the fridge and looked in with a sigh. Half a gallon of milk, fresh-squeezed orange juice, Gus's grape sodas, and my bottled water. "Crap. Only a preacher's wife would go to the beach without beer."

"Most preachers' wives I know wouldn't even have wine coolers," I said, taking out two bottles and handing him one.

Maddox chuckled as he opened the bottles, then we both spoke at once. "Where—" I began, and "Actually, I tried to call—" from him. He held up his hand. "You first, Miss Bean. Miss Willobean."

"Okay. Where'd you come from?"

"Flew from Tampa to Apalachicola, rented a car, and drove straight to your bungalow. I got this wild hair after we talked last night, and tried to call you back till after midnight, to say I was going home early and would stop by on my way. But no answer. I tried again today, before I left and when I landed, but still couldn't get you."

I nodded, leaning against the kitchen cabinet. Gus's bag of corn chips lay there, opened, and I got a handful, pushing the bag toward Maddox. "We were out crabbing last night, and today we've been swimming and snorkeling all day," I said between bites of chips. "Gus'll be tickled to death when he sees you. I left him and Lollie asleep on the beach."

"I haven't seen him in a month," he said, stuffing his mouth with corn chips. "He'll be even more pleased that I'm not here to take him home early, or disrupt y'all. I rented a room at a dump in Port St. Joe for tonight, then I'll head back to Crystal Springs in the morning. Thought I'd take y'all out to dinner." He undid another shirt button and rolled up the sleeves of his white shirt. "I was afraid I'd miss you two party animals if I didn't get out here quick, so I didn't change. Point me to Gus's room and I'll shower, get into something else."

"You've got a change with you?" I asked, and he inclined his head toward his briefcase.

"Shorts, T-shirt, and sandals, so we'll have to go informal. Real informal."

"No other way around here. You'll be thrilled when you see how well Gus's doing, by the way."

"I already am. You look more relaxed than I've seen you in months, Dean. If Gus looks half as good—"

"You're in for a surprise. And so is he when he sees you. Let's go wake him up."

"Okay." He held the wine cooler at arm's length and made a face. "This stuff tastes like Kool-Aid. Mind if I get some beer after we get Gus up?"

I shrugged. "Suit yourself. It's not my fault you don't have a taste for fine wine. Come on, I'll show you Gus's room."

Maddox rolled his eyes to the ceiling on entering. "Don't tell me that damn dog sleeps in the other bed." When I nodded, laughing, he threw the briefcase on Gus's bed, unmade, all the covers kicked off. "Gus has sounded great on the phone. Think he's doing okay, really?"

"You won't believe it. Get him to tell you about his new friend Mikey."

"He already has. Let me hurry so we can go to dinner, since I'm starved half to death. Are you?"

"The corn chips'll tide me over. Oh—something else you'll like, how Gus's appetite's improving," I said, turning to go out the door. "I'll change, too, and meet you on the porch."

His eyes moved over me in my wet swimsuit. "You look so good, I wouldn't have known you."

"Talk about a two-edged compliment," I laughed.

He was serious, regarding me. "I'm glad St. Joe's has been good for you. You deserve it, Miss Bean. I don't know what any of us would've done without you."

I looked at him in surprise. Muttering, "Why, thank you—how sweet," I turned and scurried up to my room before he could see how his remark touched me.

Although I'd sworn off tears for the week, I got choked up watching Gus's reaction when he saw his daddy. When Maddox and I climbed over the sand dunes, the towels were empty and Gus wasn't where I'd left him. My heart leaped in fear, then I spotted him playing on the edge of the beach, Gus throwing a stick and fat little Lollie plunging after it. He hadn't quite gotten the drift of it, and I poked Maddox with my elbow. "Lollie tries to eat the stick instead of bringing it back to Gus," I pointed out.

"Not the brightest pumpkin on the vine, is he?" he said, then stopped in astonishment. "Good God, would you look at Gus?"

I shaded my eyes with my hand and grinned. "I told you he looked good."

"He looks fabulous." Pushing his sunglasses up on his head, Maddox looked down at me, eyes glowing. "Jesus, Miss Bean. We'll be calling you Annie Sullivan from now on."

"Me? I can't take any credit for it." I motioned dramatically, flinging my arms out in an imitation of Celeste. "Eez the sun, the sea, the sand . . . all zee healing powers of the universe."

"Did you know he cried every single day he was home for spring break? I've been worried sick about him."

"He's not completely out of the woods yet. Remind me to tell you about the latest nightmare. But he's much better."

Gus saw me first, his arm poised to throw the stick to Lollie, Lollie wagging his tail in readiness. His mouth flew open when he saw who was with me. "Daddy!" he shouted, and ran toward him, Lollie at his heels. Maddox knelt and opened his arms, and Gus ran into his embrace, almost knocking him over. Laughing, Maddox held him close, and Lollie barked in a frenzy as Gus buried his face in his father's neck. "Daddy, Daddy—I missed you!" he said, as I blinked back tears. An elderly couple, sitting on beach chairs near the water's edge, watched the reunion with tender smiles, and even a bored jogger slowed down and smiled before resuming his pace.

Back on the deck after Gus showered and changed, he filled Maddox in on everything he'd missed out on this week, the swimming and snorkeling and boat ride and his new friend Mikey. Maddox let him get about halfway through every single event of every single moment since our arrival Sunday, then held up his hand to silence him. "Whoa. Let's go to dinner and you can finish this."

"We can't go to dinner now," Gus gasped. "We'll miss the sunset. Me and Beanie never miss the sunset, do we?"

We all raised our heads and looked out over the bay. Although we couldn't see the sun from here, we could tell by the gold tinging the water that it was hanging low over the ocean. "You two would actually moon over a sunset while I pass out from hunger?" Maddox said, sending Gus into another one of his giggling fits. He turned to me, his hands on his hips. "You've corrupted my only son and heir, Miss Bean. Turned him into a poet, dooming the family business. He'll be writing odes to tomatoes instead of what I've been doing this week, lobbying for the use of seven-dust and cow manure."

"You talk so crazy sometimes, Daddy," Gus giggled. "But I'm hungry, too. Let's go."

"Ready, Dean?" Maddox asked, turning my way.

I sat on a deck chair facing the water and propped my feet on the deck. "You and Gus go on. I'm not hungry." They needed this time to catch up on their long absence.

"Aw, come on, Beanie," Gus whined, standing with his hands on his hips like his daddy, frowning at me. Freshly showered with his wet hair plastered down, and dressed in khaki shorts and a knit shirt like his father, Gus looked much like Maddox, in the same posture.

"Beanie doesn't have to come," Maddox said, much to my relief. "We'll bring her something. Guess we'll have to go all the way into Port St. Joe, right?"

"Right," I said. "But they have some good restaurants."

"I'll show you the tacky place I'm staying tonight," he said to Gus. "You'll be real impressed."

"Just stay here tonight, Daddy," Gus said with a shrug. "There's an extra room upstairs."

I couldn't help it; I glanced up at Maddox and he winked at me. "Can't do that, son."

"How come?" Gus said.

"Well, Beanie stays in enough hot water with the church ladies without giving them something else to gossip about," he explained.

Gus frowned. "Why would the church ladies gossip about Beanie? She's the preacher's wife."

"Bingo," Maddox said.

It took Gus a minute, then he looked at me and said, "Oh." I looked away, a hot blush creeping up my neck. "Let's go before it gets dark," Maddox said briskly.

They were halfway to the front door when I jumped up, calling after them. "Maddox?" He and Gus stopped and looked back at me. "Why *don't* you stay here? I'll take your tacky room, let you and Gus have some time together."

"Absolutely not," he said, shaking his head. "I just wanted to see him on my way home, then we'll have the whole summer together. Relax. It's okay."

Maddox and Gus were late getting back, and I'd dozed off, reading in bed. Since it was past eleven, I was surprised when Gus knocked on my door. "Beanie? You awake?"

"Sort of," I said.

"Me and Daddy got you a present, so we want you to come downstairs."

Their loot was spread out on the kitchen table, Maddox and Gus standing on either side, eager as little boys to show me what they'd brought. "Look, Beanie," Gus cried as I came down the stairs, blinking in the light. "We got presents for everybody."

"Oh, thanks a lot," I said. "Thought I was getting special treatment."

"Oh, no," he said seriously. "We got everybody we know stuff—even Joe. Look at Lollie." Lollie was sitting at his feet, posed as though having his portrait painted, a sombrero perched atop his head and a rawhide chew shaped like a guitar at his paws. I groaned and looked at Maddox.

"Oh, no. Not gag gifts," I said, and he nodded.

"Look what I got Joe," Gus giggled, holding up a whoopie cushion. "I got Mikey one, too, and silly hats for Carl and Theresa."

"I can't wait to see mine," I said as Gus went into a fresh peal of giggles with each one while Maddox watched us with folded arms.

"Daddy wouldn't let me get you anything silly," he said, handing me a small box. "So here."

Opening it, I took out a tiny gold crab on a chain, then lifted my hair up as Maddox fastened it around my neck. "You guys are so sweet," I said, hugging them. "Thank you."

"We brought a key lime pie home from the restaurant. Want some?" Gus asked me.

"Sounds great. Let's take it on the porch."

After we'd eaten our pie, Gus announced that he and Lollie were going to bed, and Maddox had gotten up to go back to Port St. Joe, when the phone rang. We stared at each other wide-eyed, wondering who could be calling us this late. "Who has this number?" Maddox asked me, frowning.

"Now that you're here, only Theresa and Carl. And Ben, of course, but he wouldn't call this late."

"Then something's happened at the plant. Let me get it."

The phone had rung several times by the time Maddox picked it up, his brow furrowed. "Hello?" After a pause, his face relaxed. "Oh, hi! How are you?" Another pause and, "Sure thing." He covered the receiver and turned to me with a twinkle in his eyes. "It's Ben," he mouthed.

When I stood motionless, Gus tugged on my arm. "Good night, Beanie," he whispered. "See you in the morning." I reached down to hug him absently, my heart fluttering. Something terrible must have happened.

Gus and Lollie went into their bedroom, and Maddox handed me the receiver. He stood by, waiting to hear what was going on.

"Ben?" I said, my hands trembling.

"Hello, Dean." Ben's pulpit voice, loud and commanding, made me flinch. "How are you?"

"F-fine. What's happened?" My voice was as weak as my knees.

"Happened? Why do you think anything's happened? The caucus ran late, and I just got back into my room. First time this week I've checked my messages, and I had one from you. So thought I'd call and catch you up on the news. Why'd you think something's happened?"

I leaned against the counter. "Well, it's just so . . . late. I didn't expect you to call so late."

"I apologize for that, but you're usually up at ten."

"Ben, it's eleven," I said, and he gasped.

"Oh! I looked at my watch wrong. Did I wake you up?"

"No, but I'm about to turn in. Gus just went."

I knew what was coming next before he said it. "I was surprised when Maddox answered."

I looked over to where Maddox stood. He'd gotten a beer from the fridge and was leaning against it, eavesdropping shamelessly. When our eyes met, he motioned to the fridge, mimicked opening a wine bottle, and I nodded eagerly, glad he'd brought some back from town. I needed a whole bottle for a conversation with Ben. "Gus and I were surprised to see him, too," I said to Ben.

"I bet. Thought he was in Tampa at some kind of business meeting."

"He was. He's on his way back home, and stopped by here to see Gus, since he hadn't seen him for a while." I took the glass of wine Maddox handed me with a grateful smile.

"Surely he's not driving home this late at night," Ben said.

"No, no. He's got a room in town—Port St. Joe—and will drive back in the morning. Isn't that right, Maddox?" I asked, and he lifted his beer with a wink.

"So he's standing close by, huh?" Ben said. "I kind of wanted to talk to you in private."

"What is it?" I turned my back to Maddox pointedly. He chuckled, then went to the porch, beer in hand. I waited until he sat down, his back to me.

"We need to talk. About the way things have been—ah—between us lately," Ben said.

I sighed, rubbing my eyes. "I've said that repeatedly. But not now. Not at eleven, over the phone."

"Dr. Clark asked why you canceled the appointment, and I told him things were still pretty bad with you. You need to see him."

"Me, or the two of us?"

"Of course this affects me, too. That's the other thing I called for. It took a lot of persuading, but Dr. Vickery let us put his name up for bishop."

I put my hand over my face, too stunned to speak. "Dean? You still there?" Ben said, but I couldn't answer. What a fool I'd been to think he meant it, to believe his remorse and guilt were stronger than his ego! Like Augusta, I'd made the mistake of trusting him. "Dean?" Ben said again.

"Y-yeah, I'm here," I said weakly.

Oblivious, Ben continued. "So, the cabinet appointment's looking more like a certainty. I need to know things are going to be okay between us when that happens."

"It's great to be needed," I said.

Ben sighed his martyred sigh again, a sound I'd spent a blissful week without having to hear. "This is important to me. You of all people know how important."

There was a long silence. "Very well," he said finally, his tone icy. "I hadn't wanted to tell you, but Dr. Clark thinks you are headed for a nervous breakdown."

I closed my eyes, forcing out thoughts of John Marcus Vickery. "Ben, listen to me. We're in big trouble—big trouble—and we have to do something before it's too late."

"Let me say it again, Willodean. Dr. Clark wants to see you, not me. He didn't say one thing—you hear me?—not one thing about seeing me," Ben said, his voice loud. Evidently he wasn't sharing his room with anyone.

"Then he doesn't know his butt from a hole in the ground, and I'm not going to anyone that incompetent," I said between clenched teeth.

Ben's voice quivered. "I'll tell you, I'm so worried that I added your name to the prayer requests on the conference floor."

"Oh, God!" I yelled. "How dare you? Every blue-haired biddy in the conference will call me, trying to get the scoop."

"I refuse to listen to this," he said coldly. "I'm sick and tired of you yelling and carrying on, reverting to your white-trash background every time you have a temper tantrum."

"And I'm sick of you looking down your pious nose at me, calling me white trash. I'm sick of it, you hear me, Ben, you sanctimonious, self-righteous son of a bitch—"

His astonished gasp cut my tirade short, and I put my hand over my mouth, realizing what I'd said. "Oh, my God . . ." I whispered, "I'm sorry . . ."

"That's why I'm so worried about you," Ben said in a tight voice. "The only thing left for me to do is pray for you." And he hung up.

In a daze, I put the phone back on the wall. I stumbled out of the kitchen, stopping short when Maddox came to the porch door and stood watching me, trying to keep a straight face.

"Don't you dare laugh at me, Maddox Holderfield," I said.

"I wouldn't dream of it," he said, but his voice was barely controlled. His hand touched my arm. "Come to the porch and tell Daddy all about it."

I shook my head. "Believe me, you don't want to hear it."

"Come have one for the road, then," he said, his eyes dancing. "Then I've got to get back. You go to your room and I'll go to mine, full of fear and trembling that one day, I might do something to piss you off."

"You heard every word, didn't you?" I stumbled after

him while he retrieved my wineglass, filled it, then led me by the arm to the porch.

"Every wonderful word," he laughed. "It was the most entertaining tirade I've heard in God knows when. I was quite impressed, too; your alliteration was priceless. What was it—self-righteous, sanctimonious son of a bitch?"

I sank into a deck chair. "Oh, Jesus. I'm not believing that happened." The candle I'd lit earlier and placed on the railing flickered in the strong wind.

"Sounded pretty serious," Maddox said, the laughter gone from his voice.

"Yeah. Pretty serious," I echoed, gulping my wine.

"Whoa. You're supposed to sip that stuff, you know." When I didn't say anything, Maddox pulled a chair close and took my hand. "It might help to talk about it."

I lowered my eyes. "I know. But I can't right now. Things are bad between me and Ben, Maddox. Have been, for some time."

He patted my hand. "I'm sorry to hear that. Anything I can do? Want me to go beat him up or something?"

I smiled. "That won't be necessary."

"Well, know that I'm here if you need me, okay?"

I looked at him as the candlelight flickered off his glasses. He was right about that. He'd been there for me every time I'd needed him, ever since Augusta died. I leaned forward, put my arms around his neck, and kissed him lightly on the cheek. "Thank you for saying that." My voice caught in my throat. "Thank you so much."

"No big deal," he said, embarrassed, and I pulled back. It was my turn to laugh.

"Look at you—you're blushing!" I said. "Tell me this, why is it so hard for men and women to be friends? We've become really close lately, yet both of us blush like fools when we try to talk about it."

Maddox regarded me seriously. "Men don't know how to do friendships. Not that we don't have them, we just can't talk about them like you women do. Every time I want to say how close I feel to you, and what a good friend you've been to me since Augusta died, I feel like a cornball. I can't do it."

"You don't have to. You've said it in a hundred different ways."

"Really? I had no idea. None of this comes easy to me," he admitted.

I laughed. "Come on." I got to my feet and took his hand, pulling him up. "You'd better go to your tacky room now and get some sleep. It's bound to be close to midnight."

He nodded. "Yeah, guess so. Wish I hadn't had that last beer now."

"Want me to make some coffee?"

"No, no, I'm fine." He rubbed his face and looked up at the sky. "Hey, a full moon! Let's go for a walk, like we did that night in Crystal Springs. Remember?"

I laughed. "Of course I remember. But we can't."

"How come?"

"No windows to look in."

"You're right. I have a better idea, anyway—let's go for a swim in the moonlight."

I gasped in surprise, delighted, then sighed and shook my head. "We can't leave Gus here."

"Sure we can. Pollie, Lollie, whatever his name is, will protect him for ten minutes. I'll make sure he's asleep and lock everything up tight. Then, sober, I'll hop in my car and take off. Nothing to it."

"But you don't have a swimsuit."

"It's in the car. Come on, Miss Bean, it was meant to be. Let's have another of our little adventures."

Swimming in the ocean at night was totally different than swimming in the light of day, unlike anything I'd ever done. Mystic, divine, so magical that I made Maddox leave twice to check on Gus, prolonging it. After his last trip to the house, Maddox dove in and surfaced beside me in the darkness. "You can quit worrying now, sending me back and forth," he said. "I left a note on Gus's pillow telling him we were in the ocean, and to come out here if he wakes up. We can stay out all night if you want."

"Don't tempt me," I said. The tips of the waves were moon-gilded as they formed around us, spreading silver as they broke on the shore. "Would you look at that," I whispered, surfacing beside Maddox. Humming the theme from *Jaws*, he chased me until I squealed and splashed water on him every time he surfaced. "Stop it!" I said, swimming away from him. "You won't let me enjoy this."

"Because I'm a male, unable to show my appreciation of moonlit mysticism. To hide the depth of my emotions, I have to act like a fool." Sneaking up behind me, he tweaked my leg between his toes. "Watch out—there's a crab."

"Hey!" I yelled, splashing him furiously. "That's the second time today you've scared me to death." Laughing, he swam away from me, disappearing in the dark waters. I rode the waves in solitude, opening my eyes in the murky blackness underneath them, unable to see my hand in front of me. When I surfaced, I shook my hair out of my face and rubbed the salt water from my eyes, looking around for Maddox. He was nowhere to be seen, but I knew he was lurking around, waiting for the chance to scare me again. "Maddox?" I called, and was answered by the roar of the waves. "I know you're hiding from me," I yelled over the sounds of the ocean.

Treading water, I looked around, even though it was impossible to tell if anyone else was in the water. I shuddered, realizing I could be surrounded by sharks and not know it. Their fins couldn't be distinguished from the choppy peaks of the black waves. Something brushed my leg and I jumped, wheezing and coughing as water went up my nose. "Stop it," I yelled again. "I mean it." But wiping my eyes and looking around me, I couldn't see a thing, looking left and right, then to the horizon and the shore. No one was on the shore, no lights shone anywhere, and our discarded towels were a dark bundle like a huge octopus. "Maddox?" I called, shivering.

He grabbed me from behind and I screamed, plunging both of us beneath the dark water, me choking and sputtering. I came up before he did and tried to hold him down, but he pushed my hands off easily, surfacing and holding my wrists so I couldn't push him under again. "Guess what?" he said. "I caught a mermaid. Scared the shit out of her, too."

Giving him another push, I swam away from him as he chased me, laughing. Running to the shore, I sank beside the dark bundle that was my towel and beach jacket, tickled that I'd outwitted him. I buried my face in the towel, then rubbed my hair with it as Maddox came out of the water and sank down beside me, panting.

"I'm dying," he gasped. "My lungs are about to explode. I haven't stayed underwater that long since I was a kid."

I threw his towel to him. "Give you credit, that was a good one. I couldn't see you anywhere. I was about to work myself into a real panic."

He lay on the wet sand without moving, the towel half over his face, where it landed. "It's cold out here, isn't it?" he said finally. "Feels good, though."

"Feels great," I said. "That was absolutely fabulous." I threw my head back and shouted to the stars overhead, "Fabulous!"

"It was, until I started thinking there *could* be sharks out there and we'd not know it till it was too late," he said, rubbing his face with the towel.

"I was thinking the same thing. That was just before the

panic struck." I pulled my beach jacket around me. "Hmm, feels good in this cool breeze. You don't have anything but a wet towel."

"I'm fine. Got a dry towel, too." He draped it over his shoulders and sat up. We were right at the water's edge, and he stretched out his long bare legs, just out of reach of the lapping waves. Running his fingers through his hair, so fair it shone in the moonlight, he glanced my way. "Dean? Scoot over here a minute," he said in a light voice. "I need to talk to you."

"Uh-oh—what is it?"

"One thing is, I tried to thank you earlier for what you've done for Gus, and you wouldn't listen," he said. Settling myself beside him and crossing my legs to get comfortable, I glanced up and found him regarding me speculatively. Without his glasses, his gray eyes were clear silver in the moonlight.

"I told you, I won't listen to that kind of talk," I warned him. "It embarrasses me. Keep it up, and I'll go to the house."

"Okay, I'll shut up because I don't want you to go until I have my say," he said, staring out at the ocean. "Then you may want to, as fast as your legs can carry you."

"Uh-oh. I don't want to hear it, then."

"Okay." He grinned. "That's a lot easier on me."

I poked him in the ribs and he chuckled. "Oh, no, you don't," I said. "Now you've got my curiosity up." I looked at him in surprise. "I'll be—you're embarrassed, aren't you? Now you've got to tell me."

"All right, all right. But I can't if you look at me. Look at the ocean instead. And stop shivering. Are you cold?"

"A little," I admitted, and Maddox opened his arms, the beach towel draped across his shoulders like a cape. I moved over so that his body blocked the night wind. His arms were

strong and warm around me as we sat together without saying a word, looking up at the moon hanging high over the
dark sea, listening to the waves lapping at our feet. I snuggled
into the warmth of his arms comfortably, the beach towel
around both of us. It had been such a long time since I'd
found comfort anywhere. He shifted to prop his chin on top
of my head until I moved my head away. "You can't talk that
way," I said.

"I don't want to now," he said. "I want to sit like this
forever."

"I was thinking the same thing. Now, tell me. I promise
to sit like this and not look at you."

"Okay, but don't cheat. Here goes. A funny thing happened to me on the way to Port St. Joe this afternoon."

I smiled. "Good start. Though not very original."

"The next part's not, either, I'm afraid." He got quiet
again, and I nudged him with my elbow. "This is hard for
me, like I told you before we came out here," he said, clearing
his throat.

"Oh! I know what you're going to say, then, and you
don't have to. It's been established—we've become really
good friends, and we like each other a lot. See, that wasn't so
bad, was it? I said it for you."

He put his hand over my mouth and whispered, "Shhh."
His hand tasted like the ocean, warm and salty. "A funny
thing happened to me on the way to Port St. Joe. I couldn't
wait to get here. I couldn't drive that rental car fast enough. I
wanted to sprout wings."

"And why not? You hadn't seen Gus for a month," I reminded him, twisting my head from his hand to free my
mouth.

"True, and I couldn't wait to see him. But here's what
happened to me, if you'll hush long enough for me to tell you.
For the first time since God knows when, not just since Au-

gusta's death but maybe even years before, I was happy. Mr. Gloom-and-Doom was actually lighthearted and happy, singing along with the radio, grinning and waving at every car I passed."

"Bet you looked like a fool," I said, and his hand came over my mouth again, firmly this time.

"I felt like a fool when it hit me. And it hit me hard, Dean, so hard that I almost wrecked the car. I had to pull over, I swear. I put my head on the steering wheel, feeling like the biggest idiot that's ever lived."

I squirmed, trying to look at him, trying to ask him, "What? What was it?" But he wouldn't let go, and he lowered his head next to mine so that his voice was in my ear. "God almighty, Dean," he whispered, "it was you. It was because I was going to see *you*. Don't you know that? Can't you see it? I was terrified you'd see it on my face, in my eyes. It took all I could do to fake it when I saw you, pretend nothing was different. And that bullshit tonight about our friendship—Jesus, I almost blurted it out then. I had no intention of ever telling you, even after overhearing the conversation between you and Ben. Or maybe especially because of that, because I don't want to take advantage of your unhappiness now." He fell silent and I sat still, too shocked to move. "The moonlight made me reckless," he continued. "You don't have to do anything about it, ever, but now you know how I feel about you."

Aghast, I turned to look up at him. We'd never been this close to each other, and I frowned, blinking at him. His eyes searched mine, and I reached up and touched his face. "What are you saying?"

"You know. You know damned well what I'm saying."

"But—*me*, Maddox? Surely not me?"

He answered by taking my face in his hands and kissing me. My hands went into his hair and we fell backward, locked together. The waves pounded over us as we slid into the wet sand. The cold water brought me to my senses, and I pulled my mouth from his, opening my eyes and laying my head down on the sand. "Oh, Lord," I whispered.

Maddox chuckled, his eyes glowing as he looked down at me. "My thoughts exactly."

"Let me up," I said, pushing against his chest. "I can't breathe."

"Me neither," he murmured into my hair.

I managed to pull myself upright, facing him. My hands trembled as I pushed my wet hair out of my face. My face was hot, and my lips burned in the salt air.

"Dean?"

"Don't say anything right now, okay?" I shivered as he touched my cheek with the back of his hand. "Oh, God. And don't do that, either." I squeezed my eyes shut and his fingers traced the outline of my face like a blind man. His hands moved down to the necklace he and Gus had given me, the gold crab on a golden chain.

"I'm afraid this blows our friendship to hell," he said with a soft laugh.

"Listen to me, Maddox. Listen!"

"Okay. You're in a great position to bargain right now."

"Let's go back to the house and pretend this never happened, okay?"

He hooted. "I've got a better idea. Let's go back and make out. Somebody might see us out here."

"We can't do that with Gus in the house," I gasped. He laughed and took my face in his hands again.

"You're right. But tomorrow night, I told him he could go camping with Mikey. You know what? I love Mikey for that. When I see his skinny little butt I'm going to grab him and kiss him on the lips." And laughing, he kissed me instead.

"Dammit—listen to me," I repeated, when I could get

my breath. "Here's what we're going to do. We're going back, and you're going to sleep in the extra bedroom—"

"Likely story." Like he'd done to me, I put my hand over his mouth to shut him up.

"It's too late for you to drive in, and there's no reason why you can't stay here. Then, tomorrow morning as planned, you're going back to Crystal Springs."

He took my hand away from his mouth and pressed his lips to my palm. "Can't. When we were having dinner, I promised Gus I'd go snorkeling with him."

"After that you've got to go." The feel of his lips on my palm was weakening my resistance, and I jerked my hand away.

He shook his head. "What a heartless woman you are, sending me back to my empty and lonely house. Don't you get it? Didn't you hear what I said? If I could've flown this afternoon, I'd have done it, just to be with you."

I put my hands on his shoulders and faced him, sitting up on my knees. "Maddox, you're not hearing me. We can't do this. You know that, don't you? We cannot do this."

He searched my face. "Actually, I was hearing you, I just didn't want to."

"You've got to!" I said. "This scares me to death."

"Scares *you*? I'm the one who heard you chewing Ben out tonight, so I've got to be either real brave or real stupid."

I laughed, shaking my head. "I'm going back in now and pretend this never happened, okay?"

He rubbed his face wearily, then turned to gaze out over the ocean. Finally, without looking at me he said, "Whatever you say, Miss Bean. I might've known you'd be like this, break my heart into little pieces and throw it back at me. Serves me right."

"Will you be okay?"

"No. If you hear someone scratching at your door tonight, don't think it's Lollie."

"Maddox!"

"Okay, okay, I'll be fine. I'll take Gus snorkeling tomorrow, then go back home."

"Thank you," I said. As I'd done earlier tonight, before our so-called friendship blew up, I leaned over and kissed his cheek. Somehow, I made it back to the house, hurrying up the stairs to the safety of my room.

Even though I slept late the next morning, I was the first one up. I tiptoed down the stairs, afraid I'd run into Maddox before getting to the kitchen. The house was quiet and still and peaceful, deceptively so. Last night seemed like a dream, something that could only happen on a deserted beach, turned silver by moonlight. Two lonely, grieving people who'd been thrown together as Maddox and I had—we should've had better sense. Moonlit nights on lonely beaches could be dangerous places. I fumbled with the coffeepot, desperately in need of a caffeine fix to clear my head.

"Good morning, Dean."

Startled, I twirled around, spilling coffee beans on the floor. Maddox smiled at me as he strolled into the sunny kitchen barefoot, dressed in a faded T-shirt and running shorts.

"You sure are jumpy this morning," he said. "Look what a mess you've made. A person could slip on those coffee beans, bust his butt."

I turned my back to him, grabbing for a dishcloth. Yawning, he propped himself against the cabinet, his arms folded. "I had an awful time going off to sleep last night, and bet you did, too," he said. "Did you notice how bright the moon was?"

I kicked the coffee beans aside as I ground another batch, concentrating on making coffee as though my life depended on it.

"Must've been the moonlight that made me have such

strange dreams," Maddox continued, his eyes on me. "You know that old movie *From Here to Eternity*? I dreamed about it. There's a famous beach scene—"

"Listen to me," I interrupted. "Last night—"

But the bedroom door downstairs slammed, and with Lollie barking at his heels, Gus ran into the kitchen, throwing himself into his father's arms. "Daddy—you're here already!"

Maddox looked at me over the top of Gus's head and winked. "Yep. Got up early just so I could go snorkeling with you today. Isn't that right, Dean?"

We took a boat out and Gus showed off his new snorkeling skills. When we anchored and they went to the shore to find shells, I stayed on the boat. Helping Maddox with his snorkel, swimming together, and eyeing him warily through the swim mask had been too much for me. Whenever he swam near me, I got flustered, strangling and spitting water while Gus giggled. I was going to drown my fool self at this rate. When they returned from the shore and climbed on the boat, Gus had a broken starfish in his hand. "Come on, Daddy," he cried. "Let's see if we can fix this starfish so he won't drown."

They bent their heads together to examine the small creature and I watched from my perch on the side of the boat. Maddox took the starfish from Gus and held it with a frown, his hands gentle as he turned it over. I lowered my eyes, remembering the feel of his hands on my body as we lay together in the sand last night. My eyes were drawn back to him as though pulled by a magnet. Gus looked up at him, face shining, sure that his daddy could fix the poor broken creature. Maddox squeezed the back of his son's browned neck, his hand moving up to stroke his hair. He raised his head and his eyes met mine, and I turned away. Oh, God help me. What was I getting myself into?

· · ·

I showered and changed while Maddox helped Gus get ready for his camping trip. It would be a relief when Gus went on his trip and Maddox left for Crystal Springs. I planned to drink a whole bottle of wine and pass out as soon as the taillights were out of sight. The peace and tranquility I'd found here were shattered, and like Gus's broken-armed starfish, couldn't be put back in place.

Standing in front of a seashell-edged mirror, I patted aloe on my sun-browned face, frowning at a new batch of freckles and wrinkles. Life in the Florida sun was havoc on a Southern belle. There was a knock on my door and I jumped. Gus had been yelling for me to hurry, so I yelled back, telling him to come on in, I wasn't deaf.

Maddox strolled into my bedroom as nonchalantly as if he were walking into the kitchen. With green gel on my face, I froze and watched his reflection as he came to stand behind me. Our eyes met in the mirror, mine wide and tense, his playful. He'd gotten sun today, too, maybe too much, his face glowing. His hair was wet from the shower, and he'd changed into his uniform, khaki shorts and a white knit shirt.

"Do I see freckles?" he said to my reflection, amused.

I shook my head. "Used to be freckles, now they're age spots. Both of us got sunburned today, I see."

Hands on my shoulders, he turned me to face him. Frowning, he smoothed out the globbed-up gel on my face, and I stood still, eyes focused on a spot on the white-painted wall, just over his shoulder. I didn't dare meet his eyes. His aftershave had an outdoorsy smell, and there was a tiny place on his jaw where he'd nicked himself shaving.

"What's this mess?" He took the jar of gel from my hand and eyed it suspiciously. "Looks like snot."

"It's fresh aloe that I got from Celeste. Keeps you from peeling," I said to the spot on the wall.

"Naw, you won't peel, you're too dark. Like me, I bet you've got Spanish blood."

"My great-grandmother was the queen of Spain, so I was really surprised to be turned down by both the Junior League and the DAR," I said dryly.

Maddox hooted and I raised my eyes to his. A mistake, and I looked away. He handed the jar of aloe back. "That's better. You looked forlorn when I came in, with your green face. You okay?" he asked, raising an eyebrow.

"I'm fine," I said.

"Not upset with me?"

"No—it's not that. I hate to see this week come to an end, is all."

He looked to the open doors of the balcony, the bright blue sky and treetops, the Gulf in the distance, visible at points through the foliage. The afternoon sun sparkled off the dancing waves like thousands of jewels. "I dread going home," he said.

"I hadn't wanted to put it that way."

"I came in here because I owe you an apology," he said abruptly, staring outside instead of looking at me, his voice low. Since first meeting him, I'd loved his voice. Whenever I heard it on the phone these last months, I'd felt a response, a quickening of my pulse. I knew why now.

"For what?" As if I didn't know.

He ran his fingers through his wet hair, disturbing the neat comb tracks. "When I made the—ah—stupid-ass confession last night, I didn't mean to cause you any more grief. I wish I'd kept my big mouth shut ...." He stopped and shrugged helplessly, his eyes troubled.

"Listen, Maddox," I said. "We've become so close,

thrown together in our grief for Augusta, that maybe something like—last night was inevitable. As we said, it's difficult for men and women to be friends. A magical night in the moonlight, and things got out of hand. Let's forget it, okay?"

He smiled in relief and nodded. "Right. Good idea." He folded his arms and regarded me. "I really regret coming here and spoiling your week. You were so relaxed yesterday, looking so happy and peaceful, until I messed everything up."

I shook my head. "No, no, I'm glad you came here. Really. Gus has loved having you. It's been good for the two of you."

"He's going to be okay, isn't he?"

"He is," I said, "and so are you."

We eyed each other, still wary, and I was the first to look away. "Well!" I said with forced cheerfulness. "I'll go downstairs with you and say good-bye to Gus."

"And to me, too. I'm heading on after dropping him off at Mikey's place."

We walked companionably out of my room and down the stairs, where Gus waited with Lollie, packed up and ready to go. His eyes widened when he saw his daddy behind me on the stairs. "Daddy," he gasped, "you shouldn't go in Beanie's room! The church ladies'll gossip about you."

Maddox laughed. "You going to tell on me, son?"

Gus tilted his head, his eyes full of mischief. "Not if you'll buy me some scuba equipment."

Maddox lunged and grabbed him, throwing him over his shoulder as Gus squealed, kicking his feet in delight. "You brat—think you can blackmail me, huh?" They wrestled on the floor, laughing and knocking things over, and I watched, feeling sad. In spite of his apology and my acceptance, I was afraid my easy friendship with Maddox was gone. His touch had stirred something in me that I thought was long dead, something that had nothing at all to do with friendship.

· · ·

It had been such a clear blue day that I was surprised to find the sun obscured by heavy clouds when I took my sunset walk, a summer storm brewing to the west where the sky was dark and ominous looking. Even with no sunset to view, I walked for a long time, trying to get control of my wandering thoughts, forcing them to Gus's camping trip. Mikey's dad was taking them to a place with the romantic name of Indian Pass, and Gus'd expected to find arrowheads there. I wondered if the rain would be a problem, or if Dr. Johnson was an experienced camper. Perhaps he'd been an Eagle Scout who could make a fire even with wet driftwood, I thought, then smiled at my silliness. But anything was better than thinking about last night. I walked faster, swinging my arms and clenching my jaw. I could walk it off. I could go back to the house, drink a bottle of wine, and sink into oblivion. Maybe then I could close my eyes without seeing gray eyes, stormy as the clouds building over the ocean.

The rain held off, so I sat on the deck with my wine, a thick towel wrapped around me to block off the chill of the strong night wind. If the rain came, a covered part of the deck, like a porch roof, extended out from the back of the house, and I could move my chair there. I'd poured my first glass of wine when the phone rang, and I ignored it, afraid it might be Ben. Ben! I'd not allowed him into my thoughts all day, knowing that was a place I couldn't go now. Because of the turmoil that Maddox's touch had caused, I longed to run home to Ben and find things like they used to be, staid and predictable and comfortable. If he called back, I'd answer. I'd agree to do anything, get down on my hands and knees and genuflect when he came in, kiss the bishop's royal behind, make an appointment to see Dr. Clark—anything to go back to the way things were before we moved to Crystal Springs and our lives turned upside down.

The phone rang again and I got to my feet. I could do it. I knew exactly how to kiss up to Ben and make things right.

"Ben?" I said into the receiver.

"How'd you know it was me?" he said, surprised.

"Had to be. I'm here by myself, Gus gone camping with a buddy and Maddox back home. And, I was hoping you'd call."

"You were? I'm home now, just got in from doing Kim's wedding, and thought I'd call to see when you'd be home tomorrow."

"Tomorrow's Saturday; it's Sunday we get home."

"Sunday? In time for church, I hope?" I braced myself at the disapproval in his voice.

"It's too far a drive for that," I told him, then took a deep breath. "But I should be back for night services."

"Good," he said. A heavy silence, then he said, "Ah, I've been real upset since our conversation last night. You'd never talked to me like that, and I was shocked. And hurt. I have to tell you how hurt I was."

I swallowed, ashamed of myself. "I apologize, Ben. And I've been thinking. When I get back, I want to see Dr. Clark."

"Really? You mean, next week?"

"As soon as he can see me."

"Because of the situation, I'm sure he'll work you right in. As a favor to me."

"Good," I said softly.

"Pardon me?"

"That's good," I said, clearing my throat and closing my eyes.

"That's great, Dean—really. I had a feeling that you'd see things my way, eventually."

"How was Kim's wedding?" I asked. Oh, Ben, you know me well, I thought. Too well. You know better than anyone what a spineless coward I am. He described the wedding, told me what a good job he'd done with the ceremony, what a big honorarium the bride's father gave him. I hung up, promising I'd be home for Sunday evening service.

The phone rang again. Recognizing Maddox's voice, I sank into the nearest chair.

"You got home earlier than I expected," I said.

"Not quite there yet," he said. "I'm calling on my cell phone in a restaurant, having a beer and awaiting my hamburger, so I thought I'd see if it was raining there."

"Where are you, Panama City? Is it raining there? Are you worried about Gus camping in the rain?"

"Whoa, one question at a time. It's not raining yet, but I'm not worried. Dr. Johnson set the tent on high ground, put a tarp under it, everything. But best of all, he told me if the bottom fell out, they'd sleep in his van."

I laughed, leaning back in the chair. "A man after my own heart."

"So, what're you doing?"

"Drinking wine, sitting on the deck, waiting for the rain to start. Missing you and Gus." It slipped out before I realized it.

"Can't have that, can we? I'll turn around and come back."

I laughed. "You can't do that, silly."

"Sure I can. I can stay there tonight, and you'll be perfectly safe. We're buddies again, remember? I'll never touch you except to shake hands. Maybe a friendly hug on special occasions. Otherwise, my hands stay in my pockets. We'll sit across from each other and have deep philosophical conversations. But on platonic matters only. How does that sound?"

"Sounds perfect." Try as I might, I couldn't keep my spirits from lifting, just talking to him, and I grinned into the phone like an idiot.

"Okay. Be out there in a few minutes, then."

"Maddox!"

"Gotta go now—waitress's here with my hamburger." And he hung up before I could say another word.

I thought he was kidding me, but half an hour later, he came bounding up the steps. "I don't believe this," I cried out, jumping to my feet, my hand at my throat. "Where were you anyway—across the street?"

"Almost." He grinned. "Hamburger joint in Port St. Joe."

"Are you kidding? You liar, you!"

"Nope, I didn't lie. Just didn't tell you."

"Omission's still a sin," I said. He threw back his head and laughed, and it thundered ominously at the same time. We raised our heads to the dark sky, and the raindrops began to fall on our upturned faces.

"Here's our storm at last." Taking my arm, Maddox led me to the overhanging porch, where we stood side by side, watching the rain beat down on the dark waters of the bay. The drops and a sudden gush of wind extinguished the candle I'd left burning on the railing. "Blow out your candles," he whispered. "The world is lit by lightning."

"Maddox?"

His eyes were on me in the darkness of the night, amusement in his voice. "Yes?"

I hugged my arms against the cold wind. "Actually, I'm glad you came back, because I need to talk. You overheard my conversation with Ben, and wanted me to tell you what was going on, remember?"

"I changed my mind. I don't want to hear it."

I ignored him, looking out at the rain falling on the bay, listening to the sounds of the thunderstorm. "As I said, things haven't been good between us for a long time. It's like my life's coming apart at the seams."

"I sure as hell know how that feels."

"Tonight I told Ben that I'd go to a counselor, try to make things right again."

He reached out and tucked my hair behind my ear. "Why'd you do that?"

"The first day here, I watched a sand castle wash away in the waves. And I thought, that's the way my life is now. I don't want that anymore."

Maddox was silent so long that I dared to look over at him. He stared at the bay and didn't look my way when he spoke. "Good metaphor, the sand castle. The two of us standing in the rain, cold and wet with a storm raging around us, is another good one, don't you think?"

I shrugged. "I don't know. I guess."

"So, what you're telling me is that you're going back to resume your life with the old sanctimonious son of a bitch, huh?" he said. I expected him to be angry, or bitter, sarcastic. I'd not expected the heavy sadness in his voice.

"That's what I'm telling you." It's what I have to do, I said to myself, but not to him.

The fury of the storm let up and the rain fell more gently, making little splashes in the black bay water. Large drops pinged on the tin roof, playing us a symphony. "You called me a liar," Maddox said, his voice coming out of the darkness, startling me.

"I didn't mean it."

"No, you were right. I lied to you this morning, pretending to be nonchalant about what happened between us last night. I lied by saying I wished I'd kept my mouth shut. I'm glad I told you how I felt, Dean. And now that you're going back to Ben, I'm even more delighted, because I want you to take it with you." In the darkness, he took my hand. "I'm glad that fate threw us together here, as on a darkling plain. You know that poem, don't you?"

I managed to nod my head but couldn't speak. "One of my favorites, 'Dover Beach,'" he continued, his voice soft, as in a dream. "Like the poem says, lately I have felt as though the world has neither joy, nor love, nor help for my pain." He turned to look at me. "Maybe you'll find help for your pain by going home, my sweet Dean. I hope you'll find it with Ben, and I pray to God that you'll be happy."

I sighed, dropping his hand. He was right. Rain was blowing in on us, and I was cold and wet. "What does happiness have to do with anything?" I asked.

"You're asking the wrong person that one, my dear," he said.

The rain was soft now, a memory of the earlier storm. "You were honest with me, Maddox, so I want to do the same. I'm not going home seeking happiness, or help for the pain. I'm going home because I gave up looking for it, long ago."

Moving suddenly, he pulled me to him, and I couldn't make myself turn away. "Don't you believe there's something more in life than fear?" he asked me. "Can't we help each other find whatever it is?"

Instead of answering, I took his hand and led him into the house, up the stairs to my room. It was dark and the curtains billowed, filled with the cold wet wind that blew across the bay. I stumbled in the dark when I reached the bed, but Maddox grabbed both my hands, and I sank down blindly. He knelt in front of me, and taking my ankle, removed first one soggy wet sandal, then the other one, tossing them aside. We undressed each other as though in a fever, throwing our rain-soaked clothes to the floor. It was good to be free of the cold, clinging garments, to feel his body strong and warm over mine. We moved together as though there were hope, certitude, and joy, as though the rightness of our being together was all there was in the world. For Maddox and me that night, all we knew was the rain-kissed wind blowing across us as we came together, our bodies joined in an attempt to ease the pain of our lives.

I didn't hear him leave. I slept so soundly for the first time in months that I didn't hear the rain stop, or the soft, sweet sounds of morning. When sunlight burned my eyes and I raised my head, I saw the note propped next to me, where his head had been.

First night's sleep I've had in God knows when. I'm writing this at sunrise, watching you sleep. I'd love to wake you, but wouldn't be able to leave if I did. I must go before Gus gets here—I told him I was going home yesterday, and don't want to lie to him again.—M—

And across the bottom he had scribbled, barely decipherable: *There is something more, Dean, and I think we have found it.*

Twenty

THE SUN LOW BEHIND us, Gus, Lollie, and I pulled up the tree-shaded driveway to Mimosa Grove, the house forlorn and empty-looking in the distance. Ten days ago I left home, going to Gainesville for my audition. I had loaded my car, weak with fear yet also excited, full of anticipation. How could I have known how things would turn out?

"Well, here we are. Mimosa Grove," I said stupidly to Gus, who looked small and dejected. He'd gotten quiet as we got closer to Crystal Springs.

"I wish we didn't have to come home," he said. "Do you, Beanie? Do you wish we could stay all summer at St. Joe's?"

"I'd like nothing better. But life is funny, Gus. We can't escape it, except for occasional magic moments." Give him another one of your corny speeches, Dean, I thought. Maybe you can convince yourself.

When Gus didn't move, I reached over and undid his seat belt. "Hey—you okay?"

He nodded. "Yeah. It's still sad coming home with Mama gone."

"Remember what we talked about? It always will be." I squeezed the back of his neck as I'd seen Maddox do on the boat. Maddox . . . I couldn't let myself go there right now. The first thing I'd noticed when we drove up was the empty place in the garage where his old black Mercedes was usually parked. Thank God for small favors. When he'd called last night, I'd panicked, scurrying to my room and listening at the door as he and Gus talked. When Gus called up the stairs, "Daddy wants to speak to you, Beanie," I didn't answer, and I heard him say that I'd already gone to bed. When Gus returned from the camping trip, I'd exhausted him, cramming every minute with the things we hadn't gotten around to: biking, shopping, sightseeing, a frenzy of activities to keep me from thinking about what had happened with Maddox and me.

When we'd unloaded everything, Theresa took my arm and pulled me aside. "There's a problem with some equipment at the plant," she said. "But Maddox called and asked that you not leave until he gets here." Impeccable as always, Theresa's face revealed nothing, but I was uneasy, avoiding her eyes. Something was different about the way she looked at me, or maybe my guilt was making me imagine things. I had no intention of staying until Maddox got here.

Instead I took the kitchen phone and punched my number in. "I need to use the phone," I said inanely. I hung up when the answering machine came on. "Well," I remarked as Theresa came back from the freezer with a package of frozen hamburger meat, "that's strange. Ben's not at home or the church." He never went anywhere on Sunday afternoon.

Theresa put the meat in the microwave and punched Defrost. Tired of seafood, Gus'd asked for hamburgers for supper. "Oh!" she said, looking over her shoulder. "I forgot to tell you. Mr. Charlie Hall died last night, so Dr. Lynch is at the funeral home. Church services have been called off."

I nodded, surprised. One of our oldest members, Mr. Charlie hadn't known he was in this world for months. Still, I was surprised Ben hadn't called to tell me he'd died. "Guess I'd better go before it gets dark," I said.

"You're not going to stay until Maddox gets here, then." She made it a statement, not a question.

I looked away from her, out the kitchen window. "Uh— no, I really can't. I should go to the funeral home, too."

Theresa took out an iron skillet and began frying the hamburger patties. I jumped, hearing a car door slam outside, and gave her a quick hug. "Gotta run now, Theresa!" And I hurried out the back door, knowing I could get to my car before Maddox came into the house. There was a breezeway from the garage to the back of the house; he always entered that way.

I made it to my car, but not in. As I opened the door, I heard the footsteps behind me. Maddox's arm shot out and pushed against the car door, slamming it shut. I turned around to face him, embarrassed that he'd caught me sneaking off. "Maddox!" I said, leaning against the car, my heart pounding.

"Trying to sneak off, were you?" He grinned, but his eyes were puzzled.

"I—I've got to get home," I stammered.

"Why? Old Charlie Hall kicked the bucket, so Ben and everyone else at First Methodist's at the funeral home." His face changed as he watched me. "Didn't Theresa give you my message?"

"She did. Don't blame her," I said, unable to meet his eyes.

"Just wanted to leave without seeing me, then. That it?" His voice was low, intimate. I was pinned between him and the car, his arm holding the car door shut. I looked around to see if anyone, Theresa or Joe or Gus, might be watching us. Fireflies sparkled amidst the dead azalea blooms and green-leafed dogwood trees.

"We can't talk out here," I whispered.

"You're right, and we need to talk. So let's go somewhere else." His intensity scared me, and I shook my head.

"I can't. I've got to get home." When he didn't say anything, just kept staring down at me, my eyes filled with tears. "Maddox, please. I need some time. I've got to be alone, to think . . . after what happened with us . . ."

He relented, removing his hand from the car door. "I know. So I'm not going to push you, okay?" I wiped my eyes with the back of my hand, looking at him gratefully. He reached up and touched a teardrop with his fingertip, brushing it away. "Missed one."

I let my breath out slowly. "I wish we could talk now, but . . . I'm in a state of shock."

"Me, too." His eyes fell on the gold necklace around my neck and he reached out again, lifting the chain and dangling the gold crab from his hand. My neck burned as his fingertips brushed my skin. "Know that I'm as blown away by this as you are, Dean; don't think I'm not." Reaching past me, he opened my car door. "Okay, off you go. We have to talk soon, though. Let me know when you're ready."

I nodded, and got into the car. As I fumbled for the key and looked up, a light came on in the kitchen window, then a face appeared. It was Theresa, watching us.

Driving into Crystal Springs, I knew with a heart heavy with sin and guilt that everything in my life had changed. The woman who left here ten days ago, heading east, was gone. I drove past my house without stopping. When I passed First Methodist with its stately columns out front, I averted my eyes. Out front was a neat white sign that jumped out as if it were flashing neon: *Crystal Springs First United Methodist, Dr. Benjamin J. Lynch, Minister.* What would I do when I had to face Ben?

It wasn't dark yet; still light. Twilight. As I drove through Crystal Springs, I knew where I was heading. I didn't really want to go, but maybe I needed to. The sign on the gates read *No One Allowed in After Sunset or Before Sunrise.* I ignored it and pulled onto the winding dirt road.

Fresh flowers were on Augusta's grave, yellow mums in a marble urn. I sat down on the stone wall bordering the plot. I stared at the grave as I sat on the low wall with its sharp stones, hot from holding the day's sun, cutting into my bare legs. Why had I come? Augusta wasn't here. I didn't know where she was, but one thing was for sure: She was not here. Some people went to their loved ones' graves and talked to them, but I wasn't sure what I wanted to say to Augusta. Would I tell her that I loved her child, but didn't want to love her husband? Perhaps I'd tell her that I knew what it was like; I finally understood passion, like hers for John Marcus. It was all clear, now that it was too late to offer compassion and understanding to her. Augusta would chide my fears, my cowardice in running from love. But she knew me well; knew that I lacked her fire, her daring in living my life. I whispered as I got up, heavy with fatigue and grief, "But look where it got you, Augusta."

I had let Maddox catch me this afternoon, but I was determined to be in bed with the lights out by the time Ben got back from the funeral home. I propped a note on the kitchen table, saying that I was going to bed early. I'd see him in the morning. Again, my timing was off, because just as I reached to turn back the spread, Ben knocked at my door. "Come in," I said, sitting down on the side of the bed, resigned.

Ben entered, dressed formally in his dark funeral suit. "How are you, Willodean?"

"Tired. Didn't you see my note?"

He nodded, crossing the room. "I did. But I left the funeral home early so we could talk."

I looked down at my bare feet, unable to face him. Ben's fan club would have the last laugh: I'd turned out to be the worthless Jezebel they'd imagined from the first. "Not tonight. Let's put it off until tomorrow," I said.

Of course he was having none of that. "The funeral is tomorrow. Unlike you, I have a busy schedule. I have to do things when I can make the time."

"But, still, tonight's not the time—"

"You're not hearing me, Dean. I said I left the funeral home early tonight," he repeated for the third time.

"So what? Mr. Charlie sure didn't care."

Ben took a handkerchief from his suit pocket and wiped his face. He looked so bad that I was concerned about him. "Ben? You don't look so good. Please—let's go on to bed now, get some rest first, okay?"

"The reason I don't look good is because it's been such a rough week at conference. So many things going on—all that mess about Luke Shepherd, and the endless caucus meetings to get Dr. Vickery elected." His eyes moved over me, coming to rest on the gold chain around my neck, and although he didn't say anything, I was sure he thought I'd bought it, indulging myself with expensive doodads while he slaved away at conference.

"I wanted to make sure you wouldn't cancel your appointment with Dr. Clark again, Dean. Our little problems need to be resolved before my cabinet appointment is announced."

Our little problems are more serious than you know, I thought, but said nothing.

Ben paced, his hands behind his back. "After our conversation the other night, I did some soul-searching. And I came up with something that made me ashamed of myself. You're right: I have to take my share of blame for our problems. I've been so busy since we've moved here that I've neglected my home life."

I swallowed. "There's some truth in that, but—"

Ben held up his hand. "Let me finish. I've seen for a long time that you're struggling with your relationship with God, going through a spiritual drought—which is common in middle age—and Augusta encouraged it. It's manifested itself in hostility toward me and the church, I see now."

I closed my eyes. "There's a lot of truth in that, Ben, but—"

He stopped pacing and stood in front of me. "If you'll let me, Dean, I can show you the way back. You are lost, in a spiritual wilderness, mixed-up, confused, and angry. Guess what the lectionary was this morning—Ephesians Five! *Wives, submit yourselves unto your husband, as unto the Lord.*"

He stood over me like an Old Testament God on judgment day, staring down at me with opaque eyes. "Oh God, Ben, what's happened to us?" I asked.

"I haven't changed, Dean. You're the one who's become a different person," he said. We stared at each other until I looked away guiltily. He was right, of course. I was a different person now, not the naive, guileless woman who'd won his heart with her music. Like Eve, I'd tasted the apple, and could never go back.

Ben sighed and shook his head, his shoulders slumped in defeat. He rubbed his face wearily, then turned, his hand reaching out for the door.

"Ben, wait!" I cried out as I jumped off the bed, running to him. He turned to me astonished as I flung my arms around him. "I'm so sorry! I never meant to be unfaithful to you."

"My goodness," he said, locked in my iron grip. "It—it'll be okay."

"No, it won't! I'll never forgive myself for what I've done to you," I sobbed into his dark funeral jacket, wetting it with my tears of guilt.

"Hush now," he said in a low voice. "As I said, I haven't been blameless. I've not been faithful to our vows, either, putting my work before everything else."

"That's not what I mean! You don't understand—"

"I said hush, and I mean it," he said, giving me a shake. "I'll forgive you, and things can go back to the way they used to be. I'll help you with this, and Dr. Clark will, too. Things are going to be okay now."

Covering my face with my hands, I cried until I exhausted myself, still in his arms, seeking the comfort and safety I'd always found there. From now on, I would cling to Ben for dear life, and no matter what, I wouldn't see Maddox again.

I ran from my feelings for Maddox by burying myself in endless activities that consumed my days, exhausting myself so I could fall into a dreamless sleep at night. I drove to Pensacola twice a week to see Dr. Clark, but our sessions were fruitless, a waste of both his time and mine. I didn't talk about my feelings, I didn't talk about my music, and I didn't tell him about my infidelity. Avoiding his probing eyes, I told him my guilt was based on my inadequacy, the way I'd failed to be the wife Ben deserved, but he didn't believe me. Evidently he decided to wait me out, for he kept scheduling me for appointments, and I went, eager to fill up another day.

My new fervor pleased Ben, and things got better. We had church work to talk about again and the plans for his cabinet appointment, which were still highly secretive. He'd been right; we fell easily back into our old routine, almost as though the angry and bitter words we'd thrown at each other had never happened. Our occasional lovemaking was back on Ben's busy schedule, and I retreated to my room immediately afterward so I wouldn't have to explain my tears.

I could avoid Maddox but not Gus, who called me almost every night. Every time he said his daddy wanted to speak to me, I stalled, saying I'd call him when I got a chance. I got roses, black-red and heartbreakingly beautiful, with no card. The second time, there was a card. "When you're ready," was all it said. I'd taken the first vase of roses to the hospital, but the last one I took to Celeste. She raised her eyebrows, her eyes full of questions. She was busy with a customer, a college student with a pierced nostril and spiked hair, so I left. When I returned home, the sweet scent of roses lingered in the house, haunting me. I sprayed the entire house with peach potpourri until my eyes stung and Ben coughed while eating his lunch.

It was the arrival of the letter from the University of Florida that made me seek Maddox out, three weeks after our return from St. Joseph. Unable to sleep, I called Mimosa Grove, after listening at Ben's door to make sure he was snoring. Maddox's voice was dazed and sleep-filled, that dreamy-toned voice that had haunted me since our return.

"Dean? Jesus—I was dreaming about you," he said hoarsely.

"I didn't think I'd wake you," I whispered, looking at the clock. It was eleven-thirty. "Can we talk?"

He was instantly alert. "Of course. But not on the phone. What about tomorrow? Oh crap—I'm taking Gus to camp. Why don't you sneak off, come with us?"

"I can't, but if Gus is asleep, could I come out there now?"

"Of course."

"Let me in the back way, in the sunroom, in ten minutes," I said breathlessly. Mimosa Grove was the perfect place for us to meet because Gus, asleep upstairs, would be the barrier we needed.

Maddox let me into the dark sunroom, and we stood facing each other with the moonlight coming in eerily, shadows around us from the plants, as in some sort of surreal garden. I studied him carefully for the first time since we'd been in my bed on St. Joseph's Peninsula. He looked awful, bleary-eyed, his hair tousled. "You look terrible," I said.

He smiled, putting an arm around me. "You know the way to a man's heart, don't you? God, I've missed you!" I pulled away from him, and he frowned. "What's wrong?"

I took a deep breath and exhaled slowly. "Everything."

"Let's sit down," he said, looking at me warily, but I shook my head.

"I can't stay. Ben's asleep; he doesn't know I'm not in the house."

"Is that what's going on? Ben? Does he suspect—"

"No, but I feel so guilty! You just don't know . . ."

"I'm so sorry," he sighed, his head bent to mine. "You've been going through hell, haven't you?"

I nodded. "I can't do this, Maddox. I just can't."

He studied me but I avoided his eyes, looking down at my feet until he lifted my chin. "I told you to take your time. I'm not going to pressure you. You know how I feel, and if there's anything I can do to make this easier for you, let me know. But otherwise, you work everything out and decide what you want. Okay?" His voice was so kind that tears stung my eyes.

"I got the grant," I said, and he blinked at me, his face in shadows.

"What?"

"The women's studies' grant. The letter came today. I wasn't expecting—"

With a whoop, he grabbed me and lifted me off my feet. "Why didn't you tell me as soon as you knew? That's wonderful!"

I couldn't help it; I threw my arms around his neck as he whirled me around the room. "I wanted to tell you right away, but—"

"Doesn't matter." He grinned, putting me down. "The important thing is that you got it. I knew you would, by God."

"I've got to go," I said. "But I wanted to tell you in person."

His eyes shone as he looked down at me. "You had me scared. You sounded so remote on the phone that I thought you were coming out here to tell me to go to hell."

I made myself look at him unflinchingly. "Maddox, you've got to hear this loud and clear. I'm trying to make things work out with Ben, and this time I mean it. This is highly confidential, but it looks like he's going to get an appointment on the bishop's cabinet at the end of this summer. If that happens, we'll be moving to Tallahassee. It works out really well for me, now that I've gotten the grant, because I can commute to Gainesville."

He was so stunned that he took a step backward. "I didn't mean to blurt it out like that," I said helplessly.

"You don't need time to make up your mind, then. You already have, haven't you?" he said, his eyes darkening.

When I nodded, he lowered his head. "So. I had everything wrong," he said, his voice soft. "What happened between us didn't mean anything to you. That's what you're telling me, isn't it?"

"I'm not going to leave Ben," I said.

His face flushed, Maddox stared at me. "Tell me that you love Ben, Dean. Say it. I need to know, so I can get on with my life if there's no hope for us."

"Of course I love Ben," I said, turning my head.

"Look at me, goddammit. You're lying, aren't you? Look at me!"

"I don't know how I feel anymore. Don't do this."

He sighed. "We had this same conversation at St. Joe's. You're scared, aren't you? That's why you married Ben to start with, isn't it, because he didn't ask anything of you?"

"Don't say that," I gasped. "Of course that's not true."

"What would you have done if I hadn't come along—pretended forever that you didn't need passion? That you were happy with your pathetic life because nothing was required of you emotionally?"

"That's a horrible thing to say. And it's not true. Not a word of it is true, Mr. Know-it-all."

"Oh, yeah? Know what I say to that? I say bullshit. And I'll tell you how I know, Dean. I know what it's like to settle for a life without love, to convince yourself that you're happy anyway."

"That's not true—Augusta loved you!"

"I don't believe that Augusta never told you that she loved someone else, all her life, and that she only married me because she couldn't have him."

The letter, I thought in a sudden panic. He knows Augusta left a letter that I've hidden from him all this time! When I didn't answer, he smiled. "You have lovely eyes, Dean, and they're very expressive. They say more than you put into words."

"Maddox—" I began, but he held up a hand to silence me.

"Didn't think I knew, did you?"

"Who was she in love with?" I dared ask.

He shrugged. "She wouldn't tell me, saying that she'd gotten over him. Bull. I knew better. I think that's why she died. I think she was leaving me for this man, whoever he was."

Tell him about the letter, Dean, I told myself. Don't make him go through this torment any longer. Go home and get the letter. "I have to tell you something," I said.

"But I have Gus," he continued. "Augusta couldn't give me her love, but she gave me my son. He's all I have now. He's all I need."

That stopped me cold, and neither of us said anything as we stood, eyes averted, until we both raised our heads to look at each other.

Maddox reached up and brushed my hair off my face, tucking an errant strand behind my ear. "Go home, Dean, back to your life with Ben. You're right. You're doing the right thing. I have nothing to offer you."

"I won't ever forget that night at St. Joe's," I whispered, looking at him with great sadness, remembering the way we came together in such desperation, and the astonishing comfort we'd found in each other's arms.

"I'm not going to forget it, either. Not any of it."

Although we talked a couple of times on the phone, casually, confirming or making plans having to do with Gus, Maddox and I stayed away from each other. My frenzy of activities picked up once the jurisdictional conference of the church met and nominated John Marcus Vickery as their candidate for bishop. Elated, Ben told me to begin packing, but to keep the boxes hidden away in case someone from the church came over. He couldn't tell anyone anything until it was official.

Then the call from the bishop came, and the first Sunday in August, to the astonishment of the congregation, Ben made the announcement from the pulpit. It was his sad duty to inform his beloved church, he said, that at the end of the summer, he would be moving to Tallahassee to take an appointment on the bishop's cabinet. Loud voices from the congregation rose in protest. Overcome with grief, Vanna Faye Bell ran from the choir loft, her dramatic exit spoiled when she slipped and almost fell at Ben's feet. I put my hand over my mouth to keep from laughing out loud.

Ben also announced that our district superintendent, Dr. Jim Robertson, would be coming in from Pensacola for a special meeting that Monday night, and all their concerns, as well as the announcement of Ben's successor, would be discussed. Ben was trying hard to be sensitive to the highly charged emotions of the church, but he could barely hide his elation. That afternoon, I overheard him on the phone with Bob Harris, telling Bob that of course he didn't want to move, but it was the will of the Lord God and out of his hands. How convenient that the Lord's will coincided with Ben's ambitions, I thought with a weary smile.

The next evening, I fixed a fancy dinner for Dr. Robertson, relieved that he was driving back to Pensacola after the meeting rather than spending the night with us. Dr. Robertson and Ben had gone on to the meeting, and I was to follow when I got the kitchen cleaned up. I was loading the dishwasher when Maddox called.

"Dean? Is Ben there?" he said abruptly, not identifying himself, and my heart jumped at the sound of his voice.

"Maddox? N-no, he's at the church," I stammered. "Did you need to speak with him?"

"Of course not," he chuckled. "Just wanted to make sure you were alone."

"You're hopeless," I said, smiling. I'd worked so hard to put him out of my mind throughout the endless summer that I was unprepared for the effect his voice had on me. I felt like I'd been punched in the stomach, weak and nauseous.

"I knew he'd be at that big meeting," he said. "Carl told me about it. Listen, I need to see you. Wish it were darker, but that can't be helped. Meet me at Lake Crystal in ten minutes."

"Are you crazy?"

"Gus is at the Hernandezes', playing video games with Joe, so you can't come here. Meet me—let's see—at the covered pavilion farthest from the parking lot. See you in ten minutes." And he hung up before I could say another word. I stood there staring at the phone, my hands shaking, not knowing what to do. Lake Crystal! A weird place for a rendezvous. Or maybe not. Maybe no one else would be there on a Monday night after dark.

At first it appeared no one was in the pavilion, then I saw Maddox leaning against a picnic table. As I'd hoped, the lake area was almost deserted. "Here I am," Maddox said as I made my way over to him.

"Unfortunately, I can see you," I said. "I was hoping it would be a little darker." The pavilion was the most isolated, closest to the lake, sheltered by low-limbed live oaks. Maddox's big black Mercedes, recognizable to anyone in Crystal Springs, was parked discreetly by the main recreation building. Civic meetings were held there, and he was on the board of some of them, so if his car was spotted, it would seem he was in a meeting. Maybe. Be kind of hard to pull off, though, with the building locked up and deserted.

Maddox watched me, amused. "You should see yourself, Dean, sneaking up here, looking like one of the church ladies was going to jump out from under the picnic table. Relax. Everybody you know's at the church now, right?"

I sank down on the concrete bench next to where he stood. "What's going on? What did you need to see me about?"

He looked down at me calmly, his eyes searching my face. "Who said anything was going on? I just wanted to see you. I've missed you. You look wonderful tonight, by the way. You're the only woman I've ever known who has no idea how lovely she is."

"But, you said . . ." I replied, too jumpy to pay attention to his flattery.

"What? I said what? Only that I needed to see you."

"Don't tell me that you had me sneak out here for nothing!"

"Nothing? Give the knife one more twist. Bad enough I have to trick you into seeing me without your saying my longing for you is nothing. Don't you know about the fragility of the male ego?"

"This is not funny! I'm worried sick, full of guilt, confused and upset, and you're playing games with me."

The laughter left his face and he sat down beside me on the bench, frowning. "Jesus, Dean, you're really upset, aren't you?"

I nodded, my anger dissipated by his gentleness, which always took me by surprise. "I didn't trick you entirely," he admitted. "I wanted to call you yesterday, once Carl and Theresa told me about Ben's surprise announcement at church. But I knew this would be a better time to talk. So it's true, then? You're moving to Tallahassee?"

I shrugged. "That seems to be the plan."

"Is that what you want? Are you happy about it?"

I stared down at my feet as though the answers were written on my sandals. Shaking my head, I twisted my hands together, confused and distraught. "I don't know."

Maddox leaned his head close to mine. "What? I couldn't hear you."

"I said—that I don't know," I repeated, clearing my throat. "I'm too confused."

He put his hand on top of the fist I clutched in my lap. I looked down at his hand and felt an irrational but powerful sense of comfort. I couldn't tell him that in spite of everything—my vow not to see him again, my overwhelming guilt, my terrible fears—I had a desperate longing for his touch.

"I'm confused, too," he said, his voice low. "I never expected what happened between us. After Augusta, I certainly didn't want it. God—it's the last thing I wanted!"

"It's the last thing I wanted, too," I said. "That's why we agreed to stay away from each other, remember?"

He took my shoulders, turning me to face him. "I'm afraid I'm not able to keep my end of that bargain."

"You don't know how guilty I feel about Ben—"

"Yes, I do. Even though Ben doesn't deserve you, I feel god-awful about him, too. And I've let myself get involved with Libby again, although I didn't intend to. So I'm torn to pieces with my guilt and my need for you. I'd do anything not to hurt Ben, or Libby, or anyone. Anything but give up what you and I have found."

I put my hands over my face. I couldn't lie to myself anymore, pretend I didn't feel the same, deny my need for him. "Oh, God. What are we going to do?" I said instead.

"Damned if I know."

I laughed in spite of the tension, giddy with confusion and guilt.

"You know how I felt about Augusta," Maddox said. "But it wasn't like this. I was utterly miserable—miserable with her, miserable without her. She tormented me, drove me crazy with my love of her. But with you, it's a peace like I've never known; a sense of rightness, of coming home. Does that make sense?"

"Oh, yes." It made sense because I'd been so terrified of those same feelings, thinking surely I was imagining them.

"Guess I've never believed it could be this way. Tell me the truth, Dean—have you?"

I could only shake my head, helpless to stop this, unable to keep from going into his arms, his mouth over mine stopping my giddy laughter. We were both lost, not caring who saw us. I felt as though I were in the lake, drowning, being pulled under by unseen currents. I knew that I'd never come to the surface again, and I didn't care.

"There's a back room in the rec center that I have a key to," Maddox said, his hands holding my face. "Tiny little office, but it has a couch."

"Why do you have a key?" I asked.

"I've been chairman of the Crystal River Preservation Society for years," he said. "I knew serving on all those boring boards would pay off one of these days."

I found that I couldn't tell Ben, even though I knew now that running to the safety of my old life no longer worked. The only refuge I found was with Maddox, with the stolen hours in the back room of the Crystal Lake rec center. No longer could I pretend that a life without him was an option for me. But neither could I face Ben, tell him the truth. Whenever I tried, I turned away from the elation in his eyes as he prepared for his new appointment; his surety that all would be well with us now. He was going where he wanted to go, had prepared for his whole life, and I couldn't tell him that I wasn't going with him. For years, the more cynical of the preachers had called Tallahassee "East Jerusalem." Without a trace of irony or cynicism, Ben was going to East Jerusalem, riding in on a donkey, palm branches thrown at his feet. The pinnacle of his success was now only a few days away, and he floated through the present, living only for the moment when he left Crystal Springs for his Mecca. His joy was so palpable that it encompassed me, and he talked endlessly about how things would be once he was on the cabinet. "Just think," he said, grinning at me over breakfast on the day he was leaving for Tallahassee to set up everything for our move, "no more parsonage committees, no church ladies questioning your every movement. You'll like that, won't you?"

"Ben, there's something I need to tell you."

"Don't think I haven't been aware of how hard it's been. But it'll all be worth it now. You'll like being a cabinet member's wife, everybody kissing up to you."

"I'll be in school," I managed to say. "So it won't be like that. Actually—"

"The more I think about it, the more I like the idea of you going back to school," Ben interrupted, his face bright. "I wasn't so sure at first, but I've had second thoughts. Be good for me to have a professional wife, like Beth Vickery." He rubbed his hands together. "It's worked out well that we can move into the house Mike Stewart vacated, but I still wish you'd come with me to check it out."

"It's better that I don't," I said, lowering my eyes and despising my weakness. It was the same weakness that kept Augusta's letter locked away in my jewelry box.

Ben got to his feet. "You like surprises, but I'd rather see the house before we move in."

"Ben? Can we talk before you leave?"

He kissed the top of my head, pulling his coat on. "Gotta run. We'll talk about it when I get home!"

I went to Celeste, making her pull out the cards and crystal ball. To my astonishment, she knew about my affair with Maddox without my telling her. When I asked if she'd seen it in the crystal ball, she laughed. "No. I can see it in your face."

"Oh, Celeste, what am I going to do?"

But Celeste wasn't able to do for me what I could not bring myself to do. Instead, she insisted that I not tell Ben about Maddox. "A Pisces, you feel the pain of others too much. You must not tell your husband that you love another, or his pain will always torment you," she said.

"You know what I'm going through, don't you?" I asked. Unlike me with Ben, Maddox had talked with Libby. He hadn't mentioned me, had said only that it would be better if they broke it off. Rejected once again by Maddox, Libby was trying to get Simms back.

Celeste shrugged and got to her feet. I was afraid I'd offended her, but she opened a wooden box on her dresser and took an object out, pressing it into my hand. It was a key. I raised my eyes to her, puzzled. "My trailer at Grayton Beach," she said. "Hidden away where no one will find you. When you leave your husband, you must go there. Stay as long as you need, my friend."

"Oh, Celeste," I said, touched. "I can't do that! You might need it with what's going on with Simms."

She shook her head. "No. I'll stay here for when he comes back to me, as he will. I am sure of that, because Cups dominate my cards. You are the one who will need the retreat, for the Swords are in your spread."

When Celeste read my cards today, the poor knight with the ten swords in his back had shown up again. "It's very important that you hide away," Celeste continued. "You promise?"

I promised that I'd think about it. Then, in desperation, I confessed that I hadn't given Maddox the letter yet. Throwing up her hands, she begged me to do so immediately. "That door to the past must be closed before opening the door to the future. You will never find happiness with Maddox until you give him the letter. It is not yours to keep, and he must know its contents before he can make a new life with you, leave his old life with Augusta behind. You must not wait another minute!"

Since Ben would be in Tallahassee until the next day, I didn't have to make up excuses to meet Maddox in the rec building that night. Before leaving, I took Augusta's letter out, folding it and putting it deep into the pocket of my jeans. Celeste was right. I had to do this.

At first, Maddox and I had parked far away from each other, but we'd gotten careless lately. He went into the building first, then I followed him. As I locked my car, there was a sudden clap of thunder, lightning flashed, and the bottom fell out. Holding my arms over my head, I took off running. At the door, I fumbled around in the darkness before realizing that it was locked; that Maddox wasn't there, even though his car was under the tree next to mine. When I was late, he usually sprinted around the lake. As though my thoughts conjured him up, he appeared from behind, then grabbed me in his arms and spun me around. "Put me down and open the door, you crazy man," I laughed.

Inside the dark room Maddox flicked the switch, but no lights came on. He reached into the pocket of his jeans and grinned. "Ah-ha—matches!" Stumbling over to a table, he found a stubby candle and lit it. Going to the john, he returned with a towel, drying his face. "You look like a drowned kitten," he said, taking his towel and drying my hair, holding the back of my neck with a gentle touch. "Cold, aren't you? You're shivering."

When I nodded, he brushed my lips with his. "There's a coffeemaker here. I'll make us some coffee," he said.

"Oh, good. I've always wanted to see one that operated on candles."

Laughing, he pulled me close. "I've got some whiskey in the desk," he whispered. "We'll have a drink, take off our wet clothes, and get under the blankets on the sofa. What else can we do?"

A sound outside startled me out of a dream in which I was standing in a stormy ocean, rain pouring down on me. I was cold and alone and afraid as lightning flashed and sea creatures swam close. I opened my eyes to see Maddox next to me on the sofa, asleep, a leg thrown heavily over my waist.

I moved, and he tightened his arms around me as he stirred. The candle had long since burned out, and it was pitch-black in the room except for the light from a small window. My head was heavy and my mouth tasted of whiskey. We'd fallen asleep on the sofa, exhausted with lovemaking and laughter.

"Umm . . ." Maddox murmured, eyes still closed. "You awake?"

"We've got to get up, sweetheart, and get out of here. I have to get home." My head was on his shoulder, my lips touching the sweet skin of his neck.

"Don't do that or we'll never leave," he groaned. "Might as well take advantage of me being on top of you anyway—"

"Oh, no, you don't. Get up and look outside, make sure we can make a run for our cars," I ordered, wide awake now. I had to get home before daylight. I couldn't have someone else telling Ben before I did, and I was telling him today, without fail.

"Don't want to," Maddox murmured, his lips in my hair.

"Quit it," I said, pulling away. "You've got to get up, you hear me?"

"That, at least, has been accomplished," he chuckled.

"Hush up and listen to me. We've got to go!"

He groaned again, kissing my palm. "I can't stand the idea of putting on my wet clothes."

"Then drive home butt-naked. That'd sure give everybody something to talk about."

Fully clothed, we made it to our cars without seeing a soul. It was early morning, but dark as sin. When I got into my car, Maddox crawled in next to me. "Will you do something for me?" I asked. "I'm giving you something that belongs to you, something I should've given you a long time ago. Will you take it without any questions? And will you go home before looking at it?" I couldn't be with him when he read the letter; couldn't stand his pain if Augusta told him about Gus, as I feared.

Frowning and tilting his head, he nodded. "Okay. Sounds mysterious, though. Take it, no questions, don't look at it until I get home. Right?"

I nodded. "It'll make sense to you afterward." Except why I kept it from him, but I couldn't even begin to explain that until he read the letter. Thank God Gus was away at camp.

I tucked the letter deep in his damp shirt pocket, and Maddox patted it. "Safe and sound, right here," he said. "Satisfied?"

I smiled, my heart heavy. "And now, my darling man, you've got to go." He kissed me briefly, then got out. Leaning down to close the door behind him, I gasped, my heart giving a wild lurch.

Just as Maddox reached for the door of his car, a man with a flashlight appeared, stepping out of the shadows of the oak tree. Maddox froze, stopping dead in his tracks like a deer caught in headlights. Because the light was in his face, he didn't recognize the approaching man—the reddish hair, the short stocky body, the gleam from the top of his balding head. It was Simms Legere.

"Maddox!" Simms cried. "What the hell?" He held the flashlight down when Maddox brought his arm up to shield his eyes, like a criminal.

"Simms? What are you doing here?" Maddox countered quickly. The best defense was a sudden offense.

Simms's face in the moonlight was friendly, unsuspecting, and he shrugged. "I was out here walking, before it started raining. Evidently when I stopped to rest, my wallet fell out. Been waiting for the rain to let up to return and get it. Couldn't wait till daylight or someone else might find it, right?" He patted the back pocket of his shorts to indicate that he'd found it. "What are you doing here?"

"I—ah—got caught in the rain—" Maddox began, but Simms laughed.

"Yeah, sure. Who you with?" Turning suddenly, he shone the flashlight into my car. With my clinging wet clothes and wild hair, there was no question of innocence, and I put my head down on the steering wheel to avoid his eyes.

Simms turned to look at Maddox. "Oh, shit, man. I didn't know."

Maddox didn't say a word, and Simms shook his head in bewilderment. He lowered his voice so I couldn't hear, evidently, but in the quietness of the rain-washed night, I heard every word. "I mean, I suspected something, but . . . Jesus, you'd better watch out! Folks around here are such religious fanatics, they'll be after your ass if they find out about her, I don't care who you are."

Maddox stood motionless, and finally Simms shrugged. "Listen, man, I won't say anything, and I'll tell Libby not to, either. But for God's sake, be careful, okay?" He looked into my car again, then turning quickly, walked away. I saw then what I hadn't seen before: Libby was with him, and she stood in the shadows of the tree, watching us. She had seen and heard everything.

Everything blew up at once, and afterward, I was never exactly sure how it all happened, in what sequence, how my whole world fell apart in one swift moment. Perhaps Libby wasn't able to endure being scorned by Maddox again, and moved quickly to exact her revenge.

Maddox, whom I'd found to be the most understanding of men, was more devastated by my duplicity than by the contents of Augusta's letter, and I lost him on the same day Simms discovered us at Lake Crystal. I'd gone home and showered, changed into dry clothes when he called me. The voice that I'd loved so much was cold. "You need to come out here," was all he said.

"But—isn't Theresa there? Will anyone see me?"

"Doesn't matter," he said, hanging up.

I could stand the flatness of his voice, but not the dead-
ness in his eyes when he opened the front door and stepped
out, meeting me on the portico without letting me into the
house. In his hand he held Augusta's letter, and when I
reached out to him, he took a step backward.

"Please let me explain—" I began, but the look in his
eyes stopped me. He stood watching me with his arms heavy
at his side.

"So I was right—Augusta was running away with her
lover." He waved the letter scornfully. "She protects his so-
called good name, but it doesn't really matter who he was. I
don't even want to know. What matters is that you've known,
Dean. You've known all this time."

"I was wrong to keep the letter from you, but I couldn't
stand to see you hurt!" I cried, scared, my heart pounding.
"Surely you know that."

"You made a pact with Augusta to take care of both me
and Gus when she ran off, right? Got to hand it to you, you
did such a good job that you had me fooled. Too bad Augusta didn't stick around long enough to see how well her
plan worked. But she always drove too fast, didn't she?"

"Oh, God, no, Maddox! That's not the way it happened.
I'd never do anything like that. Please listen to me—"

"Why should I listen to you?" he said, his face dark. "I
can't think of anything you can say that I want to hear."

"I know how you feel—"

Moving suddenly, he grabbed my arms, roughly. "Goddammit, don't you dare say you know how I feel. Don't you
dare say that, you hear?"

"No, no, you're right. I don't know how you feel. But
surely you know I was only trying to protect you! I was trying to protect you, and Gus, and I never, ever meant—"

But he held up a hand to stop me, backing away. "Go

home, Dean. Please. You've got a lot of packing to do, right? Next week you and Ben are moving to Tallahassee."

"I'm not moving to Tallahassee, and you know it."

"Oh, really? The question is, does Ben know?" I flinched as though he'd struck me, the look he gave me was so full of contempt.

"Not—yet. But I'm going to tell him, I swear."

He laughed. "You seem to have a problem telling people things, don't you? Especially important, life-changing things. Guess when the moving van pulls up, you'll say oh, by the way, Ben, did I tell you? I'm not coming with you."

"I don't blame you for thinking that," I whispered, wrapping my arms around me. It was hot, stifling hot, but I couldn't stop shivering.

Maddox studied me. "You haven't gotten a place in Gainesville, have you?"

I shook my head, tears filling my eyes. I hadn't gotten a place in Gainesville because I thought I'd be with him; that we'd be together from now on. "Why did I know the answer before I asked?" he said, with a smile that held no humor. "Let me make sure I have this right. You're trying to convince me that you're leaving Ben, yet you've neglected to tell him. Then, you claim you're going back to school, but it's late August, and the semester starts when? A few weeks, and you don't have a place to live? Tell me this, Dean. Have you even accepted the grant?"

I nodded, unable to speak, unable to raise my head. When he didn't say anything, I looked up, trembling.

"I'm leaving Crystal Springs, Dean. I'm going to North Carolina, maybe permanently," Maddox stated flatly. "Carl can run things here. I'll pick up Gus at camp, then head for the hills. He's been wanting the two of us to go camping, so I'll take him until his school starts."

I took a deep, trembling breath. Augusta hadn't told

him—thank God, she hadn't told him about Gus! Of course she wouldn't do that; what had I been thinking? Because of my stupid fears, I'd lost him. "I'm glad about the camping," I managed to say. "Gus will be thrilled." I had to ask him, no matter what it cost me. "Will you let me hear from you once you get settled?"

He shrugged. "No, I won't. What's the use? I don't need you now. I can take care of myself, and Gus, without your help, thank you."

"Please, Maddox, don't do this—"

"You heard me; I don't need you. I don't want you around my son. I want you to go home."

I shook my head, swallowing until I was able to speak. "I thought I *was* home."

His eyes changed to a steely color that cut through me like a razor, and he leaned against a column on the porch. "Looks like we were both wrong, then."

I turned away and went down the steps to my car. As I pulled out of the tree-tunneled driveway, he was still standing there, leaning against the column, alone again, as on a darkling plain.

I walked into the parsonage stunned, the horrible words Maddox threw at me sharp and painful as arrows. The dead knight in my cards, ten arrows in his back, mocked me as I tripped over a box of china, packed up and waiting for the move. Standing in the kitchen, I heard a noise and whirled around. Ben was sitting on the sofa in the den, his head down. I saw his car, knew he was back from Tallahassee, but hadn't realized he was in the house. Standing next to him, facing me, was Vanna Faye Bell.

"Y'all scared me," I gasped. "I didn't know anyone was here."

Vanna Faye's face was white, her eyes wide and staring.

She looked different than she normally did, dressed in running shorts and a T-shirt, her face without makeup, hair in a ponytail. Ben didn't look up at me. Something was very wrong. I walked into the den, my heart in my throat. "Vanna Faye . . . Ben—what's wrong?"

Vanna Faye stared as though I were a ghost, and I resisted the urge to look over my shoulder. "What is it?" I repeated.

"When Ben got in from Tallahassee, I was here waiting for him," she said in a shaking voice. "He asked me to stay until you got home."

"Ben? Are you sick? Is it your blood pressure?" He took blood pressure medicine but it had never been a problem before. I moved toward him, but Vanna Faye stepped forward to block my way.

"I think you should leave him alone," she said. I stared at her, my mouth open, too shocked to speak. "Yes, it's his blood pressure, and yes, he's had his medicine. I called Dr. Brandon, and he said for me to keep checking his blood pressure and to keep him posted." Somewhere in my dazed state I remembered that Vanna Faye had studied nursing, that she worked part-time at the clinic. I saw the sphygmomanometer on the sofa, coiled like a snake, but when I reached for it, Vanna Faye again blocked my way.

"I've got this under control. The worst thing you can do now is interfere," she said. Her voice, usually so breathless and prissy, was acidic. I stared at her, seeing a different woman than the silly beauty queen I'd always made fun of. This was Vanna Faye the person, without her heavy makeup and public persona, a woman whom evidently I'd underestimated.

"Interfere in what?" I cried. Ben still hadn't looked at me. "Ben—what is wrong?"

"He has had a very bad shock," Vanna Faye hissed, "and he asked me to be here when you got in. But frankly, it'd be better if he never had to see you again."

"At this rate, it doesn't look like he's going to," I snapped back at her.

"The shock of finding out about you and Maddox Holderfield has almost killed him," she said.

"What did you say?"

"Remember, I've tried to get you to join me walking around the lake every morning? I told you that a group of us ladies had organized a group, and we walk with our partners," Vanna Faye said conversationally, and I stared at her in disbelief.

"Walk with partners? What are you talking about?" I cried.

"My partner is Libby Legere," she said, triumph shining in her eyes.

I turned from her to Ben, and finally he raised his head and looked at me. His eyes were shocked, tear-stained, terrible. "Vanna Faye," I said weakly, "Ben and I need to talk."

"Absolutely not," she said. "Dr. Brandon said I couldn't leave you alone with him."

"You told Dr. Brandon what Libby said?" I cried, incredulous.

Vanna Faye's eyes narrowed. "He's a doctor—he can't tell stuff he hears, and he needed to know what was wrong with Ben." I knew that was only the beginning. She had run straight to Ben once Libby dropped her bombshell, but it wouldn't stop there. Everybody in town would know before the sun set today. Poor Ben—his worst nightmare.

"Ben, we've got to talk." I turned to him desperately, kneeling in front of him. "Please!"

Ben's eyes narrowed and he pulled back. "I asked Vanna Faye to stay because I didn't want to be alone with you, Dean," he said hoarsely. "I don't want to hear anything you have to say."

"Please, listen. I wanted to tell you, to explain how it happened—"

But he shook his head, closing his eyes. Vanna Faye moved next to him and put her hand on his shoulder, as though to protect him from me. "All this time, you and Maddox," Ben said finally, spitting the words out like bitter medicine. "Ah! It makes sense now, why Augusta was leaving him that morning. She found out, didn't she? Your so-called best friend. How can you live with yourself after what you did to her?"

Stunned, I got to my feet. "What I did to Augusta? *Me?* I can tell you what really happened to her, but you wouldn't believe me."

"You're right about that," he said. "I don't want to hear any more of your lies. I can't stand to even look at you." And with that, he turned his face from me. Vanna Faye's hand tightened on his shoulder, and she began to cry.

Without another word, I backed away from the two of them and went to my room. After throwing a few things into an overnight bag, I went to the music room and got my dulcimer. All my other belongings were packed, ready to be moved, but I walked past them. With nothing but an overnight bag and my dulcimer, I walked back into the den. Vanna Faye and Ben were praying together, their heads bowed and eyes closed. I stood a minute, waiting to tell them that I was leaving, but they didn't see me as they cried and prayed, asking God for the strength to endure the shame and humiliation of knowing a woman so low-down that she drove her best friend to her death.

Twenty-one

AT GRAYTON BEACH, I sit on the sand and think about God. I am so moved watching the sun in the white-blue sky that my eyes fill with tears. I fall back, looking up and saying a prayer of thanksgiving.

I know now—without any doubt—that God has not left me. I have left God instead, shutting myself away from the solace I found when I first trusted in the order and rightness of the universe. I lost God because I've spent most of my life searching in the wrong places. Long before my conversion in church, I found God in the sea, in the salt wind, the sky overhead, and the white sand. The sand is beneath me now, cradling me, and it feels right. I've come from this earth and I'll return to it; its substance is mine, and everyone that I've loved and lost—my parents, my granny, Augusta, Godwin, Rich, Ben, Gus, and Maddox—are all made from the same particles.

There is much about life I'll never understand. I want it to be fair; I want retribution. I can't understand why Augusta, who never did anything except love the wrong man for the wrong reasons, is dead. Why is John Marcus Vickery, a spiritual leader, not paying for his sins? What does he say when he prays to God? I want to think that even if we're not punished for our sins, we're punished by them. But I'm not sure if that's true, and it confuses me. I wonder where Augusta is, and if she's found the peace she couldn't find here. What I haven't been able to accept is that in many ways, Augusta made her own unhappiness. I take a deep breath and exhale slowly, releasing that burden into the morning air. She couldn't find happiness or peace because she lost sight of the source of joy. Like me, she looked in the wrong places.

It'll be much harder to let go of my grief for Maddox. At night, I sit on the beach and look up at the stars. Maddox and Gus are in the mountains now, camping out, and I picture them at their campsite, looking at the same stars I see. Gus will be dozing, Lollie snuggled next to him, and Maddox will add wood to the fire, then sit back and think about things. Maybe about me, maybe Augusta. Or Libby, his first love. We all like to think there is only one great love of our lives, and maybe with some people, that's true. But I don't think so. Celeste once said that people come in and out of our lives, and we connect in some way during our time together. They all form who we are and who we become. Destiny causes our paths to cross, though I could never begin to explain how or why. But I no longer believe in coincidence. No way I believe it was mere coincidence that Maddox decided to stop by and see Gus and me at St. Joseph's. Somehow, it was meant to happen. I can't regret my love for Maddox, no matter what kind of pain it brings. Had I not come to love him, who knows? I might not have accepted the grant; might not have realized that life with Ben had cost me too much; might never have questioned the emptiness of my life. I walk the lonely sand dunes, fish the ocean in solitude, sit alone as the chilly waves wash against my feet, and know that my loss of Maddox will always be lodged like ten arrows in my heart.

I can't stay much longer at Grayton Beach. Already, I'll be starting the semester late. Walking to the town of Grayton, I called the dean of women's studies, my advisor, who—like Maddox—was horrified to hear that I hadn't made any living arrangements. But, luck was with me; a friend of hers might rent me a room. When I go into town next and call her, I have good news: There's a room waiting for me in Gainesville.

But even so, I can't make myself leave here. It's as though I've rediscovered the only part of my past that's worth saving, my love of the sea. Once I get my master's degree, I'll move to a place on the ocean. I'll teach music, and live in a weather-beaten beach cottage. There, I'll swim and fish and live out my life surrounded by the things I love best. It'll be lonely, but there are worse ways to live, as I've already found out.

Everything becomes a last: the last fish I'll pull from this sea, the last shell I'll find on the beach, and most poignant of all, the last sunset. On the day before I have to pack up and leave or lose the grant, I make plans for the last sunrise, preparing for it like a religious ritual. I go to the City Café and talk the proprietors into selling me a bottle of champagne. Champagne at sunrise! My spirits lift, and I go to bed content. Without setting an alarm clock, I awake at the first light of morning and look around the little trailer. I'll miss it all.

A soft morning dawns. Everyone is still asleep, with darkness deep in the shadows of the scrub oaks and twisted pines. When I walk to the beach, the sand is cool beneath my feet. The sky is beginning to lighten, and I run so I won't miss it. Just as I pour myself a glass of champagne, a yellow-white sun appears over the top of the pink horizon, and I raise my glass. "Oh, yes," I whisper, my glass held high.

I don't hear him come up behind me as I stand with my face to the sky, watching the last sunrise I'll see over the Gulf of Mexico for a long time. When he calls my name, I think it's the wind blowing through the sea oats. It's only when he steps closer and calls my name again that I turn around in astonishment.

Maddox looks down at me, sunglasses pushed up on his head. He appears exhausted, his eyes purple-smudged. "Hello, Dean," he says finally. "You wouldn't have another glass of champagne, would you?"

I refill mine and hand it to him. "What are you doing here?" I ask.

"What do you think? Looking for you. I had to move heaven and earth to find you, but—here you are. Grayton Beach, watching the sun rise," he says. I stare at him as though he were an apparition. "You told me once that if you ever ran away, you'd go to Grayton Beach," he adds.

At first I have no recollection of having said that. "But, surely you didn't—"

"Prowl the streets until I ran into you?" he finishes for me, then shakes his head, his smile grim. "No. Celeste told me where you were. Don't be mad with her. She took pity on me, seeing how desperate I was. I went to Crystal Springs, to Tallahassee, to Gainesville, then back to Crystal Springs before Celeste gave in."

"You drove all night getting here?"

He shakes his head. "No. Last night, after Celeste told me, I went home and got a few hours sleep. Then I came here, hoping you'd be exactly where I found you—on the beach at sunrise."

"Good Lord! No wonder you look so bad," I say, and he laughs, rubbing his neck.

"That's what I've always liked about you, Dean. You know the way to a guy's heart."

"Yeah," I mutter, sighing. "Sure do, don't I?"

Maddox points over my shoulder. "Wow—take a look at that."

The sky is pinker than before, and the new day dawns bright and perfect, the air crisp. We watch as the sun rides higher and higher, and Maddox comes up behind me.

"Are the sunrises the same in the mountains?" I ask as I shield my eyes with my hand.

"Not really," he says. "The sun floats over the mountain tops, as unattainable as God."

"I like that," I say, nodding.

A warm breeze begins to blow over us, and Maddox places a hand on my shoulder. "Dean? Could we talk?"

I close my eyes. "I really wish Celeste hadn't told you that I was here."

"I'm sure you do. The last time you saw me, I was an unbelievable asshole."

"You had every right. What I did to you was unforgivable."

"No. You did it to protect Gus from finding out that his mother was leaving me when she died, and to protect me from being hurt any more than I already was. I knew that, knew it that last morning. But I was so hurt with Augusta that I had to lash out at someone. I'd give anything if it hadn't been you."

I shake my head. "It doesn't matter. Really. It doesn't matter anymore."

"It matters to me," he says.

We look at each other warily. "Maddox," I say, "I don't know exactly what was in Augusta's letter, but it almost killed you, didn't it?"

"It was so bad, it blinded me," he says, frowning. "I can't believe I accused you of—God, I can't even say it. Just tell me this: Do you think that we can be friends again?"

I study his face. "Of course we can."

"You don't have to say that. I don't deserve it."

"One thing I've discovered since I've been here," I tell him, "is that we don't get what we deserve in life. If we're lucky, we get what we need."

He frowns at me. "Isn't that a Rolling Stones song?"

I stare at him, then his face breaks out in a grin that changes his whole appearance. I can't help myself; I smile, too, shaking my head.

"God, Dean—what we've been through together!" he says, putting an arm around my shoulder as I lean against him, my arms going around his waist. "I've been a dead man since that day we parted," he continues. "It's been the worst time of my life, worse than when Augusta died, worse even than when I read her letter."

"Want to talk about it?" I ask him, but he shrugs.

"There's nothing to say, really. The letter confirmed what I knew all along, that Augusta loved someone else, that she was leaving me. I was so angry that she ran away, that she foolishly lost her life doing so, that I went kind of crazy. But after being in the mountains, alone with Gus, having some time to think, the anger left me. Augusta . . . I can't really blame her, I see that now. I finally got it: She was just like me, an imperfect human being. She never asked me to put her on a pedestal."

"If there's one thing I do believe, it's that we all fall short. Every one of us struggles, falls down, gets back up, and falls down again. Don't you think? Being here, I've had time to get some things in perspective."

"Have you decided not to go to Gainesville?" he asks. "I found out that classes have already started when I was there the other day looking for you."

"I'm going. My advisor knows I'm coming in late."

Maddox takes my hand. "Let's walk by the water while you tell me about it, okay?"

As we walk along the beach together and I tell him about the room I've got waiting for me, a strong breeze tosses our hair and flattens our clothes against us. Maddox listens, then asks, "How long are you staying here?"

"Today," I tell him. "I'm leaving today."

"Dean?" He doesn't look my way. "Don't go. Come with me to the mountains instead."

I hesitate, then shake my head, looking forward. "No. I can't, Maddox. I have to go to Gainesville." I stop suddenly, and both of us stand in the lapping waves of the Gulf at low tide. Hoping to make him understand, I reach down for a handful of white sand and hold it up to him.

"My whole life," I say, "I've been paralyzed, trying to be somebody who isn't me." We both look at my clenched fist, gripping the sand as though my life depended on it. Taking a deep breath, I release my fingers. The sand slides between them and the wind catches it, scattering it away. "I've got to let all that go now. Don't you see that? I have to do this, for me. I've got to risk everything, even losing you, to do this."

He frowns, looking down at me, then finally, he nods solemnly. "You know I-95?" he says.

I stare at him in disbelief. "I-95? We're having a deep, life-changing conversation, and you're asking me about *highways*?"

"I can leave the mountains, get on I-95, and be in Gainesville in a matter of hours," he says. "I might do that occasionally, when I get a hankering to hear some dulcimer music. What do you say to that?"

I wipe the sand off my hands on the seat of my pants. "I say that I-95 runs both ways."

With a laugh, he reaches down and picks me up. With me in his arms, he turns around in the sea, spinning me high over the waves.

"Put me down, you crazy man," I yell, grabbing his shirt. "We'll fall if you don't!"

Just as I say it, of course we do, falling into the water, disturbing the early morning tranquility with our splashes and cries.

"You've lost your mind," I sputter, coming up from the cold waves. Maddox falls down when he tries to get to his feet, pulling me down with him. We struggle to our feet, stumbling as we slosh through the waves to the shore.

"I can get a good metaphor out of this." He grins down at me. "The two of us rising up from the tempestuous ocean, trying to get to the shore safely."

"Sounds more like a country song," I say, laughing.

The sun is high overhead now, hot and fierce, but it shines down on us with the gentleness of a mountain morning.

Look for Cassandra King's
new novel, The Same Sweet Girls,
to be published in January 2005.

1

Corrine
Blue Mountain, Georgia

ALTHOUGH WE CALL OURSELVES the Same Sweet Girls, none of us are girls anymore. And I'm not sure that any of us are now, or ever have been, sweet. Nice, maybe, and polite, certainly. All southern girls are raised to be nice and polite, can't be anything but, regardless of how mean-spirited we might be deep down. The illusion of sweetness, that's all that counts. We don't have to be sincerely sweet, but by God we have to be good at faking it. Southern girls will stab you in the back, same as anyone else, but we'll give you a sugary smile while doing it.

The question is, are the Same Sweet Girls sweet? Hardly. But one thing's for sure: We're the same. We are the same complicated, screwy, mixed-up, love-each-other-one-minute and hate-each-other-the-next group of women we were when we met thirty years ago. I guess we were sweeter then, at age eighteen; we were certainly more naive and less sophisticated. I'd like to say virginal, but that wouldn't quite be true. Not of everyone. Okay, I was. Unlike the others, I was fresh off the farm, as wide-eyed and gullible as a newborn calf. But a couple of us were already damaged, innocence long gone. Those of us with a trace of naïveté left at age eighteen were soon to lose it; we just didn't know it then. I can promise you this: Not a single one of the Same Sweet Girls has a smidgen of it left today.

We're the same, but we're also different, if that makes sense. The group—the SSGs, we call ourselves—formed when we were in college together, roommates, suite-mates, tennis or lab partners. We got our name from a silly little incident that we still relate to each other, telling the story over and over as though we haven't heard it a million times already. Finding ourselves away from home for the first time, in the intimate environment of an all-girls' school, we became friends for life. We forged our clique then, our group of six girls, and we became closer than sisters. We scheduled classes together, stayed up half the night gossiping and giggling, went home with each other during weekends and holidays. As close as we were then, however, we were only truly bound together when one of us was lost, three years after graduation. When you're in your early twenties and invincible, death is a life-changing experience, a sobering wake-up call unlike any other.

I clung to the Same Sweet Girls then, loving them as I'd not done before. Before, life was one big party, the whole basis for our friendship; afterward, we were tightly bound, as though knitted together with unseen but indestructible threads. In tears, we stood apart from the crowd of mourners at the grave of one of our own, linked hands, and promised to remain friends, to always be the Same Sweet Girls we were then. Five felt like such an odd, lopsided number that we moved quickly to fill the gap, becoming the magic six again. Too quickly, some of us thought later. But . . . that's another story, for another time.

Today the six of us do not live in the same place; some of

us are geographically separated by hundreds of miles. But somehow, we manage to stay as close as we were when living in the same dorm, all those years ago. Some years I've seen the others only at our biannual get-togethers, in early summer and late fall. There have been times when job or family obligations kept us apart. After graduation we started our careers, then we married, had babies, raised families. Things like sick children, school plays or Little League games, proms, funerals, weddings, graduations would keep us from attending our gatherings. Inevitably, when that happened, we grieved our absence from the group as though we'd never see each other again. Now that we're older, for the most part our kids grown and gone, we see each other more often, and we're all more aware of the passing of time, the shocking awareness that one day we'll attend a gathering of the Same Sweet Girls, and it will be our last one.

When I'm describing the Same Sweet Girls to other people, I usually tell them it's helpful to group us in twos. Lanier and I were former roommates, as were Julia and Astor; then there's the odd couple, Byrd and Rosanelle. (Poor Byrd, getting stuck with Rosanelle, but there again, that's another story.) Paired like that, we seem like polar opposites, but we aren't, really. I'm considered the weird one of the group, and I'll admit I've earned that honor. Most people think artists are weird, anyway, but me—I'm a gourd artist. As the other SSGs say, with much eye rolling, how many of those do you know? My former roommate, Lanier Sanders, doesn't do weird, being not only a former jock but also a nurse, which is such a prosaic profession for someone like Lanier. Lanier would have been a doctor—a good one—had she not flunked out of medical school her first year. Not because she's dumb; although she struggled in the humanities, Lanier's plenty smart in math and science. Here's the thing about Lanier—lovable as she is, she will always find a way to screw up her life. Almost fifty years old, and she is still doing it. But I don't have any room to talk, since I've been pretty good at that myself.

Like Lanier and me, Julia and Astor were college roommates. The school we attended, the Methodist College for Women in Brierfield, Alabama (nicknamed The W), paired you up; you didn't get to choose like you do in most schools, the Methodists preferring to mix their poor scholarship students in with the more privileged ones. If it hadn't been for the incident our freshman year that made us the Same Sweet Girls, I'd never have gotten to know Julia Dupont or Astor Deveaux, either one. Unlike me, a shy little art major, both Julia and Astor were hot stuff on campus. Classically beautiful in a Grace Kelly sort of way, Julia Dupont was from a wealthy old family in Mobile. Her mother had gone to some fancy boarding school with the dean of women, which was how Julia ended up at The W. It was a year after we became friends before we discovered the real reason Julia was there. Thirty years later, it still surprises me.

What to say about Astor Deveaux? How about, she and I have a rather complicated relationship. I'm not sure what kind of weird chemistry there is between us, but it's been going on since the first day we met, in an Interpretative Dance class. Lanier accuses me of not even liking Astor, but that's not quite true. I don't trust her, I'll admit, and we've had numerous clashes. But like everyone else, I'm fascinated by her. From Lake Charles, Louisiana, Astor Deveaux came to The W on a dance scholarship and intrigued everyone on campus. None of us Alabama hicks had ever seen anyone like her; we'd certainly never seen anyone so talented. Astor went on to dance on Broadway, until she got too old to get good parts. Then she moved back to Alabama, unfortunately. See?—that's what I mean. I'm always making cracks like that about Astor, and I'm not even sure why. But one thing I do know—I've got better sense than to turn my back on her.

I group Byrd and Rosanelle together because they're the most normal ones of the Same Sweet Girls (which isn't saying a whole lot, believe me). Byrd McCain is plain and simple and unpretentious. We've nicknamed her Mama Byrd, a role she fits to a tee. She certainly plays it well, and if on occasion Byrd plays it too well, giving out advice, being uptight or disapproving . . . we always forgive her. She's that lovable. Rosanelle Tilley is another story, but she's not really one of us. She's who we inherited after Byrd's roommate, one of the original six, was killed in a car wreck, and we felt the need to fill the gap. Rosanelle's also the one who unintentionally gave us our name, the Same Sweet Girls. This will tell you everything you need to know about Rosanelle—she's flattered that we named our group after something she once said, not realizing that, as usual, we were being ironic and facetious. Thirty years have gone by, and she still doesn't get it.

It all sounds so serious, telling it like this, but it's anything but. Over the years, we've developed a lot of silly rituals that I'm embarrassed to tell other people about, especially now that we're almost fifty years old. We crown a queen and have royal edicts and all sorts of stuff like that. Each year the crown goes to the one who can prove that she's the most deserving. And what does she have to do to land the coveted crown? Why, be the sweetest one of all, of course. She campaigns all year for the crown, then has to convince the rest of us that she's done enough sugary deeds to earn the coveted title. The highlight of our summer weekend is when each of us summarizes our campaign for the crown during a ten-minute presentation. Like the pope, the queen is elected by secret ballot. Naturally, the first year everyone voted for herself, so we had to change the rules. It's not considered a sweet thing to do, to vote for yourself, and if you do so, you're disqualified.

Even more embarrassing, we have our own coded language that we call Girl Talk. It's been going on for so many years that it's hard to remember where most of it originated. The punch lines of popular jokes make the rounds, but we tire of them and they fall by the wayside, due to our overuse. Our most enduring Girl Talk comes from stories we repeat ad nauseam, year after year. Lanier provided one of the lines we use most often by telling us the story of the elderly woman who was a patient of hers. When Lanier took her vital signs and asked her how she was feeling, the lady said, "Terrible, just terrible. My rheumatism's worse than ever; I can't lift my arms; my back's killing me; and I can't walk without hurting. But it's being so cheerful that keeps me going." The other two most popular Girl Talk lines were provided by Astor, years ago. When she lived in New York, her best friend was a gay dancer named Ron. Astor would take Ron shopping with her because if she picked out the wrong thing, Ron would shake his head sadly and say, "Oh, honey, *no*." On the occasions Ron didn't go with her and she showed up wearing one of her mistakes, Ron would sigh, roll his eyes, and say, "Girl, what were you *thinking*?"

With the Girl Talk, the crowning of the queen, the royal salute, the procession, and the edicts, our get-togethers have become ritualized to the point that they're pure theater, and anyone peeking in a window at us would swear we're all crazy as loons. Which we are. One of these days, we'll stop being the Same Sweet Girls and start calling ourselves the Same Crazy Fools, I suppose. Some would say that day is fast approaching. But in the meantime, we'll be the Same Sweet Girls, who aren't girls anymore, and who aren't sweet and never have been. We'll keep crowning our queen and going through our rituals and loving each other and sometimes hating each other, because we've done it so long it's become a part of us. It's a big part of who we are and how we got to be that way. It's where we are today and how we got from there to here. It's our story.

2

Lanier
Dauphin Island, Alabama

MAMA ALWAYS CALLED ME sassy, and bless her heart, my smart mouth nearly drove her to drinking. If you looked up "sweet old southern lady" in the dictionary, there would be a picture of my mama, wearing pearls with her apron. For some reason I have Mama on my mind today. Guess because it's been several weeks since I've gone to Selma to visit her in the nursing home. I feel bad when I visit her and worse when I don't. Last time I was there, she didn't know me from a houseplant. Poor Mama. Sometimes I think it was having me for a daughter that made her lose her mind. It's all my fault.

Maybe it's the dolphins jumping in the bay this afternoon that make me think of Mama and Daddy and the so-called good old days of my childhood. Actually, they were. Good old days, that is. Sometimes I think I ought to make up some dysfunctional stuff so I'll fit in with everyone else. The Same Sweet Girls say I had the best childhood of all of us, and I reckon they're right. Truth is, I didn't think about it one way or the other when I was a kid. I just lived it. I was raised in a pretty little town, Selma, Alabama, which later got famous for the civil rights stuff. But in the fifties when I came along, it was just home, where my grandparents and most of my relatives lived, and where my daddy was a judge. Mama was a homemaker and did the country club and the Episcopal church ladies and all that stuff. Actually, I spent about as much time at the country club as Mama did because I played tennis and golf all the time. So guess I had one of those—what do you call it?—idyllic childhoods.

We spent most of our summers here, on Dauphin Island, in this old fishing cabin where I've been staying the last three months. As I stand on the back deck and watch the dolphins playing around in the bay, I remember naming this place when I was eight. Lord, that's forty years ago now! Five acres of prime waterfront real estate on Mobile Bay, this property and cabin had been in Daddy's family for years without being named anything, just called the Brewer place by the locals. When we piled in the car and drove three hours south to get here, we just said we were going to Dauphin Island to our fishing cabin. (I thought it was "Dolphin" Island until I was ten.) I pitched one of my fits, insisted the property needed a name, and we should call it Dolphin Cove. Damn if Daddy didn't go for it, even making a sign in his workshop and hanging it up on the gatepost. The thing's still out front but I've got to fix it, because it's loose and flops around whenever the wind blows hard. When I first moved in here, it banged around in a rainstorm and liked to have scared the devil out of me.

I watch the dolphins jumping around, bobbing up and down like they're showing off for me, and I raise my wine-glass to them in a salute. Not a coincidence that I named this place Dolphin Cove—I've always loved dolphins. They're like pure magic to me, and I used to swim with them when I was a kid. The Same Sweet Girls don't believe that, even Corrine. First time the SSGs met here, everyone got so excited when they saw the dolphins that they almost fell off the pier. "I swam in the bay with them when I was a little girl," I told them, not dreaming they'd think I was bullshitting them. When everyone pooh-poohed me, I jumped right into the bay with all my clothes on—of course I'd had a few drinks—and swam out to where the dolphins were. I spooked them splashing around, and they took off like I was the guy who chased that big whale we studied about in American Lit. What was his name, Captain Arab? The book was *Moby-Dick,* I know, because I called it Mo' Big Dick, just to aggravate Byrd, who was in class with me that semester. Anyway, with the SSGs yelling at me to get my butt back to the pier, *right then,* I tried to grab a dolphin and almost drowned myself. Corrine screamed bloody murder and poor Julia cried until I managed to crawl back on the pier, soaking wet and sober. It was one of those things that was funny afterward but not at the time—Corrine actually grabbed me by the shoulders and shook me, like she was my mama or something. In an attempt to lighten things up, Astor said, "Girl, what were you *thinking*?" but nobody laughed, even me.

I tried to explain to Corrine that I have a thing for dolphins, like they're my soul mates or something. I figured Corrine of all people would go for that, since she's into all sorts of New Age stuff. But she was too scared and mad to listen to me. I said maybe I was a dolphin in a previous life. And Corrine said, "Yeah, Lanier, guess that's where all the crazy karma comes from." Maybe she's right. If so, I must have been one bad-ass dolphin.

I wait until the dolphins disappear from view, moving further and further out to sea, before turning away and going back into the cabin. I've put this off long enough, by God. I *have* to get the house cleaned up. It's a disgrace. For three months I've lived here like I was on a camping trip or something, and the place is a wreck. The big weekend is coming up, the annual gathering of the Same Sweet Girls, and the girls will have a hissy fit when they see what a mess the cabin's in.

The SSGs love this place almost as much as I do. The first summer after graduation, when we decided to have our first SSG get-together, we had it here. I had to beg; everyone wanted to go to Gulf Shores instead. I promised them we could go to the beach whenever we wanted to, since Gulf Shores is not that far. Once everyone got here, I was scared they wouldn't like it, since it's so isolated. Although it's *real* pretty here, there's not a blame thing to do except sit on the deck or the pier, watch the dolphins and seabirds, gossip, and get drunk. Dixie Lee was alive then, bless her heart, and she said, "And the bad part is . . . ?" which kind of broke the ice.

We didn't go to the beach the whole weekend, we just lazed around the cabin laughing and talking and drinking rum punch. Well, we did a little crabbing, too, the girls surprising me by enjoying that so much, something I'd done all my life. They loved catching the crabs, thought they were *so* cute, but did not like cooking them. Corrine grabbed my arm and stopped me when I started to drop one of the squirming crabs into a pot of boiling water. She's always been too tenderhearted, which is part of the reason she's had such a sad life. I ended up throwing the crabs back into the bay and going into town to buy crabmeat for my she-crab soup. Corrine wouldn't even taste it and still won't, to this day.

I get the mop and the bucket and the Clorox and Mr. Clean and start cleaning up. Before I tackle the house, I make myself go down to the pier. Daddy added a little gazebo-like thing with benches—another project from his workshop— and all the fannies that have sat on the benches over the years have worn them smooth as driftwood. But the benches are grimy and nasty now, so I spray them with Fantastik and wipe them off with paper towels. The walkway of the pier is white-speckled with seagull doo-doo, making it look like a crazy artist flung a paintbrush over it, so I unwind the hose and wash it off good. The queen's promenade down the pier is a Same Sweet Girl tradition, one of my favorites. We can't have the queen slipping on seagull doo and busting her royal ass, can we?

It takes me a couple of hours and several trash bags to clean up the cabin, it's such a mess. Don't know how I've let it get so bad in such a short time. The cabin's real simple, what a decorator would call rustic. Julia once called it shabby chic, but Astor muttered, "Guess I missed the chic part." There's one big central room, with plank walls and pine posts from the floor to the ceiling. The kitchen area's sectioned off from the sitting area by a counter that doubles as an eating bar. The back of the room is the best because of the floor-to-ceiling glass doors and windows looking out over Mobile Bay, with all the sofas and chairs turned to face the great view. On either side are the bedrooms, two on each side. That's it, except for the deck in back, where the steps lead down to the bay.

Plopping down on the old wicker sofa, I try not to break my arm patting myself on the back. It looks good, clean as an angel's underwear, as Mama used to say, but living here now, rather than just vacationing, I see that it leaves a lot to be desired. Truth is, it's pretty tacky. Both Mama and my grandmother furnished it with their throwaways, a few "beachy"-looking pieces thrown in, like the wicker sofa and rocker. I don't know how much longer I'm going to be camping out here, but I ought to fix it up, make it not only more comfortable but prettier. My house in Reform, now that's what you call well decorated. Ought to be; Paul and I paid a fortune to that hotshot decorator from Columbus, Mississippi, to fix it up, after we restored it. *Paul and I . . .* better not go there now, or I'll end up squalling again, and I won't get a thing done. I stand up, hands on hips, and look around. I'm not sure of the best approach for a makeover.

Repainting the walls? Putting rugs on the bare floors? Nuking the whole place and starting over?

I go outside and down the wooden stairs to the storage area under the house. Since it's on stilts, there's not only a parking area under there but also lots of room to store stuff, which Mama did after Daddy died, before she got sick and ended up in the nursing home. But rummaging through it, I don't find anything I like, except a big pink ceramic lamp that looks like a tallywacker. Being the mean person I am, I put it in the room where Rosanelle always stays, she and Byrd. Poor Byrd, getting stuck with Rosanelle every time, as though it was Byrd's fault that Dixie Lee was her roommate and Rosanelle the replacement. Once I had too much rum punch and horrified everyone by saying that the worst thing about Dixie Lee dying was how we ended up with Rosanelle taking her place. (Obviously, this was one of those times when Rosanelle didn't come.) My comment even shocked Astor, who's pretty unshockable, and everyone agreed I'd never be crowned queen again, saying such terrible, unsweet things. I felt real bad about it, I swear I did, because I didn't really mean it. I like Rosanelle fine, bad as she gets on my nerves. Truth is, I'm not a sweet person, but most of the time, I'm able to fake it pretty good.

I get this wild hair up my butt and decide to decorate, not just clean up. Except for a few nice pieces of Corrine's artwork, her gourds that look like fancy vases and bowls, everything here is so tacky I can't stand it anymore. I load up three big boxes—old-timey chenille bedspreads, plaid and floral throw pillows, faded rugs that look like they survived the Civil War, they're so old—and haul them to Mobile, to the Goodwill thrift store. Then I shop, going to Pier 1 Imports and blowing a whole month's paycheck. I buy bedspreads in Indian batiks and a red-patterned throw from the Himalayas to spruce up the sofa. I get kilim floor pillows and a green-edged sisal rug. The sales clerk, a skinny college girl with little-bitty ears pierced about fifty times, talks me into getting these *precious* hanging lamps that she calls "jewel-globed," telling me the colors are amethyst and ruby and emerald. I've always been a sucker for talk like that. Taking her advice, I buy enough scented candles to burn Mobile to the ground and smell good doing it. In a fancy kitchen store at the Outlet Mall, I splurge on bamboo placemats and at least a million baskets, every size and shape imaginable. On a roll, I can't seem to stop myself buying stuff. I've always hated to shop, which caused Paul to swear I was lacking in some essential female gene, but today, I see why it's considered such fun. By leaving the hatch open in my car, I'm able to take home two five-feet-tall ficus plants in sea-grass baskets as well as half a dozen hanging spider plants. If I can't decorate it, I'll hide it.

By nine o'clock that night, I'm worn out. I've only stopped once, to eat dry granola from the box, standing up by the sink. I emptied the fridge when I cleaned it, and my cupboards are bare; how they'll be till payday. I've never had to worry about money before, never in my life, and I feel guilty how I've always taken things for granted. You know, things like groceries and the light bill. I've found out in the last few months that nothing makes you feel poorer than being hungry. Because I haven't had to think about it in the past, I do dumb things like spending all my money buying jewel-globed lamps instead of groceries. Tomorrow I'll have to hit the crab pots again, just to have something for supper. Once the SSGs get here this weekend, though, there will be plenty to eat because our dishes have become part of the ritual.

For a bunch of weight-conscious women, we eat like field hands when we get together. Julia will have her chef fix that great chicken salad with red grapes and toasted pecans in it, which I could eat by the gallon, and she'll also bring her pimento cheese. The other girls make sandwiches out of it, but I've been known to sit cross-legged on the floor with the bowl of pimento cheese in one hand and a spoon in the other. Mama Byrd brings comfort food: garlic-grits casseroles and her tomato-and-Vidalia-onion pie. I ate a whole one the first year, all by myself, so since then, she's been bringing half a dozen, one for each of us. First time she brought that many, Astor made me mad by saying that Byrd brought one pie for the SSGs and five for me. That wasn't what pissed me off, actually; it was the way Astor rolled her eyes and carried on about me eating a whole pie. I stuck out my tongue at her and she said no wonder your ass is so big and I said you can kiss mine, and she said she'd better get started, then, because it'd take her a while. We ended up having a pure-tee fight about it.

The next year, after we'd all graduated, we had the gathering here again—the beginning of the tradition—and Astor flew in from New York with a cheesecake from some famous Yankee place up there. Since then she always brings the desserts. Not that Astor cooks them; she's about as domestic as a bird dog. Recently, she's been bringing healthy, sugar-free stuff that we all hate, things like tofu and fruit with Sweet'N Low on it. Take last year. Astor brought a *prune* cake from a new bakery in Birmingham and told us it was sweetened with fructose or something. After supper we got about half-crocked and took the cake down to the pier, where we broke off chunks of it and fed the fish.

After a thirty-minute shower (Oh, God, how will I pay the water bill?), I go to bed on new sheets from the Ralph Lauren outlet. They feel as soft as a baby's behind, which they'd damn sure better, at fifty dollars a sheet. A breeze, tasting of salt and smelling of the ocean, blows in the opened windows (that way I don't have to run the air-conditioner), and I doze off. When the phone rings, I can't think what the sound is, what has jerked me out of sleep. I think it's the alarm and I've got to be at the hospital. When I grope for the phone, a catch in my back surprises me, what I get for getting down on my all-fours and scrubbing the floors, like a pure fool. A good deed never goes unpunished. I answer without turning on the lamp. "Yeah?"

"Lanier? You there?"

It's Astor. I fall back on the pillow, wishing I hadn't answered. Conversations with Astor can be exhausting; she's nothing if not high maintenance. "I'm asleep," I tell her, throwing in a yawn for good measure.

Her laugh is skeptical. "Oh, bull," Astor says. "Don't give me that. You've got someone with you, right?"

"Listen, can I call you back in the morning? I cleaned up the house and . . ."

"Someone's there," she repeats, ignoring me. "Who is it, Roland Pierce?"

That wakes me up. "*Not* funny, Astor. Even for you, that's a low one."

"Calm down, Sidney Lanier," she sighs. "Don't get your panties in a wad." Astor tells everyone that she always does yoga while on the phone, so I picture her twisted like a pretzel, the phone hooked up to headgear. "I'm calling to see if you knew that Byrd has gone to Blue Mountain to pick up Corrine," she says.

I sit up against the wicker headboard, pulling a pillow behind me. "Byrd's gone to Corrine's? Why would she do that?" Our travel is habitual. For our get-togethers here, Corrine drives from Blue Mountain to Birmingham to Byrd's house, and they travel together to Mobile. Since moving back to Alabama, Astor's been going to Montgomery and picking Julia up. Rosanelle drives down by herself, since she usually visits with other alumni groups. That way, she can write the weekend off as part of her job. In October, when we meet in Blue

Mountain, we reverse the process, me going to Birmingham to travel with Byrd, Julia picking up Astor. Only a few times have there been any variations in our patterns. Byrd driving to Blue Mountain to pick up Corrine is definitely weird. For some reason—maybe because I'm only half awake—it makes me uneasy.

"I have no idea why Byrd would do that," Astor says, with that breathlessness she gets when she's either excited or nosing around in somebody else's business. Why Byrd picking Corrine up would interest Astor is beyond me, except she's so nosy. Since moving back she's been in hog heaven, all wrapped up in the boring little dramas of our lives. She goes on to say, "When I called Byrd tonight, Buster told me she'd gone to Blue Mountain to get Corrine. I was afraid that something might be wrong."

"Nothing that I know of. Corrine's car is a piece of crap, as you know, so maybe Byrd got it in her head that Corrine wouldn't make it to Birmingham. Probably nothing more than that." I'd almost fallen for Astor's dramatics again, gotten myself all worked up. "Guess we'll find out this weekend," I add, yawning.

"If Corrine decides to be her usual murky, mysterious self, we won't. And quit yawning, Lanier, you're making me sleepy. Oh, did I tell you, I'm leaving for Julia's right after my afternoon dance class so her chef can fix those crab cakes of his, just for me?" The way Astor emphasizes "just for me" in a playful, little-girl voice irritates me for some reason. Makes it sound like I'm supposed to be jealous or something. Determined not to let her get to me again, I say, "I love going to Julia's now, with all those servants and chefs and bodyguards hanging around."

She giggles. "Especially the bodyguards, huh? If I were Julia, I'd go after—oops . . . somebody's beeping in. Hang on a minute." Astor's back in less than that time, breathless.

"Nobody I need to talk to now. Thought it might be the nursing home."

"Anything new with Mose?" I hold my breath guiltily. I'm too tired to hear it tonight.

"Guess you could say that. Earlier today he watered the potted plants on the front veranda, in full view of a group of visitors."

"Yeah? That's a good sign, if he's taking an interest in gardening—"

Astor snorts. "He peed in them, Lanier. Can you imagine? The esteemed Mose Morehouse, rising up from his wheelchair and pissing in a flowerpot on the veranda of St. Mary's. Oh, crap—another call coming in. I'd better catch this one."

"Talk to you tomorrow," I say, relieved she's going, though the image of Mose and the flowerpot breaks my heart.

"Okay. And, Lanier? Give Roland Pierce a kiss for me." Cackling like a wicked witch, Astor hangs up.

I put down the phone and swing my legs over the side of the bed, sitting in the dark. Sometimes Astor can be more irritating than Rosanelle, which is saying a mouthful. I've been fascinated by Astor since we first met, but she can be one royal pain in the ass. Here's what is weird, though. Something about Astor makes you overlook that—which we've all done, again and again. Well, all of us except Corrine, that is. I don't get it, whatever it is between the two of them. Sometimes I think Corrine actually dislikes Astor, but then we'll all be together, laughing and talking and carrying on, and I'll wonder where I got such a notion. One of the Same Sweet Girls couldn't dislike another one, could she? We'd kick her out of the group, since it wouldn't be *sweet,* and you can't be an SSG if you're not sweet. It's an oxymoron, or whatever you call that thing. I wasn't particularly good in English class.

Corrine and I met Astor Deveaux the first day of Interpretative Dance class, our freshman year at The W. We'd heard of Astor since she arrived on campus, of course; everyone had. Anyone out of the ordinary stood out at The W, and Astor was anything but ordinary. She'd come to The W on a dance scholarship provided by some rich alum who'd made a name for herself on Broadway. We'd heard there was competition all over the southeast for the coveted scholarship and that the girl from Louisiana who got it was really something. After college, Astor went on to dance on Broadway, too, and the SSGs always planned on taking a trip up to see her in a play, but we couldn't get everyone together for that. Too much trouble. Some of us went on our own, though.

Even before our dance instructor introduced Astor as the scholarship winner who'd be assisting her in teaching the class and Astor made a theatrical bow, I knew who she was. Had to be. Since I'd never seen a real live Cajun before, I stared at her wide-eyed. "That's her!" Corrine whispered, nudging me with her bony elbow. Then she leaned over and whispered again. "If that girl's a Cajun, Lanier, I'll kiss your behind." I tried to shush her, but she added, "Bet you *anything* she's a phony." From that moment on, before they ever spoke to each other, the die was cast for Corrine and Astor's up-and-down relationship.

I pick up the phone to call Corrine, find out why Byrd is picking her up, but don't. It's an hour later in the north Georgia mountains; Corrine will be asleep. Even in college she kept odd hours. First night, I figured I'd have to go to the housing council the very next morning and request a new roommate, much as I liked Corrine. Night and day we were, literally and figuratively. But I decided to give it a little longer, giving me time to get used to Corrine's weirdness. Which wasn't just her bedtime hours, believe me. For one thing, Corrine was the first person I'd ever met who had problems with clinical depression, something I knew nothing about. I wasn't sure if that meant she'd spend a lot of time sitting and staring like a zombie, or if she'd talk to herself or something. God, I was so ignorant then! I knew The W would put me with a scholarship recipient, but I wasn't expecting an art major, which was as strange to me as clinical depression.

Then, to top it off, I found out that Corrine's "medium" was gourds. Gourds! I laughed my hiney off when she told me, but it shut me up when she hauled in a bunch of gourds that she'd won all sorts of prizes with and decorated our room with them. I'd never seen anything so cool! Matter of fact, I wouldn't have even known they were gourds if she hadn't told me. She'd carved or painted them in all sorts of really neat-looking designs. She'd even made musical instruments from some of them, little flutes and sitars and stuff. It used to make me feel really bad for Corrine when she had to sell one for spending money, because you could tell that she was attached to everything she made. She was snooty about it, too, refusing to give in to requests to make those crafty-looking gourds you see, the ones decorated like Santas or birdhouses, though she could've made a lot of money doing so. Corrine's stuff was real art, and sure enough, after graduation, she went on to become sort of famous as a gourd artist. Which still sounds funny, to tell you the truth. To this day, I can't even say the word "gourd" without getting tickled.

Both Astor and Rosanelle have told me—in strictest confidence, of course—that they think Corrine's crazy as a loony bird. Talk about the pot calling the kettle black! One thing about Astor, though. She and Corrine have their little clashes, but deep down, I can tell that Astor really admires Corrine. I know for sure that she likes Corrine a whole lot better than Corrine likes her.

The reason I know how Astor feels about Corrine is this: At our get-togethers, the SSGs are always playing these silly little games, stuff like "If you wrote your autobiography, what would the title be?" Well, one year Astor said, "Let's describe each other by using literary characters instead of adjectives." Most of the time, I like the games a lot, but for some reason, that one struck me as the stupidest idea yet, and believe me, Astor's come up with some lulus. When I pooh-poohed it, Astor told the others that I didn't want to play because I wasn't smart enough. She said that I didn't know any literary characters or adjectives, and I said, "Oh, yeah—is that right, Lady Macbeth, you frigging bitch?" I thought Julia was going to fall off her chair laughing. I ended up playing the stupid game anyway, and Astor said that Corrine was Annabel Lee, which I thought was perfect. The reason is, Corrine is really pretty but in an unearthly sort of way, if you know what I mean. What makes her look kind of ghostly is her being so pale, with big round eyes, silver and clear as water. Then she's got this long, curly, reddish-blonde hair, exactly like the picture of Annabel Lee in the American Lit book we used as sophomores.

I realize I can't call Corrine this late because she's been feeling puny lately, had some kind of bug. Which might be— it hits me—the reason Byrd has gone to get her. Corrine left me a couple of messages when I was working nights last week, saying she might not come to the SSG gathering this year since she couldn't seem to shake whatever was ailing her. Because of her being a New Ager, she's been to psychic healers and herbalists and stuff, but they haven't helped. I'd pooh-poohed the idea of her not coming, calling her back and telling her she'd never get the crown again if she didn't. And we haven't talked since. I'd just assumed she was coming. Assumptions, Paul used to say; you can't assume things in our profession. Got to have proof. He sure took that a whole lot more literally than I ever dreamed he would.

Paul. Almost every night, before going off to sleep, I have to stop myself from calling Paul, just to hear his voice.

Sometimes I literally grab one hand with the other to keep myself from picking up the phone. But tonight I have it, right here. I punch in the numbers and wait for the ring. Since I'm no longer in the house to screen the calls, his service usually answers. But ever so often, I get him instead. Like tonight. My breath catches when he answers, and I say, "Paul?"

Must've had an all-nighter at the hospital last night, otherwise he wouldn't be in bed already. "Paul?" I repeat.

"Who's this?" He's answered without thinking, sleep-dazed. I know him so well. Or so I thought. So I thought.

"Paul, it's Lanier."

"Who?"

I clear my throat, and speak louder. "It's me, Lanier."

The sound I hear is the rustling of the sheets as he moves across the bed to hang up the phone. "Paul—wait! Please, don't hang up!" It's too late. Hearing the click of the receiver, I throw the phone down. Before I know it, I'm crying again, though I haven't cried over him for days. Weeks, maybe. I've been doing so much better. Serves me right. I had to hear his voice again, didn't I? No matter that he hates my guts, that he can't stand the sight of me or the sound of my voice, I had to twist the knife. Fumbling around on the bedside table, I find a tissue, wipe my eyes, and blow my nose.

Jesus, I'm such a slow learner! Either that, or a masochist. Haven't I found out, over and over, that I can't talk to Paul, Lindy, or Christopher without boo-hooing? Christopher calls occasionally, and I always cry, even after his most recent call, a happy one to tell me about his tennis scholarship to Vandy. He's such a jock that I used to worry he couldn't deal with emotional upsets, yet he's handled this better than any of us. Lindy, on the other hand, won't return my calls or answer my letters. Everyone tells me she just needs time, that she'll come around if I let her grow up a bit. She just turned seventeen, and it's been harder on her than any of us.

I can't go back to sleep now; I've gotten myself all worked up, calling Paul and thinking about the kids. Pushing the pillows behind me, I sit up in the bed, yelping at the pain in my lower back, and open the drawer to the bedside table. Fumbling, I pull out my lesson book and fountain pen and wipe my eyes. Since I'm awake anyway, might as well write in my book. I've neglected it lately, being so caught up with settling into my new life. Plenty I need to add to it, that's for sure.

Corrine gave me the lesson book as a joke, sort of, with neither of us having any idea how I'd take to it. It was a few years ago, at a Same Sweet Girls gathering at Corrine's place in the mountains, when she brought out the book and presented it to me. "Lanier, I found this at an antiques store on Tate Mountain," she'd said, "and knew it was perfect for you."

Being Corrine, she'd wrapped it in artsy-looking parchment paper that she'd tie-dyed, or something, herself. I was disappointed when I unwrapped it, failing to see what made it so perfect for me, while the other Same Sweet Girls oohed and aahed politely. It was a child's old lesson tablet, made of heavy cardboard, with the blue-lined pages stiff and browned around the edges; the kind of writing tablet I guess our grandparents practiced cursive writing in. The neat thing about it was the way Corrine had added to it—matter of fact, it took me a minute to figure out she'd done it, that she hadn't found it that way. The ivory-colored cover was real old and antique-looking, and "LESSON BOOK" was printed in dark calligraphied letters. Above that, Corrine had added "LANIER'S." Dead center, she'd written, "When the pupil is ready, a teacher appears."

"Okay, Lanier, here's the thing," Corrine had said, sitting beside me on the floor and opening the lesson book. "You tell us how you're always screwing up, right?" "*Right!*" the Same Sweet Girls yelled together, before I could open my mouth.

Ignoring me giving everyone the finger, Corrine continued. "You've got to help the rest of us out. It's your duty to our friendship. I got this for you to put your life lessons in. Think of all the important lessons you've learned over the years from your screw-ups and record them for posterity." She handed me a fountain pen. "I got this to go with it and put purple ink in it. Real sweet of me, wasn't it?"

"Kiss my fanny," I'd said indignantly, and everyone booed me. "I'm not going to do it! It's not only that I'm a lousy writer, but I never learn from my mistakes, no matter how many times I mess up." I tossed the book in Corrine's lap, pouting.

But Corrine made me take the stupid little book back and kept telling me to just give it a try, that I'd come to love writing in it. I knew what she was trying to do, of course, so I resisted, like I've always resisted anything good for me, from spinach to studying. But the little book was so cute—and I'd never written with a fountain pen, much less one with purple ink—that I told myself I'd at least write my name in it. Then a couple of days later, I picked it up and wrote down something that my mama used to say, something the Same Sweet Girls loved and quoted over and over when I read it to them: *Honey, it will either work out or it won't.* Having it in writing kind of inspired me, so that whenever I got myself in a mess, I'd take out the little lesson book and read over that line again—it will either work out or it won't. Yep. That was sure the gospel truth. One day, in a snit, I wrote: *I keep doing the same crap over and over and expecting it to turn out different each time.*

The entries began to expand, and once I was so startled on rereading an entry that I called Corrine, excited. "Listen to this, girlfriend," I'd said. "I think I've discovered the source of all my problems! Here's what I wrote in that stupid-ass book you gave me. All my problems can be summed up in this one line." "Let's hear it, then," Corrine had said, and I'd read, *"I thought I was doing the right thing at the time."* I knew I'd hit home when Corrine, after a pause, burst into laughter. Once she told everyone, I was assigned the role of the official scribe of the Same Sweet Girls. Every time we get together, I have to read them what I've written.

Tonight I look back over the last entries as I think about what needs to be said before the gathering, what I can write to share with everyone. Lanier's Life Lessons. A few months ago, when Paul kicked me out of the house and I ended up here at the cabin, I'd written, *The Moving Finger writes "You're Screwed," then moves on.* Tonight I nibble on the tip of the fountain pen, frowning, before finally writing: *Any landing you walk away from is a good landing.*

I put the notebook back in the drawer, then yawn and stretch, trying to get the kink out of my back. Getting to my feet, I stumble to the kitchen for a drink of water, feeling my way. Then on to the bathroom to pee. When I come out of the bathroom, something catches my eye, and I move to the window that's across from my bed. Leaning over, I stick my head out, squinting without my contacts to see through the thick foliage. What I see scares me, and I grip the windowsill. I'll be damned—a light is on in the house next door. But—it can't be!—the house has been empty for years. Just yesterday, a Realtor who was one of Mama's old friends called me, asking if I'd ever thought about putting Dolphin Cove on the market. Somehow, with me and her yakking about various things, the subject came up, and the Realtor told me that the Picketts had not sold their property next door. Mrs. Pickett died a few months ago in a nursing home in Mobile—hadn't I read it in the papers? she asked. She said the house was unoccupied, what with the Pickett kids all over the world and poor Mrs. Pickett dying in a nursing home. Said she'd tried to get the Picketts to put the house up for sale, but no. She'd repeated herself, so I'm sure that I heard her right: A shame it was, a real shame that such a nice house, such an *important* house, should be empty.

I sink back in my bed, a little shaken, and pull the sheet over me against the strong salt wind. For the first time, I have second thoughts about my impulsive decision to move here. Pretty as it is, and as much as I love it, it *is* isolated. Everyone—the SSGs especially—told me I was crazy, a single woman living here alone. It was Lanier and her foolhardy behavior again, they'd said. Fools rush in where angels fear to tread, blah blah blah . . . as though anyone would ever mistake me for an angel. Well, I've been a fool going on fifty years now, all my life, and it's not very likely that things are going to change at this late date. If I weren't so sleepy, I'd pull my lesson book out again, and that's what I'd write.